About the Author

Matthew is an author from the American Midwest. He studied English and Creative Writing at Truman State University. When he is not glued to his keyboard, Matthew enjoys board games, outdoor adventures, and watching spooky movies with friends.

Spellseeker

Matthew J. Oelkers

Spellseeker

Olympia Publishers
London

www.olympiapublishers.com
OLYMPIA PAPERBACK EDITION

A CIP catalogue record for this title is
available from the British Library.

ISBN: 978-1-80074-822-4

This is a work of fiction.
Names, characters, places and incidents originate from the writer's imagination.
Any resemblance to actual persons, living or dead, is purely coincidental.

First Published in 2023

Olympia Publishers
Tallis House
2 Tallis Street
London
EC4Y 0AB
Printed in Great Britain

Acknowledgements

Thank you to Cody, Darren, and Mike, who helped me find my pen.

1.

FAREWELL

Ninety-seven. Even before removing the ticket from its housing, the number was plain to see. The ticket hung from the open mouth of the black, steel dispenser. Golden filigree began at the opening and wrapped like vines around the smooth, metallic surface. A single short prong jutted out where ticket ninety-seven met ticket ninety-eight. All supported by a red mahogany post, fashioned in such a way that it resembled a proud wolf. The dispenser rested atop the wolf's magnificent head.

Suspended ten feet above the dispenser was a large, wooden cube made of the same red mahogany. There was no apparent fixture from which the cube hung. It floated free and still, positioned to be viewable from all angles of the spacious lobby that was occupied. The number thirty-four appeared on each face of the cube in raised golden numerals.

"Serving number thirty-five," called a teller, as the position in front of her register was vacated. The golden numerals adorning the wooden cube had congealed into a pool of liquid gold on each face before the teller finished speaking. These pools morphed to display the number thirty-five in short order. A small, smartly dressed calico harn rose from one of many mahogany waiting benches, a ticket held high above his head as he bounded towards the available teller. His cotton- ball tail twitched at the chance to stretch his rabbit-like legs.

"Excuse me, sir. Are you here on official business with the bank?"

Owen was caught off guard by the direct address. Lost in his thoughts, he had not seen the middle-aged human in Orland Bank attire approach. Owen himself had not gone unnoticed, however. A quick survey of the establishment's lavish waiting area revealed several curious gazes. Some were polite enough to cast a mere passing glance, or peek out for a brief moment over opened books or unfurled newspapers. Others made no attempt to hide their unabashed stares. Dressed as he was in the freshly-pressed blues of a Spellseeker, with his left hand resting on the pommel of a sheathed arming sword, there was no wonder as to why he drew so much attention.

"No, sorry," Owen said, raising his left hand from his sword to wave the notion away. "Personal business. Just here to make a withdrawal."

"Very good, sir," replied the banker. The words were expelled as a sigh of relief. His shoulders went slack as a relieved smile thawed his chilled countenance. Pinching ticket number ninety-seven between his thumb and forefinger, the man ripped the perforated scrap of paper from its housing and presented it to Owen.

"Please feel free to take a seat while you wait for your number to be called. Refreshments are available along the east and west walls." A sweeping gesture indicated several rows of open benches, each adorned with black and gold velvet cushions. Tables with drinking water and various baked goods were pressed up against the large room's walls. The man transitioned from his gesture to a hurried walk with all the grace of a startled calf. Another look around the room seemed to indicate that any curiosity regarding Owen's presence had also vanished.

Owen made an honest, unsuccessful attempt to stifle a quiet laugh.

His sense of mirth was short-lived. As he walked to the nearest unoccupied bench, iron-heeled boots clicking against the sturdy marble flooring, Owen glanced at his ticket. *Ninety-seven,* he thought to himself. Visits to the local Orland branch were not a common endeavor in his day-to-day life. The glimmering number thirty-five above remained unchanged. Owen wrinkled his nose at the number. *I've not got all day, you know,* his thoughts continued as if willing the number to change would do any good. With a resigned sigh, he eased himself down onto the cushioned bench and raised his right leg to rest onto his left. His downward movement pushed the tip of his scabbard against the bench. Owen caught the scabbard by the body before it was able to topple and laid it across his lap. He performed the practiced maneuver without giving it any thought.

Benches were arranged in sets of three to form what could be described as open squares. Each group's open side faced inwards towards the red-carpeted walkway that led to the main counter. Five groups of benches were neatly aligned on either side of the walkway. A low coffee table, of the same ornately carved red mahogany as the claw-footed benches, was situated in the middle of each group. They rose roughly to the height of the knees of an average human. Unlike the refreshment tables, these coffee tables housed reading materials. There were copies of the current week's newspaper, a small pamphlet on the history of the Orland bank and its many services, as well as various lighter fare that seemed to be aimed at children: a book of House fables, a copy of *Learning to Light a Match*, as well as some fresh puzzle books.

"Serving thirty-six. Number thirty-six," called another teller, a young human male with a clear voice that carried over the murmur of the establishment. The number on the suspended cube morphed to reflect the appropriate progress of the queue.

Owen heard the click of his heel striking the marble floor before realizing his leg was bouncing of its own accord. He placed a firm hand on his legs to quell the unsightly show of impatience.

As he reached out to grab a newspaper, hoping to distract himself from the fact that the queue had only just now advanced to thirty-seven, he became aware of a low rumble. It was coming from his right and increasing in pitch. A casual glance revealed the sound to be coming from the nearest bench mate: a female katarl. Her black ears were flattened backward, the white fur on her face folded in response to her crinkled nose. Orange, cat-like eyes became narrow slits as she stared in apparent contempt at a small gazette held in her clawed hands. The cover of the article was difficult to make out. It had been bent and torn in the woman's naturally sharp grasp.

"Oh, gods above!" the katarl gasped. "I was growling before I even... I am so sorry if I disturbed you, Mr. Seeker, sir!"

Owen had turned his head farther than he realized to get a look at what the woman held. Rather than a casual side-long glance, his neck craned downwards to get a better view. He waved away the offense with a guilty chuckle.

"No worries, ma'am," Owen replied with a smile. "I didn't mean to intrude. You just seemed so intent on what you're reading." He pointed a hesitant finger toward the gazette.

"Oh my!" the katarl gasped. Closing the article, she was able to see the full extent to which her claws had torn the front and back cover. The title, *The Daily Flow,* was almost indiscernible. "I am an absolute mess, aren't I?" She raised a hand to her face in an attempt to mask her embarrassment.

"Come now, that's not fair. Let's have a look, yeah?" Owen held out a calm hand. "I'm Owen, by the way. Owen Raulstone."

His warm demeanor put the katarl at ease. She lowered her hand and allowed a bashful smile to unfurl, doing her best not to bear any fangs. Owen could see that her claws had retracted as she passed the ravaged gazette to him.

"Beatrice Mayweather. Most folks just call me Betty."

"Delighted," Owen replied as he accepted the article. The source of the katarl's displeasure was evident as Owen pieced together the subtitle for this edition: *How to Change the Color of a Katarl's Coat.*

"The nerve of those people," Betty grumbled as Owen flipped through the article. "The last thing I need while walking down the street is for some urchin to get a bright idea and change this clean coat to some awful shade of pink or yellow."

The Daily Spell had been in publication well before Owen was born. He remembered tearing through each new edition the moment it was released to newsstands. The pop of twine being cut that bound the fresh stacks of the gazette were burned into his memory. It was a constant source of knowledge to expand his understanding of the Flow. How it could be implemented in simple ways his young mind could not have fathomed; *Spying Crawfish, Mending Torn Trousers, Removing Rust from Ordinary Objects.* Each issue would pose some manner of problem. From there, tips and suggestions would be provided on how to best utilize the Flow to resolve said problem. To mend trousers, for example, the gazette may suggest willing a new patch of fabric to weave into the tear. That same issue might also suggest willing a needle to perform stitches, or even to will the threads of the tear to rebind. Illustrations were provided to help the reader focus on a clear method and outcome.

That was back in the days of Owen's childhood. Now, at the age of twenty-four, he heard little praise for the publication. What had once been a gateway to useful knowledge had devolved into articles on petty tricks. An issue would be more likely to detail how to rig a pair of trousers to rip at the worst possible time than to detail how to fix them.

"There has to be something you folks at the Bureau can do about this nonsense, right?" Betty pleaded.

"Unfortunately," Owen replied, rubbing the back of his neck with his spare hand, "none of the spells taught in *The Daily Flow* require licensure with the Bureau of Arcane."

The disappointment was clear to see on the katarl's face as Owen handed the ruined issue back. She received it with a half-smile. An uncomfortable silence lingered between the two until Betty's number, forty-two, was called. Brief pleasantries were exchanged as she left Owen to his wait.

After the exchange, Owen removed a small, silver pocket watch from the breast pocket of his coat. He was unable to spy a clock on any of the walls despite his best efforts. *Bit of an oversight,* he thought as he released the catch. The time was nearly half-past eight. Slightly more than an hour before the first west-bound train of the day would be leaving the station. Owen grumbled at the thought of missing the train. A flash of gold up above left the number forty-three to loom over Owen.

"Staring won't make it tick faster," Owen sighed as he closed the watch, running a thumb over the front cover. On the covering was a brass inlay in the shape of an open book. Three words, repeated three times, encircled the book: *Magic in Moderation.* A gift from the Bureau of Arcane to every graduating Spellseeker. The recipient's name was engraved inside the casing and filled with the same brass inlay. Pride swelled in Owen's chest as he turned the freshly-minted timepiece over in his hand.

Just as Owen began to accept that he would miss the first train of the day, he felt the rap of leather against his shoulder. The blows were quick and playful. More meant to get his attention than to cause upset.

"What's all this sitting about, then? Haven't you got a train to catch?"

The familiar, bright voice was that of his mother's; Danitha. She twisted her leather riding gloves menacingly as a look of mischief spread across her face. After another series of blows against her son's shoulder, she removed her wide-brimmed yellow hat and dropped the gloves inside. Long, brown curls tumbled down over shoulders as the hat was removed.

"Up!" she exclaimed. "We have places to be and people to transport there!"

"Mother, please," Owen pleaded, hoping his hushed tone might elicit the same from his mother. "There's a queue. Nothing to be done about it." He raised his ticket, thumb just below the number ninety-seven, up to her sightline.

"Nonsense," Danitha chuckled. She took the ticket from Owen's grasp and promptly tore it to pieces. Bits of paper tumbled to the marble floor as she wiped her hands of the newly made mess. Danitha pinched Owen's ear and tugged upwards. "Family doesn't wait in the queue."

Danitha's stride was full of purpose as she made her way to the carpeted walkway. As she turned on the heel of her black riding boots, she beckoned intently to Owen. He could almost hear her say, "Come along now, sweetheart." Owen was thankful to be spared at least that much. A snicker to his left. A handful of poorly concealed, mean-spirited grins from the other side of the walkway. Where once there was respect, there was now a room full of laughing eyes that reveled in the sight of a grown man being towed about by his mother. Owen could feel his face take on a very particular shade of red as he made long strides to catch Danitha.

There were eight clerks in total. They all worked in a closed-off area behind a chest-high counter. The base of the counter was made from masterfully connected sections of red mahogany. Atop the counter rested a continuous slab of granite. Small flecks of gold dotted the countertop in what was otherwise a black void. Each clerk had a small workspace separated from their neighbors by wooden dividers. A small, brass housing for interchangeable nameplates sat in plain view for those approaching the counter.

"Excuse me," Danitha started with a pause as she looked at the nameplate of the young, acne-ridden human across the counter from her, "Brandon!"

Danitha received two bewildered glares; one from Brandon, and the other from a female harn with piercing blue eyes.

"Excuse *me*," the harn replied. She had taken advantage of one of the bank's stepping stools, which allowed her to be on eye level with her current human company.

"Oh, don't mind me, dear. I'll be out of your tail in a hop, skip, and a jump!"

Owen arrived behind his mother just in time to catch the harn before she leaped at Danitha. His hands alone were not enough to stymie the stream of expletives that flowed from the harn's mouth. While not unused to his mother's occasional culturally oblivious statements, this one managed to draw out an even deeper shade of red in his face. Owen had half a mind to let the flailing woman go and allow nature to take its course. Instead, he settled for profusely apologizing on his mother's behalf until the infuriated harn had calmed somewhat.

Danitha continued to seek the attention of the poor young clerk, who appeared to be at a loss for what to do about the whole situation. He attempted to seek guidance from either of his neighboring clerks. Neither afforded him any recognition. Rather than step in to deal with the whirlwind that had landed at Brandon's station, his neighbors, Tanvi and Horace, continued to work with their respective customers as if nothing was happening.

"All right now, what seems to be the problem here?"

The voice that called out from behind the clerks sounded familiar. Owen craned his neck to look past the now cowering Brandon. Approaching the station was the same middle-aged man who had proffered the now shredded ninety-seventh ticket. His eyes first whipped to Brandon, who offered little more than a shrug in response. Owen tried to formulate an explanation as to why he was restraining one of the bank's customers.

"Oh, Ms. Orland!" The middle-aged man's voice gushed with a swell of recognition. "I didn't see you there!" He brushed firmly past Brandon, who seemed perfectly happy to become little more than a piece of scenery.

"I know Mrs. Orland-Raulstone is a bit of a mouthful, Daniel, but I am getting awfully tired of reminding you." Anyone looking at Danitha would struggle to describe her smile as anything but forced. She certainly did not attempt to conceal it.

"Right you are, ma'am. My apologies. And what brings you to our branch today?" Daniel made a sweeping gesture about the building as he spoke.

"Withdrawals." She placed a gentle hand on Owen's shoulder as she continued. "My pride and joy is freshly graduated from Eastpointe Spellseeker Academy and headed out west. Have to make sure he doesn't go hungry on the way there."

"Ah, that must make you Owen!" Daniel reached across the counter with an open hand extended.

It was not until the offer of a handshake that Owen realized he was still holding the harn by her waist. He was supporting the entirety of her weight. Owen looked down to see that the stepping stool had toppled over. No doubt a result of the harn's attempt to launch herself at Danitha. The smoldering cinders of her impotent rage were finally snuffed as she raised her hands in defeat. 'You can put me down, now' might as well have been inked across her small forehead. Owen obliged with another apology.

Hands now free, Owen extended his own. The over-eager banker grabbed Owen's fingers. A limp handshake resulted from the endeavor.

"Wish you had said something when you first arrived," Daniel

15

continued. "We could have gotten you squared away without pause."

"No, no. I'm just another customer." Owen raised his hands as if attempting to push the notion of being special as far away as he could.

A few more pleasantries were exchanged at the counter before Daniel moved to the end of the counters, where he held open a small, waist-high gate. Danitha moved to pass through the gate without a moment's hesitation. She had grown quite accustomed to barging into Orland Bank branches with the same authority that one might display when entering their own kitchen.

Owen did not share in his mother's sense of entitlement. What he did feel was yet another change in the room. An uncomfortable silence had replaced the dull murmur of business and idle chatter. Side-long glances that had been full of curiosity were now laced with dread. Any who had openly made fun now buried their faces in newspapers, hoping to be forgotten.

"I wouldn't believe it if I hadn't seen it," Venkat remarked, his hand doing a poor job of concealing his gleeful expression.

"Enough already," Rebecca snapped. "Give it a rest."

"The literal cavalry came to the rescue!" Venkat pointed over his shoulder with his thumb, indicating Danitha. "Gods forbid we have to wait in line, right?"

"It is an open cab, sweetheart," came the cool reply from Danitha. She did not bother to turn her head. "I *can* hear everything you're saying."

"Yes, ma'am. Sorry!"

Owen was doing his best to ignore the exchange in front of him. Eyes half-open with an elbow on the carriage's door, he focused his attention on nothing in particular. The rhythmic clatter of large wooden wheels on cobblestone vibrated through his arm and up to his ears. Not quite enough to drown out the scene that continued to unfold, but the rhythm helped to calm his simmering nerves. The mid-morning sun at least gave him an excuse to shield his eyes.

The two sitting across from Owen were, as might be guessed from the constant jabs, his friends. Venkat was the son of an accomplished, Bangeli textile merchant and friend to the Orland family. His skin was a very dark, warm brown with eyes to match, and he stood a full hand taller than Owen. His inviting smile hid just how sharp his tongue was.

16

Rebecca's family had no such claim to success public distinction. She had met Owen in primary school, and the two had remained friends ever since. A mess of red curls and a fair, freckled complexion made clear her northern Nirdac descent.

Both Venkat and Rebecca wore the same attire as Owen, being members of the same graduating class of Eastpointe Spellseeker Academy. Their double-breasted coats were dark blue, cutting off just above the knee. White trim ran about the cuff, breast pockets, and high collars. Each of their brass buttons was engraved with the image of an open book. Their trousers were a somewhat lighter cerulean blue, with a pair of white stripes running from waist to bottom hem. A smart pair of black boots and a sword on their belts completed their Spellseeker attire.

"Raise your chin, Owen," Venkat said, much quieter now. Owen felt the gentle tap of a boot against his shin. "Only a bit of fun. You know I don't mean anything by it, right?"

"Of course," Owen replied. His sullen expression began to recede as he turned to face his compatriots in the cart.

"Excellent," Rebecca interjected brightly. "So, where do you think we are being assigned? Discounting Southport." She raised both hands to indicate the seaside city that was their immediate surroundings.

"Orlena. Ten silver dollars says it's true!" Venkat's grin widened until it reached from to ear. "We take the train to the end of the line, keep heading west, then ride a ship down Sisir's Run. Takes us straight to Orlena. No way Second Seeker Rohit would send us anywhere less exciting!" He leaned forward as he spoke, resting his elbows upon his knees. Excited hands traced out the proposed journey as it was being described.

"Nonsense," Owen chided with a smirk. "She asked where you think we're being deployed, not where you want to spend your next month-long birthday party." The remark elicited a light chuckle from all three friends.

"If we're being realistic," Rebecca began, staking her claim, "I'd wager at least one of us is going up north to Oswyn, up north. Ten silver dollars is a bit rich for my blood, though. You'll have to make do with some candied almonds if I'm wrong."

"You didn't." The assertion rolled off of Owen's tongue slowly. Hope mixed with expectation as he questioned Rebecca. "Aldner's?"

Without breaking eye contact, Rebecca's hand moved to a leather pouch on her belt. The smell of cinnamon mixed with sugar radiated from the moment she popped the pouch's clasp. A smell that became more powerful as she lifted a green cloth bag from the pouch and tossed it to Owen. The letters *AG* were stitched onto it: the Aldner's General. Owen pulled the mouth of the bag open and grabbed a small handful of its contents.

"Oh, they're still warm," Owen mumbled as he munched. "You're the best."

"I'm aware," Rebecca replied with pride. "And I'll have them back. If I let you keep that bag, they'll be gone before we ever set foot on the train."

There was no question in Owen's mind as to the truth of that claim. He closed the draw-string bag with a somber nod, unable to hide the brief moment of discontent as he handed the bag over to its keeper. Venkat, however, was not so keen on the bag disappearing without claiming a mid-morning snack of his own. He cocked his head slightly and turned longingly to Rebecca. Resting his chin on both hands, Venkat began to blink incessantly at her. His white teeth crept out as his ear-to-ear grin morphed into a pleading smile.

"Gods above, what is that face?" Rebecca recoiled from Venkat as he continued to lean closer. Her laughter was at odds with the look of mild disgust that crinkled her nose and brow. "Here! Just make it stop." She pushed the bag into Venkat's face. Venkat let out what could only be described as a gleeful squeak as he received his prize. He was more reluctant to return the sweets than Owen, necessitating physical intervention from Rebecca. Owen shook his head in amusement, his attention leaving his friends and their struggle.

The major city of Southport rolled by at a modest clip. Danitha drove the two horses that pulled the open carriage at a reasonable canter. Fast enough to reach the westbound Federation Rail station, but not so quick that it might draw the ire of any 2nd Federation Army soldiers that may be posted at the city's various intersections.

Lucina's Lane, the road they were currently on, was one of the largest in Southport. There was enough room for four carriages to ride abreast with plenty of room to breathe and space for pedestrians beside them. The smell of Bangeli street curry overpowered any who came unprepared. Freshly tanned leather, spices newly arrived from the Scalded Mire to the south, and many other things besides all crashed over each other in a wild tide of fragrance.

It was the last main, commercial road before reaching the train station. The colloquial 'Last Road Out of Town'. Anything an aspiring pioneer might need could be found or made on that stretch of cobblestone. Hence its designation as Lucina's Lane. The many craftspeople that called the road their home knew that their patron goddess Lucina, the Builder, would be proud. At least, that was what Owen had been led to believe. Marcus Tully, of Tully's Travelers, had spoken at length of his devotion to the Inspired Goddess. Listening to the cobbler's adulations was part of the price Owen paid every time his boots needed tending. A price worth paying, of course. There was no better shoemaker in all of Southport as far as Owen was concerned. The two shared a polite wave as the carriage rolled by Tully's establishment.

"Why are we slowing down? The station is further down the road."

The polite chatter that had overtaken the back of the carriage came to an abrupt halt at those words. They were the first words spoken by the carriage's last passenger. He rode in the front of the carriage next to Danitha and was adorned in the dress uniform of the 2nd Federation Army: waistcoat and trousers of dark olive, with a red beret leaning to the right side of his head. A silver phoenix bearing crossed spears in its talons, denoting the rank of colonel, was affixed to his left sleeve just below the shoulder. All three Spellseekers came to immediate attention at the slightest hint of his gravely baritone voice.

"Pull your face out of the dossier, love," Danitha replied, unaffected by the colonel's voice. Arthur Raulstone's voice. He narrowed his eyes as he looked up at his wife with a mixture of respect and frustration, then turned his gaze to the middle of the crossroad at which they had stopped.

"Glorified crossing guard," Arthur mumbled. A female harn stood in the middle of the intersection on a raised platform directing traffic. She wore the uniform of the enlisted: knee-length coat and trousers of dark olive, with a black beret. A single chevron was affixed to her left sleeve. "Private! Make way!"

It took a moment for the soldier to locate the source of the order. Upon noticing Arthur's commanding frame, she snapped to attention and saluted her superior officer. A frantic whirlwind of gestures accompanied shrill whistle blasts as the soldier made way for Danitha to drive her carriage through. Riders and pedestrians alike did not hesitate to voice their displeasure.

19

Not all onlookers were offended, however. A Bangeli katarl waved at the Raulstone carriage as it began to resume pace. She wore the blues of a Spellseeker, the sun shining bright on her orange, black-striped fur.

"Where to?" she shouted after the carriage.

"No idea!" cried Venkat in response, leaning over Rebecca and out of the carriage. "Come and see us off, yeah?"

The katarl did not voice a reply. She merely shook her head as she started towards the Federation Rail station at a jog.

The deep thrum of the manarail engine had begun in earnest as the Raulstone carriage arrived at the station. Owen could see the engine and the many cars behind levitate above the rail. A distortion between the rails and cars blurred the hurried, red-coated porters fast at work on the other side. It looked much like a heat distortion that appears on the horizon, save for the slight purple hue.

All manner of folk lined up at the booking office, attempting to claim what few seats remained or to capitalize on last-minute cancellations. Prospective pioneers, with their travel gear and weapons, sought to push every copper penny for all that it was worth. Parents and children who desired to meet relatives that lived half a continent away. Fur traders, with their traps and snares, wanted a few days' peace before blazing trails in the Kastkill Mountains to the north. Those hoping to pass the iron gate that led to the train never lacked in diversity. Fortunately for Owen and his friends, their tickets had been purchased in advance.

"All right sweetheart, give us a kiss before you start your big adventure." Danitha leaned back into the carriage. Owen, who had been busy passing luggage from the carriage to his friends on the sidewalk, made a quick look about. He was not sure what exactly he was looking for. Perhaps a reflex from his youth to avoid the snide comments of his peers. Owen obliged his mother after passing down the last suitcase. Danitha wiped away the faint mist in her eyes before taking a firm hold of her son's forearm.

"Make us proud," Danitha said with a final squeeze before releasing Owen. She then proceeded to dig a heel into Arthur's right foot. "Go see our boy off while I mind the horses, dear."

If Arthur had felt his wife's assault, there was no clear indication of it. He merely stood and lowered himself off the carriage. All the while, he maintained eye contact with the packet of documents he held.

A porter, spying the arrival of the three Spellseekers, approached the trio with a dolly in hand. Under his arm were three sealed envelopes. He waved off the trio's attempts to load their baggage onto the dolly.

"Good day, Seekers!" The porter spoke with practiced professionalism. "I am to give these to you three, presuming that I am speaking to Owen Raulstone, Venkatesh Ramaswami, and Rebecca Hall?"

"I suppose the Second Seeker got tired of waiting for us," Venkat said, directing a smirk at Owen.

"Precisely, sir," the porter said matter-of-factly. "Said he had urgent matters to attend to and entrusted the paperwork to Federation Rail. Always happy to be of service to our bluecoats." He finished with an exaggerated salute. He then handed the three envelopes to Venkat and began loading the group's luggage onto the dolly. Putting years' worth of efficiency on display, the porter had stacked their baggage and disappeared into the bustle of the station before the trio had managed to open their respective envelopes.

Each of the brown envelopes was roughly the size of an unopened newspaper. The name of the intended recipient had been elegantly scrawled onto the front. Owen turned his envelope over to see that the flap at the top had been sealed with blue wax, the insignia of the Bureau of Arcane visible. A faint, golden glow radiated from the seal. The minor spell served as an additional layer of security and would fade should part of the seal ever lose contact with the envelope.

Owen's hand began to tremble. The envelope contained the culmination of four long years of work. Four grueling years studying the practical application of the Flow, as well as its related laws and how to enforce them, at Eastpointe. Four years of sleepless study. Four years of constant physical battery to forge his body into a shield for the people of the Federation.

"Climb the ladder. Do the Raulstone name proud."

If Arthur had not placed his hand on Owen's shoulder, the words might have caused Owen to jump out of his skin. His father's hand weighed heavy on Owen's shoulder. Owen turned his head to see that Arthur stilled, poring over the documents he carried. He removed his hand from Owen's shoulder only to turn to the next page.

"I'll do my best," Owen said quietly, his father's hollow words still ringing as he did so. Owen felt a slight tug on his sleeve. Rebecca had lowered her head to meet Owen's dejected gaze.

"C'mon, then," Rebecca half-whispered.

The trio had almost passed through the barrier to reach the train when Owen felt the familiar tap of a cane behind his knee. He turned to find a heavyset, smartly dressed man. Age had ravaged this man, leaving him with wispy traces of silvered hair. The cane returned to supporting his weight after garnering Owen's attention.

"Grandfather!" Owen said. The weight on his shoulders lessened slightly. He shook his grandfather's hand when it was offered.

"You didn't think I'd miss my grandson's big send-off, did you?" The man's laugh was labored, and as thin as his hair. "Arthur, is that you back there?" He placed a hand over his eyes, pretending to shield his vision from the sun that was behind his back.

"Henry," came Arthur's grumbled salutation.

Only upon realizing Henry Orland had arrived did Arthur Raulstone look up from his papers. In fact, not only was Arthur's attention stolen, but he made a point to fold his papers and tuck them under his arm. It was not the first time Owen had been caught in the middle of the two men. No amount of exposure, however, seemed to lessen the tension that rose from such standoffs.

"Daddy? Is that you?" Danitha called out with glee from the driver's seat of the carriage. "Ah, Daddy!" Her exuberant squeal was enough to divide Henry Orland's attention as he waived to his daughter.

"Morning, sweetheart! Just came by to wish your boy well. Oh, by the way," Henry continued, turning to Owen, "do say hello to Cynthia when you arrive. She's been heading the branch out there for a few years now. I'm sure she'd love to see you!"

"Truly? That's… wait, when I arrive—"

The question was cut short by the howl of the manarail engine's whistle. Three blasts, followed by a cry of, "All aboard!" from the conductor. The call was echoed by the porters manning the platform. Before Owen could finish his question, he was being pulled along by a now agitated Venkat who was eager to be gone from Southport. Owen looked at the seal on the back of his envelope as he stumbled along behind his friends. His brow furrowed as he confirmed the Bureau seal was still in its proper place, its golden glow shimmering in the light of the sun.

22

2.

WESTBOUND

Glass met the lacquered bartop with a welcome thump. Owen reached out reflexively towards the sound. He did not bother to raise his head, separated from the bar only by his left forearm. A single silver dollar was deposited on the table before Owen fumbled for the glass. Another familiar sound, the bottom of a glass scraping over wood, met his ears as the glass was gently pushed into his hand. Owen raised the glass in salute to the attentive bar hand.

There was no rush to attend to the drink. Another full day remained before Atherea's Spear, so the manarail engine was named, would reach the city of Elstaff. No rush to pull the glass to him. No rush to turn his head, or to open his eyes. Owen could melt into the bar as the ice in the glass melted into his whiskey.

It did not matter that the room spun while his eyes were closed. That he felt the very real danger of falling from his stool. He could fall from his seat, spew his liquid dinner across the floor, and pass out in his own sick. None of the people in the lounge car would ever see him again. Not at the edge of the world.

"Hey there, big guy."

Owen felt a conciliatory hand come to rest on his back. The welcome sensation of a light scratching at the small of his back, until the hand came to rest on Owen's shoulder. Then a light tug came at the glass in his right hand. Owen pulled at the glass sharply, wrenching it away from the would-be assailant. Some whiskey was surrendered to the table in the process.

"Not a chance," Owen mumbled. He turned his head just enough to glare at Rebecca through the narrow slit of one eye. "I paid for it. It's mine. I'm gonna drink it." Each word was slow, deliberate. As if Owen was digging through a bog to find each one.

"You can't do this all night, Owen."

"Watch me," he replied, lifting his head long enough down his drink in one labored gulp.

"He can't do this all night," Rebecca said, turning her attention to the bar hand. He was a slender katarl with yellow eyes and black fur, his white sleeves rolled past his elbows.

"Sorry, ma'am. Not about to cut off a man that tips." Owen held up another silver coin as the bar hand finished. "Especially not one that tips in dollars." The katarl palmed the coin. Without another word, he prepared another glass of whiskey and placed it near Owen.

"Right then," Rebecca said. Her glare was powerful, causing the bar hand to recoil slightly. "If you won't cut him off, I will." She grabbed the glass of whiskey without looking and, much to Owen's audible dismay, consumed the golden liquid in an instant. The drink was more powerful than she had expected. Rebecca coughed twice, though she made a concerted effort not to double over.

Watery eyes blinked away the burn in Rebecca's throat as she began to hoist her maudlin friend up from his seat. She managed to wrap his right arm around the back of her neck, then tucked her left arm around his waist. The problem, however, was not Owen's weight. Rebecca was able to stand Owen up with a single, powerful lift. Opposition came in the form of balance. Owen teetered back and forth. It felt to Rebecca as if she were carrying a sack of potatoes while standing on a ship's deck in the throes of a storm.

Owen, too, felt as if the floor was moving beneath his feet. One foot would rise just as the other fell. The liquid contents of his stomach sloshed back and forth with the rest of his body. Open eyes were no longer a remedy for the spinning sensation that attempted to grapple Owen to the floor.

A sharp, sudden pain shot through Owen's skull. His next few breaths were sucked through clenched teeth.

"Let's hope that knocked some sense into you," Rebecca muttered. She had managed to haul Owen across the aisle of the lounge car and into a vacant booth nearby. She aimed to seat Owen upright. Her friend's mostly limp body, however, had other plans. Owen toppled over as soon as Rebecca had released him. The somewhat hollow sound of his head striking the window seemed appropriate. She stepped away to get two glasses of water.

The window felt quite cool against Owen's hot, tingling face. His heavy breaths fogged the glass. Not that there was anything worth looking at. Heavy clouds hung in a moonless sky. All the fields and hills beyond the walls of the train were consumed by the complete void of night. All Owen could see was his reflection. His features were distorted, as much by the fog on the window as the fog in his mind.

When Rebecca returned, she had brought more than two glasses of water. The sound of paper aggressively whipping against polished wood cut through the quiet lounge. Owen's name was written on the front. Half of the now broken seal was visible as papers spewed out from the envelope. He closed his eyes, hoping the contents of the assignment might be lost to the darkness.

"Drink," Rebecca whispered.

Owen felt Rebecca pry open one of his swollen hands, shoving a glass of ice water into it. More liquid was not something that Owen thought he could handle. He was already bursting at the seams from whisky alone. Then Owen felt another touch. This one was gentle, almost pleading. He still could not look his friend in the eye. He did, however, drink.

Relative quiet fell over the lounge. A harn woman at the back of the car tucked back into her tome, with the previous show now at its apparent end. The scratch of thick parchment was clear to hear with every turn of the page. Warm light poured over her from the lantern hung above her booth.

No longer bound to his favorite patron, the bar hand set about snuffing the lanterns above each empty booth. A light, lingering touch on each lantern's memory glass core was enough. A simple memory for a simple task. Only three lights remained on by the time the bar hand had finished his rounds: the harn's table, the bar light, and Owen and Rebecca's table. The bar hand retrieved Owen's empty cup as he passed, replacing it with two full ones. Rebecca took one of the glasses and sipped in silence.

Constant, subtle vibrations moved through the window on which Owen rested his head. Residual energy exhausted from the manarail engine as it channeled the Flow in mass quantities, both to keep the train afloat and move it forward. The vibrations added to the oncoming numbness Owen felt in his head. The cool glass had already lost its comfort. The excessive warmth from Owen's cheeks saw to that.

"Fifty-seven percent, Becca."

Owen opened his bleary eyes as he spoke. The near-silence had become too oppressive. Rebecca's patience too loud. He did not turn his gaze to Rebecca, choosing still to stare at his distorted reflection.

"Percent of what?" Rebecca followed after a few moments' wait.

"Arnstead," Owen replied. He placed a hesitant hand on his assignment

25

papers. "The mortality rate of Seekers assigned to Arnstead is fifty-seven percent."

The silence that followed was heavier than the first. A suffocating weight had fallen out of Owen's mouth and somehow managed to land on his shoulders. He removed his head from the window and buried his face behind crossed arms on the table. Each breath was slow and measured. The smell of whiskey on his breath permeated the small fortress of arms he had constructed.

"It's okay to be afraid, you know?" Rebecca's voice was warm. Owen felt one of her hands come to rest on his shoulder. "It's not safe, what we do. We knew that from the start."

"I guess always just assumed we would be doing this together. You, me, and Venkat."

"Me too," Rebecca sighed.

"Sorry for making a mess," Owen added after a pause, forcing a half-hearted chuckle. He turned his head enough to see Rebecca with his left eye. "Ugly sight, I imagine."

"Especially for someone wearing their blues."

Rebecca managed a precarious balance between condescension and comfort as she spoke, following her remark a swift flick to Owen's forehead. She smiled at the resulting groan. Owen retreated into the relative safety of his crossed arms.

"Promise me it won't happen again," Rebecca continued, taking a more serious tone. She leaned forward to rest an elbow on the table. Her hand was raised, open, and waiting. "Seekers don't hide. Not in corners. Not behind civilians. And *not* inside bottles."

With a deep breath, Owen raised his head from the table. Rebecca's face had grown stern. Her rigid frame somewhat haloed in the lantern's warm, swaying light. Owen placed his elbow on the table and clasped his friend's hand. Both squeezed tight as they locked eyes. Without a word, the deal had been struck.

"Right then," Rebecca grunted as she pushed up from the booth, "let's get you off to bed." Rebecca tugged at Owen's hand, offering to help him stand. Owen acquiesced with a few slow nods.

Though Owen's nerves had steadied, his legs had not. The sudden force of being pulled up from his seated position required more balance than he was prepared for. Owen followed the momentum of Rebecca's pull until he collided with her. She let out an excited shout of protest before being pinned against the bar. Both struggled to regain some semblance of proper footing, Rebecca struggling to prop up Owen as he slipped while pushing off from the bar.

The mess of tangled limbs ended with Owen and Rebecca falling to the floor. Desperate, haltering attempts were made to slow their fall. Rebecca barely missed catching hold of the bartop. Owen's bumbling fingers failed to reach the table from their booth. Owen had now become pinned face-down under Rebecca, who was staring at the arched ceiling of the lounge car from her back. An altogether messy event.

Neither moved for a moment. The pair lay stunned as they reviewed the episode in silence. Owen felt Rebecca begin to shudder on top of him. The sensation was followed by a loud, poorly suppressed snort. Owen tried to swat at what he guessed was Rebecca's head. His feeble attempt broke Rebecca's restraint, which exploded into bright laughter. She doubled over as she rolled off of Owen's back.

"You're a real mess, aren't you," Rebecca sputtered between laughs.

A chortle escaped Owen as he reached out for the bench where he had previously sat. He failed his attempt with a quick slip, swearing as he did so. Owen could not help himself. The two of them laid on the floor, laughing like a pair of idiots.

Rebecca and Venkat disembarked at Elstaff after two days on the train. Once a simple junction where the Southport and New Haven rail lines met, the constant traffic allowed Elstaff to grow into a prosperous trade town. Goods from the northern town of Oswyn flowed down the Twin Rivers and Orlena shipped items from Bottom Bay up Sisir's Run, both ending up in Arnstead. From there, coaches and wagons moved items to the last Federation Rail station. Elstaff saw all of these goods, as well as those going west from the Eastern Landing.

Both Venkat and Rebecca had been assigned to Elstaff. Their assignment was to bolster the Bureau's presence in the town and to help regulate the illicit trade of stolen focuses, relics, and black-market memory glass. A Bureau representative met them the moment they stepped off the manarail. No time was spared for long farewells. Only a few words could be exchanged before Owen was parted from his friends.

Owen's destination, Arnstead, required a short layover before boarding a train on a different line. He stood quietly against the brick wall of the ticket booth while he waited for the boarding whistle to blow. The leather satchel that held his toiletries and some spare civilian clothes rested between his lower back and the wall. There seemed little for him, a stranger to Elstaff, to do but wait for his time to leave.

Two hours passed while Owen watched passengers and porters go about their business. The population here in Elstaff seemed quite similar to that of his native Southport. A diverse collection of all the races from what cultures of the Old World still thrived. Bangeli humans with their various shades of brown skin and dark hair; the Nirdac, with fair skin, hair, and eyes; and the Zumbatrans, with black skin and towering stature. Nirdac harn loped about with their large feet, tall ears falling behind their heads nearly down to their cotton tails; the Zumbatrans, both taller and leaner than their Nirdac counterparts, walked a more even and deliberate stride. Bangeli katarl, in their black-striped orange fur, carried their powerful frames with authority; golden-coated Zumbatrans exuded elegance as they strode about with pride; Nirdac katarl weaved about their taller, more imposing cousins with ease.

One individual did stand out from the crowd. Owen only caught a short glimpse in his peripherals but was fairly certain that he spied a Fieldkin. He had never seen one before. Only heard about their startling similarity to humans. From a distance, they could even be mistaken as a Bangeli, with their straight, black hair. Upon drawing closer, however, their reddish skin would become more evident. Their eyes were also too large to be human. A trait that allowed them keener sight on the fields of the Great Expanse. Or so Owen had heard.

Most kin, designated as such by the Federation due to the aforementioned similarity to humans, kept away from the East Landing. The Federation's arrival had pushed the native population west across the continent. It was Owen's understanding that the Fieldkin had moved peacefully. That they were migratory people who had little use for cities and towns. This was what he had been taught, anyway.

The blare of a manarail engine's whistle snapped Owen out of his musings, drawing his attention away from the crowds. Boarding for the line bound for Arnstead had been called. Owen gathered up his things and cut through the crowded platform. His legs were eager to find a comfortable respite aboard the train.

28

Once aboard and with baggage stowed in his private sleeping compartment, Owen made for the observation car. He had made the mistake of blazing through the only book he had brought along for the trip: the most recent Stephanie Queen novel, *Shining Tower*. There was an odd sort of mystery about the harn's writings. A sort of connection between each work. Owen's mother would go on and on about the intricacies of each story and how they tied together as a greater collection. For Owen's part, he enjoyed the absurdities that the author continued to think up. Each story seemed to outdo the last.

Without literature to keep himself distracted, Owen realized he was at a loss for how to fill the next three days of travel. The observation car seemed to him a likely place to make a travel companion. Someone who might be fascinated by the wide-open fields or rolling hills. A stark change to life amongst buildings three or more stories tall. Better yet, Owen thought, he might be able to find someone willing to trade books.

A slight shudder rocked each car as the train began to levitate. With a final whistle and a sudden jolt, the train was on its way west. Speed gathered slowly for the great engine. It would be at least an hour before the train had reached its top speed.

Owen arrived in the observation car just in time to see the outskirts of Elstaff fade from view. The observation car, positioned at the rear of the train, was built differently from the typical passenger or sleeping cars. Windows were larger to allow for greater view, and the gaps between each window were smaller. No seats lined the walls of the car. A pair of long benches were set back-to-back. Considerable space was left between the benches and the walls of the car to allow for increased foot traffic.

All these differences aside, what made the observational car stand out most from the other cars was that only half of it was enclosed. A wall bisected the middle of the car. Doors on either side of the benches allowed for passengers to walk out onto the porch-like area. The benches continued out past the wall, stopping far enough from the end for people to walk through. Chest-high rails had been erected on the exposed edges of the car to prevent any unfortunate accidents.

Owen scanned the car as he closed the entryway behind himself. As luck would have it, he was not the first person to arrive. A Zumbatran harn sat in the enclosed area with his arms crossed over his chest. A small scarlet book rested on the harn's feet, which were also crossed. The man's shoes had been tucked neatly under the bench. Pages were turned by a floppy ear that hung down over the man's shoulder.

"Hello there," Owen said, smiling as approached the fellow reader. "Mind if I take a seat?" Owen indicated the open area next to the harn.

At first, there was no response. A quiet moment passed as the harn licked the tip of his ear to turn another page. Owen accepted this silence as tacit approval and seated himself next to the harn.

"Might I ask what you're reading?"

Owen's question was met with more silence. More pages being leafed through. An expectant stare went unacknowledged. The faint smile Owen had worn began to fade as he realized he was being ignored. He pulled his copy of *Shining Tower* from his satchel in a last-ditch effort to start a conversation.

"I just finished reading Queen's latest novel, myself. A gift from my mother."

"Queen, huh?" the harn rasped. His voice betrayed an advanced age not apparent from his looks. "Too fanciful for me. I prefer my stories to be a bit more grounded." The harn half-turned his head to face Owen, clearly struggling to tear himself away from what he was reading. His eyes only briefly turned to catch an initial glance of Owen.

Another quiet moment passed. Then, seemingly out of nowhere, the harn froze. Relaxed shoulders rose and became stiff. His back straightened as nervous fingers drummed on slender forearms. A deep breath filled the harn's lungs and was carefully exhaled. He turned his head to fully face Owen. Curiosity furrowed his brow.

"Is there anything I can help you with, Mr. Seeker?"

Owen was taken aback. Not only had the harn's posture shifted, but so had his tone. Vaguely dismissive remarks had become a concerned inquiry. Owen blinked twice, his lower lip jutting slightly.

"I'm sorry if I have offended you, sir," Owen calmly replied. He half-raised an open hand to the harn, hoping to dismiss any perceived aggression. "Only hoped to start a conversation. Maybe ask if you had a book to spare, to be honest."

The harn's eyes narrowed to thin slits as he looked Owen up and down. His brow twitched as his gaze met Owen's again, followed by a sharp inhale through his nose. He then earmarked his current place in his book before snapping it shut.

"Terribly sorry, Mr. Seeker," the harn added, taking his book in his hands before sliding on his shoes. "I really should be getting back to my cabin. Good day."

There was no sincerity in the harn's words. His parting was cold, impersonal. As if he were speaking to a child's doll rather than to a person. He stood, rotated his ankles to adjust the fit of his shoes, and strode out of the observation car. All the while he kept his head turned away from Owen.

Elstaff was a speck on the horizon before anyone joined Owen in the rear car. As with the harn, Owen received a curt hello before being ignored. The observation car grew crowded as the day trudged forward. Each person who entered had the same few words to meet Owen's welcoming smile.

"Good day, Mr. Seeker."

Their hollow words were infectious. Every additional person who entered the car increased Owen's sense of isolation. He was alone among a crowd of thirty.

"Good day, Mr. Seeker. Can I help you?"

Two days into the train's journey west, the words had lost a small measure of their sting. Owen had accepted that the general populace of the train wanted nothing to do with him.

Rather than try to mingle with passersby, Owen had decided to approach the front of the train. The engine's thrum grew harsher the farther forward he traveled. Vibrations seeped into every bone and joint. A general sense of numbness, almost like a leg that has fallen asleep, took over his whole body.

The engineer who had greeted Owen was a human female. Owen guessed she must at least be older than fifty, judging from the lines at the corners of her eyes and the traces of white that streaked through her black hair. Her gray shirt was soaked through with sweat. Thumbs pulled at suspender straps that appeared to bite into her shoulders. Impatience was plain on her face.

"Yes," Owen replied, holding out an open hand. "Third Seeker Owen Raulstone. Hoping to see the head engineer."

"You're talking to her," the woman said, taking Owen's hand in her powerful grip. "Lerato."

"Ah, very good. I'm to perform an inspection of the engine while I'm onboard. Transitionary task while I make my way to Arnstead. Do you have a moment to spare?"

Owen raised his left hand to show the packet of documents he carried. Lerato looked from the papers to Owen, back to the papers, and then to the door ajar behind her.

"Nobody told me about any inspection," Lerato probed.

"Surprise inspection," Owen countered. "Can't have the place gussied up just for me."

Lerato stared at Owen hard. Her eyes examined every inch of Owen's uniform, from the tip of his boots to the top of his high collar. Something was muttered under her breath that Owen could not quite make out.

"Fine," Lerato said at last, as much to the floor as to Owen. She grabbed a small, blue towel from a rack and draped it over her shoulder. The sliding door was thrown open to make way for the two to enter. Lerato dabbed at her neck and forehead with the towel as she ducked through the doorway. Owen bent over and followed through the short passage.

Heat blasted Owen's face as he entered the manarail engine's cabin. A wet heat, thick with steam and sweat. Open windows on either side of the room did little to stifle its oppressive presence. Droplets of water ran down the metal walls until they were caught by the wind. Crimson light pouring out of the two memory glass pillars in the center of the room made the whole cabin seem more like an oven than a place of work.

"Hey chief, I thought you were on break!" The scream, barely audible over the rumbling cacophony, came from a katarl at the head of the engine. He was looking at Lerato over his shoulder through goggled eyes.

Lerato did not speak as she raised her goggles, which had been hanging about her neck, but rather pointed a thumb at Owen. The katarl raised his head slowly before turning back to peer through the engine's windshield. It was difficult to tell if the gesture was meant to say *Got it,* or *Oh, great.* Owen wasn't spared the time to think about it. A pair of goggles were thrust into his free hand.

"Eyes on!" Lerato howled at Owen. "Let's get this over with."

The nature of the inspection was a simple one. A packet of checklists had been included with the assignment papers dictating Owen's travel to Arnstead. It detailed what questions to ask about what bits of machinery. Things like whether or not the memory glass pillars were clear or clouded, and what temperature the engine room maintained. All the necessary inquiries were laid it. Owen simply had to do as the documentation asked, as Rebecca had done on the first leg of the journey, and document the responses.

The task was not an unwelcome one for Owen. He had been fascinated by the inner workings of manarail engines ever since he was a boy. The combination of intense Flow mastery and modern glass smithing was like candy for a young, inquisitive mind. Teams of people working in unison to hurtle a giant contraption of iron, steel, and wood across vast expanses of land. A dangerous task performed so well that the average passenger would barely notice the engine's hum.

This was Owen's first opportunity to view the inner workings of a manarail engine. He affixed the proffered goggles to his face with glee as he entered the cabin.

"I've got four crews operating two pillars. Twelve-hour shifts," Lerato continued, shouting every word in a slow, deliberate fashion. "Crews are made up of three people. Except for Jody. She can handle a pillar by herself."

The pillars of memory glass stood in the middle of the cabin. Transparent, red cylinders that glowed furiously from constant use. Both stood from floor to ceiling. Small veins of silver-alloy led from the top and bottom of each pillar to the main console, where the katarl at the helm manipulated the Flow output.

Three people surrounded the pillar on the left. Two were readily visible from where Owen stood, while the third appeared as a blur through the bright column of glass. Each knelt on folded wool blankets with gloved hands pressed against the column. If they were aware of Owen's presence, he could not tell. Their eyes were closed as they focused on the task at hand. The column was particularly bright around the hands of the workers. All were drenched in sweat, their suspender straps hanging loosely at their hips. On the column to the right, a single Nirdac harn performed a job meant for a minimum of three. She was relatively dry compared to the others in the cabin. The only sign of her exerting any real effort was an occasional twitch of her pink nose.

"This is very impressive," Owen said, leaning close to Lerato to avoid shouting. "I've never seen memory glass this clear. These columns must have cost a small fortune to produce."

"We're a newer engine," Lerato cried as she nodded. "Less than a year old. Senate might not know a wrench from a hammer, but they're not shy about throwing money at the Transit folks. Makes our lives easier," Lerato continued, making a sweeping gesture at her crew. "Engine this size would need twice the manpower if we had hazy glass. Gets real cozy real quick."

"I can imagine," Owen replied. The space was cramped enough already with just seven people. Twelve or more would make the sweltering conditions all the more unbearable. "Glad to see—"

Their conversational shouting was interrupted by a sudden cry of pain. One of the people manning the column to the left, a Bangeli human, was doubled-over on the slick cabin floor. He clutched one of his arms close to his chest.

Lerato was down by the man's side in an instant. She had pulled him away from the memory glass pillar before Owen could figure out where to drop the papers he held. Owen opted for jamming the documents into one of his coat pockets to be dealt with later.

"Let me see it," Lerato shouted at the injured man. He held his right arm up, reluctance born from shame as much as pain. Most of the skin on his forearm was inflamed. Small pockets of blisters on hand and wrist revealed themselves as Lerato carefully the glove from the man's hand. "Only drawback for these pillars. Easy to slip past your friction limit, burnt before you know it. Lars!"

"Boss?" the katarl at the helm called in response.

"Get Onveer out of here, see if anyone from the House is onboard before he goes into shock. Priest, Keeper, whoever you can find."

"On it," the katarl replied. Lerato took control of the helm as the katarl moved to help the injured man.

"And get someone from the night crew in here. We're gonna need to get creative with shifts."

"I can do it!" Owen called out.

Lerato half-turned at the suggestion. She seemed to look through Owen rather than at him. Silent words formed on her lips. Her head rocked from side to side in consideration. A heavy shudder beneath their feet seemed to answer whatever questions Lerato posed to herself.

"It's not on my head if you get yourself killed, you hear me?"

"Endurance training is part of the job," Owen called. He pinched his collar and raised it slightly, indicating his position as a Spellseeker. "You just need someone to pull energy, right? Not do anything special with it?"

Owen had already begun to unbutton his coat before Lerato gave her

34

reply.

"Just until we get something better figured out. Gloves are by the door."

Owen hung his coat from the hook that housed his borrowed gloves. Looking at the others that channeled the Flow into the pillars, he decided he should get his sleeves and a few of his top shirt buttons undone. Another shudder, this one more violent than the last, rocked the cabin.

An open blanket remained on the cabin floor where Onveer had been. Owen knelt on the blanket and sat on his heels. The leather gloves slid on easily. Each was lined with soft, fine fur. *Abalern fur,* Owen thought to himself, *probably to help fight any kind of feedback.*

For a brief moment, Owen hesitated. The memory glass pillar loomed over him. Crimson heat enveloped his entire body as thick, humid air stifled his breathing. Onveer's burnt and blistered arm flashed in Owen's mind. Owen unconsciously pawed at his arms with a vacant stare before violently shaking the thought out of his head.

"Hill!"

Owen looked up to see the person to his left nodding.

"What?" Owen shouted in response.

"It's like climbing a hill!" they shouted again, leaning closer to Owen. "No need to run! Find a steady pace that works for you, and you'll get to the top before you know it!"

"Okay!" Owen replied, nodding slowly as he did so.

Hands trembling, Owen positioned himself to channel. His knees were together. He placed his hands on the pillar roughly a foot apart. Three slow, humid breaths filled his lungs and calmed his nerves. The vision of a river rose in his mind as he closed his eyes. Not a river of water, with a bed of silt and stone. This river was purple. A torrent of jagged light with crests of green, raging through a void darker than any night.

Owen reached out to the Flow. He called for the great torrent to reach him, to fill him with the lifeblood of the world. A small trickle of light diverged from the greater rapids. It wound its way to Owen, slithered through shadow and nothing. Warmth began to fill Owen's chest. Not like the humid, uncomfortable heat of the train. No, this heat was calm. It wrapped itself around his lungs. Every breath Owen took became laced with the light of the world. The Flow poured into his heart, filling his blood with the very force of nature.

The small stream widened as energy continued to enter Owen's body.

Heat rose internally as the Flow continued to swell inside of him. As the heat rose to become uncomfortable, Owen began to channel the energy. What had moved about his body freely was now forced into his arms. A final push moved the energy to his hands, then through them. Connection with the memory glass pillar had been established.

With the redirection of the Flow came the all too familiar sense of friction. Unable to move as it pleased, the Flow began to resist Owen. The amount of energy being channeled came at a minor price. A feeling like fine sandpaper being gently rubbed against his arms and hands. As Owen increased the width of the conduit he had established, so too did the friction grow.

Owen found a zone of relative comfort. The sensation was akin to sliding down a mountainside covered in gravel. While not pleasant by any means, Owen felt an obligation to do as much as he could without causing self-injury. Persistent in the back of his mind was the thought that his presence could have been what set Onveer over his limit. Owen would endure this precarious slope for the next five hours.

3.

TWICE TESTED

I wonder how Venkat and Becca are getting on? Imagine it would be nice to have a familiar face from the start. Would be terrifying to start a new assignment in a new town alone. Will be terrifying, that is. Still can't believe they got assigned together while I'm out alone. On the frontier, of all places. Might be a measure of excitement if it wasn't just me. Won't just be me though. Of course not. I'll have the whole Arnstead division. Must be a tight-knit bunch with how dangerous the place is. Imagine I'll make friends fast. Always do. Been getting on well enough with these train folks, haven't I? Wait... the train!

A clear vision of the Flow had become foggy and distorted as Owen's mind began to wander, as it often did. *A minute? Two minutes? An hour? More?* Fanciful thoughts gave way to speculation of time lost. Another distraction. Owen shook his head, hoping to clear away any useless clutter.

Sweat had soaked through his cream-colored shirt hours ago. His knees ached from constant kneeling, and his arms quivered under the stress concerted effort. A return to full concentration on the Flow made his arms feel as if they had turned into a warm pudding. Owen's head hung low between his outstretched arms. Air came in ragged, wet breaths.

"All right, reel it in!" Lars howled from the command console. "We're gonna coast into the station."

Each channeler pulled away from their respective memory glass column. A collective sigh filled the quieted room. The engineer was no longer using energy to push the train forward. He would keep the train aloft while its momentum carried through to the final destination. Grunts were audible over the reduced thrum as the regulars stood and stretched sore limbs.

Owen, drained as he was, toppled over and fell with a thud. Arms splayed wide across the cabin floor, too weak to move. Blood charged into his calves and feet for the first time in hours as he forced his legs to straighten. Eyes that saw nothing, in particular, blinked against the red light.

"A full shift yesterday plus another half today, Seeker," one of the channelers said as they offered Owen a hand. He was a young Zumbatran human with an irresistible, dimpled smile. "Not bad for a rookie!"

"I quite like it down here, thank you very much." Owen attempted a smile as he spoke. Only a few words came between each labored breath. He also attempted a polite wave to decline, but only managed to raise a couple of fingers off the cabin floor.

"Nonsense!" another channeler roared with glee. Another Zumbatran, this one a female katarl. "To the lounge!"

With that declaration, both Zumbatrans took an arm each and raised Owen to his feet with a single pull. There was a brief moment where Owen's legs managed to support his weight. Only a moment, though, as his legs quickly realized that they, too, felt a bit like pudding. The two channelers caught Owen's weight before he could fall.

Sheer amazement replaced Owen's concern over his inability to function. These two had worked the same shift as him, in the same sweltering conditions, and likely channeled twice Owen's output. Yet here they were hauling Owen out of the manarail engine room with jovial spirits. A sense of respect for these people had blossomed into admiration.

"Still can't believe how much energy you guys can channel," Owen said, this time requiring fewer breaths between words. "That is astounding."

"Stop it!" the katarl purred. "All we do is move raw energy. Nowhere near what Lars and Chief do."

"Or a Spellseeker!" another channeler joined in. "You folks do all sorts of stuff I couldn't even dream about. How about you show us something fancy when we hit the rail town's saloon?"

"I think I need to be able to walk first," Owen replied. The comment brought a wave of laughter over the channels, and more than a few pats on Owen's back. They all missed the bitter undertone in Owen's voice as he spoke. The pang of guilt that punched his stomach when accepting their praise. Giddy channelers carried Owen forward all the same.

The channelers were true to their word. Just as the night before, the crew made straight for the lounge. They passed through near-empty passenger cars. Normal restraint had been cast aside. Proper social etiquette had no place on a ghost train, not among those possessed with delirious cheer. Adrenaline fueled their march more than any desire for food or drink.

One cry was raised in protest as the engine crew passed. Tucked away in a dark sleeping compartment, a lone harn scowled and grumbled. Awoken from his last period of rest before marching west to join a rail construction crew. His dissent was stifled. Not by any malice or rebuttal from the engine crew, but simply because they could not hear the harn above their thunderous chatter.

Each crew member threw themselves onto a stool the moment they arrived in the lounge car. Orders were hurled at the bar hand, a jittery harn not prepared for the sudden onslaught of business. Whiskey flowed and finger food was prepared with haste. Another trait of the engine crew that confounded Owen: their ability to drink after such an arduous task. The only drink Owen could force himself to consume was water. Even that was a struggle for him to get down more than a couple of sips at a time.

A cool, dry bartop was a most welcome reprieve. The polished surface begged for a tired face to rest upon it. It needed the warmth of exhaustion. This was Owen's delusion, at least, upon plopping his face down. It made a rather squishy sound. Like a sponge being dropped onto stone.

The conversation carried on without Owen's input. There were a few attempts to drag Owen into the crew's discussion. Questions about his line of work, the cases he had solved, if he had ever apprehended anyone of particular danger. Owen's sorry countenance eventually made his refusals for him. The engine crew decided, without saying aloud, that the poor Seeker deserved some rest.

It was not until the train had come to a complete stop that the engine crew bothered to wake Owen. The inviting bartop had claimed his consciousness less than an hour into their celebrations. What few passengers remained on the train could be heard shuffling about, gathering their belongings before departing from their cars. A brief haze clouded Owen's mind as one of the channelers gave him a gentle shake.

"Last stop, friend," they said as Owen blinked at the commotion.

Parting pleasantries were exchanged between Owen and the crew amidst a series of grunts and stretches. Shoulders were clapped on and hands were shaken with vigor. Every channeler took their turn to wish Owen well as he moved to leave the lounge car and gather his luggage. Even the injured Onveer, who was lucky to have only sustained some first and second-degree burns, was present. Wrapped hands and arms, however, made shaking hands a delicate process.

Lerato was the last to speak. She sat on a stool at the end of the bar, sipping on something blue that Owen could not readily name. A single finger, from the hand that held the glass, beckoned. Her once reluctant demeanor had softened.

"Appreciate you stepping up to help. Really do." The words were warm, her voice smooth when not shouting above a manarail engine. "If this Arnstead business doesn't work out, come talk to Federation Rail. I'm sure the Western Rose could make some space." Lerato gestured to indicate the train as she spoke.

"I'll hold you to that," Owen replied with a slight bow of his head.

The sleeping car where Owen stored his luggage was a few cars past the lounge. Suitcase and satchel were tucked in the corner of his curtained bunk. Little time had been spent there since his work with the engine crew began. Thin mattress and rough woolen blanket became largely ignored. He did not have the energy to complain about such minor trifles after fighting through a twelve-hour shift.

He shouldered his satchel and pulled the suitcase from its corner. The singular motion did not sit well with legs that still ached. Small as the satchel was, it nearly pulled Owen to the floor. Stability returned slowly as he forced himself into a neighboring passenger car to depart the train.

What met Owen as he descended the car's iron steps onto the platform did not pass for a train station, in his mind. The platform was hastily constructed and did not span the entire length of the train. There was no gate to ward off would-be stowaways, nor was there a ticket booth to book passage. Not a single porter to help load and unload baggage and passengers. Nothing but thrown-together planks with gaps large enough for a harn to fall through.

Beyond the platform was no better. A handful of small structures huddled about a single, packed-earth road. There did not appear to be any houses. At least if there were, Owen had never seen homes of this sort: no windows, flat iron rooves, and with sliding wooden doors twice the height of a man. *Warehouses, I suppose?* It seemed odd to Owen to have a place to store goods but no place to sleep.

The only building that showed any sign of life was the saloon, which was clearly labeled as such with large, painted letters across the wall that faced the train platform. Members of the train crew had already found seats on the shaded porch. Familiar faces waved for attention and called out for

Owen. He had expected to be met on the platform with further instructions. With no source of orders in sight, the barkeep seemed as good a person as any to get direction from.

Dust kicked up under each labored step. The brushlands that made up the area had been beaten down by boot and hoof. Tracks of heavily laden carts cutting through the main causeway were clear to the naked eye. Everything about the small settlement, apart from its lack of life, pointed to heavy traffic.

"Seeker!"

An authoritative call rang out from Owen's left. Unlike the curt addresses of Mr. Seeker he had grown accustomed to on his train rides west, this one put an immediate halt to Owen's stride. His spine straightened as tired legs snapped together. The suitcase he carried fell to the ground, Owen's hands opening to rest by his thighs.

Though Owen had switched to his civilian clothes to work with the engine crew, he still wore signs of his station. The sword hanging from his left hip was a clear indication of the military. No average citizen would wear a weapon in such a bold, open fashion. On his right hip was his caster pistol. Memory glass cartridges were slotted across his leather belt near the pistol, four in total. Such an exotic weapon told any military personnel that Owen was something more. A fellow Spellseeker could identify Owen with a passing glance.

"With me. Walk and talk."

Released from attention, Owen looked just in time to see Second Seeker Zanaar Abbas turn heel. Quick words matched the hurried stride of the Zumbatran katarl. Golden fur gleamed in the early afternoon sun as she beckoned Owen to follow.

"Yes, ma'am," Owen replied as he lifted his suitcase.

Seeker Abbas moved with purpose towards the western edge of the railway village. Owen nearly had to run to catch up to his superior. Much like Owen, she wore civilian clothes: a red, buttoned shirt, and brown trousers with black suspenders. The legs of her trousers were tucked into leather riding boots that came up to her knees. A blue armband with white piping was the only outward indication that she was a Spellseeker. Normally worn over the blue coat regular to the position, it now served as a reminder of her rank while in her civvies.

Two six-pointed, silver stars sewn into the armband indicated the rank of Second Seeker. Owen's armband, which was tucked away with the rest of the uniform in his suitcase, had three. The stars on his armband were also smaller. First Seeker's bands held a single star. An armband of the Chief Seeker, head of the Bureau of Arcane's Spellseeker Division, would be emblazoned with the symbol of the organization in silver stitching.

"Briefing said you would have further orders, ma'am?" Owen asked as he matched pace with Seeker Abbas. The documents that detailed his assignment to Arnstead had also spoken of a rendezvous with the Second Seeker.

"We're headed to the stables. Bureau is expensing horses for us." The cadence of Seeker Abbas' speech matched her stride: quick and deliberate. "I have business at the end of the rail. Will ride with you until then. Reports of railroad ties being stolen."

"Are the horses required, Second Seeker?"

The question made Seeker Abbas' next step falter. Her glare was one of disbelief.

"Excuse me?" she inquired.

"The horses, ma'am," Owen replied, embarrassed by timid inquiry. "Are they the... only method of transport?

"You're not walking to Arnstead, Seeker. Bureau expects you in no more than a week, not a month."

"Yes, of course. I meant more like a carriage or—"

"Listen," Seeker Abbas grumbled. "I'm in a hurry. If you want to pay for a wagon or something, that's your business. It doesn't make any difference to me. So long as you make it to Arnstead within a week, my job is done. Can't promise that any carriage will want to take on a Seeker, though."

Owen slowed, then came to a full stop. His free hand was raised and his mouth slightly agape. Eyes fell from Seeker Abbas down to the brown, dusty road. Desperately he searched for the words to describe his hesitation. None came to him that would not make him seem as pathetic as he felt. Owen chose to remain silent rather than embarrass himself further.

"I don't have time for this, Seeker Owen," Seeker Abbas sighed. "Do what you want. If I'm asked to report on your whereabouts, I won't cover for you. I'll tell them that I offered guidance and you refused. If you're not on my heels when I get to the stables, I'll assume your mind is made up."

Without pause for a response, Seeker Abbas doubled her pace. Owen's hesitation had made it clear to her that he was not ready to follow. There was no longer reason for her to expect company on her ride west. Her dust-caked boots fell hard against the packed earth. A vigorous shake of her head was the last Owen saw of Seeker Abbas before she disappeared, taking a hard right-turn around one of the warehouses at the end of the settlement.

Owen had attempted to keep up with Seeker Abbas for the first handful of steps. His hand was outstretched, reaching for her shoulder or to tug at her red sleeve. Crooked fingers anticipated wrinkled cloth. They went limp and fell, followed soon after by his arm, as Owen realized he did not want to catch Seeker Abbas.

A cold, sinking chill wrapped itself around Owen's shoulders. It felt like a blanket of frost had been draped over his back. Slight shivers stood defiant against the warm midday sun. The churning sickness in his stomach rose. Up past the slow, reluctant beat of his heart. Each beat pushed the pangs of guilt higher and higher until it hung on his face. His cheeks tingled and his brow sagged. The weight of his shame pushed down against the acute awareness of his indecision.

"Something," Owen muttered. The word barely escaped his lips. "Do something."

Heavy legs made their first attempt at a slow, measured stride. A few steps turned into a few more. The weight remained, but Owen was in motion again. He made for the corner that Seeker Abbas has disappeared around.

Signs of life began, at last, to make themselves apparent as Owen approached the warehouse. Patches of tents that had been obscured by the simple buildings came into view. Canvas tents of various sizes and neutral colors. Socks and undergarments hung from the guidewires that secured the tent flies in place. Larger clothing lines connected clusters of tents, a half-dozen or more in each pod.

Order was nowhere to be found in the tent village. Guidewires reached over and across each other. The space between tents was a dangerous alleyway of snares and iron spikes. Some tents faced into their pods, while others faced outwards. Knee-high brush blocked passageways in addition to artificial obstacles. Plates and cookware were tucked under bush and tent flap alike. Attempts to find logic in the disarray came as a welcome distraction to Owen.

Though signs of their presence were strewn all about, the actual people they belonged to were still scarce. The tent village appeared to be largely unpopulated. A cot might have a curled-up figure here, or there might be a slumped-over figure in a chair there. Those people were the exception, however, not the rule.

The only space that appeared to be alive was the mess tent. A group of harn moved around under a canvas fly that had been drawn taught from corner to corner. It looked less like a tent and more like an improvised pavilion. Small fires heated tall, dull pots of scratched copper. Practiced hands moved swiftly from cutting boards to cast-iron pans.

"You lost, stranger?"

Owen had not realized how close he had crept to the mess tent. Only a few arms' lengths separated him from the Zumbatran harn who spoke. Wide, green eyes looked over Owen with equal parts curiosity and suspicion.

"Ah, yeah, I—"

"Like you mean it, son!" the harn called, interrupting Owen's sheepish reply. She cupped a sauce-covered hand to one of her long ears, free hand continuing to mince a pair of sweet onions.

"A carriage!" Owen said, drawing a deep breath to make himself heard. "I'm looking for a carriage out of town, headed to Arnstead."

The harn raised her head in acknowledgment. Her cupped hand moved to grab the wooden cutting board she had been working on. Raising the board above a saucepot, she transferred the onions into the bubbly red sauce with a plop.

"Might be one or two down at the stables." The harn pointed her onion-covered knife at the western edge of the tent village. "If you're lucky. Safe bet is going to be a pony. Or horse, rather," she added, looking back at Owen.

Brushlands gave way to green, rolling hills over the course of four days. The change was gradual. Short grass was replaced by grass that grew as high as two feet in some areas and was never shorter than a foot. The individual blades grew in thickness, as well. A single blade might be as wide as a human finger. Yellow dots, the size of a thimble, speckled the green grass.

Shrubs and bushes had been mostly replaced by clusters of spindly trees. Trunks no thicker than a foot bowed with the gentle winds that rolled across the countryside. Their bark was thin and clung tight to the three's

44

core. Resembling birch trees in color, they were mostly white. Crimson knots dotted their surfaces. Rosy pink leaves rose and fell with the breeze.

The wind blew at their backs from the east. It wrapped around the carriage and carried the smell of laboring horses downwind to the west. Owen added this to the growing list of things for which he was thankful. The carriage on which he rode being the crown jewel of that list.

Perched out front on the driver's bench, Owen was in the perfect position to enjoy the easterly wind. It helped to reduce the oppressive heat of the noonday sun directly above. He had managed to procure a dark, woolen hat with a wide brim before leaving the manarail village eight days prior. The hat, in conjunction with the pillowed bench, made for a comfortable transit. Mostly comfortable, at least. Owen still made a point to keep his feet tucked back from the outer lip of the footboard.

"Can't imagine that's comfy." The driver playfully kicked one of Owen's boots with a wry smile. "Why do you do that?"

"Excuse me?" Owen replied, genuine confusion crumpling his brow.

"Ah," the driver before clearing his throat. Hours without use had clogged the katarl's throat with phlegm, which he discourteously spat on the road. "Your feet. Why not use the footboard?"

"Oh, the footrest." An embarrassed laugh laced its way into Owen's reply. "Don't much care for horses, I guess."

"What?" the Nirdac katarl said, shocked. "How come? They're marvelous creatures, they are!"

Owen was pleased to realize that his distancing from the crew of four horses had gone unnoticed until now. He had done his best every night to keep the carriage between himself and the beasts. At the very least, a campfire between himself and the horses was necessary. The fact that the driver trusted his team enough to leave them more or less untethered at night did little to help Owen's nerves.

"Oh sure, yes. Beautiful," Owen said, attempting to placate the driver. "Just not for me, I suppose. More the type to get places on my own two legs."

"A walker, then? Fair enough, I can respect that. Especially in city folk," he added with a slight tilt of his head to Owen. "Can't imagine it's easy to find a place for them in your Southports or your New Havens."

"I suppose not."

"Well," the driver followed, taking on a conciliatory tone, "shouldn't be more than another full day or two to Arnstead, so long as the weather holds. Doubt we'll have any problems there."

The driver pushed against the footboard, forcing his body up the backrest of the driver's bench. His head circled the carriage to take in full view of the blue sky that stretched on for miles in every direction. Matted orange and white fur ruffled about his neck as he did so. He sat back down once satisfied and gave Owen a nod of confirmation.

Apart from the heat that came with little tree-cover on the open road, the weather had been quite agreeable for cross country travel. Sparse cloud cover meant no rain to douse the carriage and road. Clear skies made for well-lit nights. The team of horses would not travel by night, of course. Bright stars and a waxing, three-quarter moon, however, allowed for camp to be pitched near nightfall. The driver could push through sunset as twilight bled across the horizon.

Gentle winds never gained enough force to lift loosely-packed dirt from the road. This far west, the road became less traveled. The earth had not been abused so thoroughly as to lose all its trappings. Softer earth made for a smoother ride, as well.

Though the road was more comfortable to ride upon, it was also narrower. A single wide wagon could travel the road. Any oncoming traffic would have to make way. Typically, the lighter, more maneuverable of the two crews would make way for the larger. The particular carriage Owen had procured was spacious enough to only acquiesce to the largest of freight wagons. One convoy of traders headed east had moved Owen's carriage off the road for the better part of two hours.

The past day and a half had been quiet, however. No unexpected company apart from the occasional flock of blue-billed Oswynian geese. Beech, so the driver was called, had pointed out a red-tailed hawk earlier that morning. It was little more than a speck to Owen. He was more impressed by the driver's keen eyes than the presence of the raptor.

A notable lack of distraction gave Owen time to do the one thing he dreaded most: reflect. Self-reflection was not so terrible most days. It was not as if Owen hoped to turn a blind eye to himself for the entirety of his life. The past few weeks, full of change and challenge, had given him plenty of fuel for thought outside of simple niceties for strangers and the like. Twice had Owen embarrassed himself in just as many weeks: once as a drunken mess in front of strangers, and another time in front of the first fellow Seeker he had seen since leaving Venkat and Rebecca.

I can do better.

The thoughts echoed inside Owen's head. He rested his head gently against the carriage as he leaned back. Pinching the brim of his hat between two fingers, he pulled the hat over his face. The cool blue sky was replaced by muggy wool. Sunlight fought to shine through the darkness Owen had made for himself.

I have *to do better. I'll explain myself when I report to the Arcanarium. Better to take the initiative than to backpedal.*

"I'm done!"

The heated exclamation came from within the carriage. Before Owen had the chance to be startled from his reflection, he was tumbling backward into the carriage. The backrest, which doubled as a door between the carriage interior and the driver's seat, had flung inward. Owen's weight resting against the door hastened the already violent swing. A large, strong hand took Owen by his collar and pulled him inward. Coarse words accompanied the human hand.

"Your turn with the housekeeper, bluecoat."

Stepping over the top of Owen and out of the carriage was a human woman. Though brawny as she was, every movement seemed to be measured and precise. No energy was wasted as she lifted herself through the door and up to the driver's seat. Sunkissed, freckled skin completed the look of a Nirdac who spent all of their time outdoors. Without so much as a glance, the woman elbowed Owen's feet into the carriage and grabbed the door.

A loud clack confirmed that the latch had been caught as the door was forcefully closed. Owen had been left in a sorry state. His head and neck supported most of his weight on the carriage floor. Shifting legs shuffled across the carriage's brown, wood-lined wall. His torso had not yet decided whether to rest on a bench or fall the rest of the way to the floor.

"Seems I managed to talk Ms. Galloway's ear off, at last."

The wispy chuckle came from the rear bench. A Zumbatran harn was seated there, his head and shoulder leaning against the carriage wall. What could be seen of his fur was black, with small splotches the color of yellowed-grass dotted across his face. He wore the outdated trappings of a Keeper of the House: a chain coat with three-quarter length sleeves, metal-plated braces for his forearms and shins, and a cotton surcoat. The surcoat was quartered in black and white, with the silver scale of Manus emblazoned on the chest. A pair of cracked leather gloves rested on his knee.

"It would seem so," Owen replied. The rest of his body flopped onto the floor.

"Need a hand, my boy?"

Warm, worldly eyes looked down at Owen. The harn extended a weathered hand.

Owen felt a hint of shame. The harn was entering his twilight years, judging from his shriveling features and thin voice. Yet here he was offering to lift a young man at the height of his life. Owen shook his head, knocking away both the offer for help and the stars that still clung to his vision.

"Quite all right, Keeper Devlin." Owen hauled himself up to the unoccupied bench he had slid down, rubbing his sore neck as he did so. "Pray tell, what set Manda off this time?"

"This time, you say?" Devlin replied with another amused chuckle. "You make it sound like I aggravate the woman for sport. I cannot help that our companion is so averse to conversation."

"You *are* rather loquacious, sir. If you don't mind my saying." Owen spoke with a polite tone.

"Rather on the nose, don't you think?" Devlin's choice of words would have suggested he had been wounded, if not for the mischievous grin he had adopted. The Keeper turned his head to look outward. Red, velvet curtains had been drawn opened to allow for some view of the scenery.

"Well, if you must know," Devlin continued, feigning a great effort, "I was discussing the manarail. The ethics of it, to be more specific. Care to weigh in with your thoughts on casual necromancy?"

The Keeper tapped a gnarled finger against the carriage window. His indication was clear despite the light layer of dust caked on the glass. A few hundred yards north of the road was the only other manmade landmark within a day's ride: incomplete manarail tracks.

Knowledge on how the tracks were assembled was public information, available to those who wished to know. Owen had the pleasure of reading about the subject in his youth. *The Magnificent Manarail: Trains, Tracks, and Where They Are Headed* came specifically to mind. It was a small, unassuming book gifted to him by grandfather Orland when Owen was eight years old. Each chapter was filled with bite-sized details and colorful diagrams. The perfect hook to garner a child's interest in the study of railways.

With the advancement of age came the advancement of knowledge. In his teen years, Owen graduated from children's diagrams to more detailed schematics. Study of the composition of the rails that comprised the track, how they were fastened to prevent wear and theft, as well as the origin of these discoveries. An understanding of practical knowledge came in his late teen years. Knowledge of who performed assembly and how they were regulated.

"I've never seen an advance team before," Owen said after a moment's pause. He slid across his bench to look through the same window as Devlin. "Not in person, at any rate."

Figures of the workers were little more than black specks on the canvas of green. A rise on the far side of the tracks served as the backdrop to their labor. The movement was imperceptible. Owen took a deep breath before speaking again.

"I have two complaints with your claim. First, there is nothing casual about the forward team of a manarail construction crew. Materials have to pass inspection with both the Bureau of Transit and the Bureau of Arcane. Volunteers are documented by the BoA. Compensation is provided to the volunteers in life under the agreement that their bodies are surrendered upon death. Contrary to popular belief, the Bureaus do not creep about in the dead of night to harvest corpses from graveyards. To call the system *casual* is to ignore the vast network of regulations surrounding the subject.

"Second," Owen continued. He had been counting out his points on his fingers, but now held up only two for emphasis. "Necromancy is not an appropriate term. No life is being returned to the bodies that are used, nor do they have any manner of agency. The bodies are merely used by the manarail technician to carry out work. It would be more apt to call the technician a puppeteer than a necromancer."

"A question, if I may?" Devlin was looking at Owen again, a playful glint in his eye.

"Of course," Owen nodded.

"Why must it be the bodies of the deceased? I understand a channeler can use any manner of object, could they not? If a body is necessary for the work, it should be just as easy to build a body of stone or metal. A scarecrow of some sort."

49

"A few problems there," Owen replied. He leaned back against the bench and crossed his right leg over his left.

"Is that so?"

"I'll start with the channeling."

"By all means, please do." Devlin also moved to make himself more comfortable. He seemed to be enjoying himself quite thoroughly.

"Drawing energy from the Flow is one half of a channeler's task. In addition to withstanding the Flow and the bodily harm it may cause, a channeler must be able to visualize their work. The task has to be clear, vivid. Almost like – well, what's the best way to put it?"

Owen's words began to trail off and grow quiet. Words came by rote to describe the mechanical and regulatory aspects of the work. The more creative aspect of channeling the Flow, however, he found much more difficult to describe.

"It's like… let me ask you this. Does it make more sense to you to see a hammer wielded by hand, or to see the tool fling itself through the air?"

"To see the hammer be wielded, sure," Devlin answered.

"Excellent. Now, does it make more sense to you to see the hammer wielded by a human or harn, or to see it be swung by a scarecrow made of straw?"

"A man of flesh and blood, of course." Devlin scratched his furry chin. Wisps of hair curled around a wizened finger. "Where does this line of inquiry lead, Mr. Seeker?"

"All right," Owen leaned forward, resting his elbows on his knees. Emphatic gestures accompanied his words. "So, much like a channeler must practice to enhance their ability to channel and shape the Flow, they must also be able to visualize the purpose they intend to enact. The less fantastical a channeler's purpose the easier it is to focus on channeling. And the same concept applies in reverse.

"Logic would dictate that a channeler should focus on a simple, realistic purpose. This allows the channeler to draw as much power from the Flow as they are safely able to. Minimal risk is applied to the channeler. A manarail technician certainly *could* will a pile of stones to perform the simple tasks required. It is much more *realistic*, however, to imagine a human, harn, or katarl doing the work."

"Even though the body is dead?"

The question was sharp. Devlin saw a flaw and stabbed it with brutal precision. A retort worked its way into Owen's throat but was caught before it could escape. His hands went limp at the wrist and dropped below his knees.

"Well, yes. I suppose." Owen was unsure of himself as he spoke. The sensation became more poignant when he met Devlin's gaze. Owen allowed an exasperated sigh to escape his chest. "I've never done the work myself. It's more conjecture than anything, my understanding of a manarail technician's mindset while channeling."

"Well, I think I understand where you are coming from, at the very least," Devlin said with a half-smile. "Perhaps necromancy *was* too harsh a term. Would 'well-regulated sacrilege' be more appropriate?"

"Is it bad that I would have to say yes?"

There had been no malice in the new terminology put forward by Devlin. His tone was matter-of-fact. The words had been chosen so well that Owen could not refute the claim.

"Having established the proper terms," Devlin began through the low rumble of laughter in his gut, "I believe you still owe me your opinion."

"And here I thought I had dodged the question." Owen pushed his tongue against his cheek. Curly, brown hair rustled as he furrowed his brow. "I guess… I guess it's not my place to say what a person can do with their own body, is it?"

"*You* are much more fun to talk to." Devlin tapped Owen's shin with the toe of his boot. "Makes me glad that girl decided to scurry outside."

It *was* a pleasant change of pace to have proper conversations. Few people had been willing to say anything beyond hello and goodbye in Owen's presence since leaving Elstaff. Not only was Devlin happy to speak to more than the weather, but the man was willing to debate. To engage in proper discussion about the world and their place in it.

The conversation was not able to continue. Two harsh knocks on the door leading to the driver's seat were all that warning that preceded its opening. No care was given for where Owen might have sat. No apology would be forthcoming should the rounded corner collide with his head.

"Javelin."

The sharp word was followed by Manda's open hand. She opened and closed her hand expectantly, though the only response she received was a grumble. Devlin's face made his thoughts clear. That simply speaking Manda's name was enough to summon her.

"I said javelin!" Manda's volume increased with her second cry. The grabbing gesture, seemingly polite by her established standards, had evolved into a quick series of snaps.

"What's going on?" Owen said. He attempted to lean around the door but was foiled in the effort. The door swung with renewed forced and smashed into his nose. Owen yelped in surprise and recoiled into the corner at his back.

"I had the geezer pegged as deaf," Manda growled as she slid through the door, catching her weight on the bench, "but I didn't expect you *both* to be so dense."

Manda's hobnailed boots bit into the carriage floor with a crunch. A bundle of javelins, tightly- bound at their necks and bases with red chords, leaned against the wall of the carriage. They had sat in their corner, undisturbed for the journey's entirety. Manda pulled one of the weapons from the cluster. The remaining six were laid on the bench under the doorway to the driver's seat. She had enough courtesy to point them away from Owen before disappearing from whence she had come.

This sequence of events was a blur to Owen. He was torn between wiping his watering eyes and feeling his nose for any signs of a break. Cautious hands probed for the stray door in hopes of preventing a second strike.

"What is going on?" Owen repeated. "Why on earth do you need a weapon?"

"Group of horses, coming up from the South," replied Beech. "Came over a hill a minute ago. Now I can see them on another. They're coming this way. Fast."

Reigns whipped harshly with that last word. Their carriage jarred at the sudden increase in speed from the team of horses. What had been a pleasant cantor climbed to a near gallop.

"I wonder who that might be?" Devlin inquired, struggling to raise his voice over the thunder of hooves.

"Couldn't see any – ah, there they are again!" Beech was shouting now. His words, spoken to the South where he looked, were barely audible. "No markings!"

"How many?" Devlin called. Authoritative presence rose in the harn with these words. He straightened himself where he sat.

"Enough to cause a problem," Manda howled.

Owen ducked under the half-door, having cleared his eyes, to look out the other side of the carriage. He pulled the red curtains open to peer through the dusty portal. Sure enough, riders atop horses cut through the tall grass towards the carriage.

Five horses were shared across ten riders. Each pair, as a mixture of katarl and humans, rode back-to-back. The person facing forward held the reigns, while the person facing backward held a recurved bow. It was too difficult to see whether arrows had been knocked or not. Distance and smeared glass made sure of that. What Owen could see for certain was that their weapons had not been raised. He slipped over to open door to get a better look.

Owen's back was to the crew of horses as he pulled himself up to the crowded driver's seat. There was no room to sit there himself. Beech was focused on driving the horses, and Manda was using all available space. She rested her left leg across the driver's bench and planted her right foot on the footrest. Her left hand, knuckles white, gripped a bar atop the carriage for securing luggage. These three points of contact kept her stable as she clutched a javelin in her hand.

There was just enough space for Owen to see past Beech. The katarl was leaned forward, allowing for a clear line of sight. Nothing Owen saw was any different from what he saw in the carriage, however. Ten riders atop five horses. Bows were on clear display but had not been drawn. They rode at an angle until they drew within fifty yards and were even with the carriage.

The manarail crew!

The thought flashed like lightning across Owen's mind. He remembered Seeker Abbas' words about crews being waylaid and snapped his head to face north. No crews were in sight. What few technicians were visible so briefly had disappeared behind the eastern horizon. He furrowed his brow, bemused.

Soft, purple light tugged at the corner of Owen's vision. It was emanating from Manda. Harsh, violet light flickered from her forearm and poked out through her rolled-up sleeve. A purple fire burned beneath her skin. When Owen looked up at her face, he saw her eyes had shifted from their natural green to a brilliant orange.

"They're here for you, aren't they?" Owen shouted up at Manda. Flow-infused eyes looked down at Owen, filled with malice.

53

"Quiet."

"If you throw that thing, I'll take you in when we get to Arnstead. Unprovoked channeling and use of excessive force."

"I said shut your gob! It's self-defense."

"Not if you attack them first, it isn't."

Those last words had barely left Owen's lips before Manda raised her left foot. The hobnailed boot was poised to jam into Owen's unprotected face. He raised an arm in defense and slid back into the carriage before the assault could be launched.

"Good," Manda spat, leaning into the carriage to grab the door. "Now stay put, bluecoat."

Rather than push his way through the door again, Owen stumbled over to the southern window of the carriage. The mysterious riders had drawn closer. They were now just over twenty yards away. Arrows were knocked. Bows were raised and ready to be drawn. Owen imagined Manda on the driver's seat, poised to launch a missile at the potential assailants.

Nervous hands began to wander. The thought of an imminent attack had Owen reaching for his caster pistol. He held it in his hands before the thought had registered. Owen closed his eyes and let a deep, calming breath pass shakily through his nose.

Non-lethal, he told himself. *Just in case.*

A metallic ping, like an errant hammer striking an anvil, reverberated through the carriage interior. The sound of the caster pistol's breach being opened had never carried so much weight for Owen as it did now. It was ready to receive a cartridge.

Non-lethal.

Fingers wracked by tremors felt along Owen's belt. They knew to slide to the left-most cartridge. The one nearest his modest Bureau of Arcane belt-buckle. Silver and glass slid snuggly against leather as the desired cartridge was pulled from its sleeve. The cartridge was the length and thickness of Owen's index finger. Memory glass made up the core and was the same color as the clear, blue sky above. The glass was housed in a silver base. Four silver prongs reached from the base to the top of the cartridge. They held the glass in place, claws to keep an explosive sapphire in place.

The cartridge slid neatly into place, pressed by Owen's thumb through the pistol's breech. A lip of silver at the cartridge's base kept the whole thing from sliding out the front of the barrel. Another metallic ping, accompanied by a pair of clicks, sounded as the breech was closed. A small slot for Owen's thumb to contact the cartridge was carved out behind the breech. Part of the cartridge's silver base was visible, along with the small hole in the base that allowed Owen's thumb to meet the cartridge's memory glass core.

Owen stood and grabbed the latch of the southern carriage door. A final breath steeled his nerves as he popped the hatch. Wind pounded the door as if telling Owen to stay inside the carriage. To mind his own business.

"Your attention, please," Owen howled. His right foot was planted on the carriage's outer iron step. With his right hand, he held the carriage door open and steadied himself. In his left hand was the caster pistol. He made sure the weapon was visible. "I am Third Seeker Owen Raulstone, member of the Spellseekers under the federal Bureau of Arcane. Any assault on this vehicle will be considered an assault on the Federation itself and met with appropriate force."

If the riders had heard Owen's words, they made no show of it. The words very well may have been lost to the storm of hooves. Owen channeled the Flow into the cartridge, arming his defense.

"Stop the carriage and surrender the box. You will not be harmed."

These words cut through the equine cacophony. They were heard, clearly and by all. Each word was spoken carefully with a boom to rival genuine thunder. It was impossible to tell who among the riders spoke. Scarves, orange and pale blue, covered their head and faces. Whoever had spoken, though, was using the Flow to bolster their speech. The words that followed were more powerful than those before.

"Continue, and we will take the box by force."

A sound like splintering wood erupted from the front of the carriage. The sound was accompanied by a powerful gust of air that nearly pushed Owen from where he stood. Dirt and grass whipped by under the carriage. Owen held fast to the carriage door, but felt more and more of his weight slipping towards the ground. Glass broke above Owen's head and tumbled down, glistening, through his hair.

Just as Owen felt his fingers begin to slip, he felt a hand take hold of his belts. He was wrenched inside the cabin with surprising force.

"Take cover, son!" Devlin shouted, hovering over the Spellseeker he had just saved.

An arrow buried itself into the carriage's interior. It felt to Owen it had already been a lifetime since he sat in that very spot. He saw another arrow as he looked through the carriage's open door. This arrow had shattered the door's window. It kept the door propped open in Owen's place. Stray bits of glass had fallen onto the floor, tinkling in rhythm with the carriage.

Beyond the frame of the door was a grisly sight. One of the riders was missing their upper torso. The rider, at what had been their back, was doubled-over, clutching the bloody remnants of an arm. Their horse, galloping without direction, peeled away from the clamor. One of the archers had dropped their bow, attention fixed on their wounded comrade. The remaining three knocked arrows. What had been a tight clump of horses now fanned out to present smaller targets.

Wood splintered at the head of the carriage. The door leading to the driver's seat had split down the middle. Half flew over Owen's head to crash into the back of the carriage. The remaining half, only connected to the wall now by its bent bottom hinges, hung limp. Bits of jagged wood mixed with glass on the carriage floor.

After this barbaric display of power, Manda reached with her still-glowing arm to grab another javelin. Her posture had become more hunched. Arrows not destined for the inside of the carriage made their way at her. A subtle dip or weave allowed the missiles to brush past her short hair. There was no acknowledgment of danger in her expression. Her eyes remained fixed on the riders. A viper that has spotted an opening, Manda uncoiled herself to strike.

"Stop!" Owen yelled as he launched himself across the carriage towards Manda. He grabbed at her waist, taking a handful of shirt and trousers, and pulled hard.

Another sickening crunch erupted from the front of the carriage. Owen was able to see the source this time: half of the footboard was missing. Manda had used the footboard to help brace her throw. The resulting force snapped a section of the rest out from under her foot. Manda had been the source of the gust that nearly pulled Owen from the carriage, as well.

This throw went wide. A geyser of dirt and grass erupted in front of the lead rider. There was no time to steer away. Horse, rider, and archer all tumbled forward and were lost beneath the tall grass. Arrows leaped out from the two remaining archers in response.

In a single motion, Manda ducked the arrows, pushed Owen down into the carriage, and rode him to the floor. Glass and wood bit into Owen's back as he landed. Manda raised her purple, energy-infused fist to come down on Owen. Owen responded by burying the pistol he still held into Manda's chest. While the action stopped her fist, her expression only grew more livid.

"What's the big idea, bluecoat!"

"The horses!" Owen spat, finding a sliver of command. "Knock them off the horses!"

The argument was interrupted by another pair of arrows. Ever alert, Manda drew close to Owen's face. One arrow dug deep into the wall, the other shattering the one intact window left in the carriage. Muscles bulged in Manda's neck as she fought the urge to launch Owen at the riders.

"Unbelievable," she growled. She was on the driver's seat again, javelin in hand, before the riders had another chance to attack. "And what do you think *you're* doing?"

"Slowing down!" Beech yelped.

"The hells you are! You stop this thing and we're dead."

"There won't *be* a carriage left to drive if you keep at it!" Owen imagined the katarl flailing at the obliterated footboard. "Give them what they want."

"The door says 'Beech Security and Transit'." The carriage shuddered as Manda smacked its side. "Shut up and do your job!"

The riders used the temporary lull in retaliation to fan out further. Rather than remain grouped, one of the riders pushed their horse faster. They maintained an increased pace until they were a full horse ahead of the carriage's team. The last rider fell back to cross behind the carriage. The vehicle had become surrounded.

Owen had counted himself lucky. During the riders' change in formation, the team that no longer had their bow maintained their position. No more arrows meant a clean shot for Owen. He could take his time to line up his shot and release. Those thoughts of relative cheer lasted for a moment.

Red fire began to swirl about the rider's outstretched hand. It and crackled and popped, leaving a trail of sparks to dance on the wind. The rider pulled their hand toward themselves, then flicked outward. A small bolt of fire crashed into the southern wall of the carriage. The force of the impact made the carriage ride on two wheels for the space of a heartbeat.

Obscenities flowed from Beech like a river, newly burst forth from a dam. To his dismay, words alone would not quench the blaze eating away his carriage a mere arm's length behind. He removed his coat to smack at the fire. The desperate angle he adopted, stretched his full length with the carriage's reign held fast in one hand, should not have been possible.

"Focus," Owen grumbled. There was no time to watch Beech fight the blaze, even as it inched across dry walls and licked at curtains. No time to curtain whatever Manda was doing. A new threat had presented itself. A threat magical in nature, that required haste in resolution.

The sharp, needle-like floor punished Owen's chest as he steadied himself. Warmth filled his arms. Flow energy moved from the shoulder, down the arm, and through the thumb to gather in the memory glass cartridge.

Blue, ethereal light shone from the breech of the caster pistol. At the same time, another gout of flame swirled around the channeling rider's arm. The thick, tangy smell of ironwood smoke told Owen there was not a moment to spare. Another blast would mean the end of the carriage and anything inside. Owen quieted his mind, save for a single thought: *Go!*

An invisible line of force erupted from the barrel of the caster pistol. The force pushed Owen's arms high in recoil. A crackling lance of air pushed out through the carriage and caught the fiery rider under their arm. They were ripped from their saddle, a nearly imperceptible shout rising over the struggle as they fell. The beginnings of a satisfied grin curled the corners of Owen's mouth. Owen's satisfaction would, however, once again be a mere moment.

A roar like a hundred furnaces being fanned in unison exploded from the tall grass where the rider had fallen. Rather than tumbling through grass and over stone, the rider was in the air. Fire danced around both of her arms. Fire that coalesced into jets of blue and red flame. The rider propelled herself up and over the tops of the grass, her back angled to the ground.

There was no grace in the effort at first. The rider spun wildly in midair, attempting to control the force she had generated. Her rotations evened out in short order, though, and it became clear that the rider had gained full control of her airborne movements. Their wanton spiral became the graceful glide of a phoenix. A phoenix whose eyes burned with an icy contempt.

The ordeal had pulled the rider's scarves off of their head and face. What remained was the face of a Zumbatran human. A dark bundle of braided hair whipped past her neck and shoulders. Her sharp jaw cut an intimidating line beneath her face.

"Amalia," Devlin half-whispered with surprised recognition.

Owen started at the name. Not because of the name itself, but because he had forgotten that Devlin was still in the carriage. The harn was seated cross-legged on the rear bench. Half of the driver's seat door was lodged into the wall to the right of his head. If Devlin had noticed, he did a poor job of showing it. His fingers were knit together, open palms faced upwards. Both hands were aglow with a faint light. It looked as if light were being shined through a sheaf of parchment.

"Asking for a miracle?" Owen said, looking at Devlin's hands.

"Pray the gods listen, if she's this angry," Devlin replied, a hint of recognition in his voice. His head turned as the rider pushed through the air until she was ahead of the carriage's horses. Another hundred furnaces were fanned from the effort.

"Last chance," Amalia bellowed. Hers were words that had been imbued with the Flow. They were enhanced again. Each word rang clear over the roar of fire and thunder of horses. Each sounded as a doleful bell calling to the dead. "Surrender the box or I will take it!"

Owen held his thumb tight against the breech of his caster pistol while Amalia spoke. The fear of destroying his arm with unfocused channeling began to shrink against the fear of what this woman might be capable of.

"Shut up!" was followed by the immediate splintering of what remained of the footboard. Manda had launched another javelin. It flew on wings of Flow and fury for Amalia's chest.

The javelin did not meet its target. Amalia, having become well acquainted with the attack, had been ready to receive it. Jets of flame were angled in a way that Amalia rose and spun all at once. She dodged the javelin as the sparrow ducks an idle tree branch. A fountain of debris rose some hundred yards ahead as if to hammer home the failure.

Amalia rose higher still, until, suddenly, the roar of fire vanished. Devlin shouted. Owen raised his pistol as both Manda and Beech clawed their way inside the carriage. The crack of red, scorching death engulfing the carriage set the rest of the world to silence.

Owen was no stranger to soreness. He was well acquainted with the ache that followed a five-mile run at dawn. Tired and bruised arms were common after practice with the sword or in hand-to-hand combat. Headaches screwed into place by booze tucked so far into the bottom of a barrel that not even a gutter hound would dare lick were a weekend ritual. The soreness that greeted him as he awoke was unlike any of these. Owen felt as if he had been stuffed into one of those emptied barrels and sent for a ride down a steep and impossibly long hillside.

Night had veiled the land in soft darkness punctured by starlight. The moon hung high above as it watched the glimmering embers of the Beech Security Company carriage. The vehicle's smoldering carcass was a beacon in the quiet hills.

Owen sat up and immediately regretted the decision. He let his body fall to the ground with a labored huff. Much to his surprise, he found his head had fallen onto something he generously imagined was a pillow. A moment of examination, more akin to Owen lazily rolling his head from side to side revealed it was a bit hard for a pillow. What's more, was that it felt as if it had… *buttons?*

A strange thought, Owen conceded. He bested the pains that wracked his body and propped himself on an elbow. The pillow, it turned out, was his Spellseeker coat. It had been neatly folded and tucked under his head with care.

"Oi, looky there! The lad breathes yet." Beech seemed awfully cheerful for a man whose apparent livelihood had been reduced to coals some hundred feet down the road. The katarl held out his hand to Manda. With a grumble, she deposited a handful of silver dollars into Beech's expectant clutches.

"Care for a bit of horse, lad?"

The cheerful katarl ripped a hunk of meat that had been rotating over a bonfire on a crude spit. Both fire and spit seemed to have been made using the remnants of the carriage.

"That's all we have, then?" Owen asked. Each word came out as a grunt as he pulled his aching body over to the bonfire. "Horse?"

"Well, ya know," Beech muttered as he stuffed his face, "waysht not want not."

"Happy enough that the gods deigned to save *us*," Devlin said. "Can't say the same for the rest of our things, unfortunately."

"*Everything* went up?" Owen asked exasperated.

"Anything we weren't wearing," Manda grumbled.

Oh, wonderful, Owen whined to himself. Deflated by a moment of clarity, Owen realized the cold truth of his situation. He was not bound for almost-certain death in the company of friends. His bondage to death was made in isolation. A burnt uniform and the tools he wore were Owen's only genuine companions on the path ahead.

"So, what was all that nonsense about a box, anyways?"

It seemed a reasonable enough question to Owen. From the sound of it, some kind of box somewhere on the carriage is what had caused the current state of affairs.

"It's none of your business, is what it is," Manda said. The words were sour to complement the snarl that covered her face. "Orland property. Not something for some bluecoat to worry about."

"Like a safe deposit box or some such?" Owen probed.

"Ask again and I'll bash your nose into the back of your skull."

"No need to be so touchy," Owen offered as he raised his open hands in a sign of peace. "Just curious is all."

"Yeah, well your curiosity can shove it."

The retort was accompanied by the display of a fist that was prepared to bash. From the look of her hand, Manda had come out of the crash no better than Owen. Scrapes and bruises poked out through shredded sleeves. She moved her arm in a way so as not to upset her injuries.

"Any chance my satchel survived the blaze?"

"What about the word *everything* do you not understand, blue?" Manda retorted.

"Well," Owen sighed, "I had some soap in there. Saw your arms were about as cut-up as mine here, so figured I'd offer a wash. Best to avoid any infection if we can, you know? No sense in losing an arm to a scratch after surviving such a blast in one piece."

"I can wash my own arms," Manda snorted. The brief pause between Owen's explanation and Manda's reply added to the small hint of embarrassment in her tone.

"Of course," Owen agreed. "Maybe we can at least boil some water? This shirt is beyond repair as it is, might as well use the sleeves for cloth."

Threads popping filled the night air as Owen tore both his sleeves from the shoulders of his shirt. The garment, battered as it was, offered little resistance. He quartered the available fabric so that each person gathered had some scrap to scrub with. There might not have been any soap available to them, but rags soaked in sterilized water would at the very least allow them to get dirt away from open wounds.

"I'm sure we could some water going," Devlin cut in. "Fine idea to do a little first aid while we have the time and the fire."

The harn shared a conciliatory look between Owen and Manda. He spoke with a placative tone that even Manda could not seem to disagree with. Though Manda refused to look Owen directly in the face, she did hold out an empty hand to receive a scrap of cloth.

4.

ARNSTEAD

"Right then, off ya get. S'far as I'm takin yas."

"Of course," Devlin replied graciously. "We could not thank you enough."

"Mhm," the squat, scruffy human agreed. "Anything fer the House."

Fate ordained to grant Owen and company a single stroke of good luck. After a day's march on worn legs, a covered wagon happened upon them. A farmer by the name of Wesley had sold his entire stock in a single day. He rode with high spirits to meet his wife and sons at home. Rare was the occasion that his journeys to town took less than a full week. With a mood so bright and positive, he was easy prey for the sad story of a group of travelers waylaid by roving bandits.

A full day of bickering from the back of his wagon had set his spirits back to where they tended to be. All four strangers, whom he felt he now knew much better than he would have liked, were dropped off on the outskirts of Arnstead. A practiced mixture of whistles and clicks had the farmer's cart turned around and destined for home. There would be no further stops along the way.

"Nice as it's been," Manda said, leering at Owen all the while, "we're gonna be on our way." The *we* of it became clear as she grabbed Beech by the scruff of his neck. By unfortunate anatomical design, the act caused the katarl's legs to go near limp.

"Ay now!" Beech shouted in reply. "What's the big idea?"

"*Security guaranteed,* my ass."

Desperate eyes pleaded for assistance. The katarl's luck continued to run sour, however, as both Owen and Devlin made a clear effort to look anywhere but at Beech. Any passersby had the sense to do the same. He had been left to his uncertain fate at the menacing hands of Manda.

"Well," Devlin coughed, "I'll be off to the House, then. You're more than welcome to join."

Every muscle in Owen's body, battered and bruised as they were, felt elated at the thought. Any large town worth finding on a map would have a House. A House would mean priests and acolytes. All these things together would mean quick and efficient healing. A thin smile crept across Owen's face, despite the pain it caused.

"An excellent idea," Owen croaked. "Lead on."

The farmer had dropped the group off at a fork on the very edge of town. One fork continued due west. A wooden, weather-beaten sign at the fork declared the road to be Main. The same post had another sign that pointed along the north-western prong of the fork: Old.

"Pragmatic bunch, these Arnstead folk," Owen intoned, a feeble attempt at humor.

"You don't know the half of it."

Devlin started down the Old Road, Owen close at his heels.

Old became more and more apt a term the further the pair walked. It skirted the bulk of the township, the Old Road, with a thin veneer of homes, huts, and sheds lining its right side. A more densely packed thicket of homes filled the left. The buildings were nothing special. Simple homes for what Owen assumed to be simple people. None stood more than a story tall. Most seemed wide enough to accommodate only a handful of rooms. Buildings with a single-minded purpose.

Simple as they were, the structures did appear to be well-built. A lack of forested area near the town itself suggested that timber had been cut away ages ago, and that further lumber would have been sourced from upriver. Possibly from Oswyn or some other village to the north. Ironwood from the north was prized back home in Southport. Word had been that a blacksmith could use the stuff as thongs to work heated steel, though Owen had never given much credence to the jest.

Quality in material and construction diminished as the road went on. Softer local woods were patched with northern ironwoods where foundations crumbled or thatched rooves sagged. Door and window frames skewed with tilted walls. A general air of poor maintenance purveyed the squat skyline.

Much that could be said of the road's homes could be said of their denizens. The newer, more spacious plots showed care for cleanliness. Wash boards and basins dotted the walls of nicer homes. Clotheslines ran two to three houses in length, seemingly shared. Landry billowed on the mild, midday breeze. Hints of vegetable gardens sprung from the breezeways between homes.

All sense of care was abandoned, bit by bit, as the houses fell into disrepair down the road. Breeches and other underclothes hung from open windows or were scattered over rooftops. Unsightly thistles poked out from the narrow slits between huts and houses.

Cramped. It was the one word that came to mind as Owen trudged along. *Grimy* jockeyed for a close second, but there was not enough space for that second thought. The crushing weight of exhaustion had seen to that. It was enough of a challenge to maintain a single thought and mind the many divots that developed as the Old Road carried on. Bits of broken glass, among the other detritus, would make for an unwelcoming fall.

One thing did improve as the pair followed the road deeper in dilapidation: the dust. Hills had once again given way to somewhat flatter brushland. Hints of trees long gone from the township could be found both up and down the river. The innards of the township itself, however, had been beaten to dust. Alleyways and well-tended gardens were green breaks in what was otherwise a somewhat browned orange. It was the inner township's only redeeming quality as far as Owen could tell. The dirt had been packed by years upon years of cart wheels and foot traffic.

"We'll be coming up on the River Ro here shortly," Devlin said, breaking what had felt like an hour's long silence. Gave Owen a bit of a start. He peeled his attention away from the squalor about them. Devlin had tapped Owen's thigh a few times before pointing down the road.

The sound of the river, somehow hidden under Owen's general disappointment of what he saw around him, now trickled into focus. The beginnings of a bridge became visible over the heads of the crowded Old Road. No more than a hundred yards away.

"The River Ro? Really?" Devlin nodded at Owen's inquiry. "How strange. I've seen Ra and Ro laid out on a map before. Thought they might have been… louder? Seemed quite large."

"The Twins flow steady enough, despite their namesake. A few spots of white where they meet to form Sisir's Run. Can see a bit from the bridge, if you'd care for a break?"

"Tempting," Owen replied, raising his brows as he chuckled. "I think I can look while we walk."

"Suits me just fine."

Hand-drawn carts slowed to a shuffle as they approached the Ro Bridge. Drivers of wagons and oxcarts clicked and pulled at reigns to come to a stop. A trio of Federation soldiers stood at the bridge's approach. Pedestrian traffic flowed undeterred around the vehicles, the soldiers paying them no mind. One tipped their beret to Devlin.

"Balance in all things, sir."

"May you be weighed fairly." The Keeper's reply was practiced, but not forced. Devlin smiled at the Fourth Federation Army soldiers as he passed. That same soldier made a strained effort to look through Owen.

"A toll," Devlin stated matter-of-factly. "Anything on wheels pays to cross."

"So, I gathered," Owen mumbled absently. It was not the boxes of copper pennies or the overt contempt for himself on the soldiers' faces that caught his eye.

"Do they *all* wear swords out here, do you know?"

"What, the soldiers?" Devlin asked, surprised. "What else would they wear, Mr. Seeker?"

"Batons, in my experience. Maybe a hefty staff if they patrolled alone. The folks that mind the streets, that is," Owen added. "I've only ever seen the rank-and-file carry sword and spear if they were off to battle."

"And who says these aren't?"

Those words were more than Owen's weary mind was ready to handle. He stopped midstride and stepped off to the side of the bridge. Waist-high rails allowed for a welcome reprieve as he looked back. It didn't sit right. A collections box in one hand with the other hand wrapped tightly around the hilt of a weapon.

"Imagine," Owen said, to nobody in particular, "drawing a sword to collect a tax." His thumb fidgeted about the pommel of his sword as he continued down the bridge.

Some among the clergy may have taken offense at someone saying the House *loomed*. There was little doubt, however, that it did exactly that. It was the only structure more than two stories tall in all of Oldstead. There was no place in the area between the River Ra and River Ro that the House of Many could not be seen.

It was not sheer size alone that brought the House to the center of attention. The House was built of gleaming white stone where other buildings were made of wood or earthen brick. Colossal doors of polished cherry stood taller than some homes in their entirety. Intricate ironwork laid into the doors depicted the symbols of the Many: the scales of Manus, Hyperios' sun, the eight-pointed compass of Sisir, Atherea's broken sword, dice belonging to Manjayra and Manjayro, and the masterful hammer of Lucina. Stained-glass windows lined the east and west-facing walls. Each depicted a tale of gods or their champions. The House was a polished diamond, cut to perfection and clear as day.

In short, the House did not belong. Not where it had been built, at any rate. The buildings that surrounded it, homes, huts, taverns, haberdasheries, and any other thing in between, were in no better state than those across the river. A cloudless day with the sun at its zenith was the only proof required. The area was not called Oldstead for nothing.

Two clear notes rang from the belltower that rose from the House's northern wall. The time was two hours past noon. Owen stood in awe, dumbstruck by the sheer dissonance that lay before him as compared to what lay behind.

Great doors pushed outward as two o'clock mass made their way back onto the streets of Oldstead. Pauper and merchant shared their mild peace be with you and their have a blessed day with the faintest façade of a smile. Ways parted at the base of the House's marble, dust-covered steps. Nary a glance was to be spared. A pair of acolytes on either side of the doors waved the procession on.

"Ah, Devlin!"

The exclamation came from a Bangeli katarl at the top of the steps. She melded with the tattered tail of worshippers that descended the steps. Tall even for a Bangeli, it was impossible to lose her in the crowd. Clean, white vestments, with iconography and trim in black, made doubly sure she could not be missed. The black scales emblazoned on her chest drew nearly up to Owen's eye-level by the time the katarl had reached them.

"Rajani." Devlin beamed as the katarl drew near. He spread his arms wide. "How good of you to welcome me."

Respectfully, Rajani raised the hem of vestments and took a knee to embrace Devlin. Much to Owen's surprise, Devlin was not the only one to emit the clattering of chainmail. The armored embrace ended after a final squeeze.

"You have to send word when you're headed here," Rajani said with a hint of friendly admonition. "Would've been sorely cross if I'd missed you. Maybe a letter, next time?"

"Couldn't be helped, I'm afraid. Here on summons from Pontiff Isaac. Hadn't the time to find a pen."

"Truly?" Rajani, still on her knee, held Devlin out to arm's length. The harn's nod set her head to an inquisitive tilt. "Odd that he didn't – *oh?*"

Rajani had not noticed Owen. The crowd, mixed her with own surprise, had blocked Owen from view. With the congregation now dissipated, Owen was painfully difficult to miss. Rajani brought herself upright and faced Owen. All pleasure had drained from her face. Fingers knit together, palms facing upward, in the typical greeting of the House clergy.

"Master Seeker," Rajani said evenly with a slight bow of her head. "Are you here at the behest of the Pontiff, as well?"

"He's a friend," Devlin grumbled, his hand half-raised in meek protest. "Truly?"

This question was not like her first. Warmth and compassion had been woven into her first utterance of *truly*. Words spoke to a colleague not seen for months or years on end. Perhaps more than a colleague, even.

Where the first question had been kind, the second was an icy inquisition. Eyes probed Owen from head to toe and back again, unblinking. Another gaze that looked both at and through him. Was it the state of his soiled uniform that gave her pause, he wondered? Perhaps she saw him as a ruffian in the guise of a station to which he did not belong? If not, it may have been the unprofessional way in which he presented himself. The white trim of his uniform was now only a few layers of dust and sweat away from matching the road on which they stood, and the blues were not far behind.

Owen could not find words to protest Rajani's scrutinous scowl. It was a scowl that had not yet committed to revealing itself. A smile that twitched at the ends, eager to jump downwards at the most minor provocation. Neck muscles taught as bowstrings. Not the slightest motion below the katarl's shoulders. He knew not the reason why, but Owen was certain that he was not welcome.

"Truly." Devlin must have felt it, as well. His tone had become placative. Measured hands moved in slow, sweeping gestures to accompany his words. "We rode together, from the end of the manarail's line. Had a bit of a dust-up with Tennerim together, as well."

Bit of an understatement, was what Owen wanted to say. Words died in his throat when he saw the change in Rajani's face.

"The Witch?" she gasped. "You aren't hurt, are you?"

"Just a touch, really," Devlin replied with a hollow laugh. "Hoped we might get some help with that."

"Of course," Rajani's ears flattened, unable to hide her embarrassment. "The House shall do its best to keep you out of my care. No matter the colors you wear. This way."

Rajani turned and ushered the pair to follow. There was a brief moment where Owen's fatigued mind tried to piece together everything the katarl had just lobbed at him. It passed as soon as it came. Any aid was welcome at this point. He felt in no position to ask the clergy to be affable while they administered it.

"Yes, ma'am," Owen murmured.

The trio ascended the now-vacated steps and passed through the House's open doorway. A short, arched hallway led to the main interior of the building. Murals of the gods and their winged seraph adorned the walls. They lacked the grandeur of the stained-glass murals to come. Dour, expressionless faces stood stark against matte backgrounds of puffy clouds. Champions of old knelt, open hands extended, to receive the blessing of the gods. Dull armor and broken weapons were scattered about the legs of mortals. Even rays of the golden sun seemed dim.

Six stands, waist-high for a human, were evenly spaced down the corridor. Their tops were smooth and circular and made of polished cherry. Each stand bore a silvered icon of the gods. Before each icon rested a silver basin. Copper pennies and silver dollars coated these basins. Small nuggets of silver or gold were visible, as well. Acolytes came to collect the vessels at the end of the corridor as Owen and company passed.

Solid white marble had carried from the steps, through the entryway, and now flowed out into the House proper with splashes of black and grey. Iron-heeled boots echoed with each beleaguered step. The sound of each footfall carried up to the high vaulted ceiling to fade away. A glance about the House showed the silent clergy hustled about on soft, leather sandals. Owen, now conscious of exactly how loud he was, made an effort to walk more on the balls of his feet.

Redwood pews filled the marble expanse on either side of a wide, wine-colored carpet. Reliefs had been carved into the back of each bench and painted in gold. One bench showed a sun whose rays interwove as they reached for either side of the bench. Another depicted many hammers and chisels carving out the relief itself. There were reliefs for each of the gods. All were unique, not to be seen on another bench in the House.

The carpet stretched from the end of the entryway until coming to a sudden stop at the edge of the transept. Gold and silver thread embellished the edges with glittering swoops and swirls. A pair of acolytes had set themselves to straightening the folds that had arisen from the day's service.

A pair of divulgence booths sat at the outer edges of the House, tucked neatly against the walls. These were the most plain of all the things this House held. No reliefs or inlays decorated their cedar construction. Symbols of the gods were nowhere to be seen. A mere set of black, velvet curtains hung the two entrances into each booth. The last remnants of two o'clock mass, those who would share what must be shared, waited for their turns to speak.

On the near-empty altar at the head of the House stood a lectern of black stone. It resembled the marble floor but did not have quite the same sheen. The light seemed to become lost in its imposing silhouette rather than be reflected. A single line of golden filigree rimmed the top of the lectern.

"You're to wait here, Master Seeker." Owen had become so enthralled by the sheer enormity of the space that he failed to notice Rajani's arm barred his path. "I will send an attendant to see to whatever injuries you may have. Devlin, please follow me."

Rajani resumed her walk towards the back of the House. Much like her fellow clergy, she moved with a quiet sense of purpose. Her black and orange tail, poking out through a small set of holes in her vestments, twitched from side to side as she strode. Devlin made as if to start, but brought himself up short.

"Apologies, Seeker." The harn struggled to choose his next words. "For your reception, I mean. Hadn't thought I would need to warn you. Suppose that a decade can change a place."

"Hardly your fault, I think."

"Good of you to say, Owen. Good of you to say." Devlin looked to the doors through which Rajani had just passed. "Well, not sure how long I will be in town, but you needn't be a stranger."

"Glad to hear it," Owen smiled. "We've plenty yet to discuss. I look forward to it."

After a short string of pleasantries, the Keeper of Manus took his leave and vanished deeper into the House. Owen stood at the edge of the transept. He was not sure what to do with himself now that he was alone. Whether or not it was more polite to sit or stand was a question of its own. Uncertainty shuffled his weight back and forth between his feet. Crossed arms unknotted to place hands on hips, which inevitably became crossed again.

"Good day, sir. I was told you need healing?"

The thin, wispy voice at Owen's back caught him off guard. He felt he had only had his back turned to the transept for a moment or two. When he swiveled about, he saw that two acolytes had managed to approach seemingly out of nowhere. That, or his innate sense of time was as flustered as his aching body. Thoughts and surprise were blinked away in tandem.

Two youthful figures stood side by side. On the right was a human male, somewhere on the spectrum between Nirdac and Bangeli. Thick, black eyebrows stood rigid just below a mop of unruly hair. His vestments were plain white. No iconography suggested the boy did not observe the teachings of one god over any other. A simple length of hempen rope served as his belt. In his left hand, he gripped a clipboard and pencil. Firmly gripping his right hand was the second acolyte.

Though of roughly similar height, the two acolytes shared few similarities beyond. Owen's initial reaction, shameful as it made him feel, was to describe her as human-*ish*. The young girl had the same basic shape as a teenaged human: two arms, two legs, a nose and mouth, early suggestions of womanhood. A passing glance would say she was human through and through.

Stark, white hair was the first sign. Not inhuman in itself, but a trait typically reserved for those who had weathered many decades. The long strands hung loosely about her shoulders and back. Her skin was almost as pale as her hair, like a child who had been locked away from the sun since birth. Faint traces of blue and purple spiderwebbed across her hands and sharp face. These lines touched her pointed ears, as well, which poked out through her waterfall of near-white hair.

What stood out most, though, were her eyes. Bright, pink irises called for attention like a freshly bloomed flower. The eyes themselves were housed in sockets larger than any human's. She almost seemed to be locked in a perpetual state of surprise or disbelief. Entrancing as they were, the acolyte's gaze was skewed. Clouded pupils wreathed in iridescent roses stared into oblivion.

Shame flared in Owen's cheeks when the young man before coughed and cleared his throat. Owen had been staring, mouth agape, for some time now. He emulated the boy's actions and straightened.

"Yes, I do," Owen stammered. Embarrassment grappled at his tongue while the young man narrowed his eyes. "Please, call me Owen."

"Of course," the girl replied. The wisp of a voice had been hers. "May I join you, Owen?"

"Oh, please do."

Owen took this as a sign at last that he should be seated, and happily obliged the young acolyte. The girl's companion led her delicately to the pew and to Owen's side. Clipboard and pencil in hand, the boy stood back to watch the proceedings.

Perhaps his senior? Owen thought. Unlike the boy, the girl bore more than a simple white sheet and hempen belt. A black scale was stitched into the bosom of her vestments. Her belt was of brown leather. Many pouches and purses had been affixed to the belt. In her free hand, she had carried a silver basin, which she now rested on her lap. The scrabble and squeak of a mouse exploring its confines rose from the basin.

"So," Owen said hesitantly, "how does this work?"

"Never received aid from the House before, sir? Oh, um, Owen," the girl added with haste.

"I can't say that I've had the pleasure, no. The need never arose."

"That would be a good thing, I suppose. If you would please tell me what ails you."

"Well, it's my arms more than anything. I feel like I've been rolled down a hill, truth be told, but the only real damage was the arms." Owen did his best to lace a smile into his words. "There's some burns on my right arm. Flow-related injury. A few deep cuts on both my forearms. Probably a few slivers of wood stuck in there, too."

"How awful," the girl replied. Concern furrowed her brow, head turned to stare just past Owen. "Expose your wounds, please, while I prepare."

The acolyte's hands moved deftly across her belt as she spoke. Fine grains of red sand were pulled from a pouch and sprinkled into the basin. The same hand retrieved a pinch of salt as her right hand took hold of the mouse, now pushing its nose about the sand. A gentle shake mixed the two

72

ingredients well enough for the acolyte. Holding the mouse steady in her left hand, she reached for a small, sheathed knife with her right.

"You don't mean to… I mean… are you...?"

"A sacrifice is required to ensure the attention of Manus. There is no guarantee our request for a miracle would be heard above others, if not." A small, sweet smile crossed her lips. The sort of smile a mother gives to a child whose dog has disappeared in the night. "There's no need to worry. It will not suffer."

A quiet titter tugged at Owen's heart. He held one of his forearms in a tender grip, his mind asking if the immediate comfort was worth the creature's life.

Swift movement gave Owen no time to protest. The acolyte slotted the knife between her index and middle fingers. Its keen edge loomed over the creature's head like a miniature guillotine. She coaxed the mouse forward with a slight tilt of her hand. As the mouse's neck was below the knife's edge, the acolyte pulled the blade down. Blood dripped through her fingers as she clenched the dead mouse in an iron fist. Droplets of blood were sanguine rain over the salt and sand.

Without a word, she deposited the desiccated body in a burlap sack that the other acolyte held open. A handcloth was draped over her gore-stained hand. The girl thanked her companion with a nod, wiped her knife on the cloth, and proceeded to clean her hands. The boy took the cloth from her when he had finished.

"Thank you," she said to the bow, nodding in his general direction. "Now then, please guide me to your wounds, Owen."

"Oh, yes," Owen muttered. In hid mild shock, he had forgotten to remove his coat. "A moment, please."

"Of course."

Muscles Owen had not previously known existed now protested his attempt to remove his coat. The buttons went quick enough, his fingers one of the few parts of his body that did not hurt. Shouldering his way out was a whole other matter. A handful of grunts and the sucking of air through his teeth was the anthem of the pitiful battle.

What remained of his shirt sleeves had already been torn away to serve as bandages. Already loose, and poorly assembled, besides, they gave little resistance. A gentle tug at a bowed knot sent the entire thing tumbling to his lap. Bruising had turned his left arm various shades of purple of green, while his right was still a warm, pinkish red.

"My left," Owen said, resting his arm in the acolyte's outstretched, cool hand. Soft fingers traced injuries. Though her touch was delicate, Owen could not help but wince as she touched his open wounds. She retraced the larger lacerations and leaned over Owen's arm. A sharp inhale just above the injuries caused her nose to wrinkle.

"Beginnings of infection," the acolyte mumbled to herself. "Open. No sutures."

Each new utterance was followed by her left hand digging into a pouch or purse on her belt. A vial of foul, sulfur-infused ichor was poured into the mixture. The concoction fizzed, taking on a greenish color. Fresh mint leaves and lemon balm, freshly crinkled by hand, neutralized the odor to some extent. Cocoa powder and a thimble of buttermilk were added after touching the burns on Owen's right arm.

"Now then," the girl said, addressing Owen again, "place your hands in mine."

Owen obeyed without question. There was an authority in her voice when she spoke of wounds and healing. Confidence was born of observation and experience. It reminded him of his mother when she would speak of horses, or Venkat recalling the contents of any wine cellar in Southport worth knowing. The acolyte grasped both of Owen's hands in her right, using her left to stir the contents of the silver basin in her lap. She raised her face to the heavens.

"Manus, hear my prayer," the acolyte began. Her stern tone had vanished. Soft words rolled from practiced lips in quick succession. "I offer you these worldly goods that you might hear me. I offer you this lifeblood that you may empower me. Wield through me your power to knit flesh. Wield through me your power to mend bone. I am your servant and vessel. Manus, hear my prayer."

Salts, powders, blood, and the rest melded into a pool of light as the acolyte spoke. There was a comfort to it. A liquid sun that radiated a refreshing warmth. It began to thicken as it swirled around her hand, like hot wax beginning to cool. When she removed her hand from the basin, the substance coated her hand. She was able to move her fingers freely as if she wore a glove.

The acolyte placed her coated hand atop Owen's. An immediate rush of vitality ran the length of both his arms. It welled up in his chest, like the last breath before a deep plunge. The smell of mint and lemon tickled the back of his nose. His breaths were cool.

"Oh wow," Owen gasped. The girl smiled at Owen's appreciation.

There was a constant intensity to the process. Its invigorating nature did not allow Owen to relax his thoughts or find a more comfortable position. The toll of the House's bell for three o'clock must have sounded over half an hour ago, but that was his guess. Not that he was able to check his pocket watch to confirm.

"Am I allowed to speak during this?" Owen said.

"It would be too late if you weren't," the acolyte replied. Her smile slipped into a cheeky grin. "The gods would not be offended, I think."

"Well, in that case, could I ask you a question?"

"I'm not Deepkin, not entirely." Mirth drained from the girl's face in an instant. "My mother was. My father is human. I hope my nature does not offend you."

"I... no. Just wanted to ask your name, is all."

"Oh, I'm sorry, sir! Owe —"

"No, no! It's fine," Owen half-shouted.

Silence wedged itself between the two. Pale cheeks flushed with embarrassment as the acolyte stirred in place. Owen would have been lying if he said he wasn't curious about the acolyte's appearance, but he had been too sheepish to ask.

"Ryleah," the girl mumbled at the floor. "Ryleah Pembrooke."

Four bells rang from the tower as the salve Ryleah had prepared dwindled to nothing. The open wounds on Owen's arms had been filled and sealed. Scars would disappear in a matter of days, he had been assured. Purple, green, and red had receded to allow Owen's natural skin tone to return. A few flexes and rotations confirmed that the muscles and joints of his arms felt as good as new.

"Thank you, Ryleah. You've done impeccable work."

"That's very kind," she replied, "but the work is not mine. Manus has restored you. Your praise belongs to him."

"Well, thanks to you both, then."

Owen ruffled the girl's hair. A friendly, fraternal gesture, he thought. Ryleah recoiled from the touch with a nearly imperceptible whimper, then drew herself up again with a polite nod.

"For you, sir."

These were the first words spoken by the young boy. Quiet through all that had transpired, he squeaked at Owen while holding his clipboard. Adolescence did not appear to be treating the boy well.

"Hmm, yes?" Owen replied.

"Your signature, please," the acolyte said. Every effort was made to ensure his voice did not crack a second time. He reached across Ryleah to present the papers, a pencil trapped under his thumb. "At the bottom. Next to the ex, below the total."

"The total?" Owen mouthed as he received the clipboard. "Is this... am I being *billed?*"

"Order of the Pontiff, sir," Ryleah spoke in hushed tones. Her hand seemed to recoil at her own words. "Reagents and ingredients do not come to the House without cost. The skills of the clergy are not honed without investment. I hope you understand."

Shame was woven thick through the last words.

"Of course," Owen sighed.

Sisir's Run coursed beneath the Bridge on Main. Flecks of white-water bit at the bridge's supports, a never-ending struggle by the river to reclaim its natural state. The base of each supporting column was lost to sight beneath the turbid waters. Green scum climbed the grey stonework. Discoloration above the slime betrayed the typical height of spring floods, an extra couple of feet.

Owen turned to rest his back against the stone railing, tired of watching the occasional canoe or raft escape the smalls rapids some twenty yards upriver. He pulled the pocket watch from his breast pocket. A sharp click flung the covering wide to reveal a time of half-past seven.

"Already?" he grumbled.

Time had slipped away faster than Owen realized. He had ventured far enough away from the House that the peel of its bell no longer reached him. A glance to the west showed a sun ready to hang its hat for the day. Lamplighters at the western end of the bridge set down step ladders to go about their work. Owen watched with mild interest as the lighters worked their way towards him.

"Excuse me," Owen asked as one of the lamplighters set their small ladder down nearby, "could I trouble you for some directions? I'm a bit new around here."

The lamplighter, a female human with graying hair and a weathered face, grunted. It very well could have resulted from her effort to climb the ladder, but Owen hoped against hope the utterance was a sign of acquiescence.

"I'm looking for the Arcanarium," Owen went on. "It would be a great help if you could point me in the right direction."

A rusted creak cut through the evening air as the lamplighter opened the case. Her left hand wrapped around the clear cylinder of memory glass inside. Clean, white light grew steadily as the woman channeled energy into the lamp. With a well-worn cloth in her right hand, she made an honest attempt to clear away as much dirt and grime from the lamp casing as she could manage. Her hands switched tasks after she finished 'cleaning' the right side of the lamp.

"Um, even a simple direction would be helpful. East or west of the bridge, perhaps?"

Owen's hands crossed his chest, one pointing west while the other pointed east. The gestured looked as feeble as his request sounded. There was no indication that the lamplighter had heard his question.

Another squeal of ungreased hinges sounded as the lamplighter closed the lamp's case. She set the small brass catch that kept the case from flying open and stepped down her ladder. With a huff, she hoisted the wooden ladder up to her shoulder and began to walk to the next lamp. The only indication of her awareness of Owen was a slight tip of her plaid cloth hat, and even that was not directed straight at him.

There was no point in going after the woman. Just as there was no point in tugging at the sleeves of passersby or hailing a member of the fourth. It made no difference whether he asked human, katarl, or harn. There was no love for his station here. Exasperation fled his lungs and dispersed amongst the thinning crowd.

Despite the onset of what Owen felt to be a justified wave of self-pity, he kept his head up. A deep breath half-steadied his nerves. *Pissing into the river won't help me find the Arcanarium.* He ran dust-caked fingers through his hair and scratched his head. Hairs joined by sweat and grease eased themselves apart. *Gods above,* he thought, *how long has it been since I've had a proper bath?* He wiped his dirtied hand on his sullied trousers. The futility of the effort was lost on him for the moment.

The Bridge on Main, a busy thoroughfare when Owen had initially arrived, had grown quiet. Carts had abandoned the way over an hour ago, the soldiers at either end of the bridge with them. People continued to go about their way in decreased numbers. No one walked alone.

Through the thinned traffic, Owen noticed for the first time a small girl. A Nirdac katarl with nappy fur. The girl waved when they made eye contact. It was a frail gesture. A strong wind might carry the girl away like a discarded newspaper.

It was also a kind gesture.

Owen crossed the thirty-some feet of the bridge that separated himself from the girl. There was no need to excuse himself as he walked. What few pedestrians remained made certain to keep a wide berth between themselves and the Spellseeker.

"Good evening, Miss," Owen said as he drew near.

"Hello!" the girl rasped. She extended an open hand, its fur patchy and thin. The dirt-packed between her hairs rivaled the grime on Owen's own hands. "Jessica's the name."

"Delighted," Owen responded, smiling as he bent to shake her hand. "Owen Raulstone. But just Owen is fine."

"Okay, *Just Owen*."

Slight wrinkling of her nose displayed Jessica's self-satisfaction at the jest. Her shoulders swung back and forth in kind.

Jessica's demeanor stood in stark contrast to her position. Frayed trousers were knotted closed where her knees should have been. A pair of ragged blankets that served as her seat likely also served as a bed. Some manner of fabric was bundled up and jammed between her lower back and the bridge. Whether it was another blanket or some kind of cloak was unclear, though its state of disrepair was evident by the colorful assortment of patches that kept it whole. Her yellowed smile was missing its top-right fang. She smiled all the same.

"You look like you're lost."

"Oh yeah?" Owen grunted as he eased himself down next to Jessica. "How's that?"

"Been runnin' around the bridge half the day. Looked like a puppy what's lost its person."

"That bad, huh?"

"Mhm," Jessica nodded. "Proper pathetic." She bobbed the remnants of her legs up and down with each syllable of 'pathetic'. Owen let slip an

78

embarrassed chortle. Jessica's smile broadened. "Where's you trying to get to, anyways?"

"I'm trying to find the Arcanarium." Owen raised his collar slightly between thumb and forefinger.

"Ahh, bluecoat can't find his house?"

"Bluecoat's new in town."

"Don't say?" Jessica said, feigning surprise. "Well, good news for you. I just happen to know where the bluecoats do their roosting."

"Oh yeah?" Owen replied. The interest raised an eyebrow without his realizing.

"Uh-huh, sure do. Sure. *Don't* work for free, though."

At the word don't, a sharp claw scraped against the rim of a tin cup. Coins clattered in the cup as it slapped down back into place against the stone bridge. Jessica's head lulled onto her left shoulder, her large, green eyes glowing in the twilight.

"I suppose not."

Twenty-two silver dollars to the House had nearly cleared out his pockets, but only *nearly*. Defeat and generosity joined as a knot in his chest. He cast his eyes upwards to the first stars of the night as he produced the last of his silvers. The gleeful titter that accompanied the coin fleeing his grasp brought a hint of a smile to his face.

"Best get to stepping then," Jessica said. "Almost out of daylight."

Jessica undid the knots at the ends of her trousers with quick fingers. Toes and calves concealed under blankets and rags slid into view as the katarl rose with sudden purpose. The katarl walked with a skip towards the western edge of the bridge, beckoning Owen to follow.

5.

LONG DAY'S NIGHT

Faint, red light emanated from the doors that stood before Owen. The light radiated from the carving of an open book. Crimson, glowing words encircled the carving; *Magic in Moderation*. These words rotated around the book, a slow and deliberate motion. No words were carved into the pages of the book. Only nonsensical marking that conjured the feeling of magic marked the two exposed pages.

Locked.

The coloration was sign enough to Owen that the door would not budge. Not without proper identification. Memories of drunken revelry with Venkat and Rebecca flooded into his mind. Stories that all-too-often ended with the trio realizing they hadn't a badge between them. Stories that ended with an exhausted scolding from Sergeant Mayes. The ensuing laps they were forced to run around the facility, drunkenness be damned, were remembered just as well.

"Couldn't hurt to try, I suppose," Owen sighed.

On his belt was a brass badge in the shape of a shield. The Bureau of Arcane's familiar symbol and motto were etched onto its face, along with O. Raulstone. Numerals below his name served as further identification: eight-seven-one-one-five. The brass face was fixed to a back of brown wood that shared the shield's profile. A thin, metal clip screwed to the back of the badge allowed it to be hung, from belt or breast pocket, for open display.

Owen pulled the badge from his belt and held it against the Arcanarium door. Small vibrations rose at the touch as if the door was mulling Owen's proposal over. The door pulsed with these vibrations three times. Crimson light diluted in the area around the badge. It was replaced with a white glow that held the faintest suggestion of blue. This new light swirled around the badge, pouring into its every crevice. No speck of dust or minor nick in brass escaped the door's examination. Owen leaned forward onto the balls of his feet in anticipation.

Then, with a long, sustained vibration, Owen's badge was repelled from the door. It was not a violent push to send a person flying away. No, the push was controlled. A measured response to indicate one was not welcome. Crimson light ate away the blue-tinted suggestion of promise.

The outcome was not a surprising one. An expected setback to add to the list of woes draped over Owen's shoulders. No attunement meant no entry. Simple as that.

Owen turned and allowed himself to fall against the door, his shoulder blades resting neatly on the pages of the carved book. There was no sign of anyone on Main Street now. The sun had fallen for the day, and the little vagrant, Jessica, disappeared soon after reaching the promised destination: Arnstead's Arcanarium, the base of operations for the Bureau of Arcane in Arnstead.

Another thump rolled out onto the still, night air as Owen knocked at the Arcanarium's door with the back of his head. A deep breath came in through his nostrils, pushed out through pursed lips. Twice more he knocked against the door. Twice more he breathed heavy breaths. Crimson red caressed his shoulders in stark contrast to the dirtied white of the street lamps.

"Well," Owen murmured, bleary eyes scanning the empty street, "what now?"

Reception had not been the only thing to grow cold, Owen realized. The cool breeze of day had turned to a bitter chill. Barren streets offered no reprieve. It was not so cold that Owen could feel his breath, but given time it would work its way into his bones. Thoughts turned to how best to weather the night. His attention had been flippant while walking to the Arcanarium. The relief of knowing where he was headed had coupled with the distracting mirth of Jessica. He could have passed by a dozen hotels or inns and been none the wiser for it.

More walking, Owen moaned internally. Idle hands, seeking some kind of purpose, wiped sleep away from heavy eyelids. They kept busy by cupping Owen's sagging features. He pulled his hands downwards, wiping grease from his nose. Another knock of his head on the door. Then another. Then a third.

Before Owen could smack his head against the door yet again, he felt himself being pushed forward. Blue-tinted white shone past him as he stumbled forward into the street. An utterance somewhere between a gasp and yelp jumped from his throat.

"Oh, hello there!" called one voice. An excited male.

"We're closed," followed a cold, female voice.

Owen spun to see that the door had opened. Two figures were haloed in the door's light as they stood in its frame. The female voice belonged to a Nirdac human. Her figure was gaunt, the pale light accentuating her narrow features. Straight, brown hair drooped over her sharp shoulder in a ponytail. Pale blue eyes sized Owen up three times over before she spoke again.

"You're Third Seeker Owen Raulstone, aren't you? The hells have you been?"

Oh, gods, Owen thought, a pit growing in his stomach, *even my people hate me?*

"None of that, Violette. The man just got here!"

The second voice, speaking to Owen's defense, was that of a Nirdac harn. Excitement extended beyond the man's tone of voice. Not only did he bound over to Owen, but whirled backward to look at Violette as he did so. A brown cottontail that matched the harn's fur twitched all the while.

"Come on, we haven't had a new Seeker in *months,*" the harn continued, turning back to Owen. "What's your name?"

"Oh, uh, Owen. Owen Raul—"

"Oh! Any specialties?"

"Well, not re—"

"C'mon! Fire drinker? Shadow hopper?"

"No," Owen raised a hand in feeble protest. "There's no—"

"Ah! Metal! I bet he's a metal bender? No? Maybe a storm tamer?"

"Enough, Lionel!" the woman called, gliding towards Owen. "You'll call the dead at this rate."

Violette's words stymied the storm that was Lionel. His verbal assault on Owen quieted to a whisper. Questions boiled in the back of his throat, but the harn managed to keep them to himself for the moment.

No longer occupied, the doorway leading into the Arcanarium saw fit to close itself. It was a soundless endeavor. Hinges carried the doors home in perfect silence. Owen would not have thought the doors closed had he not seen it happen. Crimson spilled out onto the street once more as the doors locked themselves against Arnstead's night.

"What's your situation?" Violette began before hastily raising a hand. "No, never mind. You look like that story might take all night. I'll get your initial report Monday morning after synchronization. Do you have a place to stay?"

"I, uh… not yet. No."

Owen was too tired to mince words. A more present mind would have asked if accommodations had been prepared for him, as his arrival was expected. That and a great many other questions would have been levied. Owen's mind was, however, anything but present.

The answer did not appear to please Violette. She pressed the thumb of her open right hand into her right temple, fingers fanned forwards the stars. Restless eyes moved back and forth behind closed lids. Words, too many too quickly for Owen to count, fell silently from the woman's mouth.

"Ay, Violette?" Lionel had sidled up beside Violette and began to tug at her trouser legs. Her eyes, unbelieving, snapped open to glare down at the harn.

"Excuse me?"

"Well," Lionel started, unphased, "I was headed the way of the Creaky Board. How 'bout I bring him 'round, get him a room. Then you can piece this together on Monday?"

Violette's violent expression softened somewhat.

"Sit all right with you?" she asked, looking at Owen.

"Hm?" Owen uttered pointing at himself. "Guessing that's an inn? I'm a bit low on funds. At the moment."

"I'll write it off. *Once*," she growled with renewed intensity. Violette was already taking leave of the two as she finished speaking. "And bring me a receipt. The Arcanarium isn't staffed on Sundays, so bring it to me bright and early on Monday. I suggest you take tomorrow to get familiar with the town."

Lionel danced a jig of excitement, hopped up to grab Owen's hand, and took off east down Main.

"And you're absolutely certain?" Lionel huffed. "Beyond a doubt? One hundred percent?"

"No specialty," Owen confirmed. The weight of a thousand previous confirmations hung on his words. "Not in the normal sense, at least."

"That's…" the harn's murmurings trailed off. Thoughts mingled with possibilities were counted off on his small fingers. "How *did* you pass any of the field tests? I know I tried to follow the Seeker path. Ages ago! Couldn't get my foot in the door without something special to add to the force."

"Honest? I didn't. Not at first, at any rate," Owen added in the face of Lionel's obvious confusion. "Made a go of it for each test, failed, then came back again with a focus or two. No provision states the use of a focus is forbidden. Took advantage of that—"

"And made your way through sheer force. Hah! Imagine the Founders rolled in their graves when you managed to squeeze through like that." Lionel cackled at the thought. A deep gasp cut his laughter short. "You *will* have to show me your pistol, though. And the caster shells. Never seen crystal that clear in a shell before."

Beady eyes glared at the instruments on Owen's hip. There was a hunger behind those round, black dots. The sheer intensity made Owen feel the slightest bit uneasy.

"You *will,* won't you? You wouldn't *deny* a friend the pleasure, would you?"

"Of course," Owen replied. His right hand patted the pistol twice in reassurance.

"Oh!" Lionel cried with his head on a swivel. "We're here, we're here!"

Their walk had taken them back across the Bridge on Main. In the very heart of Eaststead, right off Main, was a two-story building with lights aglow. Light poured from every seam in the way and out every dust-caked window. Where another inn might have a lamp or two near their doorway, the Creaky Board shone like a lighthouse on a black shore.

Even the blind would not struggle to find the establishment on this night. A person could *feel* the beating heart of the Creaky Board as they walked past. The crash of bootheel to floorboard kept time along with the rumble of primal drums. Shouts of glee were soared out through the open doors.

Whoever ran this place, Owen thought, did not care to remember that they had neighbors.

"C'mon!" Lionel cried, taking Owen by the hand once more. "In we go!"

Lionel hopped up and over the three wooden steps that led to the Creaky Board's porch in a single step. Another step launched the harn

84

through the open doors. He vanished into the revelry coursing through the tavern, a brown blur caught in a torrent of color.

Owen climbed the stairs one at a time, noting the effort in each step. A sharp squeak called out beneath boot when he took his first step onto the deck. *Really?* He looked down at the source of the meek sound. The signpost for the place was plain; a simple rectangle of painted black wood with the words *the Creaky Board* painted in white. There was no crest or symbol to speak of.

"A bit on the nose," he mused as he crossed the threshold.

A wall of sound overwhelmed Owen as he stepped into the Creaky Board. There was no additional clarity. The sounds somehow became less distinct upon entrance. Amid the chaos, all sounds seemed to thrum as one carnal beat.

To the right of the door, at the far end of the wall, was a raised stage. It was tucked into the corner and served as the beating heart of the night's revelry. Six drummers pounded away at a dozen drums. A mix of katarl, harn, and humans moving as one. A pair of flutes and a pair of guitars made an honest attempt to reach the crowd. It was clear in their movements, however, that they knew they acted in support of their percussion. Only an occasional howl as a drummer raised their head showed awareness for their surroundings.

Before the stage was a cleared area of the floor. Fourth Federation Army soldiers smashed iron-shod heels to the floor as they danced. Men and women in vibrant formal robes joined at their side. Grimy roustabouts who hadn't the time to clean themselves before coming from the docks fit in with the rest. Anyone who wanted to join in the dance seemed welcome.

Tables and chairs covered the rest of the floor, jammed together to facilitate the energetic display by the stage. Plates, glasses, mugs, and utensils plinked and clanked on hardwood surfaces in a steady rhythm. Fists pounded cluttered tables to add further noise to the fray. No corner of the lower floor did not participate in the celebration in some way.

A single harn, small for his kind, was easy to lose in a throng such as this. Owen stood no chance as he hung in the doorway. There would be no finding Lionel in this madness.

"Well, hey there, Mr. Seeker, sir!"

The bright words were accompanied by an arm interlocking with Owen's. He turned his head to see the dimpled smile of a Bangeli human.

The woman wore black and white serving robes, though they appeared to have been fastened loosely.

"You lost?" the woman continued. She craned her head down to make eye contact. Owen, realizing his vacant gaze had lingered on the woman's chest, snapped straight.

"I've been told so," Owen replied, a nervous chuckle accompanying his sidelong glance. The woman took a tighter hold of Owen's arm, pulled him close.

"Then let's get you a spot!"

Meticulous ducking and weaving spoke to the woman's comfort in a crowd. She moved in a way that informed Owen's motion. Wide-swinging elbows passed overhead by the breadth of a hair. Heels struck the floor just shy of Owen's feet. The two flowed through the throng until Owen was nestled at a table for two.

The table and chairs were nothing to stare at. The furniture of the Creaky Board seemed to care more for function over form. Not that to say that the chair was uncomfortable. An easy angle on the backrest encouraged melting into the well-worn down cushion. Just comfortable enough to put a tired soul at ease without putting them all the way to sleep.

"What's the plan then, blue boy?" The server had taken up a seat across from Owen, her back to the stage. Amber eyes glistened in the warm lamplight. "Here for a meal? A drink? Maybe here for the night?" she added with a smile.

"Oh, um," Owen drummed his fingers in time with the performers. The infectious nature helped overcome his nerves. "I'm a bit short, actually. On funds. Any chance you folks run on credit?"

Any sense of surety there had been when Owen started speaking had left by the time he stopped. The last few words fell from his mouth with all the confidence of a cow attempting its first flight. Though the serving girl maintained her smile, her eyes had glossed over at the word *credit*.

"Let me talk to the boss," the woman said as she eased herself out of the chair. "Just a moment." Her smile filled with exaggerated mirth. Only a hint of its deflation was visible as the woman turned and wove herself into the crowd once more.

A small suspicion took root in the back of Owen's mind: this chair would not be his for long. It ate at his already frayed nerves.

Tired, brown eyes examined the back of closed lids. The back of the chair rose just high enough to rest his head. Any hard edge on the chair had been worn smooth. *Many an anxious patron had sat just like this*, Owen mused, *with their head cradled neatly in place.* They had felt the rhythmic assault of drums forcing them deeper and deeper into their seat. There was a calming quality to the music once past the sheer volume and voracious tearing of tanned leather. Violent consistency beat his chest. Though the drumming did not keep even time with the beat of Owen's heart, he found himself waiting for those moments of overlap. Those brief points in time where it felt like the drums were speaking to him alone.

The base of the table had four legs branching off from the main support. Each leg ended in a clawed foot, in the shape of an eagle's talons clutching a globe. Owen planted his feet onto the nearest table leg and pushed back in his chair. He struck a balance on the two hind legs of the chair. A gentle easing back and forth kept Owen from bouncing his legs.

Might as well be comfortable, Owen thought. It was not long before curiosity got the better of Owen. He forced his eyes open to look around and see what he could see, working from the top down.

An interior balcony ran around three-quarters of the building, excluding the wall above the Creaky Board's entryway. Stairs that led to the second floor were tucked into the eastern wall and pushed through the floor of the balcony. Wooden handrails kept patrons who had lost their sea legs to wine and whiskey from tumbling into the merriment below. Legs and glasses poked out through twisted iron balusters where folks had given up on standing altogether. The mirth of the first floor did not dissipate when moving up to the second.

Wooden doors lined the walls of the second floor. There was enough room between the door and handrail to fit two people comfortably. *Five could fit*, Owen observed, *if comfort was not a concern.* Brass numberplates were nailed to each door at roughly eye-level for a human.

The key decorative space of the Creaky Board's main area was the northern wall. An errant hunting trophy or odd art piece could be found on the other walls, but the wall surrounding the entryway was an absolute mess of iconography. A wrought-iron set of scales with silver filigree rested beneath a window. The Bureau of Arcane's symbol, stitched into a flag of blue with a white bar, hung loosely nearby. Broken remnants of a longsword hung over the door. Representations of the gods mingled with pre-Federation flags amongst dozens of other articles Owen could not place.

"*Everyone* is welcome here!" came a sudden shout across the table from Owen, followed by the dull thud of a bottle meeting wood. He snapped his head to the source of the exclamation.

There was no doubt in Owen's mind that the woman was a proper Deepkin. Compared to the girl he had met at the House, this woman's skin was almost pure white with hair the shade of fresh snow. Pointed ears, clearly visible with hair drawn back into a messy bun, stretched the length of an extended hand. She rested a sharp cheek against a loose fist. Once following Owen's gaze to the north wall, she turned her head just enough to meet his slack-jawed expression. Eyes like rubies shimmered over a pleasant smile.

"Annabella Everbrite," the woman said. She thrust out the hand that had supported her face. "Most folks just call me Eve."

Owen, still a few moments away from the realization that he was openly staring, eased his chair down onto all four legs. He took her hand as he slammed his gob shut. The Deepkin's grip was surprisingly firm. She shook twice before letting go.

"Owen. Uh, Raulstone."

"Always happy to meet a new face," Eve beamed. "Seeing as how you're paid up, fancy a drink?"

The Deepkin moved in many ways all at once.

A thumb shot back over her shoulder, gesturing a few times. Rolling over top of the crowd on a sea of hands was Lionel. Stubby arms flew upwards as he rode the current for a moment before sinking back into the whirling torrent of people.

Her free hand reached for a bottle on the table as she spoke. Already half-corked, she pulled the bottle to her mouth. Eve bit into the cork and yanked it free the moment she had finished speaking. There was a measure of grace in the way she spat the cork onto the hardwood floor while pouring two glasses of dark, red wine. A Zumbatran red from the look of the squat bottle.

"Something special, for a new friend," Eve said with a wink.

"May I?" Owen asked as he accepted the glass, pointing at the bottle. Eve waved an open hand. Owen turned the bottle to see its label and felt his heart fall to his boots then jump to his throat in the space of a blink. "Is this—"

"Real?" Eve interrupted. The tip of her tongue cleared away the purple stain on her gray lips left by the wine.

"There was still an *actual* Zumbatra when this was corked!"

"Have a taste, before the excitement wears off."

"I couldn't! I couldn't ask the Bureau to—"

"Oh hush," she chuckled, raising a single finger to her lips. "This one's between friends."

Eve tipped her glass skyward, let the mouthful sit, then swallowed with a satisfied sigh. She poured another glass as she rose from her chair. "Cheers," she uttered, tipping her glass at Owen as she turned. Loose robes of red and yellow hugged at her waist and shoulders as she vanished into the crowd. Nothing about her manner or motion could suggest that Eve was cut from anything but silk.

Another look at the bottle confirmed Owen the date he had seen. Aruun Vintners, the label read. Established in 1487. The bottle Owen held lovingly in his hand noted the vintage in question was of the year 1556. *The year before the Upheaval,* he mused. *I'll have to write Venkat about this. Won't believe it.*

There was a pungent, spiced aroma rising from the glass. Even before Owen lifted the wine to his nose it was caressing his senses. A warm, oaky flavor coated his tongue when he finally ventured to taste. Numbness bit at his nose and cheeks as he swallowed. It dawned on Owen that it had been a full week since his last drink. Maybe even longer. Time was subjective at the moment.

A sensation crept into Owen's shoulders. A relaxation that he had not felt since his last drink with Becca. The strangeness of Arnstead blanked, disappeared from his mind.

Another sip.

Drums and howls peaked before hushing to a dull murmur.

Another sip.

Thumbs massaged deep into Owen's shoulders. Knots escaped him in a pleased groan.

Wait... thumbs?

Owen, pulled from his trance by sheer curiosity, looked down at his left shoulder. He looked at his right shoulder after a brief pause. Examination complete, his head centered as his brow crinkled in confusion.

"Whose hands are these?"

Not his own, to be sure. Those hands were happily preoccupied with bottle and glass. No, these hands were pure white. Phantom traces of red and blue interwove on the inner arm. Veins and arteries whose color could not be contained by the blank tapestry that was the Deepkin's forearms.

Another sip.

"Who are you?" Owen asked, turning his head to see this gentle stranger.

"The boss around here," Eve replied. Owen had not noticed her stand. He had not noticed Eve swing around to his back. "You seemed to be enjoying yourself. Didn't want to interrupt."

One of Eve's hands disappeared. It reappeared on the table in front of Owen, sliding away from a key that had just been deposited. Eve tapped on the black velvet that hung from the key's head. The number *17* had been stitched onto the tag in white.

"Set a room aside for you."

"Seventeen?" Owen continued in his bemused tone. "I don't see seventeen rooms up on the balconies."

"Ah," Eve replied with a bright chuckle. "That's right. First timer. How about I show you to your room?"

"Can I take the bottle?"

"Of course!" Eve shouted as she spirited Owen up from his chair, key in hand.

Unlike the serving girl who brought Owen to his table, Eve did not need to duck and weave. There was not a person in the Creaky Board that did not fold away from her graceful presence. Not a show of fear, but a measure of respect. She was taller than any human in the establishment. A touch taller than most of the katarl. Broad shoulders demanded space as she sauntered towards the stairs.

The true size of the Creaky Board became evident upon ascending the stairs. A mere twelve rooms were visible from the main seating area on the first floor. At the top of the stairs, however, a hallway opened up in the south wall. Additional doorways lined this hall before it turned to the right.

"Seventeen will be just around the corner," Eve said. Distance from the chaos below allowed Eve's voice to take on a more silken texture.

Owen's words died in his throat. Stillness had come over the air. The din of the first floor vanished almost completely upon turning into the second hallway. Drums had fallen to the volume of a whisper. The sudden resistance caused by Owen's hesitation forced Olu to look back.

90

"Noise barrier," Eve noted. She pointed to the beginning of the passage behind. A faint glint caught Owen's attention. Memory glass, black as jet, has been set into a groove of silver. Violet light emitted from its core. The groove ran the full length of walls, ceiling, and floor to form an invisible portal.

An object of such subtle beauty could not be ignored. Fascination trounced the overwhelming desire to sleep for three days on end. Owen had slipped from Eve's grasp. Eve did not resist.

The clarity of the glass was difficult to ascertain. Being a dark stone set deep into a wall saw to that. There was almost no residual heat, however, when Owen placed his hand onto the glass.

"Silver is conducting the Flow..." Owen muttered to himself, "pulling residual energy radiated from the people below. A self-sustaining focus. That's impressive."

The noise returned the moment Owen dipped his head through the field. He turned to look at his hand, snapping his fingers on the other side of the barrier. What should have been a sharp crack sounded as though it had been muffled under a dozen blankets.

"What is something like *this* doing in an inn?"

Musical laughter rolled over Owen upon withdrawing through the noise barrier.

"And here I thought you'd pulled that coat from a bin," Eve said. "A bluecoat for sure. No doubt."

"Do you have any idea how much a permit for a self-sustaining focus goes for? In a civilian, commercial setting? Whoever owns this place..." Owen trailed off. He rubbed his fingers to signify the immense wealth required to maintain an object of this quality.

"I care for my customers," Eve said, brandishing the bottle of Zumbatran red.

"You?" Owen was puzzled at the thought that just now started to sink in. A mixture of exhaustion and wine had seen that it took so long. "You own this place? A deepk—"

"A Deepkin," Eve interrupted with a nod.

"How'd you manage that?" Owen asked, as much to himself as to Eve. Only a trace of embarrassment was present in his question. The wine saw to the rest. "Honorary citizen? But even if you were, I can't imagine an honorary citizen owning property. In a township, no less!"

"Can't speak for all my kind," Eve said as she cleared his throat. "*Can* say that you're not in New Haven anymore, or wherever it is you're from. Things are a bit different this far west."

"So they are."

Eve shook her head, chuckled. The rap of the hefty key cut through the near-silence in the hallway. Room number seventeen appeared to be ready for service. Eve beckoned Owen to join.

Tiredness returned like a wave crashing against an unsuspecting beachgoer. It pulled Owen's shoulders down, tugged at his head. A yawn welled in the back of his throat before being quelled. No attempt was made to conceal the effort required to cover his mouth with the back of a hand.

Heavy steps brought Owen to the door of his room. He held out an empty hand to receive the key. The words *thank you* were mouthed silently upon receipt. Tumblers turned clacked with a quick turn of the wrist and the door opened wide.

Cozy would have been the one word that came to mind upon seeing the interior of room number seventeen. A hefty wooden bedframe was nestled up to the back wall, adorned with a mattress large enough to sleep two with comfort. Fresh white linens were held in place by a neatly tucked sheet the color of beets. An assortment of yellow-gold pillows entrenched themselves against the thick headboard.

Next to the bed stood a small nightstand. White and red candles, already lit, were housed in a single candelabra of brass. A pitcher of water rested within a simple basin. Two empty glasses crowded what surface area remained.

Nearer to the door was a stand with prongs enough for a pair of hats and coats. A rocking chair of black iron was tucked into each corner on either side of the door. Their seats and backs were made of lacquered slats of warm cherry. Small head pillows were tied onto the slats with bits of cloth from each corner.

The one word that escaped Owen's lips, however, was, "Pardon?"

Arranged in a tight line from wall to wall of room seventeen was a collection of humans: male and female; tall and short; Nirdac, Zumbatran, and Bangeli. Each one looked intently at Owen with hungry eyes. Emerald robes hung loosely about their shoulders.

Owen did not see who shrugged first.

It was a scattered affair. A gentle roll of the shoulders sent robes rustling down to the floor. Some appeared supple. Others were lithe and toned. The one characteristic they all shared beyond their race? Not a single shred of clothing remained between them.

Blinks came in rapid succession. Perhaps the trick of the light or a tired mind, Owen thought to himself. A shake of his head followed a thorough rubbing of his eyes. The picturesque specimens remained. Quite pleased with themselves, if Owen were to judge by the look on their faces.

No other word managed to broach Owen's tongue. He merely pointed a beleaguered finger at the seductive assembly of room seventeen and looked to Eve, a single eyebrow arched the point of flying to the heavens.

"Not uh... not to your liking?" Eve asked, puzzled as he looked at the crew he had assembled. A light clicked somewhere in the back of her mind. "Oh-h-h-h, I see. Katarl, then? Harn?"

The pitch of Eve's voice rose steadily with each question. Owen's expression was nothing short of flabbergasted.

"I just want to sleep."

Each word was carefully measured as Owen spoke. He hung on each syllable, a touch of desperation creeping into his tone.

Eve seemed to soften, shrank as she did so. Empathy dripped from her half-smile. The woman was like a mountain shedding its snow come spring. Two sharp claps accompanied a nod towards Eve's subordinates.

"All right, clear out."

The same softness that overcame Eve's countenance had infiltrated her voice. A few mutters escaped those who were expecting a well-paid night's work but none openly questioned Eve as they gathered their respective robes and filed out of the room. The group headed to a door without a number further down the hall and disappeared through its frame.

"Sorry," Eve continued after the group had left. "The harn said you were paid up. Figured I would make sure you were taken good care of."

"No, no," Owen stammered. "You don't have to apologize. It's just... just been a difficult few weeks. Looking forward to a bed and a roof overhead is all."

Eve took a moment to study Owen. Looked at the tattered and discolored uniform that seemed to weigh on his shoulders. Saw weapons that hung heavy on weary hips. Noted the shades of purple that had nested below sleepless eyes.

"You let me know if you need anything, okay? I mean *anything*," Eve said, laying into the word. "More water. Somebody to talk to."

There was a pause after those last words. A lingering moment of maintained eye contact.

"Anything."

"Okay," Owen replied, making an honest effort to smile.

"Okay."

A quick rap of her knuckles on room seventeen's doorframe and she was off to the stairs, to descend back into the madness of the first floor.

Though he appreciated Eve's sentiment, Owen did not wait for the woman to be completely out of sight before stepping into room seventeen and easing the door closed. The final few steps to the bed were lost to exhaustion. A clatter of glass and metal sounded as he fumbled to find a home on the nightstand for the gifted bottle of Zumbatran red.

The belt came first. A relieved sigh pushed out through Owen's nose as he hung belt, sword, and caster pistol over the corner of the plain headboard. His other garments received no such special care and became a pile, the floor now a hamper. Clothes shifted and fell until nothing but undershorts remained in place.

The bed enveloped Owen as he lay himself down. Springs eased themselves into place under his weight with a soft groan. The mattress itself, though not the softest thing, was well cared for. There were no lumps or sags to speak of. A hint of lavender and citrus rose from Owen's disturbance. Cool and refreshing in his lungs, the scent further relaxed unwinding muscles. Toes curled and splayed in the open air. Eyes closed with a great exhale of breath as a stillness fell over room seventeen.

Then he heard a creak.

Soft at first, the sound gained volume and rhythm. It was not so loud as to wake a person already asleep. It was, however, just enough noise to draw the ire of someone at the threshold of purest comfort.

Owen's eye snapped open. The sound of metallic springs continued to worm its way into his ear, to bore down into the very center of his brain. A pleasured moan, almost masked by the thickness of shared walls, snuck in to join the discord. An occasional thump mixed in with the midnight song. The sound of a headboard meeting a wall.

"Creaky board," Owen sneered, his eyes rolling into the back of his head as he reached for his bottle of wine.

6.

FAMILY BUSINESS

Quaint.

There was no better word to describe Arnstead's Orland Bank branch, Owen felt. The cathedral-like buildings that served the family back home in Southport would loom over this small establishment, an elephant gazing balefully down at a runt of a mouse. Twelve of Arnstead's bank could fit into a single branch on the coast and there would still be room leftover to throw a banquet.

This was not to say the Orland Bank branch here in Arnstead was in a state of disrepair. Quite the opposite. Four teller stations sat behind a simple walnut counter. The wood's only embellishment was the glassy sheen of its polished surface. Pens were chained to each station next to a square of golden oilcloth. Plates of glass, invisible, save for the glint, separated tellers from their customers.

To the right of the modest, double-doored entryway was a waiting area. A cluster of wooden benches and chairs that could accommodate some ten or twelve people in comfort. To the left of the entryway was a similar area to seat six. Copies of the weekly newspaper, as well as any daily extras since last week's printing, waited patiently for inspection on dark, pine coffee tables.

Walls were barren, save for overlarge windows, of any sort of decoration. The walls were papered in white and yellow stripes. Not a bright yellow or pure white, but rather like honey and cream. As inoffensive to the eye as it would have been exciting for the palette.

The one obvious carryover from the Orland branches back on the coast was the ticketing station: a black, steel dispenser with golden filigree, mounted a red mahogany post carved to resemble a wolf. Unlike the coastal branches, there was no large cube hanging from the ceiling to indicate the current call number. An ornate fixture like the ticket dispenser seemed ostentatious enough.

Half of the seating area was accounted for when Owen entered the Orland Bank branch that morning. Each of the four teller stations was occupied. No stranger to the workings of his family's establishments, Owen walked up to the ticket dispenser to grab his place in the queue. His iron-heeled boots clacked as he crossed the spotless wooden floor.

Perforated edges of the blue ticket popped with ease. *A satisfying sound*, Owen thought. One of those sounds that a person *feels* as much as they hear it. Much like the crinkling spine of a leatherbound book, or snap of a log as it splits in a fireplace. The sort of sound that makes a soul smile.

While the Arnstead branch did not have the imposing cube of its coastal branches, above each teller's station hung a wooden rectangle. The number of the customer being served appeared on the rectangle's face as if freshly branded with white-hot iron. Owen was pleased to see he was a mere seven numbers from the head of the queue.

"Hold it."

It was immediately apparent to Owen that the gruff words had been directed at him. A hand clapped on his shoulder like a vice and cleared that misunderstanding with haste.

"Think I wouldn't recognize you without your uniform, bluecoat? BoA inquiries are by appointment only. Now scram."

The first utterance had been too brief, but the words that followed left no doubt. Owen turned to find himself face-to-face with Manda Galloway. Her grip seemed to tighten as Owen turned to face her.

"Excuse me?" was all Owen managed to get out.

"You heard me," Manda replied, her face contorted with discontent. "And don't think I won't punch your stupid face right here if you try to cause problems."

Owen had enjoyed a degree of inconspicuousness as he walked the streets of Arnstead that morning. No person had recognized him as a Spellseeker. There were no hateful or untrusting glares cast from sidelong glances. No poorly hushed words of discouragement, no profane gestures to mark Owen's passing. He had merely walked the streets as a resident of Arnstead.

The clothes provided by Ms. Everbrite of the Creaky Board were to thank for his plain appearance. Nothing about the clothes was special to look at. She had provided a pair of brown cotton trousers, a set of purple suspenders to keep them up, and a red shirt that buttoned up the front. As promised, and somewhat puzzling to Owen, the clothes were a perfect fit. Owen's only alteration was to roll the sleeves up past his elbows.

Equally as puzzling to Owen as the fact that his clothes fit perfectly, was the fact that Manda Galloway was dressed in a Fourth Federation Army uniform. A knee-length coat of dark olive with brass buttons down the waist, fresh-pressed pants of the same color underneath, looked out of place on the gruff woman. Short-cut, brown hair rested beneath her red beret.

Of greater surprise were the two silver bars pinned to Manda's collar. A similar patch had been sewn onto her shoulder. Owen managed to stifle his amazement at the vicious woman's station as a lieutenant, but only just.

"No problem," Owen said after looking Manda over. He proffered his queue ticket and shrugged Manda's grip in a single motion. "Here for a withdrawal. And what are *you* doing here, anyway?" Owen added when Manda stood her ground. "Does someone of your station have the free time to be harassing random citizens?"

"Nothing random about you," Manda replied, her tone flat with cold anger.

"Is there a problem, Manda?"

"Just dealing with a troublemaker," Manda called out in response. She half-turned her head. It was a gesture to signal acknowledgment while maintaining eye contact with Owen. "Go on ahead into your office."

The source of the new voice, to which Manda responded with a protective tone, hobbled into view next to the soldier. A Nirdac human with dark, chocolatey hair that fell over her shoulders in thick waves. She carried herself with a quiet air of dignity despite the apparent limp in her left leg. The cane that helped support her appeared to be made of the same wood that housed the ticket dispenser for the bank. Its silver grip had been fashioned into the shape of a watchful wolf.

Green eyes sparkled when the woman looked up from the newspaper extras in her right hand.

"This isn't the Spellseeker you mentioned, is it? The one you shared a carriage with to Arnstead?"

The woman kept her tone flat and measured. No trace of the glee on her face was evident in her voice.

"Would have dealt with that cinder bitch if not for him," Manda growled, fighting a reflex to spit.

"I'm sure," the woman replied, indifferent. She used her cane to ease

Manda to the side. It took a few taps of increasing force for Manda to get the hint. "He seems to have grown quite a bit since I've last seen him."

"It's good to see you, too, Cynthia," Owen said as he opened his arms.

"Ah, my little Owen!" Cynthia's voice cracked as she stepped into Owen's embrace. She told firm hold of Owen's torso and squeezed. "It's been so long, cousin. So good to see you! Though I was hoping I'd get to see you in your spiffy new uniform."

Cynthia pushed Owen back and held onto his shoulders for support. The two stood almost eye to eye, with Cynthia standing taller by a mere inch. Mock dismay fell over her face as she looked over Owen's disappointingly pedestrian clothes.

"Eager to shuck tradition as ever, I see?" Owen replied. He gestured to the light brown tweed pants and unbuttoned jacket Cynthia wore. A white shirt with sky blue pinstripes begged for attention beneath the jacket. She had opted for a thick leather belt over suspenders. "No formal robes for the Branch Head?"

"Pfft." All pretense of displeasure melted back into joy. She waved the notion away, easing off of Owen and back onto her cane. "My branch, my rules. I have no use for grandfather's gilded sensibilities. Gold belongs in a vault, not set into the backs of sitting chairs."

Both chuckled at the comment. Owen nodded and cast a look around the building. His attention drawn to it, he could see Cynthia's touch all over the Arnstead branch. The lack of fanciful decoration. A simple, consolidated space. An air of efficiency as opposed to oppressive elegance. Cynthia's touch was evident wherever Owen looked.

"So, what brings you to my humble establishment? Or did you come just to see little old me?" Cynthia fanned herself with newspaper, batted her eyelashes. She maintained this performance for a few moments before a chortle ruptured her concentration.

"Came to make a withdrawal," Owen laughed. "And to say hi, of course."

"Oh, that's it?" Cynthia furrowed her brows when she saw the queue ticket in Owen's hand. "No, no, no. Family doesn't wait." She plucked the ticket from Owen's fingers and turned it into confetti that she held out to Manda. The Fourth Federation Army lieutenant received the trash with a grumble. Manda had sharpened the daggers in her eyes as she watched Owen's genial interaction with Cynthia.

"Come on, Cynthia, that's not—"

"Nonsense! How much do you need?"

There was no winning this argument, Owen knew. Not with Cynthia. He placed his hands on his hips and sighed through his nose.

"Hadn't settled on the number yet. I need to pay some folks back, get some new clothes—"

"Who do you owe, and how much?" Cynthia asked, taking on a clerical tone.

"Well, I assume I'll need a few silvers for the clothes and sundries. I owe the Creaky Board for a night's stay and meals."

"Oh ho," Cynthia interrupted, raising an eyebrow. "Do we need to talk in my office?"

Cynthia pointed past Owen, to a door to the left of the teller stations. The name *Cynthia J. Orland* was fixed to the door on a brass placard. Owen felt his face flush with embarrassment. He waved his hands from side to side in short bursts.

"No, it's not like that!"

"Tell you what," Cynthia said, pushing Owen's frantic hands back down to his sides. "Are you busy today?"

"Quite free, as a matter of fact."

Cynthia smiled, then turned her head to Manda and adopted a cold, officious tone.

"Manda."

"Yes, ma'am?" Manda replied, straightening as she turned her attention to Cynthia Orland.

"Withdraw a hundred silvers from the family account. Talk to Umesh to make it happen, then meet us at the house. We're headed there for tea. Yes?"

The question was leveled at Owen.

"I suppose so," he nodded.

"See to it, then, lieutenant."

"Ma'am," Manda said, raising a vague hint of a salute.

"Excellent. To the horses!" Cynthia called in a hushed cry. She lifted her cane and pointed to the door.

"Horses?" Owen asked. "Too far to walk, is it?"

"What, you're still not going on about this, are you?" Cynthia tapped her left leg with her cane. A hollow, metallic echo reverberated from the contact. "If I've gotten over it, I think you can, too."

What had been meant as a light-hearted jab elicited a darker expression than Cynthia must have expected. Owen did his best to laugh the suggestion off, but his attempt rang as hollow as his cousin's leg. Owen fidgeted in place and scratched at his nose.

"Yeah, you're right."

"How about you ride with me?" Cynthia asked. "We've only got the two horses with us, anyways. Was going to make Manda walk, but this works just as well."

Cynthia winked at Owen, turning the corners of her mouth into a mischievous grin.

"Sure," Owen replied, now his turn to be caught in a chortle. "That sounds doable."

After collecting a few documents from her office, Cynthia led Owen through the branch and out its back door. The exit spilled into a small courtyard shared by neighboring buildings. A makeshift stable had been erected in the cozy space. Three stable hands saw to the half-dozen horses currently hitched. One of the hands, upon seeing Cynthia, unhitched a jet-black mustang. Cynthia tossed the boy a silver dollar as she took the reins.

An appreciative whinny leaped from the horse's mouth as Cynthia stroked its face. She cooed to the lean creature and whispered sweet nothings to it. Her free hand tousled the horse's dark mane.

"Need a hand?" Owen asked, pointing to a well-worn saddle.

"Nonsense," Cynthia replied, breaking eye contact with the horse only long enough to assure Owen that she had been speaking to him and not the horse. "You could hold this for a moment, though."

Cynthia gave her cane a light toss upwards and caught it in the middle, holding it out for Owen to take. Owen furrowed his brow into an approximation of the phrase *are you sure?* The cane waggled at Owen until he conceded and took the implement from his cousin. Cynthia shot him a look of her own. *You'll see*, it seemed to say.

Confidence swelled in Cynthia's shoulders as she took a deep, calming breath. Her frame expanded as her lungs filled with hay-scented air. The air almost whistled as it pushed out through Cynthia's pursed lips.

Where her face was serene, Cynthia's hands told a different story. Veins popped from strain. Her fingers arched, seeming to play invisible piano keys on her upper thighs. A twitch interrupted her silent prelude at the crest of each breath.

This cycle of breathing and contortion was short. After she had completed the fourth breath, Cynthia opened her eyes and blinked at the harsh morning sunlight. Knuckles cracked as she simultaneously shook her hands and flexed her fingers.

"Right then," Cynthia said. White teeth glittered in a massive smile as she spoke. "Up we go."

Cynthia slotted her left foot into the saddle's stirrup. Before Owen could offer a hand, Cynthia had launched herself up and thrown her right leg over the saddle.

"That's... but your—"

"Leg?" Cynthia asked, making no attempt to conceal her pride. "Non-issue. As I said, I've gotten over it."

"But," Owen muttered. He looked at the cane in his hands, just now realizing how tightly he had been gripping it. "What about this?"

"For simple walking. Across a room, down a hall. For more complex activities," Cynthia grunted, patting her horse, "I channel."

Cynthia tugged at the left leg of her pants. A fully-articulated metal leg caught the sun's light and made an awful glare. It was visible up to her shin, where the bunched-up pant leg rested. There was the basic shape of a human's leg to it. The leg had a defined calf and narrowed down to an appropriately sized ankle. Something reminiscent of a human foot was likely tucked into Cynthia's dark brown shoes.

Though the approximate shape was correct, the surface was not whole. Rivulets ran from top to bottom. Dozens of strands joined together to form waves that were tucked over and under one another. When Cynthia rotated her foot, the strands moved in unison. It was as if raw muscle had been sculpted from silver.

"That is *beautiful*," Owen marveled. "Is that a focus?"

"When I said I channel, I meant *I channel*."

"So, you're actively controlling that thing? That must have taken—"

"Years," Cynthia affirmed. "Years, to learn how to control it. Hardly notice it nowadays, though, once I've gotten it started. Come on."

A gloved hand reached down to Owen, offering assistance to mount the mustang. There was a brief pause where Owen took his moment of preparation.

"Ah, gods help me," Owen muttered.

The clap of leather meeting human flesh bounced off of brick walls as Owen took Cynthia's hand. Both worked in tandem to raise Owen behind the saddle. He took fierce hold of Cynthia's torso, placing his head cheek against her back. Owen could feel a pitied sigh slip from his cousin's body.

"You'll be fine," Cynthia uttered warmly. "I'll keep you safe."

The red-brick building in Weststead that Cynthia called home was modest by Orland standards. It was at least twice the size of the Average home in Weststead, which was already twice the size of an Eaststead home. Oldstead was not a part of the equation. Its single floor surrounded an open-air garden in the center of the complex. Space along the southern wall had been procured for a private stable to house Nightshade, Cynthia's black mustang.

Located halfway between Weststead and Oldstead, the house was near enough to any place an Orland might need to make an appearance. The Orland Bank branch was a fifteen-minute ride south. This meant that Main Street was nearby, as well. Any prospective business owner had a short distance to travel to reach the nexus of Arnstead coin. The mayor's estate was a mere ten minutes to the east, overlooking Sisir's Run.

The House of Many was twenty minutes north, across a poorly maintained bridge to Oldstead that creaked if someone sneezed too nearby.

All of this had to be explained to Owen at a later time. His death grip around Cynthia's waist had made the woman's ribs creak. Legs like jelly spilled Owen to the ground when he dismounted Nightshade.

"I'm fine," Owen gasped. He raised a hand to stymie Cynthia's alarm as she dropped from the saddle. Planting a foot, Owen forced himself up by pushing off of his wobbling knee. "Promise. I'm fine. Just been a long time since I've ridden a horse."

"You don't say?" Cynthia chuckled. Gloved hands swished across Owen's back. Motherly sounds of reassurance escaped Cynthia as she attempted to assuage Owen's discomfort. The next swish was Cynthia pulling her cane from the saddle as she stood. "Come on, then. Let's get some tea into you. Should calm you right down. Marcus!"

Two sharp raps of her cane against the back door followed the call. Dozens of dents and scores in the white door suggested a pattern of behavior. As Cynthia reared back for another assault on the door, the beaten wood swung back to reveal a graying Zumbatran katarl. The dangling sleeve of his black and white robes leaped over his forearm as he caught the cane with his bare hand. Not a hair on the katarl's luxurious mane moved.

Owen assumed the man must have had calluses the size of silver dollars on his palm. The katarl showed no indication of pain at stopping the sculpted object, and Cynthia had not restrained herself in her swing.

"Ma'am?" the katarl asked. A dash of annoyance gave some color to the katarl's otherwise measured tone. Owen wondered if there had been a time where the katarl, Marcus, had bothered to refinish and paint the door after each attack.

"Ah, there you are," Cynthia said. She leaned heavily on her cane after Marcus opened a reluctant hand. "Timely as always. The kettle, if you would. We have company."

"Young Master Raulstone. How good of you to visit the young Mistress."

"Good to see you, as well, Marcus," Owen nodded.

"The garden, I presume?"

"Of course. Come then," Cynthia said, turning her attention to Owen. "In we go."

Through the door was a small mudroom. Various stable implements were propped against the exposed brick: pitchforks, shovels, and the like. Several pairs of riding boots had been tucked into a corner along the proper interior of the house. Gloves and hats, as well as coats for colder weather, hung from brass hooks fitted to the walls. Cynthia deposited her gloves and boots before entering the house. Owen left his boots at Cynthia's request.

"I'm amazed Grandfather let you take Marcus. Had thought he was grandfather's favorite."

"It was the first time I'd ever seen Marcus ask him for anything. Grandfather, that is." Cynthia watched the katarl glide down a short hallway and disappear around a left turn. "I have more memories of Marcus than my real father. Probably had something to do with it."

"Leaves you with quite the retinue, I'd say," Owen said. He spoke with an overly impressed tone as he began to list individuals, counting them on raised fingers. "We have grandfather's favorite attendant, for starters. Your very own officer from the Fourth. Some luck with that one."

"For the mayor, that one. Keeps his nerves easy."

"Ah, the *mayor*. There's a third!"

"Knock it off," Cynthia chuckled, leading the way to the central garden. "Comes with being a member of Arnstead's assembly. Wouldn't do the mayor much good if his treasurer got carted off in the middle of the night."

"On the assembly, as well?" Owen replied. This time his question had a genuine measure of astonishment. "I knew you were the head of the local Orland branch, but Grandfather failed to mention you had a seat on the assembly, as well. That's impressive."

"It was the least Mayor Ashby could do. This place was damn near desolate when I got here ten years ago. You wouldn't have guessed Arnstead sat on one of the largest memory glass quarries know to the Federation. Plus, you have furs coming down south from Oswyn, raw materials from forests and mines to the west. If not for Bottom Bay, we'd be the largest commercial hub in all the New World."

Some of the finer points of Arnstead's economic past and future escaped Owen's retention as he and Cynthia entered the garden. The open-air square was thirty feet on all sides. Archways of white stone lead from each red-brick wall to allow access from any part of the house. Large rose bushes, each pruned into a pleasing shape, bloomed shades of red and pink. Beds of soil reached out from the walls with lush carpets of green leaves.

Rooms lucky enough to have a window to the garden were adorned with mantles of ivy. Hanging plants dangled from iron hooks embedded into the brick. Vivid begonias that could put a sunset to shame. Petunias dotted the vibrant mix, giving any wandering eyes a cool place of respite.

Where the ground had not been replaced with fertile soil, it remained hard-packed earth. The same dull, earthen orange from the street without the oppressive layer of dust. In the center of the open space rested a fountain. A pair of seraphs, wrapped in their wings, stood back-to-back. Together they held aloft a basin from which water tumbled over their marble features.

Cynthia led the way across the garden to a cozy nook. Four iron chairs, backs in the shape of waving oak leaves, sat around a latticed iron table. She tapped one of the chair's armrests with her cane before seating herself in a different chair. The effort of moving through the house and garden unassisted exited the woman as a contented sigh. She placed her cane across the armrests of the chair, rested her arms on it.

"So, how do you find my gem of a town? The soon-to-be city of Arnstead?"

"Lofty goals as always, I see," Owen grunted as he sat. "Well, apart from nearly being blown up—"

"Ah," Cynthia snapped. "That was outside of the township."

"All right. Well, that leaves me with the constant slurs and slander." Owen began counting on his fingers again. "The glares of murderous intent, the general dissatisfaction with my presence, and the occasional attempted assault. Couldn't imagine how things could get any better, to be honest."

"Assault?" Cynthia pursed her lips. Her eyes narrowed as she looked her cousin up and down. "Who is stupid enough to try to attack a Spellseeker in broad daylight?"

"Your precious lieutenant, for one. And I have to ask," he added, raising a hand in protest, "was she *your* choice, or did the mayor force her onto you? Some kind of sleight?" Owen tilted his head downward, gazing up at Cynthia with mock reproach.

"I get my pick, actually." Cynthia's head bobbed from side to side as she batted the accusation aside. "And she does have her uses, that one."

"I'm not sure that I want to know."

"And what's that supposed to mean?" Cynthia asked musically.

Visions of javelins tearing people in half flooded Owen's memory. No, it would not be fair to say they were torn in half. It was more like a part of them had exploded, leaving bits of dangling flesh where a shoulder had once been. The sheer, overwhelming force of the attack in response to a handful of arrows that had severely missed their mark.

"Just seems a bit quick to violence, I guess. The sort who gets set off by any little thing. Not the type of person I'd expect to be a bodyguard. Shouldn't there be more restraint in that line of work?"

"Hmm," Cynthia tilted her head. "Well, I suppose she had a few more uses than being a bodyguard. But that's enough about her. Oh, tea!"

Ten years seemed to fall away from Cynthia's face as Marcus strolled into the garden. A pair of teacups rested on a wooden platter, which Marcus balanced on his hand with no sign of effort. Milk was motionless in its saucer as Marcus deposited the platter on the table. Only the slightest tinkle of the sugar's serving spoon betrayed any loss of balance.

"Rooibos," Marcus stated. "Milk and sugar, should you care for it."

"You are a delight, Marcus! Thank you."

"Of course, ma'am. Anything else, or shall I return to my duties?"

"Oh," Cynthia said, sucking granules of sugar from her thumb. She had wasted no time in preparing her tea just the way she liked it: a small dabble of milk and three pinches of sugar. A silver teaspoon clinked softly as Cynthia stirred the concoction. "Bring a couple bits of wood, could you?"

"Ma'am?" Marcus cocked an eyebrow.

"You know, like planks. I'm sure we have some in the storage room. At least four feet long, if you could."

Sudden realization elevated Marcus's features into an impish grin. He nodded as he turned to leave.

"Of course, ma'am."

Owen was too busy preparing his tea to notice. The amber liquid was more milk than steeped water by the time he was through with it. He did not bother to measure sugar in the same way that his cousin had. Sugar crunched both times Owen jammed the silver spoon into the snowy mound.

As Owen went to deposit the sugar spoon next to its saucer, he spied Cynthia's creeping hand. He rapped the spoon against her knuckles. The motion was sharp, catching Cynthia by surprise.

"Excuse me?" Cynthia sucked on the knuckle that had been struck.

"There will be no mercy for fingers that have already been licked," Owen accosted. He reached across the table to offer the sugar spoon. "You'll just have to take your sugar like a normal person."

Narrow eyes flashed at Owen as Cynthia snatched the spoon from him.

"So, this Spellseeker business," Cynthia started. "If it *is* all that bad, you could always leave. Always space for family at the branch. Not working as a teller, of course. You've suffered enough by the sound of it."

"No, I don't think so. Not that I don't appreciate the offer," Owen added over his cup. Warm, amber liquid revitalized his core as it trickled down his throat. His nerves had not yet fully recovered from the ride to the house. "No, I think it will get better with time. The notes in my briefing said Arnstead Seekers tend to start in my department. Most folks move on after a month of probation."

"Oh, well a month is not so bad. What department are you with?"

"Lost and Stolen, for the time being."

"Ugh." Cynthia shuddered. "The lack of appreciation makes more sense now."

"Dealt with Lost and Stolen before?"

"Unfortunately, yes."

"Been having break-ins at the bank?"

Cynthia crumpled into the back of her chair. She pulled her cup to her face but did not drink. Steam coiled up to mask subtle changes in her expression. Feigned drama and childish sleights melted away. There was no lack of sincerity in her displeasure.

"Some thugs seem to have taken quite a liking to our transport services." Molten steel could not have resisted the chill in Cynthia's voice. The abrupt change caused Owen to draw himself up. "I've tried a dozen changes, at least. Moving with small groups versus large. I've had heavily armed caravans, plants in civilian wagons, anything you could think of. Has made no difference. Even when a Fourth Federation Army lieutenant is charged with the task."

"The Cinder Witch?" Owen asked.

"You've had the misfortune to experience her damned crusade against me." Cynthia threw back her cup, drained the last of its contents. Desire crept into her eyes as she stared into the empty vessel. "I help the House turn a profit, and suddenly their heretic wants to burn everything I touch."

"And how does this concern Lost and Stolen?"

"The Orland Bank does not transport goods in mundane crates, Owen. People willing to pay to have their valuables shipped across the New World wouldn't stand us using apple barrels."

Realization gripped Owen as Cynthia's eyes snapped up to meet his own.

"Orland lockboxes are focuses," he muttered. "You've been reporting their theft to Lost and Stolen, then?"

"I used to," Cynthia nodded. "After a few years, I got tired of filling out the paperwork for the same response. Or lack of, rather."

"Why not file for this one, then?" Owen leaned forward in his chair as he asked. "I might be able to help smooth things over, make sure it gets proper attention."

"That's very sweet of you, dear," Cynthia cooed. "No, quite all right. Pontiff Avendale has assured me that his little heretic will be dealt with shortly. Something about bringing in a Keeper to sort the business out."

"Are you sure?"

"You're family, dear. Needn't muddy the waters with business."

"Well, if you change your mind—"

"I'll be sure to let you know."

Bluebirds twittered, settled on the seraphs in the fountain. The pair shared in sweet music as they bathed in the isolated water of the Orland house. Away from the prying eyes of street cats and miscreants with stones to hurl. White breasts rose and fell at a rapid pace. Streaks of black on their wings blurred as the birds flapped against the water.

Owen sipped the remains of his tea in silence. Cynthia seemed just as content to watch the display as he was. These spare moments gave Owen a chance to study the whirlwind of thoughts that had just been thrust upon him.

Some threads wove together quicker than others. The bit about the Orland family using focuses to transport their clients' valuables was a short leap. *The family certainly has the money for the licenses, no doubt,* Owen mused. *Still not cheap, though. Can't imagine that* every *box is a focus. Must be a special perk for wealthy clients.*

These simple threads led to frayed ends. There was no way of knowing what had been in the box that Lieutenant Manda Galloway had been transporting on their journey. Owen never had cause to inquire after the box before knowing it was magical. Knowing that fact now made no difference. Questioning Cynthia about the contents of the box would yield nothing. The contents of a safety deposit box were strictly confidential, an agreement between the Orland Bank and the customer. It was likely enough that Cynthia did not know the nature of the contents herself.

Thoughts of the journey to Arnstead lead to memories of fire and splintered wood. Owen had dismissed the thought of a handful of arrows earlier, but the voracious way they bit into the carriage door was clearer in his mind now. Danger, more present than he had ever known it, had galloped alongside him on a wave of thundering hooves.

Surrender the box, Owen remembered her say. Amalia Tennerim, the Cinder Witch. Terror to the Orlands, the House of Many, and the Bureau of Arcane alike. *You will not be harmed.*

The clatter of teacups pulled Owen from his reverie, sent the bluebirds up to dance among the clouds.

"Excellent," Cynthia exclaimed, her voice being that of preparedness. "Thank you, Marcus. That will be all for now."

"Very good, ma'am. Master Owen, a pleasure," Marcus added with a slight bow. He turned, remnants of tea time in hand, and left the garden as quietly as he had entered.

Though cups and saucers had been removed, the iron latticed table was not empty. A pair of wooden planks had been deposited by Marcus as he gathered the tea set. Each was four feet long and the rough width of a human hand. They were stained a luxuriant, glossy brown to match the floorboards of the Orland house.

Cynthia set the planks a foot apart on the table. She situated the planks parallel to each other so that they ran like manarail tracks between herself and Owen. Her fingertips rested delicately on the boards, one hand to either board. Warm, green light began to radiate from Cynthia's hands and she closed her eyes in concentration. The Flow moved through her hands and into the wood.

"What's this about?" Owen asked.

"You mean to tell me don't remember?" Cynthia replied. Her voice was faint, almost lost in the flood of power that she channeled. Veins of green light, now with a sharper emerald hue, branched out through the planks. "Our sparring sessions?"

"A bit generous of a term, don't you think? I seem to remember my older cousin routinely beating my knuckles bloody."

There was no admonition to be found in Owen's voice. Despite his words, he looked fondly on the days he spent with his cousin at the Orland's Southport estate. A great expanse of oaks and maples, of clear, rolling hills. There was space enough for a pair of children, aged ten and fourteen, to run wild.

The wooden weapons that Cynthia had fashioned in those days were crude. A product of inexperience that slowly took shape as her younger cousin grew in strength. Owen could feel the rough grip of a wooden sword-shaped from fallen tree branches. Tree bark remained for grip, or so Cynthia had said. She had mentioned something about the knots in the blade being there for character.

"I see you've been practicing," Owen said, allowing a pinch of astonishment to slip. "These are looking impressive."

Cynthia did not acknowledge her cousin's compliment. Energy continued to move through her into the practice swords she was crafting. Both weapons looked identical, despite their original boards having unique swirl patterns. Grips had the look of wire wrapping rather than a smoothed surface. There was enough space to hold the weapons comfortably in two hands. Uniform blades, with rounded edges and points, ran three feet long.

The process sounded like a tree growing at hundreds of times the normal pace. At least, that was what Owen told himself. He did not have a reference point for this collection of noises. There was fine sandpaper being rubbed into an almost smooth rocking chair. A lumberjack splitting timbers as big around as a Bangeli katarl's torso. Twigs snapping over Cynthia's knee as they played Shikaree in the woods. All this at once, and yet more besides.

Five minutes had passed before Cynthia lifted her hands from the wooden swords. One handle rested on her side of the table, the other at Owen's. She opened her eyes slowly after a handful of recovery breaths. Traces of sweat showed on her forehead, but Cynthia did not seem to mind. The look of competition burned in her eyes.

"Ever since I'd heard you were coming, I've been curious to see if those folks at Eastpointe taught you anything. Let's have some fun."

"You can't be serious?" Owen's questioning gaze looked first to Cynthia's left leg. It was a perfectly valid point, but he felt a rush of embarrassment the moment he looked. He snapped his eyes up to Cynthia's face. "Being four years my senior means less than it used to, you know. I can actually swing one of these things now."

"That's good to hear. I'd hate to have to go easy on you at this age."

"Well, don't say I didn't warn you."

"My," Cynthia chuckled, "how considerate."

A familiar look of concentration fell over Cynthia as she stood. She took one of the wooden swords from the table and deposited her cane in its place. Her left leg creaked and groaned at first, a metallic protest, but it was not long before Cynthia's stride was indistinguishable from any person who walked on two good legs of flesh and blood. Air whooshed around the wooden blade as Cynthia flourished her new creation.

"Never have been any good in telling you no, I guess," Owen muttered. The comment had been just loud enough to elicit a grin from his cousin.

Owen took the remaining sword in hand and rose from his chair. There was more to be impressed by than the practice weapon's aesthetic, he realized. Weight had been balanced in the handle to mimic a proper sword. Owen was able to flick the blade and feint with a single hand. Subtle technique would not be lost with this tool.

Satisfied with the sword he had been provided, Owen placed himself opposite from Cynthia. Both his knees were bent in preparation. He shifted his weight backward and kept his sword hand at waist height. The blade rose at an angle that leveled the tip with his eyes. It was a simple defensive stance that could handle an attack from any direction.

There was a gentle clack as Cynthia tapped the end of her sword against Owens. A declaration of readiness. Owen nodded consent.

Cynthia, holding her sword in both hands, pushed off her right foot and lunged forward. The rounded tip of her sword was aimed at Owen's right shoulder. Powerful and direct, but also messy. Cynthia's head followed her strike. She would be able to throw all of her weight into the attack, but it left her vulnerable.

The brash opener was easy for Owen to read. Reflex took over. A slight push to the right would render the hasty stab toothless. After, Owen would slide his sword down Cynthia's and catch her with a tap on the skull. Simple, efficient revenge for a childhood of busted knuckles and bruised wrists.

Owen's first surprise came when he moved to deflect Cynthia's thrust.

Rather than catching his opponent's weapon with a swift jerk to the right, Owen found there was no thrust to catch. Instead, there was a slam of boot and metal against packed earth. Cynthia planted her left foot and killed her forward momentum. She pulled her head back at the same time to avoid any potential counterblow.

Owen's second surprise came with Cynthia's display of precision.

The initial thrust had not been a threat in itself. It had served as a hook. A *feint*. One baited to temp Owen's guard. There was no crossguard in the way to stop Cynthia as she snapped her sword to the side, out its thrust, and brought it back to land square on Owen's exposed knuckles. Wood struck thinly covered bone with a hollow plonk.

A sharp yelp escaped as a shock of pain ran up Owen's hand and through his wrist. The pain was exacerbated by how unexpected Cynthia's maneuver had been. He let his wooden sword fall to the ground with a muted clatter. Owen rubbed his battered knuckles with his free hand, air flowing sharply between clenched teeth.

"Very clever," Owen grunted.

"The lieutenants have their uses."

"Ah, so that's how it is." Owen bent down to grab his sword after a final shake of his reddened knuckles. He held the sword with both hands now, his stance shifted to accommodate. "You're only going to catch me napping once."

The snap and crack of wooden weapons clashing echoed off the brick walls for the better part of an hour. Blows were struck and returned between both combatants. Owen, supremely confident at the start, learned to respect his cousin's precision. Cynthia's strikes were fierce. Every feint was as devious as the first, though plenty were more so. She afforded Owen no room to be careless.

Before long, Owen shared in Cynthia's excitement. Their smiles grew as their faces reddened from the strain. Cynthia was forced to remove her jacket and roll her sleeves up to her elbows. This was, in its way, a victory for Owen. Never had he forced this much effort from Cynthia in their youth. A sense of elation welled in his chest as he heaved each new breath.

The fun came to a sudden stop with the sound of a metallic snap. Cynthia's left leg went lax as she moved to pivot her foot, and she crumpled to the ground with a surprised gasp.

"Cynthia!" Owen called, matching his cousin's surprise.

"No, it's all right," Cynthia gasped. "Maybe a little *too* much fun is all. Haven't sparred like that in a while."

"Seems that way. Here, let me help you up."

"Don't be silly." Cynthia waved away Owen's hand. She jammed the tip of her sword into the ground, used it to force herself upright. "I'm alri—"

Cynthia's protests were cut short by another metallic twang. As she fell backward, her prosthetic leg wrenched itself loose and slid away. Bare metal lay exposed on the garden floor. Sunlight glared on the newly detached limb. Owen looked at the spectacle with abject horror.

"Hadn't pegged you for the type that got off to beating up cripples." The words rolled into the garden shortly before Manda Galloway made her entrance. She wore a nasty smirk befitting her comment. A jackal happening upon a fresh corpse could not have looked more pleased. "Looks like he did a real number on you, ma'am. Broke your concentration and everything."

"Enough of that, lieutenant," Cynthia snapped.

Owen looked from Manda back to Cynthia. There was more to see now that battle fervor had left him. Clearer eyes saw that Cynthia's face was closer to purple than red. Sweat drenched the collar of her shirt, caused it to stick to her chest. Distant eyes looked at nothing in particular as Cynthia focuses inwards. An empty hand clutched absently where her left leg should have been.

The wooden sword clattered to the ground before Owen realized he had dropped it. His cousin was exhibiting clear signs of Flow exertion. Their fun had forced Cynthia to channel too much energy, to overdraw the Flow.

"I'm sorry, Cynthia," Owen muttered. "I didn't realize—"

"Enough. Both of you," Cynthia grumbled. She managed a pathetic smile amid her panting. "I'll be fine. You don't have to apologize for our fun."

Without warning, Manda tossed something in Owen's direction. The object hit him square in the chest before he could register the movement. It plummeted to the ground and gushed silver dollars onto the garden floor. A leather coin purse with the Orland wolf stitched into one side. Owen could feel on his chest where the edges of coins had struck him.

Manda made no sign of apology. She had not bothered to see if Owen caught the bag or not. A handful of steps had her at Cynthia's side.

"All right, ma'am. Let's get you outta the dirt."

No protest deterred Manda, though Cynthia assaulted the lieutenant with quite a few. Manda ducked her head under one of Cynthia's, grabbed the metal leg, and brought everything up with her in a single motion. There was not so much as a grunt from Manda. Quiet duty guided her arms.

"If you want to make it up to me," Cynthia said, "stay here as my guest. At least until you have a place of your own. Wouldn't do to have family bunking at the Creaky Board, after all."

Cynthia's voice was fragile now, a cracked sheet of glass ready to shatter at the mere suggestion of contact.

"I would love to." Owen nodded softly.

7.

SETTLING IN

Noon had come and gone by the time Cynthia finally pulled herself away from Owen. The pair had worked up quite an appetite. Both the sparring session and hours of recounting years gone by played a part. Childhood years that were spent together. Years of young adulthood that were spent apart. There was no topic off-limits as Owen and Cynthia chatted through anything and everything that came to mind.

The discussion could, however, last forever. As the head of the local Orland Bank branch, there was a never-ending cascade of duties to which Cynthia had to attend.

"Just this one morning probably sets me a full day or more behind schedule," Cynthia moaned. "Not that seeing you isn't worth it."

"Oh, no," Owen said as he waved away the notion of offense. "Contracts to sign. Budgets to approve. I understand completely."

"You don't know the half of it," Cynthia replied through a hollow chuckle. "Anyways, that gives you time to go through some of the list I made for you. They won't all have their doors open on a Sunday, but you should be to get through a fair number of introductions. The ones I've put stars next to."

"Yes, Mother. As you command, Mother."

"Shut it," Cynthia said through a more genuine smile. Owen offered a similar smile in thanks as Cynthia departed for the bank branch.

It was a bit overwhelming, the list that Cynthia had provided. A tailor, a pair of bakeries, a few general stores. Leather goods made the list. A couple of metal workers and smiths, too. The list comprised the names, professions, and addresses of any establishment that Cynthia thought might be of use. Each one came from the top of her head and was inked directly to the page. A stunning feat of memory that did not pass Owen's notice.

To complement the list was a small, rolled map of Arnstead. Marcus had dug around Cynthia's study to find the article in question. Individual

114

structures were omitted in favor of clean lines. The scrap of paper did, at the very least, provide names for the streets. It was more information that had to go on before receiving the map, and he thanked Marcus for the effort.

Before attending to any of the locations that Cynthia had left a star next came the matter of settling with the Creaky Board. The thought of the Bureau filing an expense for an establishment such as the Creaky Board did not sit well with Owen. He felt that having rumors before he had managed to set foot in the building was not a smart decision. Whatever bill had been raised could be paid with ease from the generous withdrawal Cynthia had allowed.

Settling with the Creaky Board first also put Owen on the same side of the rivers as Frontier Finds. Described to Owen as a small bookstore that also served as the town library, it was a place Owen was keen to visit. He counted his graces when Cynthia mentioned that the place was open on Sundays and every other day besides. A quick tour of Cynthia's study had revealed to Owen that there was little in the home in the way of reading material. Ledgers and addresses dominated the shelves of the Orland Estate. If Owen was to keep his sanity at the edge of the known world, he knew that a steady supply of good books would be a must.

Owen continued to enjoy the anonymity that came with wearing street clothes as he left the Orland Estate to locate Frontier Finds. People excused themselves if they bumped into Owen or stepped on one of his feet. Occasional nods of 'hello' came from storekeepers trying to drum up business. It was an altogether new experience compared to his arrival the day before.

According to the map provided by Marcus, Frontier Finds was located in the Eaststead district. That would put Owen on the same side of town from which he had arrived. A trip down Main Street and over the Bridge on Main was simple enough. There were no turns that might cause Owen to lose his way. Just a straight shot down the busy causeway that was at the core of Arnstead traffic.

Simple directions ended on Main. When Owen had crossed the Bridge of Main and made his way to Eaststead, he needed to turn left. The street he was looking for was four streets down from the bridge and seemed to be named Alder Street. Counting streets turned out to be a better method of navigation than looking for the street signs themselves. Most signposts were not tall enough to be read over the crowds. Some streets did not bother to house signposts at all. It was by no means welcoming to newcomers with improvised maps.

As Owen turned further and further into the heart of Eaststead, away from Main Street, the crowds began to thin. The streets were by no means abandoned. People came and went in opposing directions just as on Main Street. The difference here was that Owen could read what signs were available without having to stand directly under the sign itself. A nice change of pace as Owen turned this way and that to locate Frontier Finds.

Disappointment in signage continued when Owen managed at last to locate the store in question. It was a tiny establishment dwarfed between two larger houses. The second floors of the surrounding complexes loomed tall over the single-story bookstore. Jutting out from the doorway of Frontier Finds was a small sign. It bore the namesake of the store popping up from the pages of an open book. The whole sign was wood-tone and easy to miss. Much to his displeasure, Owen managed to walk past the establishment twice before realizing it was there.

The door to the building was light and swung freely as if inviting Owen to enter. A small bell over the inner doorframe tinkled. Notes like crystals danced through the shop before petering out into nothingness.

"Hello there!" came a muffled salutation from somewhere within the store. "I'll be with you in a moment."

"Of course," Owen replied in his best guess as to where the sound had originated from.

What Frontier Finds lacked in height it appeared to make up for in depth. The building was structured like an enormous hallway. Owen guessed that it be twice as long as its neighbors. He wondered if walking to the back of the shop would lead to a doorway for a different street with new neighboring buildings on either side.

Books lined the long walls of Frontier Finds as far as the eye could see. This is not to say that there was some trick of the light, or that the shelves went on forever. Additional bookshelves cluttered the floorplan in such a way that it was impossible to see from one side of the building to the other. It did not matter how much Owen shuffled between his feet. The shelving units were too tall for him to see over the top of, as well. All Owen could see were shelves upon shelves of books.

The sight sent a shiver of joy down Owen's spine. Frontier Finds was far beyond what Owen had expected. Its diminutive exterior did not do the extensive interior justice of any kind.

Quiet footsteps wormed their way into the appealing silence. Louder with each step, the unmistakable sound grew closer. The steps were shuffled. A foot would drag rather than rise. The loud thump of a heel meeting the wooden floor would follow. It a messy sound. The sort of noise that accompanied a struggle.

"Is everything all right back there?" Owen could not help but ask.

"Oh, sure," came the labored reply. "Everything is— wait, no. No!"

First came the sound of a single book thwacking against the floorboards. Another book followed. This one sounded like it landed on its spine. The source was close enough that Owen could hear the pages unfurl as the book splayed its contents open to the world. Then, all at once, came a thunderous roar of books tumbling to the floor. Too many to count.

Owen took his first steps away from the entrance to seek out the source of the noise. He *felt* the cascade of books. It was a heavy sound. The type of sound that might accompany a crushed foot or a nasty fall.

"Hello?" Owen called out as he searched. "Are you okay? Can you hear me?"

"Yes, yes. No need to fuss. I'm right over here."

He's close, Owen thought. Owen was sure the smooth, chocolaty voice belonged to a male. Each word uttered brought Owen closer and closer through the labyrinth of shelves until he finally found the origin.

Covered by a small pile of books, a Zumbatran human sat on the floor between a trio of oddly angled bookshelves. He wore robes of red and yellow that seemed a touch too large for his frame. Owen guessed, from the wrinkles around the man's eyes and the slight sag of his cheeks, that the man was on the backend of middle-age. The man swiveled from side to side as he stacked the books that weighed him down. He seemed more disappointed than hurt.

"Uh, w-welcome to Frontier Finds," the man said, sparing the briefest moment of attention to Owen before looking back to the books. "My name is Olufemi. How can I help you today?"

"I think maybe you need a bit of help first, don't you think?"

Olufemi did not complain when Owen knelt and began to stack books. The two of them finished the task wordlessly. When Olufemi stood, half the books cradled in his grasp, Owen followed suit. They navigated between shelves until they reached the front of the establishment. Olufemi deposited his stacks of books on a countertop that had been obscured from the entryway. Owen did the same.

"Thank you," the man sighed. "Truly. You were a great help there. And how might I be able to assist you today, now that we've gotten my struggle squared away?"

Olufemi let out a sigh of exhaustion with his last few words. The exultation of a job well done. Owen gathered that the man must have been at this kind of work for quite some time before Owen's arrival at the store. Judging from the dented spines on some of the books, this had not been an isolated fall.

"I'm Owen. New in town, and my cousin gave me a list of places I should visit. Your place here was at the top of the list."

"Awful generous," Olufemi chuckled. "Not many people would place a library at the top of a sightseeing brochure."

"I meant to ask," Owen paused for a moment to compose his thoughts. "Is this place a library? My cousin was not sure. She listed it as a store *and* a library. What exactly is this place?"

A broad smile cracked Olufemi's winded face.

"Frontier Finds is whatever you need it to be. Need to borrow a book? I'm here for you. Looking for something to keep? I can help with that, too."

"How about stationery?"

"For letters and the like? Maybe some drafting of your own?" Olufemi raised an eyebrow before nodding. "I can certainly help with that, as well. Is that why you're here?"

"In part. It would be nice to have something sturdier to write on than the garbage that the Federal Post provides."

"They do the best with what they have," Olufemi replied. This time a note of sternness melded into his words. "I wouldn't judge them too harshly."

"Fair enough," Owen nodded. "The stationery is more an afterthought, really. I'm mainly here because I was told this is the best place to find books. I've just moved to Arnstead for work. Got here just the other day."

"Looking for something to help keep you sane at the edge of the world?"

Owen blinked twice, stunned by the accuracy of the man's statement. The bewildered look elicited another series of chuckles from Olufemi.

"Well," Olufemi continued brightly, "as luck would have it, I aim to fulfill that very purpose. What could I interest you with, Owen? Something old or new? Fantastical? Historical? Or possibly something wild and horrific?"

Each descriptor was accompanied by a gesture to a different set of shelves. Olufemi's hands moved with a calligrapher's grace through the open air.

"I guess I'm not so sure. Any old thing would do in a pinch."

"There's no pinch here," Olufemi said, placing a comforting hand on Owen's shoulder. "Tell me, what did you read last? Maybe that will help us make up your mind."

Owen had to wrack his brain for the answer. It seemed like a simple question on the surface, but the last week felt as if it had taken the space of a year.

"Well," Owen puzzled, "I suppose the last thing I got my hands on was the most recent Stephanie Queen novel."

"Oh! You mean *Shining Tower*?"

"That's the one."

"You don't happen to have it still, do you?"

The Zumbatran was electrified. The slight hunch in his posture was gone as if it had never been there in the first place. Expectant eyes leveled themselves on Owen.

"I'm sorry to say that I don't," Owen replied. "Went up in smoke a few days ago, along with most of my things. Part of the reason why my cousin made the list for me. These aren't even my clothes."

"How awful," came Olufemi's deflated response. "I'm sorry to hear that. If it's any consolation, my stock has suffered a similar setback. The caravan carrying my copies of the novel got hit by the Cinder Witch. Was hoping you'd be willing to part with your copy so I could at least have the one to lend."

Memories of arrows and fire spilled into Owen's stream of thought.

"What did the Cinder Witch want with a wagon full of books?" Owen thought aloud.

"Oh, I hardly believe she was after my stock," Olufemi replied with a bitter chuckle. "I imagine I just got caught in the crossfire of whatever scheme that woman has. It's all in the past now, nothing you need to worry about. Now how about we visit a few shelves of fiction? Something to get both our minds off this rotten world of ours?"

"That sounds delightful."

8.

REPORTING FOR DUTY

A sense of grandeur accompanied the word *Arcanarium* in the minds of the Bureau of Arcane employees. Large grounds with well-kept lawns were moats of green around a veritable castle of law and regulation. Heavy doors restricted passage between departments to only those who had business being there. Each exterior wall would be as thick as a small home and tower over any nearby structure brave enough to be erected in the Arcanarium's presence.

Inside an Arcanarium buzzed an army of clerks responsible for any number of activities. One person may be responsible for approving zoning requirements for magically worked farmland, determining what focuses could be used to work that land, and how many certifications each farmhand would be required to possess to legally work. The next clerk may have a more granular, single-minded field of specialty. Perhaps the responsibility of receiving certification applications in one of the few publicly accessible areas of an Arcanarium. No matter the breadth or complexity of their specialty, each clerk was a necessary cog that ensured the Federation did not collapse into magical anarchy.

Offices were carved out in an Arcanarium for members of the Spellseeker division. Each was a space for a Seeker to complete any clerical tasks their position may entail: paperwork related to detained suspects, filing reports on contraband focuses, requisition of new citation pads. These offices were large enough to ensure efficiency but small enough to minimalize distraction. A Seeker's office was a sterile place to allow an officer to record their duties performed in the field.

The most well-reinforced walls in an Arcanarium were those that separated the Research and Development divisions from their neighbors. Bright minds flocked to these beacons of progress. It was in the Arcanarium of New Haven that Tanya Karlovac produced the first self-sustaining, memory glass-powered light fixture. The Arcanarium of Andrasta, the Federation's capitol, saw the creation of the world's first focus at the hands of Hiral Mannan. These great minds, and many others besides, tamed wild and terrible magic in the name of progress. Thick walls encased these places of discovery more for the protection of those outside than to prevent intrusion.

It was with high hopes and expectations that Owen approached a building that looked an awful lot smaller than his tired mind had committed to memory.

Packed into the minuscule shade cast by the diminutive structure was a sweaty assemblage of people. A person with cataracts the size of a silver dollar might be forgiven for calling the horde a line. Shoulders bumped against shoulder as each person jockeyed to be next through the open doorway.

There was no doubting that it *was* the Arnstead Arcanarium. Owen was able to see half of the Bureau of Arcane seal on his approach from the east. Double doors, propped open by the grumbling mass of people, were clear as day. Unbelieving eyes looked from the door to throng, then to the building itself.

The Arcanarium stood no taller than any of its Weststead neighbors. The nearby buildings were mostly of the two-story variety where the Arcanarium seemed to have a single floor. Owen backed a few paces in the direction he had come. Peering down the alleyway, he was able to see that the walls housed windows. Simple, pedestrian *windows*. Not even a bar over the glass to give would-be trespassers a second thought!

Transitionary, Owen assured himself. *Must have been a fire in the old building. Or just the public building perhaps? A satellite licensing office?* He knew there was only one way to be sure, of course; get inside and ask the staff. Another look at the dense wedge of people in the doorway elicited a tortured sigh. The prickly thicket was anything but inviting. Owen's shoulders tensed on reflex as he drew himself up to approach the door.

"Excuse me," Owen said. The confidence in his voice surprised him, emboldened him to speak louder when no heads turned. "Excuse me! Official business. Please clear a path."

A few heads turned.

"I'm on business, too!" shouted a member of the crowd, masked by their peers.

"Same," chimed another.

"Been coming here three days straight," moaned a third. "Technicians' license expires tomorrow. Be damned if I have to get certified *again!*"

"Lost my cert the same way last year," spat a fourth anonymous queuer. "Had to take a written exam. And pay the certification fee. *And* pay the late renewal fee!"

"You did not!" shouted the first speaker.

"Oh, I did! Cost me ten silver dollars, all said and done."

"Unbelievable," wailed a new, fifth voice.

Each speaker carried a greater heft of annoyance than the last. What once had been a disorderly group of irked individuals was taking on a new form. A sense of communion spread like fire in an autumn forest.

"Spellseeker business," Owen howled over the crowd, hoisting his badge on high for those who could not see his tattered uniform.

A lot of heads turned.

Owen could feel the wave of newly shared ire wash over him. Glares soaked in contempt peered over shoulders and in-between legs. All eyes had become fixed on the self-identified Bureau official. People going about their business stopped in their tracks. Loiterers across the way raised lowered heads. Owen's peripherals had become filled with unabashed stares.

Fifty-seven percent.

The thought stopped his heart, turned his stomach. A high mortality rate among Spellseekers had meant to Owen that his post was dangerous. Villainous organizations would lurk in the shadows to upset law and order. Your average thief would have enough notches on their belt to make a veteran soldier take notice.

Pure malice, radiating from the people before him, told him otherwise.

"I only need to pass," Owen said, fighting to control his wavering voice. "No cause for alarm. Simply let me pass."

In what seemed to be the longest minute of Owen's life, he saw members of the crowd turn to each other. Hushed whispers reached his ears as little more than shapeless noise. Their glares remained steady all the while.

No words were spoken as a pair of katarl by the door stepped backward. A small gap opened in the doorway, which tucked through without hesitation. The space was small, designed to be uncomfortable. Owen brushed against both katarl as he passed. Fear rose higher in Owen's chest. It would take the slightest misstep, he felt, to snap the tension that bound these two towering figures. Their eyes lingered like knives in Owen's back.

A small measure of relief settled Owen's nerves when he saw the ordered nature of the Arcanarium's lobby. The mass of people inside had been formed into a snaking queue that consumed most of the available area. Brass posts connected by rope provided a clear path for those lucky enough to have entered the Arcanarium proper.

Another path emerged from the front doors, this one peeling to the right and hugging the wall to the corner. It did not weave through the innards of the lobby as the other path did. The path was devoid of bodies, as well. Imperfect alignment between brass posts suggested that this narrow path had been wider at the day's start. Owen was forced to turn his shoulders to avoid any unwanted contact. He had realized that the less attention he drew, the better.

The tight path turned left at the corner and continued to follow the wall. There stood a wooden door, the symbol of the Bureau etched into its center. It seemed to be a smaller version of the main doors. Crimson light radiated from the Bureau symbol. Owen jiggled the knob, already knowing the effort was futile. He removed his badge from his belt to perform a similarly hollow gesture.

"That door is for *staff only*," croaked a voice from Owen's left. It was the sort of voice that seemed to come more through the nose than through the mouth.

When Owen turned his head, he was able to make out a sliver of a counter through the writhing queue. Behind the counter was seated a wrinkled heap of a female human. Red-rimmed glasses sat low on a crocked nose that methodically twitched from left to right, left to right, left to right. A shaky, wetted finger flipped to the next page in the packet before them. Nails the color of glossed sunflowers reflected light from the lanterns overhead.

More importantly, Owen could not see another person behind the counter. Some other clerk that might have noticed Owen reaching for the door. The leathery bag of a person was too fixated on the documents before her, much to the discomfort of the Nirdac katarl who had provided them, to notice. Owen raised to the tips of his toes. He leaned back to the side, and even hopped once. There seemed to be no one else. He raised his badge to the door once more, eyeing the clerk.

"Final warning, sir; *staff only.*"

There was no indication to suggest Owen had been seen. The clerk did not turn or raise her head. No noise had been made that rose above the bitter murmurs of those in the queue, but there was no mistaking it. The voice certainly matched the clerk's appearance.

"Excuse me, there," Owen began, "…clerk. I *am* staff."

The name of his station caught in his throat as Owen surveyed the more or less docile crowd. Instead of announcing his tittle, he raised his badge so that the clerk could see it. Rather, they *would* be able to see it if they had turned their head. The loud thumb of a stamp meeting a pad of ink was followed by the subsequent, firmer thump against the front page of the katarl's packet.

"Next," the clerk whined. The katarl, ready to be gone from the Arcanarium, skipped past Owen on their way along the wall to the front doors. Owen's forehead crinkled into a frown.

"Excuse me?" he called after the clerk. "Any chance you could let me through? I need to report to Violette. For synchronization." Owen waggled his badge for good measure.

"Are you applying for a new license or renewing an existing license?"

No recognition. Not even a hint that they had heard Owen. The clerk had already moved on to service the next person in queue: a fidgety Nirdac harn with a black and white coat. The phrase 'new license' eked out of the general murmur. A sound like gravel shifting under a loaded wagon gurgled from the clerk.

"New licensure for Flow-assisted Agricultural Certification requires completion of requisition form RF-119 in conjunction with a completed RF-1B form for General Requisitions. I only see an RF-119."

Alarm spilled over the harn's countenance as he reached inside his coat. The nervous man produced a small packet of papers. With an effortless hop that brought him momentarily to eye-level with the clerk, he thwacked the papers onto the counter. Empty hands began to fidget after he returned to the ground. The clerk managed to sift through papers in a way that its sound sheered through the dull discontent that filled the air.

"Very good," the clerk continued after a moment. "As you are requesting new licensure, you are also expected to have passed a written exam specific to the nature of the licensure in question. Do you have your original test results or a notarized copy of the same?"

The harn's eyes opened wide at the request. Unsure hands moved slowly into his coat, pawing over every inch of his torso in a desperate attempt to find what he knew was not there.

"Do you have your original test results or a notarized copy of the same?" The clerk seemed to be able to hear the harn's quiet, stuttered response better than Owen. "If you do not have the appropriate paperwork, I cannot grant the requested licensure. Please return when you have the previously specified documentation, as well as the seven-dollar fee for new licensure. Have a blessed day and may the Many watch over you. Next."

There was pause neither for breath nor compassion in the clerk's speech. Even the farewell at the end felt devoid of any emotion. This, of course, was not the concern of the next person in line, who gladly stepped forward to take their turn.

Fascination at the severity of the Arnstead Arcanarium's processes held his attention. He watched another two people cycle through their requests before remembering why he had come himself. Further calls continued to garner no attention. Not knowing how else to proceed, Owen raised his badge and placed it against the door for the third time.

As before, the clerk did not turn to observe Owen's actions. She did not speak. With a practiced lack of care, the clerk slipped a hand beneath the counter for a moment before returning to the paperwork before her.

An alarm blared from somewhere behind the clerk. It was a piercing wail that bit at the ears of everyone unfortunate enough to be in the lobby. Only the clerk maintained a keen focus on the work before her. Judging from the clerk's expression alone, it would be safe to assume that there had been no alarm at all. Owen gritted his teeth as he clapped hands to ears.

Then, as quickly as it had come, the alarm was cut away in an instant. The moment was accented by the ferocious slam of a heavy door. Hands dropped slowly from the ears of people in the queue. Heads turned from side to side in mild confusion, attempting to puzzle out what had just occurred. The source of their collective relief wasted no time in presenting herself.

Violette strode into view next to the clerk.

"We've talked about this, Sam," Violette said. The small chain that affixed pen to clipboard clattered as she set the lot down on the counter. "That button," she continued, reaching down to turn off the concealed contraption as she did so, "is for emergencies. Are there any emergencies here, Sam? I don't see any murderers, Sam." Violette waved a hand at the folks queued in the lobby. "Nothing is on fire, Sam. I don't see any problems, *Sam*."

The clerk pointed a wizened finger at Owen.

"Attempted break-in."

Violette followed Sam's finger and turned her head over her shoulder to see Owen, pointing to himself with a concerted look on his face. Nostrils flared. It was the crack in Violette's steely clam expression. Gnashing teeth followed as she ripped the switch from under the counter and hurled it against the far wall with a savage grunt. The alarm housing exploded in a shower of springs and gears.

Eerie silence gripped the room. An unknown variable forced the queue into stillness, as though the whole collection of people could avoid being seen. All eyes were locked on Violette as picked up her clipboard and, looking at nobody in particular, went back the way she had come. Heartbeats thrummed in ears as people began to breathe again.

"Next," called Sam, as though nothing had happened.

Slowly, the crimson red of the door changed to ethereal white. It swung inward to reveal a red-faced Violette, chest heaving to reclaim air that had been screamed away.

"In," she muttered.

Owen complied.

The soft swish of sandaled feet whisked Violette down a long hall. The door behind Owen whispered shut behind as he moved to follow. A door to the immediate left had a small placard that read *Reception*. Glancing over his shoulder, Owen saw the door behind had a similar sign that read *Lobby*. A metallic snick broke the quiet of the hall as Violette turned the knob of a third door, beckoned for Owen to follow. This third door's placard read *Handling*. A removable nameplate below the room's designation read *Violette Woods*.

Violette glided into the room. Keeping a firm grip on the door, she made room for Owen to enter. The space inside was small, clean. A modest desk, which Violette seated herself behind after Owen had entered, sat against the wall opposite the door. Metal filing cabinets straddled either side of the desk, allowing just enough space for the woman's slight frame to squeeze through. A collection of opened file folders was scattered over the

126

green oilcloth that covered the desk's center.

To the right of the desk was mounted a map of the New World. A casual glance indicated the map was kept well up to date; it bore features not present on the maps Owen had studied on his train ride to the frontier. Push-pins of various colors held notes in place on the map, though the hasty scrawls were beyond Owen's power to comprehend. Another map, this one of Arnstead and its surrounding territory, adorned the opposite wall and was similarly marked and pinned.

On the wall directly behind Violette's desk was the most noteworthy feature of the entire room. Small, wooden boxes, the size of pen cases, hung from bronze racks mounted to the wall. Some boxes were rounded where others had a rigidly defined shape. A handful of the boxes were natural wood tones. Some were painted, flat or glossy, with any number of colors. The one feature they all shared was a small plaque engraved with a name.

Ticker-tape lurched haltingly from one of the boxes, a waved piece that looked to be made of ivory rather than wood. Violette sighed at the sound. She did not bother to look over her shoulder, well aware of what the *tick tick brrr* sounds signified. The box spat out almost two full feet of paper before it quieted. Violette turned, noted the box as she ripped the paper from its housing, and dug through a filing cabinet as she began to read.

"Go ahead and take a seat," she mumbled absently. "I'll have yours once I get this filed away."

"Good news, I hope?" Owen ventured as he sank in the lonely chair at the center of the room.

Bitter murmurs followed by a sharp click of the tongue against the palette were the closest Violette gave to a response. Ticker tape rolled through her fingers as she scanned the information. After a final click, she folded the message in half three times and pinned it to the map of the frontier. The pin was chosen with care.

Satisfied, the woman reseated herself. From a drawer, she produced a pair of small, wooden boxes. These boxes were rough-cut with uneven surfaces. Each bore a small nameplate with Owen's full name, but they looked nothing like those on the walls besides.

"This one's yours," Violette said. She pushed one of the cases forward, opening it to reveal that it did contain a fountain pen. It was blue with thin, silver fittings. A small capsule of ink, tucked into a recess on the inside of the case's top, was held in place by a leather strap.

"During your probationary month, I expect a report every day before sundown. Channel once to make paper, then again to send your message." Violette placed her thumb on a small circle of memory glass fitted next to the case's nameplate. No light was generated from the initial channeling, but the sending of the quickly scrawled *Hello* did produce a dull sheen.

"You shouldn't notice the effort within the town," she continued. "Takes more energy the further you get away from town, though. Not that you'll be operating outside the town anytime soon."

"How long if I wanted to send a message to, say, Southport?" Owen asked.

"Can't," Violette replied flatly. "The boxes only talk to each other. For you to report to me, and for me to confirm receipt. Any other correspondence would go through Federal Post like normal. Hand me your badge."

Owen cocked his head, confused by the breakneck shift in topic. Violette proffered no explanation. She simply held out an impatient hand until Owen had done as she asked.

"This takes a few minutes," Violette sighed. Another message box on the wall began to spit out a report. "Shape your message box however you want while we wait. The more unique, the easier it'll be for me to recognize you."

"Hmm?" Owen closed the box that was now his, placing two hesitant fingers on the one that would stay in the office. "They seem quite serviceable this way, don't you think?"

Violette raised an eyebrow.

"I mean," Owen continued, "all the other boxes have been done up rather nicely. I think mine might stand out a bit more if it was just left as-is."

"Doesn't have to be perfect." Violette's concentration remained on the badge, which now glowed. Her hand radiated a thin emerald aura. "Don't have to add or change anything, if woodworking isn't your thing. Can just shave some bits off. Can't imagine a Seeker hurting themselves over something so small."

"Simple taste, is all," Owen half-chuckled, raising a hand in friendly dismissal.

"Well," Violette grunted. She pulled her hand away from Owen's badge in a sharp motion, allowing it to plonk onto the desk. Smoke rose from the sizzling piece of metal. She pulled a kerchief from her breast pocket and pushed the badge towards the pair of message boxes. "You can always change it later, I guess. Just make sure you knock first. Lost and Stolen is at the end of the hall. Last door on the left. Connolly's expecting you."

Violette replaced the kerchief in her breast pocket as she grabbed the other half of the communications pathway. She seemed to know where the box was going to reside, as Violette placed the rough box on the rack without pause for thought.

The snap of paper filled the room as Violette tore the new message from the rack and began to read. This message was half the length of the first. Judging from the quiet nods and lack of clicks, its contents seemed to be more positive, as well. The message was folded over once and placed under a pin on the map of Arnstead proper.

Visible confusion warped Violette's sharp features when she turned to see Owen still in the room.

"Out."

"Yes, ma'am!" Owen said, the woman's tone forcing him to straighten on reflex.

"Oh, and take that with you," Violette added, pointing to the door before Owen had finished standing. "If you *insist* on wearing the thing, gods help you, make sure it's in proper condition."

Hung from a coat hook on the room's sole door was a fresh-pressed uniform in Spellseeker Blue. It bore the correct number of stars in all the right places. A yellow-brown tag clipped to the right sleeve showed Owen's exact dimensions. Correct sizing for trousers was on the tag as well. The trousers themselves were folded neatly over the bottom of the coat hanger.

"Yes, ma'am."

Owen gathered as much warmth as he could muster for the reply. His nerves were still strained from the whiplash suffered in transit between the Arcanarium's doors, its lobby, and the notable chill in Violette's office. *A kind gesture, especially amid strife and suffering, should not go unnoted.* The words, a favorite of his father's, rose from heart to mind as Owen slipped into the hall.

"The last one on the left, then," Owen muttered, closing the door behind himself.

The hallway was no overlong. Eight doors in all, each some eight feet apart, lined the left wall. A final, ninth door was set into the end of the hallway. Each was cut from a single slab of ironwood and was painted a warm, inoffensive brown. Placards were fixed to the right of each door about five feet from the ground.

A frown replaced Owen's brief moment of mirth as he looked up and down the right side of the hallway. Glass windows ran down the length of the hall, one opposite the gap between each doorway. He turned his perturbed expression back to the locked lobby door. The point of having a door so thoroughly secure that led to a place easily accessible by an average brick was beyond him.

To distract himself from the idiocy of the windows and the, admittedly pleasant, floral arrangements between each, Owen read the placard next to each door and their associate names as he passed.

The third door, neighbor to Handling, was labeled *First Seeker*. This room, Owen knew, would be where all disputes would come to be settled. Any decision that could not reach a conclusion would be made here. The First Seeker was to an Arcanarium what a branch manager was to a bank or a principal to a school. Only the Chief Seeker, leader of the entire Spellseeker organization, could speak to Arnstead's Arcanarium with greater authority.

Best be in the newer uniform before I introduce myself, Owen thought, looking at the nameplate below the title: *Akheem Albarn.*

Next down the hall were two rooms that shared the same designation: *Violent Offenses.* Owen would have guessed the rooms to be conjoined if the half-dozen names below either placard were not unique. It seemed like a large number of dedicated Seekers. These were Flow-assisted violent offenses, after all. The Arcanarium would not step on the army's toes be in non-magical offenses, and the department could feasibly draw on officers from other departments if the situation were serious enough.

Fifty-seven percent.

The number began its chilling crawl once again from the base of Owen's spine. Though he could not yet read the department names or their associated officers, it was easy enough to see that the Violent Offenses department's headcount dwarfed any other department's headcount. Sure, the average citizen of Arnstead had been less than friendly during Owen's stay so far, but none had threatened his person. *Maybe not overtly,* he corrected himself.

Owen quickened his pace. An eagerness to find distraction propelled him forward, now only catching the departments in passing; Magically Missing Persons, Magical Misdemeanors, and, finally, Lost and Stolen. The door at the end of the hall was marked for *Research and Development*.

Two nameplates had been slotted beneath the *Lost and Stolen* placard. Owen was surprised to see his full title already in place: *Third Seeker Owen Raulstone*. A minuscule swell of pride forced his thumb over his badge at seeing the nameplate. His name was at the bottom of the short list. Slotted above was another full title and name: *Second Seeker Aaron Connolly*.

A triplet of sharp knocks on the door to Lost and Stolen drew a readied reply.

"Come on in, while the day is still young!"

Lost and Stolen at first, second, and final glance appeared a complete and utter mess. Wayward pages from any number of files or reports kicked up from the floor at the simple motion of the door opening. Metal filing cabinets were loosely pressed up to dimly- lit walls, their contents bursting from drawers whose latches had buckled. Corkboards sat atop the filing cabinets were eased against the upper reaches of the walls. The boards were held in place only by topless boxes that teetered on the rounded edges of the cabinets.

On the wall to the right was a map of Arnstead. Much like the maps in Handling, this one had push pins holding bits of paper in place. This map, however, must have had thirty for every *one* of Violette's. Further chaos coated the map in the form of yarn strings being tied between various pins. A veritable web of blues, greens, yellows, and reds rendered the highly detailed map almost unreadable.

Nestled in what vaguely might have been the center of the room was a small desk. It stood no more than a foot and half off the ground. The word desk would have been an overstatement. A pair of well-concealed lines that marked the 'desk' into thirds. There was a nagging suspicion at the back of Owen's mind that the surface was three footstools pushed end-to-end.

"Ah, rough around the edges, *indeed.* And here I thought I'd heard Violette's first joke."

The remarks came from the harn seated behind the ramshackle desk. He was Nirdac, his long, relaxed ears resting on his hunched back. Warm brown eyes looked up an assortment of papers that didn't seem to belong to any one particular file. Over his shoulder, Owen could see a wrinkled set of Spellseeker blues being bullied by three stacks of boxes.

"Seeker Connolly?" Owen ventured. He flashed a salute, weaker than he meant, as a matter of precaution.

"Aye, that's me. Though Aaron suits me just fine."

Each word was round and warm, matching the harn's physique. There were slight hints of the northern Nirdac accent. Just enough to know it was there, but not so much that it made conversation a challenge.

"Have a seat, why doncha?" Aaron patted the box of files he was sitting on, gestured to a cluster near Owen. "Plenty to talk about. No need to waste our legs just yet."

A slight twitch pulled at the corner of Owen's left eye. A look around the front of the room told him that using boxes as seats was common practice. Box tops bowed to the point of breaking. Smushed corners and buckled edges spoke to poor quality in material.

Owen found the closest box he could consider intact, pulled it towards the desk, and felt it crumple beneath his weight.

"Right then. A bit about us," Aaron started, placing a hand on his chest, "then we'll talk about how you fit in. Sound fair?"

"Of course, sir."

"So, Lost and Stolen, then. Name pretty much says it all. Folks come to the bureau to file a complaint, that they've lost a registered focus or relic. That, or it's been stolen. Either way, folks file that complaint with Sam up front and it gets sent back here."

One of Aaron's small hands patted a stack of papers on the right of the desk. The collection of documents rose from a wooden receptacle, stopping just before the crest of the harn's head.

"Our process is simple; verify the documents have been completed in their entirety, visit the claimant for questioning, recover the reported article to the best of our abilities. Easy enough, innit?"

"Seems straightforward, sir."

"Excellent!" Aaron cried. The sudden surge of boisterousness gave Owen a start. "Now I know it doesn't sound exciting, this Lost and Stolen business. All the transfers spend at least a month here, though, to help 'em get their legs underneath 'em. Like a probationary period, if you will. So don't worry about any specialties going to waste or whatnot. You'll have your time to shine."

"Sounds fair, sir."

"Easy going," Aaron remarked as he eased back against a stack of boxes. "I like that. And speaking of *you,*" he continued, leaning into that last word. Aaron sifted through papers and folders on his desk. Finding what he wanted, he held it between thumb and forefinger and extended it to Owen. "Your file is awful threadbare."

Owen accepted the folder with a curt nod. He had never seen the contents of his personal records before. The thought of a threadbare record spoke to him of black bars covering test results. Perhaps redacted accounts of any by-the-book loopholes that saw him through his time at Eastpointe Spellseeker Academy.

What Owen did *not* expect to see was a collection of recipes and preparation methods for the Misty Lake moose.

"Sir?" Owen wasn't sure what else to say as he turned the folder around to reveal its contents.

"What's this?" Aaron grumbled, snatching the folder. "Oh bother."

The harn pitched the file over his shoulder. Grumbles and half-swears continued to stream from Aaron's mouth as he rooted about his desk. His discomfort grew louder as he was forced to expand his search to neighboring boxes.

"Aha!" Aaron shouted, bringing himself back to rest in his seat. A new file was caught between his fingers. He double-checked the yellow-brown folder's contents before handing them to Owen. "*Your file.* Not much in there. Was hoping you might be able to tell me about yourself, and any specialties you think might assist Lost and Stolen."

Threadbare did not begin to describe the lack of detail that was present in the correct file. There had been more substance to the moose recipes than to Owen's career file. He understood that the assignment to Arnstead was his first, but Owen expected there to be at least *some* detail about his time at the academy.

Within the folder were three pieces of paper. At the top was Owen's graduation certificate from the Eastpointe Spellseeker Academy. It was a hefty piece of paper. Most of the certificate's face was filled with flowery language in silvered print. There were a few useful bits of information, however, such as the date of graduation and Owen's Spellseeker identification. The second document was a few pages bound together; the written oath signed by all Spellseekers. They served as a more binding version of the graduation certificate.

At the back of the folder was Owen's physical, noting simple information that one might expect from a physician's report. It was here that Owen saw, at last, some form of tampering. His eyes had raced first to the 'Disabilities' section of the report. He was only half-surprised to see that it was blank. A pang of guilt rose like a lump in his throat.

It's fine, Owen told himself. *It's just Lost and Stolen. He doesn't need to know. I'll cross that bridge when I move to a real department.*

"So then," Aaron spoke after a protracted silence. "Tell me what there is to know about Third Seeker Owen Raulstone."

"Not much," Owen replied, his voice meek. He snapped the folder shut and handed it back to his superior. "Not yet, that is. Arnstead is my first assignment after graduation."

"First, huh? A tough lot," Aaron smirked, though not without a hint of consolation.

"I have not developed any specialties yet. Leadership thought that a tough environment might be what I needed, that Arnstead might be able to finish what the academy had started. I'm like a blank slate."

Owen stopped himself before his fancies carried farther than he could manage. There was nothing on hand to check his story against, as evidenced by the file. That did not mean that an unnecessarily complicated story would not lead to further inquiry.

"Well, if that's all there is to it..." Aaron paused to give Owen a moment to interject. "Then I guess I'd best get to filling that slate in. Plan for today is to keep it simple, as I've said."

The harn slip from his well-worn perch onto the office floor. Loose sheets of paper crinkled under his sandaled feet. Each pivot set a new patch of the floor to a lively rustle. With a quiet *Aha!*, Aaron returned to his seat with what appeared to be a remarkably fresh stack of papers bound by twine.

"These," Aaron said, setting the bundle down on his desk, "are Official Complaint Forms. OCFs for short." He produced a small pocket knife and cut the twine with a satisfying pop. "The entirety of Lost and Stolen revolves around these sheets of paper. These are our lifeblood. Without these, we aren't doing anything.

"Over here are the ICFs: Initial Complaint Forms." Aaron patted the tower of loose paper that loomed up from his desk, rooted in a wooden receptacle. "Sam fills these out up front as folks come in to file complaints and send 'em back here. We take the information from the ICFs and transcribe them over to the OCFs. Making sense so far?"

"Question, sir," Owen stated, raising a finger to pause Aaron's lecture.

"By all means."

"This seems awfully redundant."

"Not much of a question, there," Aaron posited.

"Okay," Owen allowed. He grabbed a blank OCF and the ICF from the top of the pile, looked at the pair side by side. "These are almost exactly the same. The information is just housed in different places between each form. The only thing that's going to different is…"

Owen stopped when he noticed the date in the top left corner of the ICF in his hand.

"This complaint was recorded almost three months ago. Is this the oldest one? The one from the top?"

"Should be, yep," Aaron nodded.

"And how often do you get new complaints?"

"*We* get new complaints almost every day."

"Exactly how far in the hole are you right now?" Owen asked hesitantly.

"Exactly how far in the hole are *we*," Aaron added again. Rather than give a straight answer, he grabbed the entire stack of papers and set them in front of Owen. A pale, yellow light shone from the emptied receptacle as a new sheet of paper materialized. The same light poked through the single paper as a second appeared beneath it.

This process continued for two minutes until the stack had been replenished in full.

"To answer your question, I've no idea."

9.

THE GRIND

"Look who it is, fellas."

"Oh, Mr. Seeker, sir? Made it a whole day, sir?"

"And look at those fancy new duds!"

"Almost looks like a real person now, doesn't he?"

"Almost!"

Several of the faces gathered out front of the Arnstead Arcanarium looked familiar to Owen. They had been emblazoned into his memory the day prior. A few of the faceless voices in the crowd rang familiar, as well.

"Good morning," was Owen's flat reply. He made a powerful effort to keep his emotions in check, to avoid starting yet another day on the wrong foot. Owen made a mental note to check which foot hit the floorboards first on the next morrow.

"May I pass?" Owen asked the morning throng.

"Oh, of course, sir!"

"Right this way, sir!"

A small gap opened to allow Owen passage. The overwhelming sense of dismay from the day before had been replaced by a thick smear of feigned respect. While Owen preferred the sarcasm to threats to his person, it felt at the moment that the margin was thin.

"Try not to set off any *alarms* today, sir."

Owen stiffened at the remark, immediately regretting it. A snickering wave fell over those who saw Owen's reaction. It spread like a flood through the leering crowd. Guffaws, nurtured by the communal sense of ridicule, sprouted in pockets as Owen tucked inside the Arcanarium.

The crimson door transitioned slowly to ethereal blue-white at the touch of Owen's badge. At the very least, Owen thought, he would rob them of the satisfaction of triggering any alarms for a second time. Owen cast a fleeting glower at the reception desk. Sam, processing the paperwork of an uneasy Bangeli human, paid him no mind.

Mischief and ridicule faded as the lobby door whispered shut behind Owen. The main hall of the Arcanarium, if it was right to call it that, was a quiet place. No work sounds penetrated any of the doors he walked past. He imagined the *tick tick brr* of message boxes spitting out reports from Handling. Rousing discussions on how to capture the latest menace filled his imagination between the doors to Violent Offenses.

Iron-heeled boots hammered out a measured pace as Owen strode down the silent hall. A final clack echoed in the space as he stopped before the door to Lost and Stolen, knocked twice.

No response.

Another pair of knocks followed shortly after and received the same response. That is to say, none. Owen sniffed, pulled his pocket watch from the breast of his coat. Fresh wool crinkled as it was pulled back from its pocket. The snap of the new brass button took on a short but vivid life before dying away.

"Seven-thirty."

Owen mumbled the time to door as much as to himself. The watch was closed with an annoyed click, replaced in his pocket as Owen looked down the hallway. Still, he found himself to be the only person. He checked the handle to Lost and Stolen, found it to be locked.

Just as Owen leaned in for another lash at the door, he heard the faintest creak. It was a noise like an ungreased hinge doing its best to avoid persuasion. *There it is again*, Owen thought to himself as he turned to look down the hall a second time. The noise seemed to emanate from one of the windows in the middle of the hall.

One of the window latches seemed to jiggle. Subtle at first, then almost to the point of snapping the latch in two. Another two attempts saw the latch pop free from its housing. Windows swung outward into the alleyway. As the windows opened, up jumped Second Seeker Aaron Connolly. He cleared the jump from ground to sill with apparent ease.

"Oh!" Owen gasped.

"Hello there, Owen," Aaron called, full of cheer. "Beaten me here, have you? Your enthusiasm for eye-hemorrhaging paperwork is impressive. I'd expected you to be *at least* an hour late."

"Wouldn't dream of it, sir," Owen said, collecting himself to attention.

"Enough of that." Aaron waved away Owen's formal countenance as he dropped down into the hallway. The harn waved another hand behind. Both windows pulled themselves closed at the motion. The latch threw itself into place after. "Remind me to grease the window catches, would you?"

"Of course, sir," Owen affirmed with a nod. "If I might ask, sir?"

"Yes, go on."

"Do you, uh... always take the window in, sir?"

"What kind of silly question is that?" Aaron replied, feigning offense. "Of course, I do! Think I'd be daft enough to use the front door? Don't tell me you've been coming in through the front."

Blood rushed to Owen's cheeks. Embarrassment and jealousy fought for the dominance of his expression. Aaron, seeing the color in his subordinate's face, decided not to press the matter.

"Anywhoozles, you needn't worry much about paperwork today. You've had your crash course for the office work, so today's a day for stretching your legs. We'll be out knocking on doors."

"Very exciting, sir," Owen replied, seeing Aaron look up for a response. "Can't wait."

"Excellent! Let's pop into the office and grab the necessities, then off we go."

Aaron bounded down the hallway to Lost and Stolen, his sandaled feet a hushed murmur on the wooden floor. He dressed in casual street clothes as he had been the day before. Brown trousers were held in place as much by his generous girth as the blue suspenders over his shoulders. The buttons of his plaid shirt seemed to groan a little with each step. Golden-brown hairs poked out from the slight gaps the shirt could not quite cover.

The only thing Aaron wore that signified his position was the badge on his hip. He pulled the object from the waist of his trousers and held it to the door of Lost and Stolen. A familiar glint of ethereal blue-white. There was no Bureau symbol on the door. Just a small patch of light next to the door handle where a locking mechanism would reside.

"No need to wait for me in the hall, next time," Aaron called out over his shoulder. "If Violette did her job right, your badge should be able to open Lost and Stolen. And Violette never does her job wrong."

"Yes, sir. Good to know, sir," Owen sighed. He closed his eyes to hide their rolling into the back of his skull.

Owen pulled the door closed as the two slid into Lost and Stolen. There was an impressiveness to the musty chaos that gripped the claustrophobic office. It was the sort of disarray that would put a whirlwind to shame.

A tornado might actually make it cleaner, Owen mused as he watched the Second Seeker.

Necessities spoke to Owen of several things. To start, the man needed to be fully dressed. The sad state of Aaron Connolly's Seeker blues put an involuntary crease on Owen's forehead. Though better was better, and a crumpled coat was better than no coat at all. There would be a sidearm for certain. A sword was common for a Spellseeker. Not so much for a harn, however, so perhaps a dagger or some small focus for defense. Idle hands rested on his sword and pistol.

What else? Owen wondered. He enjoyed the thought exercise, decided to run with it.

Weapons and uniform aside, documentation would be a must. Aaron had suggested the day before that the Official Complaint Forms would be used. The thought of an entire day's efforts going to waste was more than Owen wanted to consider.

Something about questions. Uses them as a reference, I wager. Get all of our details squared away before we actually hunt anything down. Makes sense. No use in chasing deer before you've seen their tracks.

"Done! Ready, Owen?"

The exclamation and subsequent question caught Owen off-guard. He had only half-registered them. Lost in his thoughts, he had been prepared to spend the next half hour guessing at what the day might hold. Immediacy gave rise to suspicion.

"Is that everything, sir?" Owen asked an incredulous air.

Golden-brown fur was still visible between buttons struggling to hold the line. There wasn't a single weapon, that Owen could see, strapped the harn. By all accounts, Aaron seemed to have just slapped a portion of yesterday's work onto a clipboard.

"Ah, yes!" Aaron cried with the suddenness of stubbing a toe. There was no time for a sigh of relief on Owen's part. No window long enough to thank that his mentor had some measure of sense and order. Aaron grabbed a pen from his desk and slid it between above the papers on his clipboard. "Wouldn't be getting much done without that, would we?"

"I suppose not, sir," came Owen's beleaguered reply.

Aaron did not seem the slightest bit bothered.

Two gentle taps on the door grabbed the attention of both men.

"Mail."

The single word was immersed in Violette's signature chill.

"Grab the door, would you?" Aaron asked, gesturing at the door with his clipboard.

Crystal blue eyes looked through Owen as she handed him a pair of mail packets bound with red ribbon. Both packets rested atop a hefty brown folder. Violette rested a slender finger on the larger envelope as she spoke.

"Boss wants this done before the week is out."

Aaron squirmed under Violette's scrutiny, nodded.

A sense of ease fell over the men's shoulders as Violette pulled the door to Lost and Stolen closed, like a warm blanket on a bright-yet-chilled morning. Sandaled feet in the main hall turned to silence.

"Well then," Aaron sighed as if he had just now begun to breathe again, "let's have a look before we go. See what's so important."

"Of course, sir," Owen said.

The larger envelope was clearly for his superior. Owen left the small packet of envelopes labeled for Aaron on the brown envelope and passed them over. Each letter the barn had received was of a different size. The packet they formed was loose, barely held in place by the red ribbon. The binding had to be wrapped around corners and at odd angles to keep everything in place.

Aaron's attention was not on the letters. They were tossed absently onto his desk as soon as they had been received. He was more concerned with the formidable accordion folder. String, secured at the base of the folder, whined as it was peeled away from a pair of tin discs on the lip. A pop signaled the death of the string. Pressure from the aggressively packed documents forced the folder open.

As Aaron busied himself with the contents of the folder, Owen looked over the two envelopes that had been addressed to himself. These were of similar size and had been bound more neatly. Two red ribbons kept both envelopes firmly in place. A blue wax seal had been stamped on the back where the ribbons met. The small circle depicted a caricature of a woman riding a speeding horse, a mailbag hung from her shoulder; The Federal Post.

Wax responded with a satisfying crack as Owen tore away the ribbons. The letter on top had the return address of his family's home in Southport.

He shifted his parents' letter to see the second. Though he was not familiar with the street address, 17 Olthorn Plaza, there were only two people he knew in Elstaff.

Warmth overtook Owen. Sudden warmth, the kind that brings heat to the back of a person's eyes and sets their nose open like a faucet. The sort of warmth that comes from a sense of belonging, of being remembered. Owen traced the addresses with an excited hand before tucking the letters inside his coat.

A new barrage of knocks at the door of Lost and Stolen gave both Owen and Aaron a start. The attacks against the door were erratic, and they did not cease until Owen pulled the door open to reveal an electrified harn. It took a few moments for Owen to register the familiar face. The associated frown took half the time.

"Morning Lionel," Aaron grumbled. It was the first time Owen had noticed a sense of agitation in his superior's voice. "And what can the fine folks of Lost and Stolen do for you on this most peaceful and quiet of days?"

Words were not a part of Lionel's reply. Rather than his intentions, he bounded up alongside Owen and snatched the caster pistol shells from its leather housing.

"Excuse me!?"

Owen's exasperated protest flew past Lionel without garnering any attention. The harn bounced a few times towards the windows in the hall. He held the shell up to catches stray traces of sunlight. The amethyst memory glass took on an iridescent quality as Lionel began to channel energy into the shell.

"I'll have that back," Owen demanded as he followed Lionel into the hall.

"Hush hush," Lionel replied. He raised his free hand in a distracted attempt to stop Owen. "You said I could take a look. I'm getting to know him."

Lionel's eyes glistened as he assigned sex to the small device, a name surely to follow. Reverent fingers manipulated the delicate work of art in his hand. Silverwork, meticulous in dimension, was smooth and polished. The object seemed more like a jewel than a weapon while in the harn's curious grasp.

"Yes, and now you've looked at it, Mr. Eilhart. I'll have it back, please."

"What? Without trying it out?" Lionel pleaded. "Would be a crime. A crime! Let me use it."

"No, not in the hallway."

"That dangerous?" Lionel flicked a glance at Owen. The obligation to know lit a fire inside Lionel's eyes. "In there, then?"

"No," Owen replied, following Lionel's nod at the door to Research and Development. "Now, if you'll hand that back, we have—"

"At least tell me what it does!"

"It stuns people!" Owen cried. His patience had worn thin, and the harn's goading demeanor did little to abate his frustration. Owen grabbed at the shell, missed.

"They seize up? Like a shock?"

Lionel ducked another attempt at his newly acquired treasure.

"Yes!"

"Can I try it?"

"Mr. Eilhart, you're standing in the way of a Spellseeker in the line of duty. That shell is a tool used to perform my duties and I'll have it back!"

"All right, all right, enough shouting," Aaron called from inside Lost and Stolen. He set the accordion folder down on his desk and stepped into the hall. "Go ahead and let him see the thing, Owen."

"Sir?"

The brief sense of elation Owen felt at receiving backup was torn away.

"He'll never shut his mouth, this one," Aaron said. He threw a playful punch into Lionel's shoulder, who adopted a devilish grin. "Let him hurt himself with the thing. He'll give it back once he's singed a few hairs off."

"Promise!" Lionel added with an emphatic nod.

"Sir," Owen started. He shook his head in a hopeless attempt to rid the situation of its absurdity. "These are tools, to be used in the line of duty. We can't wait here all day for him to finish blowing himself up!"

"And we won't," Aaron affirmed. "We'll not be up to anything dangerous today. No need for the pistol. Or even the sword I'd wager, but I'll leave that up to your discretion."

"But, sir—"

"Can't be wasting the whole day, Owen," Aaron interrupted. "Said so yourself."

There was no mistaking Second Seeker Aaron's tone. This was the closest thing to an order he yet given. His lack of patience with the situation was clear as day.

Owen did not agree with this. Heart sinking in his chest, Owen pulled his pistol from its holster. A flick of the weapon by the finger guard had him holding it by the barrel. Owen felt the weight of his security there in his hand.

Lionel snatched the pistol as if it were a candied apple. He held out his other hand, waiting for the three remaining shells to join the amethyst one in his palm.

"I'll be keeping the sword, sir. If that's all right."

Bitterness dripped from Owen's lips as he deposited the remaining shells onto Lionel's greedy palm.

"Very good," Aaron consoled as he returned to the office to grab his abandoned clipboard. "Now, where did I set you?"

No thanks escaped the elated Lionel Eilhart. Only imagined possibilities emerged between chortled fits of laughter. Lionel did not even think to ask what the remaining shells did. The prospect of learning for himself was far too tantalizing for anything like a proper line of questions to stand in the way. He darted through the door to Research and Development without looking back.

Owen stood alone in the hallway, a forlorn pillar of cold rock jutting from a river of silence. A certain sense of nakedness emanated from the empty holster on his hip. Not the sort of abashed nudity of being happened upon during a bath. No, this was a different kind of naked. It felt like being drawn by horse miles into the wilderness, only to have the rope cut as the horse continues to speed along. His right thumb hooked the lip of the empty holster.

First one deep breath.

A second breath, and then a third.

I'm not alone, Owen rationalized. *Even without the focus, I'm not alone. I'll be fine.*

Self-talk came to a sudden stop as Owen noticed a door opening down the hall. It was the third door from the lobby, after Reception and Handling.

"First Seeker," Owen murmured.

Akheem Albarn, First Seeker of the Arnstead Arcanarium, stepped from office into the hall. He was Zumbatran, with skin black as night. Coils of ash-brown hair were together by a blue ribbon and fell to the small of his back. Dark fingers pulled at scraggly hair on his chin as he examined a dossier. Despite his impressive size, moved with silence and grace.

Large steps carried the First Seeker past Owen. The man stopped at Lost and Stolen, knocked twice on the door that had been left slightly ajar. A crackle of intensity surrounded Akheem. It was as though the air around him would crash with thunder at the slightest whisper.

"Gods above, what—"

"Second Seeker Aaron Connolly."

Smooth, baritone words set Aaron's back straight as a flagpole. There was no aggression in the First Seeker's tone. Nothing hostile made Second Seeker Aaron stand at quiet attention. Akheem's rolling, deliberate speech commanded attention all its own.

"Looking for the new Seeker. Need to ask him about last night's report."

"Behind you, sir," Aaron replied. "In the hall."

The First Seeker turned. A line of surprise had been drawn on his face.

"Ah, didn't see you there," Akheem said.

Somehow this made Owen as if he had been stripped further.

He whisked the thought away and drew himself up to proper attention. With a clear view of the First Seeker's face, Owen was able to make out the remnants of a burn scar that ran up Akheem's neck to his left ear. A singular flaw to otherwise sculpted features.

"Sir?" Owen ventured.

"You mention being attacked, between the end of the manarail and Arnstead. Claim that the civilians you rode with identified one of the attackers as the Cinder Witch. One Amalia Tennerim. Is this true?"

"Yes, sir."

"Did you witness the attack with your own eyes?"

"Yes, sir."

"Good," First Seeker Akheem affirmed. He took a step towards Owen as he rifled through the documents in hand, made a few notes with a blue and silvered pen. "Now, was the nature of this person's assault physical, magical, or miracle?"

"Seemed magical to me, sir."

"Seemed?" This word did bite. The First Seeker stabbed at the casual uncertainty of Owen's speech with a knife-edged tongue. "I need facts, Seeker. Certainty. If this witch is throwing fire granted by gods, then she's a heretic. The House's problem. You, *Seeker*, are our only specialist that has

144

seen woman's work. Is she a heretic, or a criminal?"

"Criminal, sir," Owen said, his face burning. "Her fire came from the Flow."

"Good," the First Seeker sighed, easing back. "Now I have a lever to jam under that Pontiff's idle ass."

The First Seeker waved a hand as he turned and walked away, a signal that Owen and Aaron could return to their business.

"Seen worse first encounters, I have," Aaron said after the First Seeker's door had closed. "All our new folks spend their probation with me. Let me tell you, I've seen some *bad* feet get put forward."

"Thank you, sir."

All Owen could think about was that First Seeker Akheem Albarn reminded him so much of his father.

"Right, then, hands out from behind your back," Aaron said, heaving a deep sigh under the oppressive noon sun. He proffered the clipboard packed with Official Complaint Forms to Owen.

"Are you certain, sir?" Owen replied. His words came out in staccato breaths as Aaron jabbed the clipboard into Owen's ribs. "You don't think I should observe longer?"

"We've been at it half the day. You're a clever lad, right?"

"We have visited *two* claimants, sir."

"Twice the points of reference you'd had before the day started," Aaron posited with a cheeky smile. "Sounds like quite the foundation, to me."

This was another request just shy of an order, Owen realized. It felt wrong to acquiesce to a suggestion rather than obey a direct order. The broad grin on his superior's face made it feel all the more loathsome. Owen snatched the clipboard from Aaron's hand and began to scan the details of the topmost claim.

A dusty breeze curled down the road. The wooden sign hung next to the open doorway of Parn's Apothecary creaked in protest. Both mortar and pestle on the sign retained little of its gray paint. Flecks wafted away to join grating dust on the wind. Shutters on the shabby building's windows, whose green paint fared better than the sign's, were bound tightly by chains.

Owen climbed the two stairs up to the porch in a single step and proceeded through the doorway. A counter stood five feet from the door. The surface of the counter was barren save a single jar of rock candy. Each piece went for half a copper, according to the hand-drawn paper sign pasted the jar's interior. Shelves adorned the wall behind the counter at various uneven intervals. Jars and tins of all manner of herbs lent Parn's Apothecary its welcoming, earthy aroma.

Only a small portion of the building was dedicated to the front room. The storage area, visible through another open door behind the counter, led back into darkness. A Zumbatran harn and her two children waited patiently in wooden chairs. The mother read to an attentive toddler while bouncing an infant on her knee.

"Have your order, ma'am. Take one in the morning and one in the evening. Should clear your cough up in about a week."

The rasped words came from an aged Bangeli human. He ducked out from the storage area with a brown paper bag curled in his knotted hands. The harn gathered her children, paid the man a dollar and two coppers, and hustled past Owen out the front door.

"Help you, sir?" the man asked, leveling a curious gaze at Owen.

"Yes, hello!" Owen said as he cleared his throat. "Would you be Parn Coates? Proprietor of Parn's Apothecary?"

"Who wants to know?"

Phlegm gargled in the man's throat as he coughed into his elbow. He pulled the pair of wire-frame spectacles from his nose and proceeded to thin the grease on the lenses with his shirt. Amber eyes narrowed, adding more lines to his naturally crinkled brow. Owen tried to look past the undercurrent of disgust in the man's voice and chalked the question up to poor eyesight.

"Second Seeker Owen Raulstone, of Lost and Stolen. Here to inquire about a stolen focus, a refrigeration unit."

"Oh, got some news for me?" The man's shoulders pulled back, ears perked. Owen had his attention now. "Yeah, I'm Parn."

"Excellent, thank you. Can I confirm a few points from your claim?"

Parn's sudden excitement tempered.

"I guess, sure."

"Can you confirm for me whether the item was presumed to be lost or stolen?"

"No, genius, but I put my money on stolen."

The man pointed to one of the windows behind Owen. A glance revealed that one of the window panes had been shattered. Jagged edges remained in place from the time of the robbery. The scratch and scribble of

Owen's notes on the OCF filled the room.

"Can you confirm that the focus was reported missing as soon as its absence was noted?"

"Almost *three months* ago to the day," Parn replied, agitation rising in his voice. "Been having to pay some kid five coppers a day to make ice for me. *Every day*. For *three months*. You know how much that cooler focus cost me?"

Owen checked the paperwork in hand.

"Reported value of stolen focus was fifteen silver dollars, sir."

"Know what that means, bluecoat?"

"It means," Owen sighed, "that you have paid eighteen silvers worth for ice since the filing the initial report, sir."

"It means that I'm losing money trying to keep Arnstead alive!" This last comment came as a heated shout. Neck muscles tensed beneath loose skin as Parn continued. "It means I have to throw money at some peddler because I can't make ice to keep perishables from going bad. Money that I could have invested in another focus instead of waiting on some bluecoat to pull his thumbs out of his ass! It means I have to sink another fifteen silver into a new cooler focus. Wanna tell me how much I'll have to pay to get it registered with you people?"

"I don't know, sir," Owen said, deflated.

"What do you mean, *you don't know?*"

"I'm sorry, sir. I can ask the reception dep—"

"Let me see that," Parn spat, pointing to Owen's clipboard. He raised a slab of the counter and tucked through the opening. An open, wizened hand was thrust out before Owen. The calloused palm quivered in rage. "Gimme that paper."

Owen pulled the OCF from the clipboard in compliance, handed it to Parn. The page had been torn four times before Owen was able to raise any protest.

"Get out," Parn growled. "I'm done wasting my time on you people. On waiting for nothing."

"Sir, if you would just give me a chance to—"

"Out!" wailed Parn.

The disappointment in the man's eyes twisted a knot in Owen's stomach. Owen wanted to kneel and sweep the papers together. Wanted to gather his thoughts and get through the process so he might be able to help.

It didn't feel right to abandon the man, even if he had flown into a rage. The claim was certainly under the jurisdiction of Lost and Stolen. Owen might be able to do something if Parn would let him.

Owen caught sight of the shattered window again as he turned to leave. He wondered if the man chose not to repair the window, or if he simply could not afford to. The thought weighed on him as rejoined Aaron outside.

"A bit heated, that one," Aaron said in a hushed tone. He tapped the outside of Owen's thigh gently with a few knuckles. "Get the report squared away?"

"The claimant has withdrawn their request, sir." Owen's dutiful reply rang hollow. He didn't bother to hide the sense of guilt that hung heavy on his shoulders. Aaron pursed his lips to the left, gazed into Parn's Apothecary.

"Not everyone wants to be helped, I suppose."

"I don't suppose that was the problem, sir."

Aaron took the clipboard from Owen with a solemn nod and started towards their next location.

Parn's Apothecary was located a street over from the western bank of Sisir's Run, south of the Bridge on Main. Their next claim, from a tannery in Eaststead, would take them to the other side of the bustling bridge. Elbows bit and shoulders shoved. No soul crossing the bridge that day could afford to reach their destination any later than now. At least that was how it felt to the Spellseekers as they were jostled about in the crowd.

The general lack of consideration bit at Owen's nerves. A native of Southport, he was no stranger to navigating a large crowd. Perhaps it was the heat, Owen thought. They almost shared a longitudinal line, Arnstead and Southport, but the oceanside city was much cooler this time of year. Sisir's Run could not hope to battle heat the way the ocean could.

Heat permeated every pore of Arnstead during the day. It was not the dry, clear heat that the dusty roads might suggest. That fine-grain dirt came from the town's constant traffic. Vegetation was ranged from sparse to plentiful the further a person walked from the Bridge on Main. No, the heat of Arnstead was wet. It clung to your neck and back. Dripped from your armpits down your sides. To move through a crowd in Arnstead was to slide and smear, to become caked in orange-brown silt.

Lack of consideration started to make more sense when looked at through the lens of heat. A person drenched in sweat, to the point of swimming in their boots, stopped caring about the people around them after a while. Personal comfort became the primary concern. One nudge here, another shove there. No one bothered to notice. It was too much effort to protest such minor trifles under the sweltering Arnstead sun.

Traffic settled once off the bridge. It thinned considerably more as they made their way three streets north. The smell of fish, freshly caught and butchered, wafted out from small stalls and booths along the river. A curious glance past the stalls showed Owen small boats moored to wooden posts. Nets rained droplets of water into Sisir's Run before falling with a splash. There was something he would rather be doing, if only for a moment; hike his trousers and stand knee-deep in the river. Owen waved the thought aside as he turned to follow Aaron, who had ducked into a building on their right.

"We'll do this one together, yeah?"

Aaron held the clipboard up to Owen, smiling eyes promising some measure of support on this second attempt.

No clever name adorned the sign hung next to the tannery's door. The sign bore no name at all. It featured a crude depiction of a hide being stretched over a rack. *Tannery* was written under the hide in white letters. Bits of the white paint had run down to the bottom of the sign, permanent imperfections on the simple signage.

Owen stepped into a lively workspace that smelled of apples and cinnamon, laced with an honest day's sweat. The dessert-like smells combatted the rank of perspiration quite effectively.

"Are you sure we're in the right place, sir?"

"Sign said *Tannery*," Aaron replied without much thought. "Sounds right enough to me."

Owen narrowed his eyes into a glare for a brief moment before poking his head outside. The sign *did* read *Tannery*, and it *was* fixed to the doorframe. However, the smell was all manner of wrong.

There was exactly one tannery Owen ever had the misfortune to frequent. In his younger days, Owen accompanied his mother on errands about town. Good behavior and a mindful attitude tended to result in a bag of cinnamon-roasted almonds. It was only the tannery, across the street from the leatherworker's shop where Mrs. Orland-Raulstone took her saddles for repair, that managed to put Owen in a foul mood.

It was not a normal sort of bad smell, the odor that emanated from the tannery near Worthrom's Leather Goods. Not like the stink of mud that had baked for three days in the sun. Not like the stench of a stable in dire need of shoveling. No, those were smells that could be tolerated, dominated by a powerful spirit. What saturated the air of the tannery was akin to death that's been pissed on for weeks straight. It was a smell that demanded both lime and nose plugs.

"Help you folks?" came a cry from deeper in Arnstead's sweet-smelling tannery.

A Bangeli katarl stepped out from a small doorway, too small for her comfort, and joined Owen and Aaron in the standing room. The room by the doorway, already cramped by two Spellseekers and an assortment of packaged leathers and hides, became quite full.

"This place smells *wonderful*," Owen replied. The words came as a surprise.

"Oh, thank you," the katarl replied. "Husband baked a pie last night. Brought it in to share with the hands."

"Aww, that sounds lovely," Aaron grumbled. It was not a jealous sound, but the sort of primal appreciation that comes from a stomach rather than a formulated thought.

"Might be a bit left, if the hogs didn't demolish the whole thing yet. Care for some?"

"Maybe in a moment, if you'll still have us," Owen said, tempering Aaron's agreement before it was spoken. He held the clipboard up to remind his superior why they had come. "We're here on behalf of the Arnstead Arcanarium's Lost and Stolen department. We understand you filed a claim for a missing focus."

"Ah," the katarl replied. A wary undercurrent slipped beneath her welcoming tone. "Makes sense. Blues and all."

"Could you confirm your name for me?"

"Namita. Namita Anand. Should be listed as the one that filed."

"You are, indeed. Thank you," Owen nodded, copying the name into the appropriate of a blank Field Survey Form. "And the date you initially reported the focus missing?"

"The exact date?" The katarl's black lips sputtered like a horse as she forced out a sigh. She scanned the low ceiling with rolled eyes. "Been a few months at least. Couldn't give you the exact date."

"Perfect, thank you."

More scribbles.

"Have any news, by chance?" the katarl ventured. "Now that we know who's who and all that?"

"If I might ask another question?" Owen deflected. Namita drew a long breath through her nose, huffed it back out, then nodded. "The nature of the focus, you reported that it was related to your work here in the tannery. Was it some sort of scenting device that has since been replaced?"

"What?" Namita chuckled, caught off guard by the nature of the question. "Gods above, no. We work hides the kin's way. Takes half the time, and doesn't smell like a piss-stained corpse to boot. No, the focus was a barrel for making glue out of scrap. Used to take weeks before we could drain the water out. Took only a couple days with the focus."

"Ah, that makes *much* more sense."

A greater number of scribbles.

"So, about that news, then. Have any?"

"We're here to perform a cursory investigation," Owen replied. This attempt at deflection did not sit as well with the katarl as the first.

"What, you're just getting started? Is that it?"

"Think of it as a friendly follow-up, ma'am," Aaron said, breaking his attentive silence. "We came by to assure you that case is being worked, and to see if maybe any details were left out from the initial report."

Owen was relieved by the interjection.

Namita was not.

"If I knew where the thing was, I wouldn't have bothered to report it. Told you everything I knew when it was fresh in my head," Namita said, pointing to the clipboard. "Now is there anything you want to tell me, or can we quit wasting each other's time?"

Time slowed to a painful crawl. It was the moment before a disaster. He was aware there was nothing he could to avoid confrontation, but the world wanted to give him a minute to think regardless.

The knowing resignation in the katarl's eyes cut deeper than the shouts from Parn in his pharmacy. Rage had erupted from the human with little provocation. It felt as though the man had been looking for an excuse to be angry, to yell at someone. What the vent was about would not have mattered. Owen just happened to be there when the cork popped, and took the punishment head-on. With the katarl, it felt different.

Namita had been wary of the Spellseeker station. Owen had no delusions on that point after Namita took a careful study of every woolen thread in his coat. There was patience there, though, unlike with Parn. Namita had not immediately jumped on Owen as if he were a disobedient child. She had waited carefully for Owen to work through a handful of questions. Even when she realized there was no news to be had, she had not devolved into a screaming mess.

"No, I think that will be all, ma'am," Aaron replied, once again taking the weight of response off of Owen's shoulders. "We'll refer to your original report and advise as soon as we have an update. C'mon, Owen."

"Thank you for your time, ma'am," Owen added as the pair turned to leave.

"Damned bluecoat."

Those scornful words had waited, patiently, for the Spellseekers to leave the tannery. They slipped through the door, crawled into Owen's ears like a spider looking for a new home. Owen froze mid-step. Only a single bluecoat was being called out. Once again, Owen felt himself become an object of scorn.

Aaron pulled at Owen's sleeve to keep him walking forward.

"Let's get some food."

No conciliatory remarks accompanied Aaron's words this time.

The pair trudged in silence, Aaron leading the way as Owen followed behind with heavy, unwilling feet. They did not walk far before Aaron stopped. He mumbled something to Owen about the fish on the eastern bank of Sisir's Run being quite good. Maybe even the best the harn had ever had. A few coppers changed hands, and the Seekers each found themselves holding a fried fillet half-wrapped in last week's newspaper.

Crisp skin melted away as Owen took his first bite. The taste of the fish itself was unfamiliar, almost sweet. Fresh, flaky meat fell apart in his mouth and went down easy. It was a good find. No doubt.

Owen struggled to convey the pleasure to Aaron. What Owen managed to contort his face into could not be construed as a smile. Nothing that felt so hollow could pass for real, he reasoned. The best way to show appreciation, Owen thought, would be to finish the fish without a word. He licked the residual grease from his fingers without thought.

"No sense in lying, I suppose," Aaron rumbled. He took the greasy newspaper remains from Owen, combined them in a ball with his own, and launched the remnants of their lunch into the great, meandering river. "Folks don't take kindly to our type around here. Trouble separating the person from the uniform, I guess."

Aaron trailed off. He watched the balled-up newspaper bob a few times before being lost to Sisir's Run. An idle hand reached up and scratched the back of his head between his ears. Twice he attempted to speak. Both times the words were caught in his throat, causing the harn to sink into himself.

"Take the day tomorrow," Aaron said at last. His tone was one of telling a child that there was, in fact, no Solstice Spirit. "Get yourself some clothes. Something plain."

"You're saying I shouldn't wear my uniform, sir?"

Defeat rode openly on Owen's words. He saw the expression on Aaron's face change from conciliatory to pained.

"Look," Aaron whispered, placing a hand on Owen's knee, "I've been doing this for a long time, Lost and Stolen. Twenty-seven years and some more besides. Sometimes I forget what it's like to be new in this place. A place that doesn't want your help, that thinks you're a waste of space. Good for nothing."

"I don't understand it, sir. Why all the bad blood if we're just here to help?"

"Lost and Stolen is a part of the whole, Owen. We're not Lost and Stolen to them. We're the Bureau."

"But still," Owen protested.

"I know." Aaron raised an unsteady hand. "I get that you want to help. You don't know how much I appreciate that. Most of the recruits that roll through can't think about anything but when they get to move on. I haven't had a dedicated report stick around for more than a couple of months in..."

Aaron did not manage to find the number. If he did, it must have been too embarrassing to share.

Where Aaron remained silent due to a loss for what to say, Owen's silence was born of guilt. There was nothing about this post, from the two days he had seen of it, that seemed like appropriate work for a trained and certified Spellseeker. This clerical work was beneath him.

It was still his job though, Owen thought, even if it was just a short stop on his way to a different department of the Spellseeker organization. If it was worth doing, it was worth doing right. With a little luck, he might even be able to do some good.

"Anyway," Aaron said at last, "people seem more willing to work with you if you show up in civilian clothes, mention as little about the Bureau as possible."

"Understood, sir."

the Creaky Board felt like a different place during the day. With most of Arnstead's people hard at work during the day, the main floor allowed a person enough room to breathe. There might even be enough space to stretch with some luck. Staff carried themselves with a knowing grace that was difficult to pick out in the night's crowd.

Most notable was the noise. Brash performances of classic comedies and assaults of primal, thumping music were replaced with audible conversation. Patrons who could afford to take long lunches gathered around secluded tables. Silken formal robes whispered while people of import talked about money and land. Dockhands and miners, a few minutes to spare between the lot, sat at the bar in the back for a quick meal of bread and beer.

A solo fiddler, perched on a stool on the Creaky Board's stage, sawed her gleeful take on old Nirdac melodies. Bits of Bangeli flair were woven into unexpected places. She made the classic songs her own, joy evident in her wide smile. Every note brought a new motion to her swaying form as the performer felt her way through each tune.

Owen, entranced by the sweet melodies, was brought back to reality by the feeling of delicate fingers at his neck. How could hands be so delicate, he wondered. Precise, practiced digits began to unbutton Owen's coat. He tilted his head back and confirmed his suspicion.

"Can I help you?" Owen asked, his smile tainted somewhat from weariness.

"Thought you looked uncomfortable," Eve replied. She had gotten halfway down Owen's coat before bringing her hands to Owen's shoulders. Powerful thumbs bit deep into Owen's knotted shoulders. "Should I stop?"

Muscles gave way as Eve probed for the spots that ached the most. Tension, built throughout the afternoon, melted away.

"You're going to make me fall asleep, Eve."

"Ah, far too early for that," Eve said in a friendly growl. She smacked her hands against the sides of Owen's arms. The resounding clap snapped Owen to attention. "Night hasn't even started yet. How was work today?" she added, cutting off Owen's protest. "Enough paperwork to make your eyes bleed?"

Owen stewed on what to say for a moment, thought better of it. Instead, he swallowed his remaining half of a glass of a particularly bitter stout in a single gulp. It was the sort of gulp that hurt his chest for a minute or two afterward. Owen clenched his fist and pounded his sternum twice for good measure.

"That bad, huh?" Eve groaned. She pitched a low whistle to the ceiling as she settled back in her chair. "You wanna talk about it?"

Yes, was Owen's first thought.

"I shouldn't," Owen mumbled with a limp shake of his head.

Desperately, was a close second.

"You don't have to tell me anybody's name," Eve prodded. She pushed a few gentle fingers against Owen's forearm. "Simple stuff. Is it the people you don't like, or the work itself?"

"Can I say both?"

"Course you can," Eve chuckled. "Get that around here sometimes. No fun fighting a belligerent drunk off a girl half his size."

"Yeah, I imagine not." Owen looked through the bottom of his empty glass, staring at the table through a lens coated in suds. "I guess... I just expected to be doing something more. Tracking down rogue mages or putting a stop to trafficking rings."

"Grand stuff," Eve nodded. "I get it. But it's only been a couple of days, yeah? I can't imagine they'd let a rookie loose on Arnstead's underbelly. Some nasty folks around here."

Eve cast a sweeping glance around the Creaky Board's main seating area. She did not linger too long on any particular gathering, but it was enough to get a point across. The staff at the tavern seemed friendly enough. That did not necessarily extend to the clientele.

Owen deflected the notion with another gripe.

"Nasty, all right. Folks back home didn't treat Spellseekers like this. There was respect, I mean," Owen continued with a bitterness he failed to stifle. "People back in Southport knew we were there to help. That we had their backs. Here? My Second Seeker... my boss, told me today that it's easier to do my job if I don't wear my uniform."

"I could see that," Eve said in reply. Owen huffed and slapped his glass back onto the table. A little harder than he had meant to. "No, really. The BoA... it takes a lot. Folks out here, they don't always have a lot to give. You hear all sorts of sob stories in a place like this."

One of Eve's white, delicate hands waved around the Creaky Board. She had eased herself forward in his chair as she spoke, resting her elbows on the table with arms folded over each other. It was clear that her attention was undivided.

This behavior was most of the reason why Owen held back from making some snappy retort. From laughing off the notion of the Bureau of Arcane abusing the citizens of the Federation. Owen knew that the woman's words were earnest, even if Eve had perhaps been misinformed. He could imagine aggravated business persons coming in to whine to a barkeep about submitting improper forms. Not paying correct licensing fees. People who tried to cheat the system and got caught.

These doubts swirled about in Owen's head. He kept them to himself. There was no sense in spoiling Eve's good intentions.

Candles that smelled of lemon cast an uneven light over the guest bedroom of the Orland house. The room was spacious, twice the size of room seventeen at the Creaky Board. A person could pace the room in thought without fear of bumping into the four-post bed, with its red canopy and thin purple curtains. Floral-pattered chairs, with a small couch to match, surrounded a coffee table in the center of the room. It felt as much a guest parlor as a guest bed.

Pushed up against the room's single large window was an oak writing desk. Bits of stationary littered its surface. An inkwell and pen were tucked in the upper-right corner, away from the open letters glowed in a mixture of twilight sun and candle flame.

Owen had eased into the desk's chair after a long day of settling into Arnstead. Suggestions from Cynthia and Marcus had led Owen to two exemplary tailors. One, a gruff Zumbatran harn whose hands shook so fiercely it was a shock to see him thread a needle, made work clothes that could stand fifty years in any mine on the continent. The harn had come at Marcus' recommendation. Eve, on the other hand, had pointed Owen to a Bangeli seamstress of some renown. Both had taken Owen's measurements and promised completion in a few days – the benefit of a healthy purse.

The remainder of the day had been spent with no particular goal in mind but to wander. Owen took full advantage of the street clothes he had been given. For the first time since leaving Southport, Owen had felt welcome when he entered places of business. Store owners shook his hand rather than spit in his palms. Random passersby were willing enough to offer directions if they were not in too much of a hurry. It felt like he had stumbled upon a whole new town simply by walking into a wardrobe.

To top the day off, a hot bath had been prepared for Owen upon his arrival. It came as a surprise. He had not given Marcus any guess as to when he would return. He certainly had not tossed a copper to an urchin to deliver a message. It was there waiting for him when he returned to the house, all the same.

"Always been clever, that one," Owen mumbled to himself. A half-dry towel still hung about his neck. He dabbed at wet patches in his hair, making sure that no water dripped on the letters he craned over.

His initial expectations had been correct. The letter marked from Elstaff had been sent by Rebecca Hall. After a paragraph of salutations and asking after Owen's wellbeing, she finally began to detail her exploits with Venkat. Becca indicated that her words spoke for both Venkat and herself. Though she had written that it was to save Owen the bore of reading identical letters, Owen had imagined that Venkat had simply refused to take the time. It was a notion that stung, but came as no great surprise

Details of their missions so far, of which Becca noted there had been three, were sparse. This was not for any lack of explanation on Becca's part. Large sections of the letter had been redacted. Rough, hand-drawn bars of black ink kept any specifics to the necessary minimum. Owen understood it was protocol. All correspondence detailing Bureau facilities or operations had to be closely monitored. Still, it did not make a conversation between friends feel any less violated.

What Owen managed to glean from the remainder of Becca's letter was that both her and Venkat were in good shape. No injuries to speak of. Their activities so far had been limited to smaller, disorganized trafficking. The pair had not been assigned any work related to larger rings, but Venkat was hopeful. The fact that the letter itself had been redacted also suggested that Becca and Venkat were working out of a facility large enough to have dedicated postal staff.

The second letter followed a similar format to the first:

Dearest Son,

Hello! I imagine you are doing well. I imagine you have cleaned the streets of Arnstead down to the last lamp thief! Your father pulled some strings and told me where you had been stationed. Who knew you would be

sent so far from home? I know you will do both your father and I proud!

How has the frontier been treating you? I hear there are all manner of savages that far west. Those kin folk are thicker than blood. Hear they drink plenty, too. Blood, that is. You be careful around those things. Won't have you coming back to me like a grape left to the sun! You'll have to tell me about all the other dangers you've seen. All the beasties and what-not. I expect you have a dozen stories for me to share already!

Home has been quiet without you and your friends. Your father enjoys the silence, but I find it to be absolutely dreadful. Gives me an excuse to get out with the horses, though. The Ramaswamis have made for delightful riding partners of late. All manner of stories coming their way from their boy Venkat, but I am sure he has shared all manner of things with you. Color me jealous!

Anyway, that's all from us for now. Business as usual around here. Make sure you give me all the details you can. I am expecting a book from you!

Love,

Mother

A second, and considerably smaller letter had been tucked behind the page from Owen's mother:

Owen,

I trust this finds you well. Arnstead is a good opportunity. Plenty of lawlessness to bring under your thumb. Climb the ladder and make me proud.

Best,

Father

Warmth radiated from Owen's cheeks. Not from the joy at receiving word from his friends or mother. It did not stem from the cup of rooibos Marcus had left on the writing desk, either. This warmth rose from a well of shame. Smiling cheeks became weighed down by its tingling waters.

Make me proud.

Owen read the short message from his father three times. Each time he came to those last words, he felt a renewed pang of embarrassment. Owen had never known three words to cause so much discomfort.

"I'll figure something out," he assured himself. Papers shuffled as Owen moved the letters aside. Grabbing the pen and drawing ink from the well, he began to craft his responses. "I *will* make you proud, at last."

158

10.

EXPECTATIONS

It took three weeks for Owen's life to settle into a monotonous rut. He took tea and honeyed toast in the morning, courtesy of Marcus. There was no conversation in this morning ritual. The food was waiting for him in the dining room. Marcus would already be on to a different task. Cynthia was the only person in the house who rose after dawn, well after Owen was on his way to the Arcanarium.

Pride demanded that Owen enter through the Arcanarium's front doors. He could not stomach the thought of skulking in the alley, waiting for Second Seeker Aaron to come by and pop a window latch with a spell. Owen held his head high and refused to acknowledge the insults of the caterwauling crowd at the Arcanarium's entrance. It was impossible to ignore the comments completely, though, even if he managed to avoid outward acknowledgment. Being called a rotten blueberry or a withering bluebell or any other such name had a way of grabbing his attention. There was no lack of creativity in the Arcanarium's morning mob, Owen conceded.

From morning to lunch was the time of paperwork. Despite his best efforts, the stack of ICFs never seemed to dwindle. Owen could churn out dozens of OCFs from the stack of ICFs and never make any visible progress. New forms replaced completed ones with impressive urgency.

Matters had only become worse when Aaron spoke had introduced Violent Complaint Forms, or VCFs. These forms were to be filled out when an ICF had any suggestion of violence in it. The VCF was put together with the ICF into a folder. When the folder had amassed ten pairs of complaints, it was to be slipped under the door to Violent Offenses.

"Doesn't matter which door," Aaron had advised. "All gets to the same place, far as I'm aware. I tend to alternate between the doors."

These words of wisdom, and a few others besides, were the last that Owen had heard from his superior for a full two weeks. Now that someone had come along to file paperwork and get initial casework straightened, the Second Seeker was able to hit the streets and attempt to resolve some complaints. This left Owen the thankless job of sifting through paperwork in silence from morning to noon in the musty office of Lost and Stolen.

Sun battered his eyes with murderous intent when Owen finally stepped out of the office each day. Once he had completed a smattering of forms, it was time to hit the streets of Arnstead. Saving the legwork for the second half of the day helped wake him from the tedious slumber induced by OCFs, ICFs, VCFs, and any number of the other CFs that Owen was unlucky enough to stumble upon. Sam, the sole receptionist for the Arnstead Arcanarium, snuck all manner of forms that Second Seeker Aaron had failed to mention into Lost and Stolen's work bin.

As with entering through the Arcanarium's front doors, pride demanded that Owen wear his Spellseeker blues while he performed initial casework. Hiding in street clothes struck a sour chord with Owen. Even if his superior not-quite-ordered him to wear anything but his uniform. Despite the insults that Owen knew would be slung at him in passing, or jammed into his face by the particularly feisty. None of that mattered. Wearing the uniform just felt *right*.

One more week, Owen thought. Arnstead's afternoon sun beat down on him like a spiteful teacher armed with a ruler. Sweat pooled in the small of his back and drenched his armpits. Pride demanded he wore the cumbersome, sweltering blues. *I've managed without getting stabbed or beaten. No infractions at the Arcanarium, despite a complete lack of supervision. Only gotten lost twice… maybe three times. Just one more week and probation will be up. Can move to Magical Misdemeanors. Get my feet wet before landing at Violent Offenses. Just one more week.*

One more week.

"One more week until what, darling?"

The brittle words startled Owen. He had been sure that he had said 'one more week' in his head rather than aloud. A quizzical look from the gray-black, Zumbatran harn in front of him confirmed otherwise. Owen's cheeks sank imperceptibly as he pondered how much he had spoken aloud.

"Sorry, ma'am, I was distracted."

"Oh, well that's a shame," the harn, Julia Thatch per her ICF, moaned. "Here I was thinking it would be one week and I'd have the little contraption back."

Each word was a struggle for the woman, whose body trembled with age. A gnarled oak branch fashioned into a cane did little to help Julia remain steady. She propped a shoulder against the squat doorframe to her tiny residence for good measure.

"Again, apologies. That was not my intention," Owen said, his speech mechanical and cold. "Remind me where we were if you could?"

"Talking about the thingy. The focus," Julia continued with casual rhythm. Her voice was fresh leather being stretched for the first time. "I'm a preserver. A pickler, if you will. Salt beef and pork, too. I get leftovers from farmers and butchers, then make my money back when the snows come down the plains. Folks pay a polished penny for something they can't get elsewhere. Come winter, I've got what they want. Follow me so far?"

"Yes, ma'am," Owen nodded.

"Good. Well, turns out it's not just us folk topside that wants a bite of cow now and then. I get all sorts of critters that try to tear into my cellar. Greedy little monsters try to make off all my goods, leave me poor and hungry. S'why I got myself that magic contraption. Something about it that those critters don't like. Supposed to smell bad or something, not that I've ever noticed. Does a fine job. Still with me?"

Another affirmative nod from Owen.

"So, one day I come down to the cellar, got a newly sealed jar of eggs to start pickling, and wouldn't you know it? The damn contraption is gone, and half my beef with it! About screamed when I saw the critters running amok down in my cellar. Dropped the jar of eggs, too. Ran upstairs to grab a skillet and ran the thieving monsters out. Have to sleep down there now. On watch all the time! Wouldn't be so bad if Emmet hadn't gone to see the gods two years back, bless him."

"I'm sorry for your loss, ma'am."

"Oh, don't be silly. Not your fault," Julia said warmly. "What would *really* make me feel better, young man, would be if you could help me get that contraption back. Would make my life all sorts of better."

Brace yourself, Owen thought. A ritual he had taken up in preparation for delivering unwanted news.

"Lost and Stolen aims to help you recover your focus as soon as possible. My purpose here today is to verify your initial report and gather any additional details that may have surfaced. An associate of mine will return shortly to facilitate recovery."

161

Here it comes.

"Shame," Julia said. Owen winced. "Guess the cot's staying in the cellar for now. You all right, young man? You look like you're about to get punched?"

Tension had contorted Owen's face more than he realized. Both eyes were hammered shut, his brow creased. His lips had drawn inward to leave a scant trace of their existence. A thin, pink line dug into his apprehensive features.

The shameful display melted away as Owen became aware of it. He relaxed his face and shoulders, cleared his throat in embarrassment.

"Apologies, ma'am," he mumbled.

"You sure say sorry an awful lot, you know that?" The feeble harn watched Owen nod affirmation, try to distract himself with scribbles on his clipboard. "Do you want to come inside? Have a seat, maybe some coffee? You look like you could use some energy. I've got a bit of lemon cake, too. Should help put a little hop in your trot."

"I'm sorry, ma'am." The reply was reflexive, as was the hand that rose to wave Julia's suggestion away. Apologies had become second nature over the past three weeks. "Just wish there was more I could do to help."

"Don't worry yourself," Julia smiled. "Said your friend would be by soon enough, after all. What's another week with a frying pan in the cellar? You sure you don't want to step in, though?" she added. Her curious inflection betrayed a sense of concern. "You look awful tired, young man."

"It's all right," Owen said. He returned her smile, albeit more wearily. "Your kindness is plenty, and I have other stops to make. Thank you for your time, ma'am."

Julia was the fifth call Owen had made that day. Tucked away in a slanted shack of a home at the edge of Oldstead, it had been the last place he expected to get a breath of fresh air. Before Julia had been a pair of businessmen in Weststead and a family in Eaststead whose intruder alarm had been stolen.

The fourth call, made on his way to Julia's home, was also in Oldstead. Where Owen's previous calls that day had been met with mild indifference, the venomous day laborer had no pleasantries to spare.

"Find me at work and waste my time, will you?" the irate Nirdac human had asked. "My time feeds my family. Wasting my time is starving my children!"

Colleagues of the man muttered bitter agreement as the day laborer raged on. Idle hands slung tools over shoulders, fidgeted at worn and splintering handles. Owen could not help but notice. More and more of his attention was drawn from his clipboard to the growing crowd. Off the heels of this near disaster, speaking to Julia had felt like the discovery of an oasis after a week in the desert.

This sense of elation followed Owen as he left Oldstead by way of the Dusk Bridge. The bridge connected Oldstead to Weststead, crossing the River Ra. Knowing these facts was enough to help keep Owen's mood afloat. It spoke to his increasing knowledge of Arnstead. Three weeks in the town had given him a strong sense of which major roads would take him where. Knowing where he was headed felt just as good as knowing how he would get there.

Owen's destination was the Arcanarium. His first couple of days had taught him a lesson in overestimation. With a clipboard packed to a point of bursting, he had hit the streets of Arnstead. Purpose filled his steps as he moved from claimant to claimant with fierce dignity. It was much to his surprise then when the sun had begun to set after only his sixth call.

The lesson was met with acceptance rather than disappointment.

It is a new town, after all, Owen had reasoned. *A new job that wanders new streets will take some time to acclimate to. I'll get faster with time.*

That had been three days prior. Now he was returning to the Arcanarium to gather new complaint forms, with five completed reports tucked under his arm and hours left before the sun retreated for the day.

With time on his side, Owen decided to take an unfamiliar route to the Arcanarium. The road from the mouth of the Dusk Bridge would take him almost directly to his destination if followed southwest. A turn left from the bridge would follow the River Ra until it became Sisir's Run. Owen had yet to have cause to walk the road along the western river banks. Now seemed the perfect time to remedy that fact.

Mud had been the defining characteristic of the eastern shores. Thick river sludge was smeared over every stall on that side of Sisir's Run and up the River Ro. Roads near the river banks had an almost viscous quality about them as if the rivers had reached up and slapped the substance there with mucky hands. It was the type of stuff that stuck to boots and stained clothes.

The western shores were a whole different world by comparison. An embankment of mortar and stone spared the West River Road, so it was called, from the rivers' slimy attacks. The packed dirt of the road offered no threat of slippage. What struck Owen most about this change was the smell. Walking down the East River Road presented not just the danger of filling your shoes with mud, but also tacking a film to your nostrils that reeked of mud, fish entrails, and loathing.

Fresh-baked bread was one of the many scents that floated on the air of the West River Road. A general lack of river muck invited different businesses. Fishmongers were replaced by bakers and fruit stalls. The two rolled into a mouthwatering mixture as Owen passed a small shop named Sisir's Sweets. A lemon and blueberry tart, Owen learned after poking his head into the establishment. His presence was welcome when it became clear he had entered for his own personal interests than that of a Spellseeker's.

Seems to be the pattern, Owen thought. He sucked the last, sugary remnants of the fruity confection from his thumb as he neared the intersection of the West River Road and Main Street. *Weststead is nice, though twice the price,* Eve had commented in passing one evening. Though Owen stayed at the Orland Estate now, he still visited the Creaky Board for food and musical entertainment. That, and Eve was the closest thing Owen had to a friend in the town. Cynthia was rarely home. Owen still had yet to meet any of his fellow Spellseekers.

"There's nothing you can find in Weststead that you can't find here in Eaststead. Can't deny the quality, though."

The addition had been met by the thwack of a folding fan against Owen's head. It was accompanied by a baleful look from Annabella Everbrite, fan in hand, as she navigated the bustling seating area of her establishment.

It wasn't just the quality of goods that differed, Owen realized, between Weststead and Eaststead. More buildings were constructed from brick and stone, as opposed to the wooden structures in Eaststead. There were even some roads in Weststead that had begun the process of cobbling their surfaces. It made Owen think back to Cynthia's words. About how Arnstead would not remain a frontier town for long.

Serene musings faded as Owen made the right turn onto Main Street. Pulled from flakey pastries and the future of the township, his attention fell on a rising clamor. It was quiet at first. The mere suggestion of disturbance whispered on the early evening breeze. One shout. Another.

Dust wafted up to the west. An odd sort of cloud, as if something heavy had fallen from a roof to the road. Another cloud puffed up as Owen watched. This one was nearer and slightly to the right. By the time the third cloud had risen, he started to walk towards the disturbance. Cries of dismay sent his right hand to rest on his caster pistol.

Cutting through the crowd, just ahead of each cloud of dust, was a Nirdac katarl. He had abandoned any sense of civility, running on all fours like a common beast. Terror guided his erratic movements. As a frightened fox bounds between tree and brush to flee a hound, so did this katarl weave between knees and ankles. A fleshy forest that hid him from what pursued close to the heel.

Fangs like knives glistened in the snarling maw of the Bangeli katarl that gave chase. No less than two hundred pounds of muscle pushed its way through the crowd, already giving way thanks to the smaller katarl's efforts to escape. Powerful legs propelled the orange and black-striped woman past toppling observers too slow to make way. She did not require the use of her arms to grasp at extra speed. Long strides and a clear path showed the Bangeli to be making gains on her prey.

A glint in the eye of the Bangeli katarl told Owen that the speed of the woman was unnatural. There was more propelling her movements than powerful legs alone. This katarl was channeling the Flow as she closed on the smaller, terrified katarl. The only thing that seemed to prevent the Bangeli from overtaking the Nirdac katarl was the crowd of people that choked the Bridge on Main. An unrelenting obstacle that refused to provide a straightforward path for any pedestrian, much less the one trying to move at supernatural speed.

The pair were a few arm lengths away from Owen when he first saw the Bangeli katarl eye's glint with the effort of channeling. Adrenaline poured into his veins as he drew his caster pistol, slotted the amethyst cartridge into the pistol's chamber. Conviction rooted his left foot in the path of the chase before him.

This is why I'm here, Owen thought.

"Spellseeker!" he shouted at the Bangeli katarl. "Halt or be fired upon!"

Owen stood firm as the slight Nirdac whipped around his legs. The frightened man grazed Owen's left leg as he passed. There was a brief moment where Owen feared he might lose balance and be trampled by the oncoming wall of feral aggression.

"Final warning!" Owen called.

Ferocity gave way to confusion for the span of a single heartbeat. The Bangeli katarl shifted her attention from the Nirdac to Owen for the first time. Another moment saw confusion replaced by a redoubled fury. The Bangeli's face seemed to say, "How dare you!" There was not time enough for the Bangeli's lips to match her face.

The crackling rush of purple was quick to give on the streets of Arnstead. A single, strained breath pulled energy from the Flow and into Owen's arm. Little effort was required to call it forth. More troublesome was the matter of damming the torrential flow of power once it had been unleashed. Too much energy would see the caster pistol cartridge, the target of Owen's channeling, burst in a wild amplification of the focus's intended purpose. Dozens would lay stunned on the Bridge on Main in the aftermath. The lucky ones, at any rate.

Owen did not allow such distractions to enter his mind. Purpose drew his attention to the raging Bangeli katarl who drew closer still. Necessity capped the Flow before it erupted in a fit of chaos. With caster pistol locked on target, Owen focused on a single thought: *Go!*

Violet light tore the air apart as it leaped from the caster pistol's barrel, wrapping itself around the Bangeli katarl like a fishing net. Strands of light burned through clothes and fur as they clawed at the katarl's flesh. She had no time to react. The katarl crumbled to the ground in a sizzling heap.

Thunder cracked from the barrel of the pistol after the light flashed. Terrible, chest-shattering noise that muted terrified screams. Those surrounding the event cast themselves aside in panic. Some fell where they were and cowered. A pocket of space had formed around Owen and the convulsing katarl. He holstered his pistol and raised both hands high.

"Everything is okay!" he shouted, his ears ringing in protest. Owen spun slowly to speak to every onlooker in turn. "The situation has been resolved. Feel free to go about your business!"

Few among the crowd bothered to look his way. An uncaring air swept over those in the immediate area. People gathered themselves, dusted themselves off, and continued about their days as if nothing had happened at all. What was another body in the middle of the road? Or so their even strides seemed to say between calm breaths.

Calm was the furthest thing from Owen's mind. An adrenal hammer pounded his temples as he towered over the Bangeli katarl. His hands, now free of his weapon, trembled ferociously. He took one in the other to stop the sensation as he continued to marvel. This was the first time he had ever been forced to use the amethyst cartridge. The lines of violet light had left blackened rows of fur in the woman's orange-black coat. Charred tears, yellowed at their edges, marked where the shocking lines had burned her cream-colored cotton shirt.

The smell that arose from the katarl was beyond offensive. Burnt hair mixed with what smelled like urine. Rolling her flat onto her back with his bootheel, Owen was able to see the stain where the katarl had soiled herself. A dry groan rumbled up from the katarl's throat as she plopped onto her back. Occasional spasms still wracked her body.

Right then, let's get you squared away, Owen thought with a smile.

Owen produced a pair of manacles that hung from his belt near the small of his back. Their short chain jingled at the sudden freedom. They continued their bright tune as Owen bound the katarl's wrists and clamped the restraints shut. A small key sealed the manacles and was tucked into Owen's pocket. He stood, wiping nonexistent sweat from his brow with a satisfied whistle.

"Mighty fine catch there, Mr. Spellseeker." Through thickening traffic, Owen was able to spy a familiar face. Jessica, the waif from his first day in Arnstead, was nestled amidst her sparse belongings. "Seemed ready to tear the smaller one to bits, that one."

"Good day, Jessica," Owen beamed. "Sorry to see you've lost your legs. *Again.*"

"You seem a different man today." Jessica gave no acknowledgment to any legs that she may or may not have. "Awful proud of yourself."

"And why not? Like you said, the other katarl would be in pieces by now if I'd not stepped in. Speaking of which," Owen added distantly, "you didn't happen to see where he ran off to, did you?"

"You know him? The Nirdac, I mean?"

"Can't say that I do. Why?"

"Stopped a rampaging Bangeli for the man," Jessica noted. "Askin' after his wellbeing, too. Doesn't seem the sort of thing you do for a stranger, does it?"

"It's my job when magic is involved." Self-satisfaction was evident in both Owen's tone and smile. His spirits had risen too high to care about hiding that fact for the sake of professionalism. "It's also my job to know why these things happen. Was hoping I might be able to get the Nirdac's side of things."

"Sounds important."

"It is, my dear Jessica."

"Maybe a whole *silver's* worth of importance."

The probing smile told Owen that Jessica's last statement was more of a question. Innocent questions had led the way to a financial transaction once again. Owen could not help but puff a thin blast of air through his nose.

"I could get the story from half a dozen different urchins and still not spend a whole silver in the process."

"Oh-hh?" Jessica reeled. "But those other urwhats wouldn't be half as pretty as your own Jessica, now, would they?" The girl laced her fingers under her chin and blinked rapidly at Owen.

"I'll take my chances with this one down at the Arcanarium." Owen prodded the Bangeli's ribs with the toe of a boot as he spoke. "I may take you up on your offer later, though. Can't imagine you'll have *walked* far."

The office of First Seeker Akheem Albarn was a well-ordered place. Not the sort of neatness that comes from the meticulous arrangement and rearrangement of its sparse furniture. It contained only two wooden chairs, one behind and one before the slight metal table that served as a desk of sorts. There was no coat rack next to the door. Blank walls housed neither hat hooks nor pictures of any kind.

No, the neatness of Akheem Albarn's office was the type that comes from neglect. Furniture could not be out of place because it was never touched. A complete lack of storage space would suggest that the man visited the room as infrequently as he could manage. Only a pair of sealed envelopes resting on the metal table's green surface indicated any semblance of use.

It was across this table that Owen now found himself. High spirits had abandoned him by now. The plummet had begun upon the Bangeli katarl's awakening. Cold and controlled, she had demanded that Owen search her right pocket. His brief search produced a scrap of metal; the badge of a fellow Third Seeker. She was in the First Seeker's office, as well. A fresh set of clothes and a truncated bath did little to calm the brooding fire in her eyes. The katarl stood with her back to the wall in fierce silence.

Next to Owen was Second Seeker Aaron. He had been summoned to the First Seeker's office as news of Owen's escapade spread through the small Arcanarium. The harn's usual easy demeanor was nowhere to be found. Perhaps left in the office to Lost and Stolen, or cowering in the alleyway beneath a window left slightly ajar. Here, in the First Seeker's office, Aaron Connolly was as stiff as a corpse. The harn did not dare even to quiver as he stood next to his only subordinate.

None of these things made Owen feel small. The scant furniture made him feel central to the room, reminded him that he was the focal point of the day's affairs. Caustic sneers from the Bangeli Seeker came close. Her presence kept his recent failings at the forefront of thought. Aaron's presence made Owen feel, by comparison, in command of the proceedings. What made Owen feel insignificant was the empty chair behind the First Seeker's table.

A major investigation had been decimated by Owen's failure. His choice to step in the way of the Bangeli's pursuit had thrown months of preparation into the bin. Money spent on bribes had now been wasted. Faces once blurred and insignificant against the dust-caked visages of Arnstead had been made. Lives lost were now lost in vain. All details the Third Seeker had hurled at Owen with relentless savagery on their shameful walk to the Arcanarium. None of her words hurt Owen more than the fact that First Seeker Akheem Albarn seemed to have no time for Owen's colossal mistake.

When the First Seeker entered his office, at last, Violette Woods gliding close behind, an icy stillness fell over the room. Aaron's fidgeting fingers snapped to attention at his sides. The Third Seeker's venomous features hardened into a blank slate of stone. Not a muscle twitched as the First Seeker lowered himself into his chair. Ash-brown coils bobbed about his ears and shoulders before falling still to match the room. Violette slipped a folder into First Seeker Akheem's outstretched hand. He dropped the folder to the table with a snap, causing papers to creep out from the unsealed edges.

"Tell me why you're here."

The First Seeker's words cut through the still air like a fork of lightning. Sudden and sharp, they left a sickening vacuum in their wake.

Uncertainty pulled at Owen from the edge of the void ripped by the First Seeker. Dozens of minute hands pawed at Owen's face like frozen needles. They pulled him forward, hunching him over towards the First Seeker's table.

Flicking his eyes from the floor up to the First Seeker, Owen thought he was the only one to feel silence between them. The First Seeker had not yet bothered to look at Owen. Dark eyes watched dark fingers rest on the wan envelope. An idle thumb picked at the papers that bled from the envelope's sides.

I'm sure he already knows, Owen thought. *He must know. That he was called here to deal with the mess I made. To serve as an intermediary between Lost and Stolen and folks from Violent Offenses. Maybe to make sure that Bangeli doesn't tear me in half?* The Bangeli katarl remained stiff as a board nailed to a wall.

"Sir," Owen began, his throat suddenly dry. His tongue protested the words even as they tumbled from his mouth. "We're here, sir, because of my failings. Because sir—"

"Let me ask again," Akheem interrupted. The First Seeker's words were a gavel, silencing the room without question. "Why are *you* here, Mr. Raulstone?"

When First Seeker Akheem's gaze finally beheld Owen, all those cold, invisible hands that had teased at Owen's face stopped. They joined as one and clenched Owen's heart in an icy grip. What had remained hidden behind the First Seeker's tone and mannerisms crystalized in a brief moment of eye contact.

Malice.

"Well, s-sir, *I* am here because of... because of my choices today. Choices that hindered an investigation being conducted by Violent Offenses." Owen nodded to the Third Seeker still at attention. "Choices for which I am dearly sorry, sir. I can assure you that I will not be so careless in the future."

Full lips pulled inward, tucked into the early suggestion of a frown as the First Seeker listened to Owen ramble. The stream of words had increased in pace as Akheem's displeasure became more and more apparent.

"If I may, sir," Owen continued, not leaving any room for the First Seeker to interject, "it may behoove us all to introduce me to everyone, sir.

The rest of the Arcanarium, I mean, sir." One of the First Seeker's eyebrows vaulted at the suggestion. As if the sheer audacity of the notion was enough to upset the otherwise stoic visage of Akheem Albarn. "It's just that, knowing the faces of everyone, it might... help? In the future, I mean, should another incident like this present itself. To me. In the future."

The First Seeker absorbed the mottle of words. He was a sponge for Owen's feeble attempts at misdirection, or for the justification of actions. Nothing Owen said was enough to sate the First Seeker's desire. A stoic need to have his single question answered. *Why are you here?* Each excuse or assertion had been sucked up in turn, yet Akheem Albarn still waited for more.

Words failed Owen. His jaw hung loose, mouth agape, as his mind dug for thoughts that would not surface. All had become a blank slate before the question. *Why are you here?* Owen's hand open and closed as if grasping for an adequate excuse. Splayed fingers curled and strained with the effort.

"I'm not sure, sir," Owen muttered, at last, defeated. "Not sure what you mean, sir. I thought I was here to be punished. Reprimanded, at the very least."

These forlorn phrases broke the Bangeli katarl's resolve. She let out a snort as if suppressing full laughter. It was a short lapse. The First Seeker seemed not to notice, or, if he did, showed no sign that he cared.

A soft swish of paper drew Owen's attention back to the green table's surface. The First Seeker had opened the folder provided by Violette. Akheem's cold eyes turned from Owen down to the revealed pages. Stuck pages fought against Akheem's touch, forcing him to lick his thumb to look through the documents. He skimmed the collection through twice before he spoke.

"Self-Defense Certification: failed. Self-Defense Certification, second attempt: failed. Tracking Certification: failed. Tracking certification, second attempt: failed." Each time the First Seeker uttered the word *failed* he snapped a glance at Owen. "Flow Suppression Certification: failed. Three failed attempts at that one, Mr. Raulstone."

"First Seeker, sir," Owen questioned, "are those my records? From Eastpointe?"

"Channeling Certification: passed. With honors, even? Fancy that," the First Seeker added with a look of sharp disbelief. "Ah, this is more like it. Pursuit Certification: failed. Twice failed, that one."

"Excuse me, sir," Owen protested. "I admit, I did fail most

certifications on the first attempt. However, with the accommodation of focuses to complement any deficiencies in Flow concentration, I was able to obtain my certifications. Everything should be documented in those records!"

"One more time, please."

"I'm sorry, sir?"

"About your certifications, *Mister* Raulstone," Akheem said. The First Seeker leaned into the word *mister* as if throwing a punch. "Tell me again, how did you pass?"

"With the accommodation of focuses—"

"With *accommodation*." Another verbal blow was thrown at Owen's face. "What your records say to me, *Mister* Raulstone, is that you're a Spellseeker that damn well can't cast a *spell*!"

First Seeker Akheem snatched Owen's records in a single hand and crumpled them into a jagged ball. After a final squeeze, Akheem launched the ball at Owen's face. The ball caught Owen square in the nose and caused him to flinch.

"At first glance," Akheem began again, leaning forward on his table, "I would have assumed these failures to end a career, not launch one. That was until I saw the name, of course. I know that name. *Raulstone.* Second Federation Army royalty, that name. The name has been tied to an officer in the armies for the past hundred years. When I saw that name — your name — it got me wondering. What kind of favors could a *Raulstone* call for? What strings could they pull, to save face in the light of such a failure?" The First Seeker made a slight sweeping gesture at Owen. Frigid contempt dripped from every word. "The kind of favor that lets some waste of space with Concentration Deficit slide into a Spellseeker's seat?

"I can't say I know what would possess someone like you to enlist, much less cheat their way into a position as a Spellseeker. What I can say, however, is that your delusions end here. Any thoughts of grandeur or status you had are dead. You have no ambition beyond pushing papers and scribbling notes with Seeker Aaron, *Mister* Raulstone."

"First Seeker Akheem, I—"

"No," the First Seeker growled. "You don't speak. You don't cause problems. I have half a mind to drag your precious name through the mud, to drag you kicking and screaming to the Fourth Federation Army barracks down the street. There's satisfaction in watching privileged pissants like you squirm when they're booted down to Private."

Akheem took a deep breath, forced it out through his nose as he leaned back into his chair. The worn wood creaked against his weight while the rest of the room maintained its unsettled quiet. Time itself seemed to draw to a disquieted halt. No clock was present in the barren room to mark its passage.

There was no sense of reprieve in the stillness. The First Seeker's verbal assault may have come to an end, but Owen had withdrawn too far to notice. His gaze was locked on a particular knot in the wooden flooring. That spot, insignificant on any other day, had become a lone outcrop of bedrock. It was the anchor that held Owen true against the tide of truth that shook him to his core.

Of all the bitter, mishappen scabs of fact that clung to Owen, the First Seeker had found the most vulnerable. Practiced ferocity had ripped away little thick skin Owen had on the subject. Shame burned his crimson cheeks. Owen gripped his pant legs to reassure himself against a growing feeling of nakedness.

The First Seeker spoke again. His words were distant, carried across a river on a fragile wind. Owen fought against the words as hot tears, barely held in check, began to well in his eyes.

"Do we have an understanding, Mr. Raulstone?" Akheem Albarn muttered again. Owen did not have the strength to resist him a second time.

"Yes, sir."

"Good," the First Seeker grumbled as he rose. "Chitra, you're with me. Let's see if we can't salvage some of this mess before the weasel disappears for good."

Third Seeker Chitra nodded and followed the First Seeker out of the office. She made no effort to conceal a low growl as she passed Owen. The two were gone, the door closed behind them, without another word.

Breath found Owen again as the door closed. He fought back the urge to gasp, instead of taking breath one deep, quivering lung-full at a time. To exhale was to fight back tears. The small office became a misty haze.

"When you find the time, I need you to complete this."

Owen snapped to attention. As he wallowed in self-pity, he had forgotten that others still inhabited the room with him. Composure failed him as Owen wiped his eyes to see Violette holding a small packet of papers out to him.

"It's an incident report," she continued. "I would prefer it before the end of the day, but... there's no rush."

There was an odd cadence to the woman's speech. Gone was her usual frozen tone. Though she did not speak with warmth, there was a mildness to her. Perhaps she felt some measure of Owen's discomfort at the situation.

"Of course," Owen said. He gripped the packet of papers with a numb hand.

"Complete it as best you can. Just slide it under my door when you've finished."

"Yes, ma'am."

"All right," she mumbled. There was a quick squirm, as though Violette was not entirely sure what to do with herself. The moment was brief and passed without much note. "I'll leave you to it, then."

Violette glided past Owen and let herself out without a sound.

The incident report weighed heavy on Owen's leg. It bounced on a knee that had begun to move on its own. Papers warbled as they jostled up and down in the pale blue folder. Curiosity beckoned Owen to open the folder, look through its contents. Responsibility demanded that he plan his responses for the questions contained within.

Owen's last shred of dignity denied the folder's existence.

Unwelcome thoughts wormed their way through the cracks of his tattered composure. Possible futures set themselves before his mind's eye. He could see himself wrinkled, with gray hair and eyes cloudy with cataracts. Feeble hands worked a reluctant quill in rote motions. Empty forms replaced those that had been completed in the office of Lost and Stolen until Owen's wizened head fell limp on his cluttered desk. The violent thunk drew no attention.

Half a dozen futures more flashed through Owen's mind. Some ended in senile shame, as with the first. Others saw death. The last, which Owen thought most likely, was a vivid vision of his father reclaiming the Raulstone name from his son. Owen was left without name and rank. Abandoned at the edge of the world to find his way.

A soft, warm hand took hold of Owen's. The only other person in the room, Aaron, knelt to catch Owen's listless gaze. A tight squeeze of the hand and a proffered half-smile spoke for the Second Seeker when he failed to find any words of substance. Reassurance of any kind was welcome. It did not matter that Owen had forgotten the harn was in the room, that his superior had failed to speak on his behalf. Not that there had been anything to say.

174

11.

REALITY

"Ah, Megan! Just in time," Owen howled as the Nirdac server approached his table. "Was worried I might have to go without for a minute."

"Can't have that, can we?" the cheery woman replied.

No light shone through the glass she placed before Owen. Light foam swirled amid the dark, bitter liquid. The drink had been freshly poured. Owen craned his head to see the suds form a thick head at the top of the glass. Strong scents of coffee and oats rose from the glass to cradle Owen's receptive nose.

"Very much appreciated, dear!"

The pale serving girl had not waited for Owen's thanks before leaving. It was the end of the week, Last Day's Eve. Those who could spare a day's toil and not fear hunger or eviction would do so. Sunday was a day of rest. Fewer obligations on Sunday meant more fun to be had the night before. Patrons of the Creaky Board and staff alike knew no greater creed.

Dancers flitted before the stage like moths riding firelight. Pairs wheeled to form trios that went on to accept more. Sashes pulled from robes, twirled above the crowd like ribbons caught on the wind.

Bare hands pattered against taught drums held between crossed legs. Though they drove the night's proceedings forward, they were not the star of the show. That privilege was carried across the stage by a Bangeli chanter. Azure sashes bound a loose, cerulean robe that gave her the appearance of a roiling sapphire. Brave were the dancers among the audience who tried to follow her motions as she sang.

Breaks in the Bangeli woman's chants were not a time of rest for the crowd. When the chanter joined the crowd to rest her voice, a pair of shrill Bangeli violins took her place. The instruments, dwarfed by the Bangeli katarl who wielded them, brought new life to the floor. Men and women elbowed through each other for a chance to be paired with the chanter.

While the people of Arnstead danced and sang and fought and laughed,

Owen drained another beer at his table for one. Before him was his message box. His link to the Arnstead Arcanarium. With pen in hand, he scribbled and scrawled between drinks. He did not think about what he wrote. Instead, he recorded his reflections on the day's events as they floated up to the top of his mind.

"And then I shocked her." Not only did Owen pay little attention to which thoughts he scribbled onto paper, but he mumbled them aloud as he did so. "Zap! Dropped her right to the ground in a steaming heap. You should have seen the way she twitched. Makes her tough front in the First Seeker's office laughable. But anyways, that was apparently the wrong decision. The little weasel she was after seemed to be a big something or other. Wouldn't know for sure, since none of you people tell me anything anyways."

"Not that I'm blaming you directly, of course. You're just the handler. You know, the person that keeps tabs on their Seekers. Makes sure they have what they need. That they aren't getting into too much trouble. You know, being helpful and what not."

The silvered pen bounced as it drew a large X through the last paragraph. Owen scratched furiously at the back of his head with his free hand. He kept scratching until the abused patch of skin felt a little numb. There was no telling whether or not that sensation was borne of scratches or booze, but Owen relented regardless. A sharp grunt replaced the rapid motion to vent frustration.

"I don't mean that. Not all of it. Would mean a lot if you responded to my reports with more than just 'Report received.' Maybe some advice. A little encouragement. Something. I don't know. Thanks."

Owen signed his name and slipped the missive into his message box. The message required a bit of folding, on account of length, to fit into the box. He made a fold down the middle, then down the middle again. Not a neat fit by any means.

Neatness was not a requirement for function, however. Pressing his thumb on the small memory glass fitting, white light popped through the seams of the little box. A trio of slight vibrations accompanied the light. These lights and vibrations told Owen that his message had been sent. He tossed his pen back into the box and slipped it into his pocket.

His mind cleared of complaints about the day, Owen grabbed his drink and slumped back into his chair. Wooden legs sighed with age as they followed Owen's weight backward. He tossed one leg over the opposite knee and tipped the chair backward with his planted foot. The beat of the drums on-stage informed the slight rocking motion Owen adopted. He took another deep drink while he moved, slightly out of time, with the beat.

Another set of vibrations grabbed Owen's attention before he could melt into the sounds of the night. This was a pair, as the message received. Not wanting to abandon his newly found comfort, Owen leaned forward to deposit his glass on the table. Just enough of the glass rested on the table to prevent a tip. A person breathing at the table could easily dislodge the precarious balance.

There wasn't space enough in Owen's mind for more than two thoughts at a time. The potential loss of his drink was pushed aside by the receipt of a message and the desire to read it. Numb fingers felt for the suggestion of the message box. The first attempt came back empty-handed, but the second produced the prize. Owen snapped the box open to see a small scrap of paper. It had only two sentences written upon it.

"Third daily report received. No further reporting required for —"

The note had been ripped to shreds before Owen finished that second sentence.

"Hilarious," Owen spat with bitter contempt. "More than 'report received' indeed."

Owen slammed the message box onto his table. His hand enveloped the box as he did so, pressing the contraption against the table's surface. The resulting shock sent Owen's glass, still half full, tumbling to the ground. A stabbing plink preceded the sound of shattering glass. Bits of glass rode on a wave of brown suds over the floor.

Wet feet shuffled away from the new mess. Though Owen's table was near the wall opposite the stage, there was not space free of the sweating mass of dancers. It was hard to tell if the collective shuffle had been away from the beer or in time with the Bangeli chanter's motions.

"Quite the collection you have there. Run out of room on the table, I see?" Eve's keen smile cut through the crowd. "You don't mind if I save the rest, do you?"

Eve raised a hand high into the muggy air. At first, Owen thought the yellow haze around Eve's hand to be a trick of the light. After a few moments, however, a pair of wooden trays became visible. They moved through the air above the crowd like boats on a roaring river. Raised hands

177

were rocky outcrops to be dodged and weaved around. Eventually, they settled on Eve's raised hand. After placing Owen's glasses onto the trays, three at a time, she sent the pair back the way they had come.

"Huh," Owen exhaled. "Never seen you channel before. Didn't know you could concentrate."

"Nothing fancy. Just for things around the place," Eve waved a hand. "Like having an extra set of hands. Imagine you'd put me to shame, Mr. Blue."

Eve looked down at the scattered bits of glass on the floor just in time to miss the ugly sneer that crumpled Owen's face. It was not a look of malice. More a reaction, as if Eve had jammed a finger into an open sore. Owen wiped the look away as Eve knelt to deal with the mess. A small brush and dust pan was produced from Eve's robes. The tinkle of glass was almost drowned under the chanter's refrains.

"So, Mr. Magic," Owen began, "how long have you—"

"Sorry, friend," Eve interrupted as he tucked his brush away. she forced herself back to a standing position with a grunt. "Can't stay overlong. Saturdays are always like this. I'll look for you once the crowd thins, yeah?"

That last bit was shouted over Eve's shoulder as he disappeared into the throng. Owen watched as his head bobbed in the crowd for another moment before being lost to the swell.

"Yeah," Owen mumbled. "Later."

The idea of being sober enough to remember a conversation that might take place an hour from that moment was not one Owen would place a bet on.

"Made room for another round?"

The baggy end of Megan's black sleeve drooped over Owen's shoulder. She leaned in to deposit another glass on the emptied table.

"As if I could say no to you!" Owen roared. His head lulled backward to rest on the crook of Megan's neck. An exulted laugh barreled its way upward from Owen's chest. While Megan did not recoil from Owen's touch, she did turn her head from the laugh that assaulted her ear. Not that Owen noticed. As soon as the glass hit the table, he was leaning forward to examine the newest offering. Megan, a fuzzy blur of black and white robes, slipped away when given the chance.

Bubbles the color of mahogany welled up from the dark abyss that filled the glass. As the bubbles began to fade, only the black beverage remained. The sort of blackness a person sees the moment after they blow out a candle. A sudsy, starlit sky as clouds devour what little light a moonless night has to offer. Its smell was rich and dark, like wisps of chocolate wrapped in something nutty.

"Is that… peanut butter?" Owen mused.

Another, deeper whiff of the beer piqued Owen's curiosity. He had all manner of stouts and porters, dark ales, and all the like. For every type of beer he had consumed, he felt he must have tried at least a dozen varieties each. Never before this night, however, had he ever smelled the suggestion of peanut butter in a beer.

Hesitation denied Owen his chance at the first sip of his beer. While he was stuck pondering the absurdity of using peanut butter to flavor a stout, the glass was ripped from his hand. The bottom of the glass was tipped to the ceiling before Owen knew there was a need to protest. Two, three, four, and few more powerful pulls at the glass left it empty. The offender slammed the glass down onto Owen's table.

"Yeah, it's peanut butter," Violette Woods gasped. She shook her head at the intensity of the drink, then pushed another chair up to Owen's table backward. Violette dropped herself onto the chair and flung her arms forward over the chair's back. She let her arms dangle. The middle of the backrest became a roost for the woman's sharp chin.

"Excuse me?" was all Owen could think to say, so shocked he was by Violette's sudden appearance and display.

"You're excused," she grumbled. Violette's chin remained planted on the backrest as she spoke, causing her head to bob up and down. Scarlet suspenders bowed in response to slack shoulders and a hunched back. Violette had become a portrait of exhaustion in the time it took to sit down.

"Come here to gloat?" Owen moaned.

"To make sure you didn't make a *second* career-ending mistake in a single day. Am I too late?" Violette added, sizing up Owen's sloshy demeanor. "You haven't tried to arrest half the wait staff, have you?"

"I haven't, *thank you.*" The petulance in his thanks made Owen wince. An awkward moment passed as both watched the chanter flit about the stage. "How did you get here so fast, anyways? I sent that last message…" Owen checked his pocket watch, "…five minutes ago?"

"Fifteen," Violette responded. Her gaze remained fixed on the performance, golden light from the stage illuminating her pale face. "It was fifteen minutes ago. I left the Arcanarium after you sent your *second* excuse for a daily report. That was an hour ago, so an hour and fifteen together."

"How'd you get the third message if you'd left already?"

"Brought the box with me." Violette pulled the massage box that matched Owen's out of her pocket. The small box pulled her eyes from the stage. She studied the box as she turned it over in her hand, end over end. Every groove on the bare surface had its turn to bask in the light of the stage. "Not a short walk, from here to the Arcanarium. There's never just *one* raging, booze-fueled message in my experience. Not like you're the first."

There was a brief flash of crystal blue as Violette turned her head just enough to see Owen. Not a reproachful glare or with eyes of knives, at least not that Owen could see. Violette afforded Owen little time to decipher the look. She turned her face back to the stage.

"Not the first to make a fool of himself in front of the First Seeker, and half the town besides?" Owen ventured.

Curiosity replaced much of what had been hostile in his tone. He realized that Violette was not here on a simple mission of reproach. It would have been easy to drink Owen's beer, shout in his face, and stomp off into the darkening evening without a glance backward. From what little Owen could see of Violette's face, her look was one of contemplation rather than anger.

"Not the first to make a fool, no." Violette placed a corner of her matching message box on the table, held it in place with the tip of her index finger. The gentle force from her thumb spun the box in lazy pirouettes. "The first Spellseeker to try and arrest a fellow Seeker? A first in my eight years here, yes."

"Ugh, gods above," Owen sighed as his forehead met the table. The force made the empty glass jump. Violette lost her precarious hold on her message box, which fell with a hollow clatter. "I don't understand. I have been here for almost a month. I'm already working out in the field on my own. Why haven't I been introduced to the other Seekers? Apart from Seeker Aaron, the only other active Seeker I've been introduced to is the one I incapacitated. That wouldn't have happed if I'd known my fellow Seekers. Is it too much to ask?"

"You're Lost and Stolen. Not much need to know folks from other departments if you stick to your duties."

"To push papers, you mean?"

"You wanted my advice?" Violette's lolled over to cast a crooked look at Owen. Thin, brown eyebrows arched high in question. A moment passed before she sniffed at Owen's silence. "Do you?"

"Yes," Owen mumbled. The words were spoken into crossed arms that rested on the table. Owen had tucked his face into the shelter of his elbows.

"Akheem doesn't like the idea of you."

"Hah!" A snort accompanied Owen's laugh from within his pitiful fortress of shame. "You don't say?"

"The *idea* of you," Violette continued after smashing a clenched fist into Owen's shoulder. "Arnstead is your first professional crossing. A look through the First Seeker's service records doesn't show any mention of a Raulstone, at least not on the surface, so it's not you or your family."

"Through his service records? When did you—"

"It's been a busy day. Needed to make sure there wasn't a conflict of interest between you and Akheem. My job is to make sure you can do yours. If he's going to be on your case, it has to be for good reason.

"Anyways," Violette continued, "no sign of a grudge. My guess, then, is that he doesn't like the idea of a Seeker with limitations."

"One that can't concentrate well enough to manifest a spell, you mean."

"Yes, that. Your Concentration Deficit. Speaking of firsts, you *are* the first Seeker I've seen with that notation on their record."

"Quite the black mark, huh?" Owen slid his arms far enough apart to cast a questioning look at Violette. Her hawk-like attention was focused elsewhere. A raised hand beckoned for a server. The agitation on Violette's face suggested she had been locked in this pursuit since Owen had hidden away. "I'm a bit surprised you never said anything. About the deficit."

"You passed your tests. How long it took you, and the surrounding circumstances, are not my problem. Plenty of business for a Seeker to handle besides chasing crooks down dark alleyways."

A short exchange with a harn server distracted Violette from her line of thought. Two glasses, overflowing with an amber ale, were firmly planted on the table before the Zumbatran left. Violette pressed one of the glasses against Owen's arms before taking a deep gulp from her own. There was no rush in her this time. The glass was back on the table after two swigs. Violette thumbed away a spot of foam from her upper lip before she continued to speak.

"Maybe not what you want to hear, but you're actually well suited for work in Lost and Stolen. Most Seekers out here look at the department as a stepping stone."

"Seeker Aaron said as much," Owen said. He had lifted his head high enough to partake in the ale, sipping lightly at it. "Said folks change departments as soon as their probation is up. Once they've gotten familiar with the town."

"That's about the size of it. Aaron gets a Seeker up to speed just in time for them to abandon Lost and Stolen. I think that's part of why Akheem doesn't like the idea of having you around."

"How do you mean?"

"Well," Violette grunted, "let me give you some insight." She took another swing and squared her chair to face Owen. "The First Seeker oversees some dangerous territory. I'm sure I don't need to tell you how bad the turnover is for your kind in these parts."

"Mortality rate of fifty-seven percent," Owen chimed. "For Seekers assigned to Arnstead, I mean."

"Did your homework. Good. The trouble is that the Bureau continues to rule Arnstead as a township, despite how fast it's growing. That keeps our minimum staffing requirements for the departments low. Violent Offenses, for example, has a minimum staffing requirement of four Seekers."

"*Four?*" Owen choked on his beer as much as the word. "It's a department of twelve, isn't it? How did it get so big?"

"Akheem's favorite loophole. A department that meets minimum requirements cannot actively seek out new personnel. However, no regulation prohibits a Seeker to willingly transfer between departments, so long as both department heads approve."

"So Lost and Stolen is Arnstead's revolving door?"

"Makes it hard for Akheem to get more Seekers into other departments if the open slot in Lost and Stolen doesn't stay open."

"What, you think I want to stay in Lost and Stolen?" Owen said, pointing a finger to himself. "Who says I want to stay?"

"Who says any of the other department heads would take you? A Spellseeker who can't cast spells. Even if Aaron wanted to get rid of you, one of the other heads would have to accept you."

"Are you saying the First Seeker won't force them to?"

"Not his choice. The department heads get the final say on all transfers. If they get their toes stepped on, they'll raise the flag to Central. Besides," Violette started before downing the last of her drink, "you heard it from

182

Akheem's mouth. He's already resigned to you staying in Lost and Stolen. Not that he has to be happy about it."

"You don't think he'd try to force me out?"

"Like I said, department heads —"

"No, not from Lost and Stolen." Owen shook his head. His head had grown full with all the information Violette was dumping into his lap. Between her and the steady flow of alcohol, it had become difficult to keep track of which thoughts were in his head and which he had said aloud. "From the Bureau. That he'd try to get my certifications revoked to get me out. Or maybe set me up for another big mistake, or…"

"Or get you killed?"

Violette finished the thought that Owen struggled to speak aloud. It had not entered his mind before now. Repercussions for the day's events had, to Owen, both started and stopped at being condemned to a career in Lost and Stolen. Long days of meaningless toil for minimal recognition. He would be yelled at for the rest of his life. Screamed at. Things would be thrown in fury, at him as often as past him. Death was new.

The idea of death was nothing new. Owen had grappled with the idea of dying in the line of duty ever since receiving his assignment. That he might meet his end in pursuit of a dangerous criminal was not a new consideration. That his end might come as he served as a shield for some innocent child was no strange thought.

For the first time, Owen came to the sickening revelation that his dutiful death might not be valiant. A stranger's knife in his back, paid for by someone that Owen knew, seemed bitterly possible. Thoughts rushed through Owen's mind faster than he could combat them. *How much does it cost to have a Seeker killed? Would it be the First Seeker that pays? One of the Violent Offenses Seekers? Would they do it themselves? Could I stand against them? Should I resign?*

"Not going to happen." The firm words were accompanied by an equally firm grip on Owen's shoulder. Violette's piercing blue caught Owen's gaze and held it. "My job is to make sure you can do yours. Got it?"

Violette's grounding touch slowed the morbid assault Owen led against himself, as well as the pace of his heart. He raised his glass in a toast to Violette Woods. She returned the gesture, one corner of her mouth raised in a pained smile.

12.

HALLOWED GROUND

A motion was the first sensation to return. Something very much like motion. The world seemed to spin. Not that Owen could see this motion. His eyelids remained shut against the fear of harsh morning light. Curious fingers clutched at the warm sheets that enveloped him, then down to the mattress atop which he was nestled. A pat on the chest and shoulders confirmed that he was not swirling about. All signs pointed to a bed that perfectly sedentary and ready for more sleep.

His head disagreed.

Owen tossed from his right shoulder onto his left. From his left shoulder onto his back, then flopped over to rest face down on the bed. There was no escape from the sensation. He felt as if he were being sucked down a drain that never cleared. Around and around, he circled, but was never quite pulled all the way through. A perpetual tugging at the back of his head refused to relent.

Morning's light was harsher than expected. When Owen opened his eyes, defeated, at last, it was not for long. Shafts of light cut through the small gaps between the curtains and the window. A groan creaked out from Owen's dry throat as he clamped his pillow over his head. His swollen tongue ran over teeth encrusted with the previous night's mistakes.

The room continued to spin.

Minutes of bitter struggle against the morning whirled past with no sign of improvement. Giving up on the prospect of further rest, Owen swung his feet over the bed and was surprised to see that he still wore his socks. And his work trousers. And his Spellseeker coat.

"Saves me the time, I suppose," Owen grumbled. He clapped his hands twice against his cheeks and tucked into the washroom across the hall. After a splash of water on his face and a quick effort to clean and rinse his mouth, Owen made his way through the Orland house to its conservative dining room.

Intimate was the one word, above all others, that described Cynthia Orland's dining room. Two doors led into the room, one from the hall and another from the kitchen. The walls were free of windows to ward away inquisitive glances. Landscapes of the New World's western frontier adorned three of the four walls. The fourth was decorated with a cityscape of Andrasta. Gleaming, warped towers grasped at the sun like ancient oaks, while smaller buildings clamored for what little light reached them at the city's floor.

Furniture was sparse following the owner's taste. A wooden chair sat on each edge of a small, square table. Black velvet cushioned the seat and back of each chair, their feet carved into the likeness of a wolf's paws. The table had no such intricacies. It merely served to house plates, glasses, and, for those who particularly comfortable, elbows.

Much to Owen's surprise, the table had been set for two that morning. He had grown accustomed over the past week to Cynthia having breakfasted and left the house before he ever woke. Today was different. Cynthia sat in the chair furthest from the hallway door. With a fresh edition of the morning newspaper in hand, she read as she munched on a slice of jam-smeared toast. The black robe she wore, laced here and there with crimson, gave Owen the impression she had not been awake for long.

"Morning, cousin," she said, flashing a quick look over the crest of her papers. The hand bearing her toast waved its little finger. "Take a seat. Marcus! Owen's risen from the dead, at last."

"Yes, ma'am," came the servant's muffled reply from the kitchen.

"You seem awful relaxed," Owen croaked as he pulled out the chair across from Cynthia and sat. "The dust on your tracks is normally settled by the time I'm here. Expecting a slow day at the bank?"

"I should hope so," Cynthia replied. Her tone was playful, tempered with disbelief. "Bank's closed on Sunday. A busy day would mean something bad for business."

"Ah-h-h, Sunday." The chair groaned as Owen eased back in realization. "Completely forgotten."

"Seems so, bluebell," Cynthia laughed. She was peaking around her papers to look at Owen in his Spellseeker blues. "You want to go get changed? Have a proper Sunday morning with me?"

"I don't think so. Should probably visit the office today, Sunday or not."

"Really now? Didn't expect it was *that* bad."

"What do you mean?"

"Let's just say I heard you coming home last night before I saw you."

"Sorry," Owen replied, shaking his head, "still don't follow you."

"And you don't even remember?" Cynthia folded her papers forward so she could see her cousin. Her eyebrows arched so high they seemed to be flying away. "I hear singing outside, well past midnight. A sorry attempt at what I assume must be Eastpointe's anthem. Something about justice and what not. Then you come stumbling through the door on some woman's shoulder, point down the hallway, and say, 'The bed is that way, madame!'"

"I did not," Owen gasped. His eyes grew so wide they might have popped out of his skull. A hand wandered up to cover his slack-jawed mouth.

"Oh, you certainly did," Cynthia laughed. "Not a minute later, the woman comes back down the hall, tells me she's put you to bed, then just... strolls out into the night!"

Owen ran his hands over his crinkling brow and through hair, which he had not bothered to wash. Knotted strands broke apart from each other, his fingers a plow that churned the brown waves. The fact that he had not bothered to trim his hair since leaving Southport was a fleeting thought. It held no candle to the immense embarrassment that Cynthia was shoveling at his feet.

To stand square in the path of the Violent Offenses department was not enough for drunk Owen. *No,* Owen thought to himself, *drunk Owen knew only how to exacerbate problems. Drunk Owen insisted on inconveniencing the one person at the Arnstead Arcanarium that made any show of useful support. Drunk Owen got so out of hand that Violette had to walk him home and tuck him into bed like a sick child.*

The sound of a glass being placed on the table lifted Owen's head from between his hands. Marcus had placed a tall, thin cup of something in front of Owen. The gray-gold katarl gave a nod of encouragement, set down a plate of toast and jam next to the glass, and turned back towards the kitchen.

"What is that?" Owen asked after Marcus.

"Juice, sir. You're welcome."

"Right, thank you," Owen replied to the servant's thinly veiled admonition. "Umm, may I ask why it's... orange?"

"Of course, sir." Marcus' tone evened out in response to Owen's politeness. "Carrots. Mixed with ginger and apple, to help remedy last night's revelries."

Cynthia snorted, now back behind her bastion of weekly news.

"Ah," Owen nodded. "Of course."

To see the door of the Arnstead Arcanarium closed was a welcome sight. As with any other Bureau facility, doors were closed to the public on Sundays. This meant the usual sneers and jeers were nowhere to be found as Owen approached the building. Those who would be lined up to sling abuses were busy with other matters around town. Some would be peddling wares, others plying their trades, while others still might be clustered inside the House of Many for Sunday prayers.

What these denizens of Arnstead were doing at the moment was of no concern to Owen. The fact that they did not stand between him and the Arcanarium doors was enough to raise a contented smile. The doors gave way to Owen as he presented his badge. Crimson light was replaced by ethereal blue as he stepped inside, closing the door behind himself.

Silence.

So quiet was the Arcanarium's lobby that Owen could hear the clocks adorning each wall tick out of sync. The empty queue coiled up to the vacant reception counter like shed snake skin. Not even Sam sat at their place behind the counter. Owen had half expected to see them there, having never seen the person move from that spot. He had developed the unreasonable suspicion that Sam was bound to the desk in some way and unable to leave.

Owen moved with a leisurely stride along the right-hand wall of the lobby. There was no rush today. No expectation for him to be here at the office, to be doing anything that remotely resembled work. Each lazy fall of his iron-heeled boots against the wooden floor filled the entire lobby.

Leaving the lobby and entering the main hallway, Owen's steps became quieter and gentler. It was a concerted effort. Anyone who might have business in the Arcanarium's lobby would likely have no business with him. Owen had no interactions with Sam. To have seen them would have been little more than brief displeasure, soon whisked away as he left the room. The same could not be said for the doors lining the hall.

It was on the tips of his toes that Owen walked past Violette's door. No amount of carrot juice, or time, for that matter, would prepare Owen for his next encounter with his handler. Part of him thought it might be best to get the awkward discussion of last night's events over and done with. The other, greater part of him was already halfway down the hall before allowing his heels to touch the floor. *Another day,* he thought as he passed the door to Violent Offenses.

There was another confrontation he did not look forward to. Though he had only met a single member of the Violent Offenses department, Owen was confident that he had made enemies of the whole lot. The department had more Seekers than any other two departments combined. The department responsible for dealing with the darkest, most brutal people a Seeker might encounter in the line of duty. Just passing the door made Owen feel a touch sick to his stomach.

Chitra Possummay, Third Seeker.

The words were engraved next to Violent Offenses' second door. They caught Owen's attention, caused him to hesitate before the door. He wondered what it meant to be assigned to the first room or the second. Did one crew handle individuals while the other dealt with organized violence? Perhaps the first room full of hardened veterans, and the second room housed transfers eager to cut their teeth? Maybe the two rooms were connected by some passage that made the separate doors irrelevant?

In that brief moment, Owen realized how little he knew about the place he worked. Beyond the fact that he barely needed a second hand to count the number of coworkers he could recognize by face. The other offices remained a mystery to him. With how much Lost and Stolen varied the offices of the First Seeker and Violette, there was no telling what the other rooms might look like. He tried not to dwell on the thought. Whatever chance there had been of observing other departments before had now evaporated.

A pair of deep breaths helped quell the anxious rise of thought. Remembering his purpose, Owen continued down to the end of the hallway.

As Owen drew close to Lost and Stolen, little more than an arm's length away, he noticed something: a noise. Unlike the lobby, Owen had been the sole source of noise in the hallway. His breath was all that had stirred the air, his boots all that had disturbed the silence. From inside Lost and Stolen, however, came a scratching sound. A familiar scratching sound, at that.

"Someone there?" Owen rapped his knuckles on the doorframe as he spoke. The door, already ajar, opened without resistance.

"Oh!" A supremely startled Second Seeker Aaron shot up from his seat. Long, floppy ears stood tall as twin flagpoles. Whatever papers the harn had in front of him scattered themselves into the office's vague excuse for corners. Wild eyes calmed when they fell on Owen's inquisitive face. "Ah, good to see you, Owen. Hadn't expected to see anyone else in the office today."

"I see that, sir. Apologies for startling you."

"Nonsense," the harn scoffed. "Just as much your office as mine. Used to being the only soul in the building on Sundays, is all."

Of the few people Owen might have expected to see in the Arcanarium on Sunday, Seeker Aaron was the last. The state of the office, Owen felt, should have been clear enough a statement on the subject. Yet here Aaron was, plopped behind his makeshift desk on the one legitimate day of rest to be expected in a week.

"What has you in the office today, sir?" Owen asked.

"The same thing as you, I imagine," Aaron chuckled. "Always something to be done in this office. Reception may not hear complaints on Sundays, but they sure do make up for it during the week. Come on and have a seat then."

Owen found it difficult to believe that Seeker Aaron came to the Arcanarium that day because he had destroyed his career prospects the day prior. The Second Seeker's efforts seemed more the type to present an image of staying afloat despite a welling backlog that would make a beaver blush. An attempt to make it look like he was the man to lead the team, to keep the cushy seat afforded to a do-nothing department like Lost and Stolen.

Whatever the Second Seeker's motives were behind his Sunday attendance, and whether Owen had guessed correctly, was of no real consequence. The two were here together. *Might as well make the best of it,* Owen thought. He nodded, said 'sir', and pulled over as pristine a box as he could find to sit on.

It did not take long for Owen to realize he was a disruptive presence for his superior. Glances were sly at first, signaled by a brief pause in Seeker Aaron's scribbles. Owen had thought these to be interruptions for thought or to check the time at first. There was no telling how long Seeker Aaron had been there, or how long he planned to stay. Could have been that he had popped into the office to kill time before a lunch engagement.

The glances became stares as time went on. Seeker Aaron would pause, look up to Owen with mouth slightly agape, then look back to his papers with a shake of the head.

"Something you would like to say, sir?" Owen ventured, tired of pretending he had noticed his superior's looks.

"Hmm? What's that?" The Second Seeker turned his head from side to side. He made a great show of the effort as if there was anyone else in the room Owen could have been speaking to. Owen had not bothered to look up. He kept his eyes focused on the OCF in his lap. When Seeker Aaron spoke again, the brightness that had been in his voice earlier was gone. "I was… was just wondering, I suppose."

"Wondering what, sir?"

Awkward silence gripped at Seeker Aaron's throat. Words struggled to leap from his chest out through his mouth. It was difficult to tell whether it was the choice of words with which he struggled or the act of saying those that he had chosen. Limp hand gestures failed to push the conversation further. A hand wandered behind the harn's head and began to scratch at the back of his neck.

"It's all right, sir," Owen sighed. "You don't have to say anything. What's done is done."

"How about we get some air?" Seeker Aaron responded after a sigh of his own. "Put together a few urgent OFCs this morning, could use following-up on sooner rather than later. Up for a walk?"

"Of course, sir," Owen nodded with a feigned grin.

Packing their business was a quick affair. Due to Owen's surprise at seeing Seeker Aaron, he had not bothered to take off his coat or sword belt. He had but to file away the handful of OFCs that he had completed. It was a small handful of documents. Little time had passed between Owen's arrival and the Second Seeker's decision to hit the streets.

Seeker Aaron's preparation was as quick as usual. He had a bundle of OFCs bound and ready to go. The harn snapped his suspenders over his shoulders as he stood, then tucked his long ears back under a brown, wide-brimmed hat. A couple of light steps, clipboard tucked under his left arm, and he was around his desk and out the door of Lost and Stolen. Another pair of lengthy strides put the harn just under one of the windows that led into the Arcanarium's alleyway.

"We can take the front door, sir," Owen called after Aaron. "Sunday and all."

"Hah, too right. Old habits and all that."

The disquiet of unspoken words followed the pair of Seekers as they walked the streets of Arnstead. Pleasantries were made when appropriate. They excused themselves when they got in the other's way or bumped into one another. Simple words. Phrases worn beyond meaning and uttered out of habit rather than with purpose. Unwillingness to speak on the previous day's events walked between them like a specter, whose steps wrought a bitter chill.

When they arrived at their first location, a crumbling hut on the southern tip of Oldstead, Owen extended his hand to receive the respective OCF document. Rather than provide the clipboard or papers, Aaron strode up to the door himself and knocked gently on a door that looked ready to fall from its hinges. The Second Seeker flashed a polite smile over his shoulder before the residents answered the door.

Watching Seeker Aaron perform verification work felt something adjacent to wrong. It was a duty the harn had only made example of twice before handing the reigns over to Owen. The casual tone with which the harn spoke, how he leaned against the doorframe. How little effort Aaron put in redirecting the claimant when their conversation shifted from a stolen water pump to which types of fish were biting in the nearby rivers this week. Professionalism, judging from Aaron's display, was a complete mystery to the man.

As his superior meandered through confirming sections of an OCF, Owen noticed something. Not something that manifested throughout the discussion or a clever turn of phrase that sprouted from nowhere. What Owen noticed was an absence; the human who had filed the complaint had not sworn at Aaron a single time.

Agitation was present during the confirmation of every OCF in Owen's limited experience. Even the kindest people he had serviced showed some manner of discontent. A tired sigh when Owen did not have a specific date of resolution to promise. Threats to raise additional complaints to some higher authority within the Bureau. Promises of broken windows and shattered bones. There had always been some level of aggression shoved his way. Without exception.

Lucky break, Owen reassured himself. *Finds the one carefree soul in the whole town. I'll have to note the address.*

191

The dour humor with which Owen placated himself was drained of its bite when the next call showed similar results. The claimant, an already bitter-looking Nirdac harn missing half of an ear, warmed to Seeker Aaron like a tippler to a fresh bottle. What started as a forbidding grimace had melted into a familial grin by the time the two were discussing how best to layer the contents of a sandwich.

Luck was not limited to these two initial calls. Of the next four calls the pair made, they left three of the claimants with smiles on their faces and the light of confidence in their eyes. The fourth claimant was left holding their sides in laughter as Seeker Aaron chuckled through his farewell.

Harsh rays from the noon sun entrenched Owen further into his troubled disbelief. Following the harn from corner to corner across Oldstead, head bare against heat that drenched his neck and underarms in sweat. The heavy Spellseeker coat that Owen insisted on wearing hung heavy on his shoulders.

Sore, cramped feet called out for a moment of respite that he would not allow himself. Competition blazed within Owen even as the sun burned from above. Whether it was one final call or another hundred to be made, he would not be made a fool of by the portly harn that seemed to waddle from house to house. Aches and pains could be pushed down. His time at Eastpointe had taught him as much. What he could not forget, could not repress, would be defeat at the hands of someone so far beneath himself.

"Last call, I think. Before we grab some lunch."

The Second Seeker's words snapped Owen away from his dark reflections. A small pit of shame formed in Owen's stomach when he saw Aaron's conciliatory expression awaiting an answer. He wiped the sweat from the back of his neck, sniffed at the dust-ridden air.

"Sounds lovely, sir."

"Right, then. In we go!"

Owen picked his head up for the first time in what felt like hours, his neck resisting the efforts with all its sinew, to see he stood before the white walls of the House of Many. It felt a fitting place to end the first portion of their day. Faint bells had marked the passage of time. At times their call had been a weak chime on the wind. When closer, the call of the hour became a booming proclamation. More than a match for the clocktowers of Southport or New Haven.

Midday mass was drawing to a close when the pair entered the main chamber. The priests of Arnstead flanked the podium, where a man in unfamiliar clothing spoke to the silent pews. People were packed shoulder to shoulder. So full were the pews that some had been relegated to standing at the back of the chamber near the entryway. These inconvenienced folks showed no visible distress. They stood shrouded in contemplation as they soaked in the words of the speaker.

Lucina seemed to be the topic of the day's sermon. Bits and pieces rose to the edge of Owen's awareness. Something about the construction of a glittering tower back in the Old World. A place of power erected before the Upheaval shook the foundations of the world. The suggestion that a single man built the tower in a week, with little more than a nearby quarry and a hammer gifted by the Builder herself.

Most of the talk passed Owen by. He had nothing against the idea of the gods or their practices. Far from it, knowing they had played a role in saving his life on the ride to Arnstead. The Many had little influence on his life before then, was all. His most vivid memories of anything related to the House was his grandfather's general detest for the institution. That, and the nagging thought at the back of his mind every time he saw Cynthia. Pointless conjecture about what might have been her fate if not for grandfather Orland's hate. Whether or not his cousin might still have both her legs.

The snap of a book sent Owen's dark thoughts skittering back from whence they had crawled. Members of the congregation began to rise. Blessings were shared between neighbors. 'Have a blessed day', 'May the Many watch over you.' Praise was spoken in the names of each of the gods in turn as the gathering filed out of the pews and spilled out from the House onto the streets of Oldstead.

What blessings the congregation had to share amongst themselves were withheld from Owen as they passed. Evil eyes had become the norm whenever he wore his Seeker blues. The sheer number of grimaces and sneers that enveloped him now was overwhelming. Concentrated disgust like he had yet to experience, compounded by the not-so-gentle thrum of a hangover on its way out. Owen raised his eyes above the flow of people and did his best to acknowledge as little of the hate as possible.

Against what felt to be his best judgment, he allowed himself a sidelong glance at Aaron. An imperfect view. The dense crowd made it difficult to spot the harn. Not so dense that it was impossible to make out a smile and the occasional wave to a familiar face among the congregation.

The people wrapped around and between the Seekers as they went by as water that flows between a pair of sandbars. One island was small, inoffensive to those who noticed. The other was a tumor. Not a place to moor a vessel, but one upon which to dump refuse. Mothers would warn their sons and daughters of places like these. That dirty islets such as these were best left undiscovered. Dirty looks and dirty words had begun at last to make Owen *feel* dirty.

Once the flow of bodies begun to thin, the man leading the day's sermon took notice of Owen and Aaron. What had barely been a glance was redoubled into a confused stare. The expression seemed to be one of confusion, at least. Arnstead's House was a large one. Though Owen's eyes were not poor, it was difficult to be sure of the man's exact expression from the other side of the chamber.

A heated approach left little doubt in Owen's mind that the man was no more pleased to see a Spellseeker than any four of his flock combined. Purple robes, trimmed with red and gold, whispered over the marbled stone floor. His back was straight, his head tilted forward with anticipation.

"What's this, then?" the man sneered, stopping an arm's length from Owen. The man's fingers knit together, palms facing upwards, to form the Many's principal gestures before folding both arms tight across his chest. Silver rings on either hand housed sapphires and emeralds of various sizes. "The Bureau is welcome in the House by appointment. I have not been made aware of such an occasion."

"Pontiff Isaac, I presume?"

Aaron was able to get the short question out before Owen had time to formulate a retort. Likely for the best. The wave of contempt Owen had experienced as the congregation left the House had brought him near to seething. *Sounds like we are not welcome then,* was where Owen had landed. He allowed the remark to die in his throat.

"You would be correct, child," the Pontiff said. Hair that was more gray than black jostled as the man turned his attention down to the harn. Unlike the members of the congregation, the Pontiff's white, creased features did not soften. "And I presume the two of you are here together?"

"Spot on," Aaron chimed. "This one is with me. Came to follow up on a report we received. Any chance you could point us to a… Rajani Basak?"

"The caretaker?" Pontiff Isaac uttered the title with impatient surprise.

"That would make a heap of sense. Claims mention something about unrest in the catacombs. Some missing—"

"Enough. You there," the pontiff called, one narrow finger pointed at a nearby acolyte. "Find Rajani. Summon her here, where our guests will be *waiting.*"

Fierce command propelled the pontiff's final word at the pair of Seekers. There would be no room for doubt in the man's intent. To suffer their presence in the House was more than he desired. They were to step no further into the home of the gods without supervision. The young acolyte, Nirdac katarl with an orange coat, sped away from bucket and brush to comply with his master's command.

"Hyperios help me," the pontiff muttered as he turned to leave Owen and Aaron. "Can nobody in this backwater House do their damned job without..." His words trailed off as the pontiff made his way to the back of the chamber, eventually disappearing through a doorway.

"Couldn't wait to be gone, that one." Aaron tapped Owen's leg as he spoke. Mischief played across the harn's face. "Imagine he's a fun one to dine with."

"Couldn't say, sir."

A sharp pang of jealousy prodded Owen. There were few things he would have loved more at that moment than to walk away from the harn without repercussion. Aaron's words repeated themselves over and again in his mind. *This one is with me.* The sort of thing a person says about a dog that's broken its leash and torn through a garden.

Might as well have a leash, Owen brooded.

Tense body language was clear enough a signal to Aaron. Pursed lips pushed up his left cheek as he turned from Owen to find a seat on the vacated pews. If there was no conversation to be had, the harn seemed content to rest his large feet.

Relief, slight but sweet, washed over Owen. He had dodged another attempt at forced dialogue. The mental fortitude required to maintain his image of indifference had begun to outpace his reserves. Clenched fists unwound with concerted effort. His toes no longer clawed at the soles of his boots, attempting to dig through leather in search of more solid purchase. Tension melted throughout five breaths. In through the nose, then pushed slowly through dry, cracked lips.

No longer rooted in place, Owen followed Aaron's lead and took a seat on a nearby pew. His choice of seat was across the aisle from Aaron's and two rows back. Owen sank onto the bench until his head could rest on the rounded edge of the backrest. Another couple of deep breaths, in through the nose and out through the mouth, helped ease his eyelids shut.

The western wall caught Owen's attention when he felt ready to open his eyes to the world again. Specifically, the windows. The afternoon sun shone through the stained-glass stories of the gods and their heroes. Damarae sacrificed herself in a ruby shower of blood to birth gorgons of emerald green. Stars glimmered like fireflies in a sapphire sky as Sisir led the great explorer Ibattua to the shores of the New World. Their reflections danced across the marble floor as the sun shimmered with dreadful heat.

More stories availed themselves of the sun's light. A total of six magnificent windows lined the western wall, all paying homage to some great deed or other. Another six lined the eastern wall. Only those two of Damarae and Sisir were familiar to Owen though without much thought. The gods themselves were easy enough to decipher, but the details of their stories were lost. Passage of time had claimed most of what little he knew of their tales.

Lack of knowledge did not dimmish appreciation of their beauty. The windows were just as much a marvel to Owen's tired, frustrated eyes as they were to the most devout among the House's congregation. *How long did it take to make these awesome murals?* he wondered. *How many people came together to craft a single window?* These were the first instances of stained-glass Owen had ever encountered in person. An Old World form of expression encountered at the edge of the civilized world.

Tired feet called for attention. Now able to rest, their aches and pains became more present. They had time to complain while no longer on duty. A position that Owen envied. Though his throbbing headache was on the way out, it still made its presence known while his thoughts lacked focus. Closing his eyes against the nagging sensation only increased its presence. Punishment for yet another of the litany of mistakes he made the day prior.

Can't imagine Becca would be pleased, he thought with an internal groan. They had been her last words to him in person. A warning against drowning himself in liquor and beer. Especially if the cause was some manner of bad news. An attempt to drown his misery under a river of alcohol. Her caution rang clear with every thump of his headache, her words of caution the clapper to a bell of self-inflicted misery. *Was always right, she was. Somehow.*

Sandaled feet signaled the slow approach of a priest. Their measured pace was noticed just before they had reached Aaron's pew. Owen cracked an eye open, with much effort and twice as much displeasure, to see a familiar figure. Her name had not drawn any recognition itself. The tall frame, tall even for a Bangeli katarl, was another matter and harder to forget. Narrow, slitted pupils glowered at Owen from green eyes. Rajani, Priest of Manus, had not forgotten Owen.

"Come to us, in uniform, on the day of rest?" Her tone was dismissive, the way one talks to a long-forgotten friend that has come begging for coin. "What have you managed to break this time? Should I send for Ryleah?"

Owen allowed his open eye to slide closed. For a moment, he pondered with a furrowed brow as to why he continued to receive such abuse on a Sunday. All he had to do was walk out the door with a vague salute. Tea in the garden awaited his presence, as did the soft embrace of an afternoon nap. The thoughts faded like an acrid puff of smoke taken away by a warm wind as he stood.

"Official business this time, ma'am." An officious air surrounded Owen as he pulled himself up, straightened his arms against his sides. "My superior has the details. Related to a previously filed claim with the Lost and Stolen department."

Silence filled the air between Owen and the priest. The look that danced across her face was a familiar one. Almost every claimant Owen had dealt with made the same series of expressions or some permutation of them. Disgust at the uniform became confusion, followed by a brief moment of recollection, then the realization that whatever had been lost or stolen had been so for so long that the claimant had forgotten the case altogether. Some people had their claim closer to the front of mind than others, but the process was near-universal.

Rajani's eyes jumped from Owen down to Aaron as her memory availed her. Flared nostrils indicated that the katarl did not like what she was looking at. Owen followed her gaze to find that Aaron, the infallible Second Seeker of the Lost and Stolen department, had fallen asleep where he sat. Owen's eyes reached for the top of his skull as he suppressed a growl.

"Seeker Aaron," Owen called. Not quite a shout, but loud enough to draw the attention of the clergy members going about their business. It was enough to do the trick. The harn started with a violent thrash. A quick look

197

from the walls, to Owen, then to Rajani seemed to bring Aaron back to reality.

"Ah, you must be Rajani," Aaron grunted as he forced himself to stand. Small hands straightened built-up folds in his shirt. Ears that had popped up on reflex flattened back behind Aaron's head. He bent over to retrieve the hat that his ears had launched into the air. "Caretaker for the catacombs?"

"I am."

The katarl knit her hands together in the House's traditional greeting. It must have been a motion of reflex, Owen thought. The same way that he salutes Aaron when coming or going. Though less aggressive, her countenance remained far from what would be considered welcoming or warm.

Aaron showed no sign of concern. He hardly seemed to notice that the woman he addressed was nearly three times his size. As with any other claimant, he produced his clipboard and began to take notes as he spoke.

"Excellent! I am grieved to hear of your plight here," Aaron waved the clipboard at Rajani. "Terrible business you've reported. Just to make sure, broad strokes, the catacombs are not at rest?"

"To put it mildly, yes."

"And if we were to put it less mildly?"

"I wouldn't typically call for the Bureau," Rajani sighed. "But we have a severe shortage of Keepers. More than anything, I just need for you to help confirm whether there's Flow involved or not. If I need a Keeper, or…"

She trailed off, making an off-hand gesture towards Aaron and Owen. Agitation hung from every word the katarl spoke. Natural movement evaded her. When not speaking or pointing, she was wrapped in absolute stillness. A statue of some holy figure from days gone by. It was clear that Rajani wanted the pair of Seekers gone just as much as Owen wished to leave. Likely more so.

"Well, no worries there." Scribbles filled the heavy air between Aaron's speech. Each harsh scratch of the pencil against paper grated against the group's collective patience. "Here to help. As much as we can. So, what exactly is going on downstairs?"

Rajani drew closer before speaking. A few quiet, deliberate steps to allow for a hushed tone.

"Offerings are going missing." The katarl's eyes flitted from left to right, then back to Aaron. "Tokens for the departed. No sign of where they've gone, or how they were taken. Nor of how the thief managed to enter the catacombs. I prefer to think some cretin used the Flow to sneak their way in, but fear something may have grown restless."

"And when you say *something*, you mean—"

"Something dead."

Infectious dread poured out from Rajani. What had once been a stoic visage with trappings of disgust was now the very face of distress. Change of this magnitude, so sudden and with the most minor provocation, brought with it a primal fear. The sort of innate terror that sends gooseflesh crawling over a body.

Owen was not immune to this change. The accustomed routine had been thrown to the side of the road. Before he realized it, his body had broken its stand at attention and leaned closer to the priest. Eagerness to know more swirled with the gloom that would accompany the knowledge. He was spared the affliction of goosebumps, but the fine hairs on his forearms began to prickle.

"I can block the dead," Rajani continued. Her voice adopted a nearly imperceptible tremor. "Turn them away if their will is weak. But I am no warrior. My place is to guide the passage from life to death and to care for the remains of the departed. I lack the skills to quell the restless and the time to learn them. I pray these skills will not be needed."

Those last words bore a vulnerable plea. A request that rode on a building urgency in Rajani's voice. Righteous indignation felt a distant memory in the face of the katarl's newfound sincerity. Clenched fists shook as she spoke. The act of calling for the Bureau of Arcane's aid must have felt like a defeat in her mind.

All this rising tension fueled Owen's desire to know more. Here was a plight worth the time of a Spellseeker. A priest of Manus, a disciple of life and death, feared for the safety of her House. So great was her terror that she would invoke the aid of an institution for which she and her clergy bore such obvious contempt.

Owen knew little of death and what lay beyond. He had yet to know the death of a family member. One that he truly knew, at least. Not some distant uncle or cousin that he knew only through stories or portraits hung in the Orland estate back in Southport. His closest encounter with death had been the brief flashes of Manda Galloway eviscerating the highwaymen that

199

attacked their coach. That felt like a lifetime ago, though in truth it had been a matter of weeks.

The secular nature of his upbringing had labeled death as a simple inconvenience that all must face. A matter of course. Once the time allotted you had expired, that's all there was to it. No place to go but the funeral pyre, then a short trip to wherever your bones might rest: a mausoleum for the well-off; a slot in the local catacombs for the average citizen; a plot of dirt for those who could scarcely afford the shovel. Mantras and songs of life after death were for the masses who failed to enjoy their time in life.

From such an upbringing, it was no wonder that Owen jumped at the idea of death. Bones fastened together by some angered soul who sought vengeance for sleights unpunished. Phantasmal beings inflicting the world of living with their malicious intentions through spite alone. Not the casual necromancy performed by channelers. Mere puppetry. This was the stuff of nightmares. From stories Cynthia would use to scare a young Owen in the uncertain dark of night.

"I pray your skills won't be needed, either," Aaron replied. His words were even and quiet. "And I pray that we can be of service."

"Can you defend yourself?"

"If needs be."

Aaron's fingers flicked and waved as if he were dancing a coin across them. There were no silver dollars to tumble back and forth. Instead, red and green sparks popped from his knuckles. The suggestion of fire. An odd mixture of colors produced licks of an unnatural flame. What joy and warmth had remained in the harn's face was drained away. Fierce determination took its place. It was a look as unnatural for Aaron as was the color of his flame.

It occurred to Owen that this was the first time he had seen Aaron channel the Flow for any purpose besides sneaking through one of the Arcanarium's windows. Practiced hands made the summoning of flame appear effortless. Of the handful of thoughts that cropped up from the display, one dominated Owen's mind. *Why would a person stuck in Lost and Stolen for so long be so proficient at making fire from nothing?* It was not as though Aaron had lit a match and manipulated the resulting fire. He had not even struck flint to steel and borrowed the sparks.

The display smothered any doubt Owen had possessed of the harn's skill with the Flow. Despite all appearance, there was something to be respected within the tubby ball of fluff. Owen still felt that Aaron was a joke of a Seeker, but now at least acknowledged him as a joke with some bite.

"And you?" Rajani said, turning to Owen. "You survived the Cinder Witch. I assume you have skill?"

"Some," Owen said with a nod. He placed his left hand pointedly on the hilt of his sword, his right on the grip of his caster pistol.

Rajani raised an eyebrow. Words came to her but seemed to die in her throat. She shook her head. With a great hand, she scratched at the nape of her neck.

"Simple steel might be enough for a thief, but it would not bite some of the things we might face. We may need things that burn," Rajani nodded to Aaron. "Things that corrode. Do you have anything like that?"

"I... let me think," Owen said. There was some absence in his words. His mind considered what he might be able to do to meet the priest's requirements. Fingers, suddenly desperate, rolled over each of his caster shells. The power to stun, to fire targeted wind, to cut through steel, and the last shell. Possibility after possibility flitted through his mind.

"Mr. Seeker?" Rajani asked, impatience taking seed in her voice.

"A moment," Owen pled, raising a hand to ward away her inquiry. "Just a moment. Let me—"

"It's all right, Owen," Aaron interrupted. "You've done enough for today. On Sunday, of all days. Go home and get some rest. I'm sure we have a long week ahead of us."

"I can help, sir. Allow me time to return to the Arcanarium. I can grab a few focuses from Collections that would useful, sir."

"Our good Rajani has waited long enough, I think. Her claim was filed earlier this week and got fast-tracked to me for review. Having spoken with her, time doesn't seem to be agreeable to us."

"But, sir!" Owen took a step forward. Open hands extended themselves to the harn. "Surely two would be better than one. Even if I was just to cover the rear, it would—"

"Already have two, Owen." Aaron gestured to Rajani, who raised her slumped shoulders in a show of reluctant pride.

"Three, then, sir," Owen protested. "Three would be better than two."

"You're relieved." Flat and gray, the words staked their claim on the marbled floors of the House of Many. Aaron held a firm gaze at Owen. "Whether you go home or visit Collections is your choice, but you will not be accompanying us to the catacombs. That's an order."

Limp hands fell to Owen's sides as the phrase rolled over him. The sheer weight of the words summoned by someone so small had stunned him. Owen had expected disappointment. To be ashamed to have an association with a Seeker so set on minding their own business, one who did their best not to cause a disturbance. A man who readily shirked the uniform of his post rather than face confrontation.

Fierce little eyes looked over Owen, from the tip of his boots to the top of his shaggy head. Aaron rested a hand on his round hip. Expectation was the expression he had settled on as he continued to watch Owen. What had been a watchful gaze slowly melted into a glare of indignation.

"Have I made myself clear, Seeker?"

Reflex took command of Owen's tired frame. His hunched back snapped to attention. One hand rose to salute while the other grafted itself to his thigh. Owen felt himself a clockwork toy soldier at that moment. Moved into position by the flip of a switch, all before he realized what had transpired. His feelings on the matter bore no merit on his actions.

"Sir!"

The verbal response came without own provocation. His body had accepted the command of his superior officer before his mind. Too tired to refute the matter, of course, Owen remained still in rigid acceptance.

Another scan from top to bottom, followed by a pointed nod, signed Aaron's approval. Maybe not approval. Perhaps closer to tolerance. A second look of confirmation after Aaron had turned and left with Rajani cemented the sense of suspicion. This one was softer, at least. Not a whip of a glare, but a slow rise of eyes from the floor up to meet Owen's valiant attempt at a resolute expression.

There were no words to be had in this parting of ways. The Second Seeker had said his piece and given his commands. Expression failed to materialize on Owen's tongue. Even if there had been words to share, to shout, they would not have escaped him. A bitter, impotent rage closed his throat against all manner of speech. The only sound he could manage was a frustrated grunt as Aaron and Rajani disappeared through a doorway at the back of the House.

Rooted in place, Owen stood as a pitiful monument to inaction and shame. Again, he was denied the opportunity to help those in need. Spellseeker duties had been deemed too dangerous for him. The tasks of the lowest department were above his capability.

I passed, Owen thought to himself. Ominous clouds of thunder and loathing wracked his brain. *I was certified. Every time I failed, I got up and tried again. I fought through all the jokes, and the snickering, and the sneers. I earned my coat. I* earned *my rank.*

It made no difference. Self-talk and inward praise did not clear the storm that brewed inside. Nostrils flared as the blackness poured down into his heart. Mad with hate, his heart pumped the poison through core and limb. Tension locked his muscles in place.

Owen fought against himself to lower his salute. He held the trembling hand out at shoulder height, open palm faced upwards. Joints creaked at the effort.

You're better than they say, he thought, looking inward. *You know you are. Find it!*

Amidst thrumming thunder shouted thoughts, Owen reached out for the Flow. Closed eyes saw the purple stream that crackled and popped. Terrible lightning to match his storm. The river of light pulsed at his presence heeded his call. Tendrils of purple light coiled towards him. An immortal snake that stretched the world over. Weaving back and forth, it felt its way to his hand.

There was no change to be seen when Owen opened his eyes. The clergy went about their business. Shafts of colored light poured in from the western windows. Damarae's emerald gorgons flitted across a marble canvas. Nothing betrayed the power that flowed through the world and into Owen's accepting grasp, but he felt it all the same.

The power is channeled. Now make your spell.

A new stillness overtook Owen. Rage and disgust coalesced into rapt anticipation. Sound fled the world around him, replaced by the hum of the Flow. The transference of the world's latent energy caused a vibration so deep that Owen felt it in his very bones. Power thrummed within him.

Anything, he prodded. *It can be anything. A fire!*

Fingers curled into a spider's death. Each digit quivered. The image of conjured fire rose to the front of Owen's mind. Bright, brilliant flames in lavender plumes.

Focus!

A single spark jumped from his palm and died in the air, leaving a purple and green memory.

That's it! I have it.

Two sparks.

I knew I have it. Eastpointe be damned. Father be damned!

Owen leaned forward as he waited for another spark that would not come.

Come on!

As Owen strained his wickedly bent fingers harder and harder still, the once vivid image of lilac fire dulled. The heat of the imagined pyre in his hand cooled to room temperature. Murmurs and shuffling of priests and acolytes filtered in through the thrum of the Flow. What had been the clearest spell Owen could remember to this point in his life faded into obscurity. The hope he feebly grasped after was nothing more than stagnant air.

"Gods damn it!" A sharp kick into the side of the nearest pew accompanied Owen's frenzied scream. He flung himself down onto the bench as his toes began to throb. "I almost had it. Always almost," Owen added after a pained pause.

Always almost.

A spell on the cusp of being cast. Perpetrators fled and were gone by slight misjudgment. Friends assigned together, but without him as the final link in the chain. Owen had never spoken the powerful words aloud.

Always almost.

A life lived at the edge of success. To always see the success of others and to never taste that sense of achievement for himself. Wealth and status afforded by his mother. Allowance to try and try again in the face of defeat, all a favor for his father. Dark truths shrouded in a veil of ignorance. The light could pierce that shield only when assisted by the blistering cold rays of an unbiased sun. Below the uncaring light of life could Owen's flaws be exposed in a way that he understood.

The weight of it all hung about his neck like an overlarge pendant of stone. Owen stretched his arms out over the pew before him, rested his head there against the collapse of his self-perception. A titter here and hiss of whisper there told him that sidelong glances were shot his way. *As they should*, he supposed. To blaspheme so carelessly in the House was sure to offend those who called the place their home.

What does it matter? Owen reasoned. The weight of his head had put his hands to sleep, jamming needles into each finger. *Can't imagine things growing worse. Messing this up any further would a noteworthy feat, I think.*

Boots sent an echo throughout the House as they marched in even step. A foreign sound in this House of shuffled whispers. Something solid to latch onto. The steps drew closer, and louder until they died at the far end of Owen's pew. He turned his head just enough to peep over his arms at the source of the noise.

"Bad timing, by the looks?"

"Hello, Devlin," Owen croaked, exposing a touch more of his face. Enough to solidify the Keeper's suspicion. "Sorry I haven't called on you. For tea."

"Nothing to worry about, my boy," Devlin replied. The rich voice was a soothing balm. An anointment of ignorance to Owen's seared soul. "I was not worried. There is much to be taken in once arrived in a new town. An old harn like me knows he rests at the bottom of the list."

"Hah!" Owen snorted into the crook of his elbow. "You have no idea."

The harn looked past both scoff and retort. With the same measured steps, he approached Owen's side.

"Care to indulge a Keeper's presence?"

Owen's face sunk back between his arms with a deep breath. He had stayed overlong in the House. It was less a knowledge of social graces, more that he could feel the piercing glares of the clergy who still suffered his occupancy of the pews. Their watch burned like daggers pulled fresh from a forge.

Still, Devlin had a way about him. The harn spoke with an unadulterated warmth that demanded attention. Greetings alone from the man were a hot cup of cider against a frigid winter's eve. Owen did not have the strength to resist such a kindly aura. With great effort, he pulled himself up to rest against the back of his seat and turned his head to face Devlin.

"I would be delighted."

Wood creaked as Devlin eased himself down next to Owen. Fully garbed in the mail and tabard of a Keeper of the House, even a harn could make sturdy craftsmanship take heed. A traveler's pack on the harn's shoulder played its part in bowing the bench. Across his lap lay a flanged mace, a new addition since their time together. Last of the new gear was a narrow heater shield cut to match Devlin's stature. Glossy black scales had been painted onto a matte white background.

"Look like you're off to war," Owen said as he took in all that Devlin carried. "I had thought the caretaker said this House was fresh out of Keepers. Imagine she would love to have you."

"If not for war, her plight would be at the top of my list," Devlin assured. "Faces come and go so quickly in these parts. I always try to help a familiar one when I can."

"New orders? Or finishing what brought you?"

"We've word that Amalia torched another caravan two days past. The Cinder Witch, that is," Devlin added for Owen's sake. "Pontiff Isaac takes about as much kindness to her name as he does to the woman's thievery. Didn't seem to bother him *too* much before she stole the Orland box, but sin's a sin, I suppose."

"What, the safe deposit box from the carriage? The one Manda was charged with?"

"That's the one. Had been called in to make the raids stop. No mention of violence in the summons. Once that box was taken, though? Madness and screams from Pontiff Isaac. Talk of taking Amal – the Cinder Witch's – head."

"Quite the heel-turn," Owen return, incredulous.

"It's true," Devlin nodded. The gesture bore a weight with which Owen had become familiar.

"So, you are off to battle, then. A rough lot."

"True. Though it comes with the territory, I'm sad to say." Devlin tapped his knuckles on the face of his shield. "Not to say I won't try to reason with her, of course. But I wouldn't mind an extra pair of hands if it does come to blows."

Devlin eased back as he finished. Both feet rose, unable to touch the ground as a result. The comic nature of the display was behind the harn's suggestion.

"What, you mean me?" Laughter, deflated and lacking commitment, tumbled out from Owen. Disbelief coated the finger he pointed at his face. A gentle smile from Devlin affirmed that he had not spoken in jest. "If I could, maybe. There would not be a job waiting on my return if I did."

"The House never has got on well with the Bureau of Arcane, I suppose. Imagine it would be hard to explain away chasing down a heretic of the House."

"Not that I don't want to help," Owen assured. "I'm sure I at least owe you my ability to walk, if not my life entirely. You put a fine point on the problem, though."

"Not your fault, son. If the Pontiff had wanted help from outside our walls, he would have cut all ties with Amalia. Her channeling the Flow is excuse enough to label her a rogue mage. Would make things simpler."

"I know the Bureau *wants* to help if that's any reassurance."

"That so?" Devlin asked, surprised.

"Wasn't more than a few weeks ago the First Seeker was asking about the Cinder Witch. I think he wants to charge out and deal with her, maybe as much as your Pontiff."

"Might as well squeeze a lemon over the sore," Devlin laughed. "Well, I suppose it can't be helped."

"Suppose not," Owen nodded. A morsel of the shame banished by Devlin's presence crawled back up his throat. Part of him felt that he had said too much. The Bureau's business was just that: the Bureau's. What the First Seeker asked of Owen was of no concern to anyone outside the organization.

"That's time enough wasted," Devlin murmured. "People to meet. Provisions to grab. All the fun you might expect of tracking someone who doesn't want to be found."

Both men proffered weary smiles as they shook hands. Neither was in a hurry to do what was demanded of them next. Somber steps carried the pair from the pews out the front doors of the House and down the dust-coated marble steps.

Dust lay as still as it knew how in this town. Those who would have kicked it up into a frenzy had departed the House for their homes, or wherever they needed to be on a Sunday. A couple of peddlers were still in the process of closing down shop; a shoe-shiner packing her brushes into a cabinet-like stool, and a pair of young harn wrapped-up trinkets of suspect quality.

"Strange," Owen said, as much to himself as to Devlin. A bid to not be the first to leave the House's steps. "How quiet it is, I mean. Sundays at home were never this quiet. People in Southport always had somewhere to be, regardless of what day it was."

"Peaceful, aye."

The harn did not look up at Owen when he responded. Devlin looked out at Arnstead, his eyes steady yet unfocused. It was a look that tried to pull in the entire town all at the same time. The sort of look a sailor gives his family before weighing anchor to cross the world. Watching made Owen uncomfortable, unsure what to do with his hands. He crossed his arms tight over his chest and gripped at either arm.

"Don't forget to call when you've gotten back." The attempt to disrupt the moment's unease made it stronger still to Owen. He kicked at a patch of pebbles nestled on one of the House's steps. "For tea, that is. You can call on me at the Orland estate."

"If you do change your mind," Devlin started as he began to go his own way, "I'll be headed back the way we came. Dawn tomorrow, to the East."

Part of Owen thought he had said too much to the keeper, that the Bureau's business was its own and the House could manage itself. Another part, prodded by sore feet and a headache just starting to mend, felt that First seeker Akheem could take a long run off the nearest cliff.

13.

MAKING A CASE

"Ms. Orland is with a customer. You're welcome to wait if you have an appointment. The clerks up front can help you, if not."

Next to the door of Cynthia's office was an unfamiliar face. They bore the fatigues of a Fourth Federation Army officer and the trappings of a sergeant, but Manda Galloway they were not. The particular soldier was a man, for starters. A Nirdac katarl who stood half a hand shorter than Owen. His speech was a matter of routine, not the harsh indictments in which Manda spoke. Flecks of dirt stuck to the sides of his claws drew as much of the sergeant's attention as Owen did.

"Any idea when they'll be done?"

The katarl made no indication that he had heard Owen's question. Clean nails appeared to have won out as the top priority.

Not wanting to cause a scene, Owen dropped the line of inquiry and leaned himself against the nearest wall. There was just enough space to slot his shoulder between the large windows that offered a splendid view of the neighboring brickwork. Enough commotion had risen over the past few days to sate a lifetime's desire for attention. Today was the start of a new week. Along with the new week came a new plan.

Time was no friend to Owen's scheming. The planning and procedure of weeks' worth of time had to be condensed into this single day. Hurried words to Marcus that morning had sparked a fire that would seal the day's dealings. The first hurdle in a series of three. Behind the office door of Arnstead's Orland Bank branch lay the second: Cynthia herself.

A voice in his head, the dark sort of voice that reveals itself only upon embarrassment or ridicule, was glad that Owen had no means to form a spell. His gaze was so hotly fixed upon the red mahogany door that he might have set it ablaze by mistake. The moment of self-depreciation was enough to turn his head away from the solid frame and wolf-head knob.

It's not going anywhere, Owen assured himself. *Neither is she.* He threw a fleeting glance back at the door before adjusting himself to watch the doings of the bank's customers. Just in case.

To watch a person go about their business was an odd exercise. A leathery old woman struggled to crane her neck up to a teller. The pain was evident in her expression, even from half the room away. The hand she jammed into her lower back suggested the contorted creases in her face were born from the agony of her aged form.

Placative gestures from the young teller behind the counter made the situation less clear. His left hand wandered from the back of his pale neck to a packet of notes next to his register. In his right, he held a pencil that tapped vigorously on the countertop. One of his hands would occasionally raise to calm whatever new question the elderly woman posed. A circular conversation by the look of it. Owen wondered at the nature of the details. Missing funds from a family account? Dispute of some charge applied by the bank staff? Whatever the nature of the problem was, the approach of a manager indicated it was beyond the teller's ability to solve.

People became puzzled when it was time to hurry up and wait. Distractions that bore no repercussions for the watcher. As long as the watcher remained discreet, at least. Owen enjoyed the advantage of being the sort of person most folks did not want to linger on for long. The only people Owen had found that enjoyed gawking at his presence was the surly crowd that gathered in front of the local Arcanarium. He was quick to shake the thought from his mind.

Amidst his dozens of guesses and suppositions, Owen became aware of a muffled sound. *Voices,* he thought. Not the sort of stifling that occurs due to distance or from a face tucked behind a furtive hand. Those noises were plentiful among the scattered denizens of the lobby. What had caught Owen's attention was the strained sound of aggravation pushing through solid wood.

"Not what we agreed upon! This is robbery. You are a thief!"

The accusations came from the direction of Cynthia's office, though the lack of reaction from the sergeant on duty gave Owen pause. No reply was given. That, or whoever proffered the reply had a much cooler head. An accurate assumption, Owen felt. The voice he had heard, muffled as it was, sounded like it came from a male. Would leave Cynthia as the one to lay out a measured, thoughtful reply.

So long as it's just the two of them.

Open, eager ears picked up the banter of bank tellers. Idle chatter between customers and the scuff of their shoes against the floor. Further comment from the agitated voice remained absent.

Anticipation pulled Owen so far from his center of balance that he nearly fell. What could have been a harsh tumble towards a hard, unwelcoming surface became instead a frantic shuffle that lasted a panicked moment. Owen's left hand thundered out against the nearby wall. Another effort that missed disaster by a margin of inches, with his hand finding purchase uncomfortably close the glass window. Both hands patted and smoothed his Seeker coat as Owen straightened himself.

"Do you require a chair, sir?"

Of all the things that might have grabbed the airy sergeant's attention, it was Owen's near-miss of the floor. Orange eyes, stained with amusement, flicked up to watch the Seeker. Even a ready source of entertainment was not cause enough to draw the katarl's full address.

"Quite all right," Owen stammered over a rush of adrenaline. "Thank you."

The sergeant returned his attention to his hands. What humor could be gleaned from the moment had been sucked dry, its husk tossed aside in favor of a more practical matter. An embarrassed survey of the lobby told Owen that the sergeant had been the only person to notice.

Ten minutes passed in relative silence. Owen had abandoned his watch of the bank's customers in favor of monitoring the nearest clock: a simple wall-piece hung above the tellers' counters. The gentle tick of the seconds hand was lost under the quiet talk of business and the occasional creak of a wagon or cart from the street, but the movement of time was visible enough. Owen counted, with a squint, what looked like twelve minutes from his stumble before more muffled words could be heard from Cynthia's office.

"The farm. I can't pay you – away from me!"

The man's voice again. Words were harder to pick out than the first time. Whatever gave rise to his temper now, it was not so egregious as what had first offended him. These last words sounded more like a defeat than a challenge. A resigned plea for favorable terms after a decisive battle.

As before, there was no audible reply to the man. Not in the form of speech. A few moments after the man's last words, the sounds of furniture scraping across the wooden floor squeezed out from under the door. Uneven footsteps approached the door. The wolf-head knob turned, suddenly alert, and signaled the door's opening.

"As always, Mr. Pattal, it is a pleasure to have had your company." Cynthia stepped out through the doorway, halting the door before it met the neighboring wall. The weight she placed on her cane would have been impossible to see if Owen had not known to look for it. Cynthia's free right hand made a sweeping gesture from the interior of her office out to the bank's lobby. Straight fingers pointed a clear indication to the front doors. "Should you have any further questions about the specifics of any of our contracts, you are always welcome to schedule time. We have, however, run over. You can see my next appointment is already waiting."

Cynthia passed a sly look to Owen before turning her head back to the small Bangeli human, Mr. Pattal. Small might not have been the right word. Rolled shirt sleeves revealed sinewy arms. The middle-aged man's shoulders were broad enough to garner attention. If not for the way he hunched over in the office's lone guest chair, Mr. Pattal may have been an imposing figure.

Those were things that may have been. Any fight that may have lived inside Mr. Pattal's dull, brown eyes had been quenched. Wide shoulders remained slumped as he stood to leave. Shuffled steps brought him past Cynthia without a farewell to speak of. Twice Mr. Pattal brushed against other customers as he left. Both times the offense was dismissed, as easily as the man himself. Pride had no place in Mr. Pattal's countenance.

"What happened to that one?" Owen asked in awe, waiting for Mr. Pattal to disappear completely from the bank's doorway before he spoke.

"Borrowed more than he can pay back. More than once. Enough about business," Cynthia added with a dismissive wave. "What's got you darkening my door? Something that can't wait until supper?"

"Meant to talk to you last night. Would have rather had the day ahead of me."

"That's the trouble with spending the day at play," Cynthia moaned with a roll of her eyes. "Business tends to catch up with me. Spent the evening meeting with people to talk about this or sign-off on that. The struggle never ends."

"Rings under your eyes might have told me," Owen jabbed. "Lovely shade of purple, by the way."

"Hilarious," Cynthia scowled. "Out with it, then. Before my next *actual* appointment shows."

"Well, here's the thing." From under his right arm, Owen produced a clipboard. He waggled the item in his hand while flashing a set of blank documents at his cousin. A wry smile leaped over his face as Owen looked from his papers to Cynthia. "I've got some business I was hoping you could help with."

"All interactions with the Bureau of Arcane will be conducted according to my prior knowledge and by appointment only."

Cynthia's change in demeanor was instant. The playfulness of Owen's tone crashed against her rigid defense as a ripple challenges a dam. Relaxed muscles snapped to attention, drawing Cynthia up to her full height. A light toss of her cane allowed Cynthia to grip the tool at its center and forgo its assistance. Cynthia had eliminated any outward sign of weakness in the space of a breath.

What took Owen most by surprise was the change in his cousin's stare. She had met Owen with a mixture of exhaustion and familial kindness. A look that told him Cynthia was willing to hear what he needed, despite her fatigue and busy schedule. There was no warmth in her gaze now. The mere mention of official capacity had frozen her eyes into glassy sheets of emerald.

Owen recoiled, seeing the pikes that been raised before him. His presence was no longer a welcome one.

"No cause for alarm," Owen chuckled. To make a show of humor required unexpected effort. Owen could feel his laugh ring hollow as it left his breast. "I promise. Shouldn't take more than a couple of minutes."

"The tellers up front can assist you in making an appointment, Mr. Seeker." The bitter chill of Cynthia's gaze poured into her speech with practiced ease. She turned from Owen to enter her office. "Take a ticket. You will be called when it is your turn."

"Cynthia!" Owen uttered, aghast.

Reflex pushed Owen forward in step with Cynthia. He reached forward with a gentle hand and clasped Cynthia on the shoulder.

That had been his intent, at least. Before Owen could rest his hand on Cynthia's shoulder, the hand of the nearby Fourth Federation Army sergeant had batted his advance aside. Claws bit into Owen's forearm. Owen had thought it was the thickness of his coat sleeve that repelled the katarl's claws, that kept those needles from breaking skin. The controlled features on the sergeant's face told another story.

"Only warning," the katarl said, clear enough for Cynthia to hear. He retracted his claws and tossed Owen's arm to the side.

"Cynthia," Owen pleaded past the katarl, "just hear me out. Five minutes and I'll be out of your hair. Please."

"Five minutes?" Cynthia hesitated in the doorway. Though the frost had not thawed entirely, there was a sliver of compassion in those two small words. Enough of a change to give Owen a ray of hope.

"If you don't like what I have to say, I'll see myself out. No more complaints."

A crack formed in Cynthia's glacial shoulders. They fell a hair's breadth and no further. She sighed a single word, keeping her back to the problem at hand.

"Fine."

Another step carried Cynthia back into her office. Displeased calm tempered her way to the branch's throne. She leaned her cane against the left arm of the chair as she lowered herself to the black velvet cushion. A groove worn into the edge the armrest fit the can like a jar of flour to a baker's cupboard. Cynthia planted both elbows on the orderly surface of the desk, resting her forehead against knit fingers.

Where Cynthia had entered her office with a less than subtle sense of resignation, Owen bounded forward with all the energy of a puppy unleashed. He might as well have stuck his tongue out at the sergeant as he passed by. Instead, Owen contained his mockery within a grin that pocked either cheek with small dimples.

Slender hands continued to tick while out of sight. Owen had bought himself a short amount of time, he reminded himself and knew better than to waste it with boasts and taunts. Half a minute had passed before he seated himself, Owen was sure. He did not wait to be addressed. The closing of Cynthia's office door punctuated Owen's silence.

"Brass tacks," Owen said, turning from the door to face Cynthia, "I want you to fill out an ICF."

"Excuse me?"

"An ICF. Initial Complaint Form." Owen crossed the room to place his clipboard down on Cynthia's desk. His fingertips turned the surface to be legible from Cynthia's perspective, then gave the blank forms a gentle push in her direction. "People fill them out to report focuses that have been lost or stolen to, well, Lost and Stolen."

"And what am I meant to have lost, cousin?"

"Orland safe deposit boxes, they're focuses, correct? They have bits of memory glass that seal the container like a lock."

Furrows lined Cynthia's forehead at the thought. Her head tilted back until narrowed eyes looked out from over the top of her interlocked fingers.

"They do," was Cynthia's flat affirmation. "What of it?"

"I seem to remember, on my journey Arnstead, a certain army lieutenant who was *very* protective of a box. A box that resembles the ones grandfather commissions for the Orland Bank."

Owen leaned further and further forward with each word. Questioning inflection pulled him towards the target of his inquiry. Cynthia remained frozen in place behind a mask of hands.

"I've already sent Manda to recover the box. She rode out this morning with a crew of her choosing. Why should I go through the headache of involving the Bureau?"

"So, it was meant for the Pontiff, then. Manda's riding out with the Keeper. With Devlin."

"The ownership of a deposit box held by the Orland Bank in confidential information. I am not at liberty to—"

"No, no!" Owen waved away the notion of prying into the matter. "It doesn't matter to me who the box belongs to. It's enough for me, for the Bureau, to know that the box is a focus and that it's important. My circumstantial knowledge doesn't affect this case."

"Potential case," Cynthia corrected.

"Cynthia," Owen pled. "I understand. You have business with the House, and you don't want anyone to mess with that. But seeing that box returned would be big for me, too. I *need* a win right now. Let me help. Please."

Out of words, Owen eased back from Cynthia's desk and seated himself in the lone guest chair. Both hands clapped together to further cement Owen's pure intention. He had nothing to hide from his cousin in this venture. What would benefit Cynthia would benefit Owen just as much, if not more so.

Redemption.

The mere thought of it was enough to make Owen's hands tremble. Win the trust of an influential institution for the Bureau of Arcane. Retrieve a focus of significant importance in the name of the Lost and Stolen department. Subdue a known criminal who, by all evidence, should have been labeled as a rogue mage long ago. All these opportunities lay at Owen's feet.

One small detail had prevented Owen from riding out to meet Devlin and company at dawn. The smallest detail. Something that felt so inconsequential in face of the reward that it had almost been overlooked.

None of this was official.

There had been no claimant that approached the Bureau to report a crime. Paperwork was missing that would sanctify action. To be a Spellseeker was not enough. Owen required proof that something had been taken. If the First Seeker was to kick down the Orland Bank's door in search of verification, Owen needed absolute certainty that Cynthia would not simply shrug the inquiry away.

It felt like an honest portrayal. Owen knew he was better off speaking the truth to Cynthia. No lies or half-truths to trip over if the discussion progressed. Though he spoke as a Spellseeker to a representative of the Orland Bank, there remained an element of family. He would not have been let into the office otherwise.

A statue coated in the first frost of winter would have moved more than Cynthia. Would have proffered some manner of expression, as well. If she searched her mind for an idea to share or complaint to raise, there was no indication. Her slate-faced stare was locked firmly on the Spellseeker who had invaded her sanctum. Wolves starved for weeks could not have stared at a doe with such intent.

"Well?" Owen ventured. "What do you think? Another set of hands to help bring home the prize?"

No reaction. Owen might have gotten more of a reply from the chair in which he began to squirm.

Time crept into Owen's periphery. The clock in the lobby had been too far away to hear. A small, steel clock, nestled on a corner of Cynthia's desk, was close. So close that the gentle grind of clockwork could be heard beneath the harsh tick of the hands. Frantic eyes flitted to the device long enough to see its face was directed toward Cynthia. Hands slick with sweat gripped the arms of the guest chair.

"Hmm." Owen's attention flew back to Cynthia at her first sound in what felt like hours. "I fill this out and you go join the hunt. Just you? No other Seekers in tow, dragging red tape all the way?"

"Just me!" Owen eagerly snapped.

"And I have your assurance that your aim is *just* to retrieve the box? Not to invade the privacy of my customers?"

"The purpose of Lost and Stolen is to retrieve what has been stolen. And to punish any culprits, if there are any."

Air rushed into Cynthia's nostrils with a harsh sniff.

Something! Owen thought to himself. The barest of gestures. Neither good nor ill when judged alone. *Still*, he told himself, *something was better than an emotionless void.*

Cautious was the hand that probed the blank ICF documents. A single hand. Cynthia did not rush to grab the papers. It was as if her hand stalked them, watched from a careful distance before any prod or poke. Two fingers came to rest at a corner of the pages. Twin carrion birds deciding whether or not their quarry had well and truly died.

Cynthia's free hand coiled into a half-fist. The motion, whether habit or consciously made, continued to obscure her mouth. No emotion would be gleaned from there. Her eyes, however, had wandered down to the clipboard.

The first scan was quick. Cynthia had flown through the fields of the top page. Curious emeralds lapped up the details of what would be required. She plowed through the second and third pages of the blank ICF, saw the fourth was the beginning of a new form, then lay the pages to rest where they had been.

"I fill these out, you open a case, and the deposit box comes back to me?" Cynthia looked up at Owen. The points had sounded more to him as a statement than a question, but he nodded all the same. "Am I limited to these three pages, or can I supply addendum pages? For clarity's sake."

"You could file a complete collection of the Federal Encyclopedia if you wanted. The three pages are the bare minimum. We always meet with claimants in person to sure-up the details, anyway. Think of this like skipping an unnecessary step," Owen added with a satisfied smile.

Knuckles rapped the office door from without. Four short taps on the mahogany barricade.

Light as they were, the knocks caused Owen to start in his chair. Nerves pulled taught as a bowstring had finally snapped. Business with Cynthia had been more of a demanding affair than he expected.

Owen knew of her practical nature. To argue with her in their childhood had near always been effort wasted. The subject was immaterial. From deciding a day's course of play to what should be packed for lunch, her say was final. Finality reached by reason. No cream for days spent running woodland paths. It would spoil while they lost themselves among autumn leaves. No scouring Pittwell Creek for swirled stones during early spring, lest they encounter a withered pocket bear fresh out of hibernation.

When Cynthia arrived at 'no' after giving a suggestion proper thought, Owen knew there was little chance she would be swayed. It was both a relief and a terror to know that his future once again rested on her powerful shoulders.

"Yes?" was Cynthia's annoyed reply to the knocks. Her head tilted to the side to look past Owen, as though she were speaking to the door itself.

"Nine-o-clock is here," came the sergeant's unenthusiastic response.

"Morning, Ms. Orland." A new voice, impatient. Like a teacher grown tired of a particular student's brazen curiosity. "I've some questions regarding the budget for our roadways, on behalf of the mayor."

Cynthia's face could not have soured faster if she had bitten into a handful of fresh lemon after chewing on a handful of chili peppers.

"Cancel my nine-o-clock, sergeant."

"Excuse me?" called the newcomer, stunned at such offhand dismissal.

"And everything leading up to noon, for that matter. And fetch the notary that's on duty today."

"Excuse—"

"Yes, ma'am," the sergeant interrupted.

Muffled protests subsided. The amusing sight of the katarl escorting some stranger by their ear out to Main Street popped into Owen's mind. Close on the heels of that image came a realization.

"Wait," he asked, directing his attention from the office door back to Cynthia, "through to noon?"

"That's what I said." As she spoke, Cynthia reached into a desk drawer and produced a stack of clean, white paper. "Though you'll be lucky if we're done by then. Come back at four, just in case we go long."

"Four?" Owen eyed the neat pile of papers as Cynthia drew fresh ink into her pen. "You know I was joking about the encyclopedia, right?"

"I have a contract to write," Cynthia muttered. Commands were given, her attention now divided itself between the blank ICF and notes she scribbled on the blank pages. "I'm sure you have business to attend to before you leave. Spend your time wisely. I'll have my part done by the time you get back. Promise," she added with an emerald flash of a look at Owen.

"No mistake there," Owen admitted. "I guess I'd better be on my way then?"

A nod was the only reply Owen received.

"One thing, before you go," Cynthia said. Owen had already taken hold of the doorknob and was about to leave. He half-turned, his pulse redoubled at the thought of some further stipulation to their deal. "How do you plan to catch them? Manda and company, I mean? I doubt you'll be catching them by foot."

"Spoke with Marcus before I left the house," Owen replied. Relieved, he loosened his death grip on the doorknob. "Told him I'd be leaving town for a week or so, asked that he saddle a horse and gather the essentials for me."

"Such confidence!" Cynthia chuckled. "All right, get out of here."

14.

PREPARATION

Main Street was in the full bustle of mid-morning activity. For Weststead, it meant the arrival of carts and wagons from the frontier. They carried material goods from all stretches of the freshly explored expanse. Flat carts of raw flickerwood timber and pre-cut ironwood from the Flickerwood proper pulled by oxen. Names like Alder & Sons or Flatwood Lumber were painted in fine, uniform lettering the larger carts. Their contents were taken to warehouses north of Main. Smaller carts, with their untidied piles of cinched-down cedar and pine, ambled on to the tradespeople of Eaststead.

Covered wagons, their cream-colored canvases stained bright red from the dust at the Gods' Hands, hoarded all manner of precious metals and stones. Silver bars, extracted and forged at the O'Connor Mining Company base to the southwest, kept under strict guard until reaching Arnstead's mint. Uncut sapphires and rubies clattered in barrels behind ecstatic prospectors; solo operators as happy to be home alive as to have found paydirt.

Perhaps most precious of all was the constant flow of raw memory glass from the nearby quarry. Half a day northwest of Arnstead, the largest known deposit of memory glass in the New World was mined day and night. Some of that precious cargo stayed in Arnstead to be used by its tradespeople and citizens. More went east to Elstaff. From there, the raw material could be shipped by train to the major port cities across the east coast. More still went across the Middle Sea to the Old World.

Foodstuffs. Exotic plants. Wild beasts, dead or alive. More materials than the average person could fathom. A logistical nightmare for even the savviest among Arnstead's merchants.

The bounty and wonders of the New World offered Owen the best shroud he could have hoped for. Not accounting for the handful of individuals that would cut a Spellseeker a wide berth, Owen was able to walk down main as a relatively inconspicuous part of a greater, uncaring crowd. A joy he was not always privy to while off of Main Street.

So great was the cover afforded to Owen that he was able to pass within a few feet of the Arcanarium's exterior queue without notice. None of the usual sneers or insults. He was most thankful for the lack of spittle that was often launched his direction.

Owen cut through the flow of Main Street to approach the Arcanarium. His target today was not the front door, having already passed through them earlier this morning. He moved instead toward the vacant alley that separated the Arcanarium from the neighboring building. In that alley would be a window. Left slightly ajar from his furtive escape that morning, it was his ticket to reentering the building unnoticed.

Luck appeared to have held out. Mischief danced across Owen's face as he approached the window. A quick look from right to left over the sill showed the hallway to be empty. Owen afforded himself a victorious smile as he eased the window open, then awkwardly straddled his way inside.

"Learned *something* from Aaron, at least," Owen whispered to the empty hall.

Well-oiled, no doubt due to its constant use, the window closed without a sound. Only the metallic pop of the latch slotting into place signaled his presence. Owen doubted that suspicion would be raised if he were happened upon now that he was back in the Arcanarium.

Expectations had been set that Owen would be in the office all day. After yesterday's excitement, he had said to Aaron, he felt it would be best to ensure some paperwork was getting done.

"We're just two, after all," Owen had said. "I appreciate the exposure to our methods, but the ICFs won't be transcribing themselves. We could alternate, perhaps? One day I work in the office, the next I can work claims with you?"

The claim was not absent merit. Owen was glad that it was enough to give Aaron pause. Something for his superior to chew on. More importantly, it would keep them apart for the day while Owen went about preparing for his gambit. He would return to the Arcanarium with a great enough achievement that his sidestep of regulation would have to be overlooked.

Aaron's eventual agreement to the proposed schedule had bought Owen the precious time he needed. With Cynthia working on filing her official claim, there was but one task that remained. Preparations for the journey ahead were to be made.

Simple preparations had been completed before Owen left the Orland house that morning. A quick conversation with Marcus ensured that the bare essentials would be ready for Owen by that evening. Rations for the road, bedding, and other small sundries would be packed onto the most well-mannered horse that could be found.

No stranger to Owen and his feelings regarding horses, it had been difficult to keep his conversation with Marcus to the most meager details. The fact that it was for official business had slipped early. This led to the question of why a family horse was necessary, why the Bureau of Arcane could not supply for their own? What Owen's redirections lacked in grace or subtlety they made up for in efficiency.

Ill will was not a matter of concern for the interaction. Owen saw the katarl as more of a watchful uncle than a family servant. Owen understood the importance of divulging only as much detail regarding Bureau operations as was necessary. It had been a tough decision to overshare with Cynthia about his plans. Additional breaches of protocol would have been to press his luck too far.

The last measure of preparation was located within the confines of the Arcanarium. Within each Arcanarium was a location to store focuses and other magical equipment. In smaller locations, which Owen assumed Arnstead might qualify as, this storage space was often combined with articles that were seized in the line of duty. Illegal focuses or the materials to make them, for example. The most common place to keep all of these items was as far away from the public as possible.

Owen took a deep breath to remind himself that he did belong in the Arcanarium. Each step he took down the hall felt more and more like he was trespassing. As if someone may tap him on the shoulder and escort him from the building at any moment. Peak distress came and went as he passed the doors to Violent Offenses. Of course, no one came to stop Owen or stand in his way. The clack of his iron-heeled boots on the hardwood floor did not warrant the bat of an eyelash. His place was here. Down at the end of the hall and to the left, in the broom cupboard of an office that was Lost and Stolen.

Except Owen did not turn left.

In front of him stood the door to Research and Development. He had never been given a proper tour of the building, but this seemed to be the furthest room from the general public. Barring any secret tunnels or well-obscured passageways. What better place to find all manner of magical odds and ends than R&D, he reasoned.

One courtesy knock. Enough to say he had done so if Lionel Eilhart was in the room. The excitable harn's name was the only one listed under the Research and Development placard next to the department door.

R&D was no different from the other departments of the Arnstead Arcanarium. Staffed to the absolute lowest threshold imaginable. Any department that did not have 'Violent Offenses' in its title was blessed to have more than two people on its roster. Favoritism at its most glaringly obvious, and without a care who knew.

On one hand, Owen felt a pang of pity for the lone individual, annoying as he may be, that was responsible for the entire R&D. On the other, the thought that Lionel may be too preoccupied to notice Owen's incursion added fuel to Owen's ambition.

Slow was the hand that turned the doorknob. As motivated as Owen felt, he still wanted to avoid any unnecessary confrontations with his coworkers. One slip of the tongue could be enough to plant a seed in a curious mind. What use did a Seeker stuck in an office have for sifting through Collections? None was the deflated response that came to Owen's mind. He shook his head at the thought. If an excuse was needed, he reassured himself that he would be able to craft one.

Best to not need one, though, Owen reminded himself.

The knob to R&D turned with ease. If there was a lock on the other side, it had not been engaged. Another blessing long overdue. Owen pulled the door outward with the presence of one who was meant to enter.

Noise that rivaled the peak of a thunderclap erupted from the doorway the moment it was ajar. There could not have been a greater intensity had a bolt of lightning struck an arm's length away from the door. Owen's left hand flew to his ear. His right clutched the doorknob as he shouldered the door closed with a panicked shove. The ear-splitting crack rang in his head even after the door had been shut.

Quiet resumed in the hallway when the door to Research and Development clicked closed. No echo of the cacophony remained to suggest it had ever existed. It was like placing a lid over the enclosure of a common cricket.

Owen flopped his back onto the door and slid down to its base. He sat wide-eyed, ears pounding as he waited for his heart to slow. Short gasps forced their way through his mouth until he wrested control from his reflexes, forced slower breaths through his nose. Something in the violence of that sound had reminded him of fire. The animated flame that ate at the sides of the stagecoach. A blaze stopped only the graces of the gods, begged for by Devlin.

Air flowed in through his nose. Owen could feel the expansion of his lungs, the rise and fall of his chest. Muscles relaxed in his abdomen. Knees unlocked themselves and toes unclenched. Control was regained, piece by piece.

A deep breath preceded Owen's second attempt at entering Research and Development. He did his best to present a sense of belonging but felt the wrinkle in his visage. There was no great explosion the second time. Silence welcomed him as the door was opened wide. Owen took two hesitant steps inside and closed the door behind.

The large, open floor space of Research and Development set it apart from the other rooms of the Arcanarium. White tile, gleaming under incandescent memory glass lamps, took the place of hardwood floors. Patches of tile were covered with deep scores. Some were charred and jagged. Other spots were smooth though still uneven as if water had spent decades eroding the tile.

Furniture was sparse. It gave the room an eerie sense of vacancy as if there should have been furnishings for a dozen or more people. Two wooden chairs and a green-faced chalkboard surrounded a wooden desk that had seen better days. A leg was propped up on what looked like a stack of books. The corner nearest the chalkboard was missing. Likely blasted away, judging from the protrusion of splinters.

Lionel scratched notes of some kind on the chalkboard with unrestrained enthusiasm. There was more white on the board than green. Short hops were required to reach the few blank areas that remained.

Distracted, Owen thought. *Perfect.* He took a careful step to his left. The only other door visible in the room shared the wall with the entrance. His foot hit the hard tile just as he registered his mistake. What plans Owen had for stealth were spoiled by the echo of his iron-heeled boot.

Lionel snapped around at the sound.

"You big sneak," the harn shouted, his face lighting. "Thought you were going to sneak by without a hello?"

Bare feet thumped across the open floor as Lionel ran to greet Owen.

"Sorry, friend." Owen scratched the back of his head as he stammered the phrase. "Didn't mean to intrude. You seemed like you were busy and I was just passing through."

"What, to Collections?"

"That's right," Owen nodded.

"Oh, Aaron send you over to grab some goodies for a bust?"

Opportunity continued to strike the hot iron.

"Exactly. Didn't wan—"

"What's the deal this time?" Lionel bounced as he spoke, long ears twitching at attention. "Last time was a hoarder stealing her neighbors' plumbing filters. Time before that was a gang of street kids running through fancy folks' pockets. Before that was... Uhm."

Excited eyes dimmed somewhat under the strain of reflection. Lionel flitted from one broken patch of tile to another as he dug through his memory. Seemed like Aaron managed to keep R&D busy.

"He was thin on the details," Owen started, "but told me what he needed. Two focuses: something flame retardant and another that can dampen a person's ability to channel the Flow."

"That'll be a pyro, I imagine. Sounds more like Violent Offenses work," Lionel added. A twitchy hand scratched his singed chin. "Nothing says a pyro can't be a thief, too, I suppose. Oh, or maybe they've got a den with some flame traps!"

"Couldn't say," Owen shrugged. "That's the door to Collections over there?"

"Hmm? Yeah, that's the one," Lionel said, following Owen's gesture. The initial guess had been correct. "You'll need my badge to get in, though. Nobody gets in without me except the First Seeker. Not a problem. Aaron's the forgetful type. Never remembers to tell the rookies when he sends them on an errand."

"That sounds about right," Owen agreed with a genuine laugh.

"Was about done with what I was doing anyways, but you being here reminds me...!"

A fit of realization overtook Lionel. With an eager smile and no explanation, he took Owen's hand in an iron grip and began to lead the way to the battered workstation in the center of the room. Stumbling steps carried Owen behind the harn. More than once he nearly toppled to keep pace with his excited company. Each of the harn's leaps accounted for two

225

of Owen's faltering strides.

"What's the rush?" Owen's voice jumped up and down in line with his uneven gait.

"I've been working on something you're gonna like. Over here!"

Approaching the desk, there was no question in Owen's mind what Lionel had been working on. An iron pipe with a crudely affixed wooden handle sat on the middle of the desk. Space had been cut out from the top to allow a caster room enough to be jammed in. The muzzle of the device had been blasted apart, with jagged bits of metal pointed away from the barrel's center.

Two caster shells were visible. One, a clouded swirl of yellow and orange, was half-lodged in the makeshift pistol. It seemed a fair assumption, given the state of the weapon, that this was the source of the explosion Owen heard when he opened the R&D door. The other shell was a deep sapphire. Lamplight from above pierced the shell in a way that made a robe-like corona glimmer over the desktop.

"Been working on these since I saw your pistol," Lionel said. He released Owen's hand to dig hungrily through the left drawer of the desk. Shifting paper melded with the clatter of loose metal. "Thought you might be wanting more at some point. Didn't wait to ask."

"Oh, that's..." Owen trailed for a moment. He could not help but look at the sorry state of Lionel's testing device. A protective hand draped itself over Owen's caster pistol. "That's quite thoughtful of you."

"Wanted you to try it while you're here, then we dip into Collections for a good rummaging. Aha!"

Half of Lionel's torso had been engulfed by the drawer before a triumphant hand lifted a wooden doll. The rest of Lionel followed soon after, landing back on his feet with a huff and a fiendish grin.

The doll itself was nondescript. Not even a doll, for that matter. It was rigid at its joints. Featureless approximations of arms were grafted to the figure's sides. Legs were fused into a pillar of wood. If not for the clear inclusion of a head, the figure would have looked to be little more than a smoothed block of wood.

Warm light, like noonday sun filtered through a rustle of oak leaves, encased the figurine. Lionel began channeling a spell. The Flow's energy moved through his arm, into his hand, around the object. A semblance of serenity blanketed the harn.

"Should do it," Lionel mumbled.

With his brief moment of peace behind him, Lionel pulled the figurine and launched it away from the desk. The object pinwheeled until it struck the white tile floor with a hollow thud. There was a single bounce. When the figurine reached the apex of its arc, it froze in place.

Nothing happened.

The figurine was suspended in midair. Light from Lionel's spell blanketed its small frame in silence.

When they vanished, without warning or provocation, the figurine expanded into the shape of a human. The process was slow. Wood popped and cracked as arms and legs separated from the trunk and took on a definition. Convulsions rocked its frame. Head and neck whipped violently as if trying to escape one another.

A minute had passed before the figurine had taken the shape of a mannequin. It was as if a human baby had grown twenty years before their eyes. Barrel-chested and broad-shouldered, the creation would have looked at home working in a silver mine. Legs and arms had full articulation. The fingers and toes, even, had knuckles and bent in all the right ways.

The newly formed mannequin floated to the ground with the grace of a goose feather. Only the slightest clack suggested its feet had made contact with the tile floor.

"Nicely done," Owen muttered. His eyebrows peaked so thoroughly he could feel his ears lift.

"Almost makes you sad it's for target practice."

"What, with that?" Owen pointed a concerned finger at the blasted caster pistol on the table.

"Of course not," Lionel laughed. "That's what we've got your for!"

"Oh no, no, no!" Owen backed two steps away from the devilish harn. "I'll not be blasting the muzzle out on my pistol, thank you very much."

"Hmm?" Lionel cocked his head to the side as if Owen had just spoken in the language of the Kin. The harn followed Owen's gaze until they both looked at the shattered remains on the desk. "Oh, goodness no! Not the yellow shell. Just started work on that one today. The blue one is what I want you to try."

"And how long have you been working on the blue one, pray tell?"

"Well… I suppose – I guess the day after you arrived, it was? At least a week, to be sure."

"A week?" Faith instilled by Lionel's handicraft with the mannequin evaporated. "A wee – These took months to make!"

Owen pulled one of his four caster shells from his belt. He did not give any thought to which he retrieved. The smooth cylinder rolled from side to side in his outstretched palm.

"Ah, yes, the purple one. The one that shocks folks, you said. Wouldn't happen to be how Chitra got those nasty scars, was it?"

"Word gets around, I see," Owen snapped as he clutched the shell.

"What if I told you that blue shell there could do the same job *without* making your vict— I mean, the culprit— all crispy-like?"

Indignation fumed through flared nostrils. Owen had no control over the reaction. Embarrassment heated his cheeks to a rosy red as he slotted the purple caster shell back into the leather belt ring.

Hop off, you furry runt!

Rosy embarrassment deepened to crimson shame.

The thought had risen so suddenly. What shocked Owen more than the words themselves, though, was that he had to bite his lip to keep from shouting them. A taste of wet iron dotted the tip of his tongue. Blood spilled to prevent further indignation.

Words of grandfather Orland. Deeply entrenched in the family, passed on to his children through frequent use. Coarse language that Owen had heard from his mother. Language abhorred by his father. Its use in their household had subsided as years carried on, but not so completely that Danitha Orland-Raulstone was free from its casual clutches.

Remarks about hopping down a forest path. Mention of stalking down alleyways. 'All fours' made an occasional appearance, as well.

That was all his mother. His mother and grandfather talking. Not himself, Owen thought, as he struggled to unclench his jaw. Fingernails dug themselves free from sweaty palms as fists faded.

"Sorry," Lionel whispered unprompted. "Didn't mean to offend."

Betrayed by body language. Embarrassment. Shame. Rage. Resentment. The heartfelt apology mixed them all into a sickening lump in Owen's stomach. A pit that wanted to drag him down to the floor.

Lionel had done nothing wrong. He had merely spoken a truth that Owen no longer wanted to hear, reminded Owen of failure. Incompetence that was still too close to home to jab at with comfort. Gossip from around the Arcanarium had cut deeper than expected.

"The blue one, you said?" Owen asked softly. It was the closest thing to an apology that he could muster. "Then you'll let me into Collections?"

"I'll even help you hunt," Lionel nodded.

To credit the craftsman, Owen conceded that the blue caster shell was far more appealing to the eye than the yellow-orange one. Silver had been wrapped around the end that sat on the table. A casual glance would have suggested that the item belonged on Owen's belt alongside the other four.

Light shone evenly through the shell when Owen raised it to the lamps above. The clarity of the shell stood up to his scrutinous inspection. Looking through the small cylinder of memory glass was like peering through a pair of spectacles that had been tinted blue.

What surprised Owen most was how well it fit into the chamber of his caster pistol. He only remembered the one occasion where Lionel had the device in hand. No measuring tapes had been wrapped around the barrel or muzzle. Lionel had not produced any hidden rulers or any other type of tool. He created a caster shell to fit the dimensions of Owen's pistol by feel.

The shell gave no resistance as Owen closed the pistol's chamber. No sound but the pistol's mechanisms sliding into place. A silent symphony that brought a hint of mirth back into Lionel's expression.

"Give it some juice," Lionel said, "and fire at the chest."

Enough time had been wasted. Half-excuses had gotten nowhere. Rather than continue trying to circumvent the issue, Owen leveled his pistol at the mannequin's chest and began to channel. The Flow moved through his arm, through his hand, into the shell. Sapphire light rippled out from the breach. A single word formed in Owen's mind.

Go!

The caster pistol gurgled. An odd sound, like water flowing into the hole left by a stone removed as the tide comes in. Pockets of air gasped at water's suction. The noise lasted just long enough to assign a sensation. Next came what sounded like a railroad tie smacking the surface of a placid lake after a hundred-foot fall.

Recoil accompanied the loud crack. It was not so powerful to jam Owen's wrist, but enough force to warrant note. More than he was accustomed to with his shells.

Water launched from the barrel of the caster pistol in conjunction. The stream matched the circumference of the barrel, and severed itself after a few feet of water had emerged. Tremendous speed propelled the length of water into the mannequin's chest with a splash. Upon making contact with the mannequin's chest, the water began to wrap itself around the wooden torso. Arms became bound the sides. What had started as a stream of water became liquid rope.

Before Owen had time to think on the practical application, much less ask if there even was one, the water began to freeze. The mannequin's arms were locked in place faster than Owen could comprehend it had happened.

"Yes!" Lionel cried. Hands clapped rapidly as he continued. "Perfect, just perfect. Now, aim for a leg!"

Owen obliged, curious to see how the outcome could differ.

Sounds and recoil remained unchanged. The initial stream of water seemed no different, either. It was on contact with the mannequin's leg that change manifested.

Water latched onto one of the mannequin's ankles. The spell did not settle for making a block of ice around the foot below or crawling up the leg above. Instead, the liquid rope swung around the mannequin's ankle until it found the opposite leg. Ice formed around both ankles as they were pulled together and frozen into a single block.

The mannequin, without any means to stabilize itself, toppled to the tile floor like a bundle of firewood.

"That's quite impressive," Owen murmured. He turned the pistol over in his hand. Inspecting either side revealed no damage. The chamber slid open with ease, allowing the blue caster shell to fall into Owen's free hand. "Cool to the touch."

"Hope is that it keeps everyone involved alive, though maybe not kicking. Promise to let me know how it performs in the field and it's yours to keep."

"I can agree to that," Owen smiled. He made a point to establish eye contact with Lionel for the first time since entering R&D. "Thank you, Lionel."

"Ah," Lionel grunted as he waved off the praise. "You don't need to thank me. This is what I love. Speaking of, I think we have a storeroom to plunder."

"That we do."

It seemed that no force could suppress the harn for long. Enthusiasm propelled each footfall as a child called to dinner after a long day at play. The confrontation had been forgotten in favor of a more enjoyable pursuit.

Expectant murmurs trailed behind Lionel as he bounded.

An enviable trait, Owen thought, to be able to expel negative baggage on a whim. Lionel made the act seem effortless. The sting of Owen's hateful thoughts was still too near to allow for a clear conscience. A lesser part of himself. Malformed opinion impressed upon him that would cast a shadow on a bright soul, even in the face of kindness.

"I can do better," Owen told himself. Renewed purpose imbued his stride with vigor. "I *will* do better."

Time spent in Collections had passed without mark. A windowless area hid from the sun and prying eyes alike. Spiral stairs led downward from the connecting door in Research and Development to the cavernous space. Flow-stoked sconces lit the shaft with a purple haze. Crooked shelves formed a damp, bending labyrinth that concealed all manner of trinkets and baubles.

For all the surfaces that could be seen and touched, Collections was a place where sound died a quick death. Stillness imposed itself on the most subtle attempt at motion. Owen grew thankful that he had not visited the repository alone, though Lionel's glee in walking the dour halls was not shared.

The adventure was short, thanks to Lionel's cryptic knowledge of every knot and turn that Collections had to offer. Enough time to grab two focuses, a cloak and a dagger, and be on their way back to the surface.

"The cloak eats fire," Lionel had explained. Sheer excitement allowed the harn to speak through the gloom. Even then, he could only manage short bursts. Each word was made to count. "Dagger inhibits flow after the cut. Happy hunting!"

Goodbyes were brief. Promises to share information and the typical well-wishing shared between colleagues. A mention of lunch. A noncommittal response.

Having gathered what he came for, and a little more besides, Owen snuck his way outside as he had done that morning. This time without leaving the window ajar.

"Not sure what you call a meal at three in the afternoon, but here we are."

White stew quivered in a pair of wooden. Chunks of potato and morsels of shredded chicken protruded through the surface. A sprig of parsley atop creamy, still bubbling broth. The pleasant aroma rode upwards on columns of steam.

Olufemi placed a bowel on the table in front of Owen, then set the second across the table for himself. Dark hands halved a small loaf of bread. Soup climbed eagerly through the porous half-loaves as they were dunked into place.

"Right, then," Olufemi grunted as he seated himself, "what manner of favor does my number one patron have in mind?"

Droplets of soup fell from Owen's half of bread as he drew it out. Disturbing the chicken and potatoes enhanced their smell. He let the steady stream of drops subside before taking his first bite.

"Gods above," Owen attempted to say through a full mouth, "this is delicious."

"Hey, now," Olufemi retorted. He licked his wooden spoon clean and waggled it at Owen. "You don't get to march into my store like a storm cloud, ask for a favor, then dodge the question when food's ready."

"Can't let something tasty get cold. Unless… is it better cold?"

"You sleep with somebody's wife?" Olufemi asked, looking around the odd choice of location that was the Creaky Board.

An involuntary snort wracked Owen at the suggestion. Bits of broth and potato climbed halfway up to his nose. He coughed at the burn, shaking his head as he reached for a glass of water to make the awful sensation stop.

"Somebody's husband, then?" Olufemi pressured.

"No," Owen coughed.

"You, uh…" Olufemi quieted as he leaned forward, "you need help hiding a body or something?"

Owen glowered at the notion.

"Some interesting favors you're in the habit of doing."

"Never said I had." Olufemi looked away as he ate another spoonful. "Just covering the usual asks."

Relative calm at the Creaky Board allowed the pair to eat in silence for a time. An odd time of day, coupled with it being a Monday, meant a small crowd. This afforded a typically busy man like Olufemi the chance to breathe.

For Owen, the moment of peace was a break from thoughts of gloom and toil. Idle chatter dispersed the clouds that loomed on the horizon.

Talk of favors gave way to less important things. Comments about the weather, that the muggy heat saturating the air would continue to worsen. Assurances that the heat would be missed when the bitter chill of winter came to stay. An argument about whether or not a single location could have unbearable summers *and* frigid winters. Further assurances that it was the truth.

Business came next.

"I wish I could say this was an inconvenience," Olufemi sighed. "That being carted out of my store in the middle of the afternoon would be bad for business. You know, when you first arrived here in Arnstead, you were the first person to darken my doorstep in over a week."

"Must be nice," Owen chuckled. "Hard to imagine a job where there's not always something to be done."

"Plenty to do," Olufemi said, feigning offense. "I'm entertaining a customer right now, aren't I?"

"Yes, I suppose so."

The look on Olufemi's face told Owen that the time for distractions was over. It was time to discuss what Owen had come to discuss. Doom, gloom, and all the rest.

"Right," Owen began with a labored sigh. "So, I was hoping you could do me a favor."

"Uh-huh."

"I've got a letter that might need delivering."

"What, directions to the postmaster, then?" Confusion riddled Olufemi's brow. "An awful lot of stink to ask for directions."

"I don't need to send it now. Hopefully, I won't need to send it at all. But if it does need sending, I won't be able to do it myself. I'm going away for a while."

"Guessing it's no vacation, then." Confusion melted into realization. He may not know the specifics, but Olufemi had gotten the vague idea. The danger that was involved. "Work-related? I'm sure one of your Seeker pals could hold onto a death note."

"Yes, and no."

"How is this not a yes or no?"

Owen drummed his fingers on the table. the Creaky Board remained near empty. Its tables were absent of any familiar faces beyond the waitstaff. Still, he spared a second look to ensure he had not missed some shadowed nook. The third look served to calm his nerves.

233

"Yes, it's work-related. No, because work doesn't know that I'm leaving."

"Sounds complicated," Olufemi murmured over the top of his glass.

"More than I'd like."

"And how long am I supposed to hold onto this letter?"

Muffled crinkling of paper escaped Owen's coat as he produced the letter in question. An unassuming envelope bent at a slight curve from time in a breast pocket. Black lettering popped on the yellowed paper. The address to his family home in Southport brought a sudden mist just behind Owen's eyes. He flipped the letter over to reveal a nondescript wax seal. No markings from the house of Raulstone or Orland. A plain circle pressed into the dark blue wax.

There was a sudden urge to shred the letter. Rip the paper to bits until there was nothing to read and no hope to assemble it.

Doubt wedged itself into the moment of weakness. *Why am I doing this?* Owen asked himself. *I screwed up, but bad enough that I need to leave a death note? That I should risk my life to get into the good graces of people who don't respect me? Who might never respect me? I can play the long game. Work the desk at Lost and Stolen for a few years, maybe earn back my chance for something else. Just a few years.*

Years.

The weight of the word crushed his hand, pressed it onto the letter below. It was the only word that hit quite as hard as 'maybe' in his mind.

"Two weeks." The words came out as a croak. Owen said it again, as much for himself as for Olu. "Maybe three to be sure. If I'm not back by then, send the letter. Already has postage and an address. All you have to do is take it to the post office."

A crowbar raked over sheets of glass would not have sounded more grating than the scrape of Owen's letter across the table. For a moment, he could not remove his hand. It was the last precipice.

When Owen finally pulled his hand away, it was a sharp motion. The recoil of touching a stove that was yet to cool. He could feel that heat rush to his face. Pins and needles jabbed his cheeks. Scratching at the sensation brought no relief, but Owen was uncertain what to do with his hands.

"You sure I'm the one?" The question was soft. Olufemi's hand hovered next to the envelope. "You said you had some family in town, right? Or maybe—"

"It needs to be a friend, Olufemi. It needs to be you."

Olufemi straightened at being named a friend.

It was a strong word for someone he had known for less than a month. That much Owen conceded, but he also felt there was no other person he could turn to. Someone impartial to the situation was required. The family was out of the question, and anyone from the Arcanarium would have been absurd.

Of the people Owen had consistently interacted with in his short time in Arnstead, Olufemi felt like the safest choice. The person that would ask the fewest questions. Olufemi had no stake in the matter at hand, no reason to open the letter.

Olufemi was also the first person to offer his hand to Owen. Outside of work or obligation, Olufemi had offered both ear and time when they could be spared. He was the closest thing Owen had to a friend in Arnstead. The designation of friend may have been a large one, but it had not felt false.

"All right, friend," Olufemi whispered as he placed his hand on the envelope.

"Thanks, Olufemi. Really appreciate this. With half a mind and a bit of luck, I'll be back to grab that from you in no time at all."

"You'd better," Olufemi said with a whisp of a smile. "You've only just got here, after all. Would be a shame if you kicked the bucket before your first harvest festival."

"That so?"

"Oh yeah, folks come in from all around Arnstead. Farmers, villages from out west, all sorts. Isn't a better time to make new friends than at harvest."

"Well, that's something to look forward to, then."

Rigid stone gave way to a softer expression. Owen held a hand out to Olufemi, who reached past the hand to grasp Owen's forearm. Owen reciprocated the gesture with a new light in his eyes. They shook twice before releasing each other.

"When are you off?" Olufemi asked. With business out of the way, his posture eased. He draped an arm over the back of his chair and let his head rest on the raised shoulder. "Anything I can get you for the road?"

"As soon as Frontier Finds pulls you back, I think. A family retainer put together some travel supplies and packed them on a horse for me. Haven't looked through it, but the man is usually quite thorough."

235

"Wow, a retainer. Must be nice."

"Knock it off," Owen replied. Mild annoyance tempered his jesting tone.

Another handful of minutes vanished as Owen and Olufemi bickered about the merits of family servants. Like how a person would never have to do their laundry, but be at a loss if the need ever arose. Light fare that would be forgotten by the next sunrise. The sort of inane prattle shared between strangers who waited for different trains at a quiet station.

It felt to Owen like it had been ages since he had enjoyed this kind of talk. Not since his time with Rebecca and Venkatesh on the train to Elstaff. What had in truth only been a month or so ago seemed a lifetime away.

Owen wondered if it would have been prudent to write a second note addressed to his friends.

An overlong pause signaled that it was past time for Owen to depart. The newly minted friends shared another handshake, followed by a quick embrace. Confidence and reassurance radiated from Olufemi in equal measure. Owen held on, lapping up as much of the energy as he could gather.

A clap on Owen's shoulders signaled the last farewell. Olufemi pulled himself away. The speed with which he made himself busy told Owen that there was plenty to do around the Creaky Board. Owen stepped out from the establishment knowing that he had made a wise choice of caretaker.

"Oh! One last thing before you go." Olufemi stepped out of the Creaky Board to meet Owen once again. From a leather satchel slung over his shoulder, Olufemi produced a thick, leatherbound book. A great tree was etched into the front cover. Leaves swirled around the dying oak in a flurry of yellow and orange. The title read *Home of Trees*. "It's an odd one. I'm not quite done with it yet, but I think you could use it more than I right now."

Sure enough, there was a bookmark tucked somewhere in the last third of the book. Owen took the volume in hand and thumbed through the first few pages. The paper was thick yet supple, a well-loved tome that had been rifled through dozens of times.

"I'll make sure it comes back," Owen said with a knowing smile.

"You'd better," Olufemi chuckled before heading off in the direction of Frontier Finds. He gave Owen one last, reassuring clap on the shoulder.

The same summer air discussed in the temperate confines of the Creaky

Board awaited incursion with open arms. A wet, sopping veil that doused the air, but never seemed powerful enough to keep dust on the ground. A gritty film that collected on shoes and trouser legs was the result. Stronger encouragement to remain indoors was difficult to come by.

Owen stepped out into the humid air as the doors to the Creaky Board swung shut behind. Hitching posts stretched to the left and right of the building's entryway. It was too early in the day yet for the space to be crowded with all manner of rideable beasts. The people of Arnstead had hours of sunlight yet to toil under.

Room for a dozen horses was occupied by a single creature. The horse was stocky and a bit low to the ground. Patches of black and brown mottled its saddled and pack-laden body. Speed was not the first word that came to mind when looking at the horse, but that suited Owen just fine. He preferred it that way.

"Hello, Oatmeal."

Owen spoke to the horse with the same apprehension that accompanies greeting a freshly noticed mountain lion.

Getting the horse to the Creaky Board had been a simple enough endeavor. Marcus dropped the reins into Owen's trembling hands. Then, with those straps of leather bound in a steeled grip, Owen led the creature to their shared destination.

The street is too busy, Owen had told himself. *Can't go hurting anybody the second I climb onto this thing.*

Owen told himself something similar as he unhitched Oatmeal from her post. Anyone watching Owen's hands would have been forgiven if they thought he manipulated the iron-clad jaws of a bear trap, rather than the reins of a mild horse that was content to drink from the convenient water trough.

"Uh-huh," Owen stuttered. "Yup. That's a good girl. Just... keep not paying attention. We're doing great."

Leather reins had been tied into an amalgamation at the hitch. Any sailor worth their salt would have averted their eyes at the horror. Owen was no sailor, and the towering presence of Oatmeal did his nerves no favors.

Tremors wracked his hands as he struggled to free his horse from the post. Each swish of Oatmeal's tail or clomp of a hoof caused Owen to jump, further exacerbating the issue. A steady stream of expletives muttered under his breath helped Owen remain focused. His knowledge of profanity had been exhausted twice over before he managed to untie Oatmeal.

"Ah-h-h. There we go!" Owen half-shouted. "That wasn't so bad, was it? All right then, Oatmeal, we're headed east."

Oatmeal kept her muzzle submerged in the water trough for a moment before obediently following the pull of the reins. Saddlebags jostled in time with the clop of her powerful hooves.

Owen's eyes remained fixed on the eastern horizon as he marched, legs stiff with primal fear.

Traffic thinned upon approaching Arnstead's outer limits. Homes were sparse to match. Turned heads were more noticeable now that the ocean of people had trickled down into a meager pond. It was the first time that Owen had welcomed the looks of curious loathing. They helped distract him from the phantom sound of crunching bones that sounded with each hoofbeat.

Seeking further distraction, Owen pulled out his pocket watch. The time was just past four. He clicked his tongue at the loss of time. It was pleasant while it had lasted, but Owen had not meant to spend over an hour at the Creaky Board. He had not expected the errant to require more than ten minutes.

Devlin and company had ridden from where Owen now stood sometime that morning. As close to dawn as they might have managed.

"Nine hours behind," he grumbled to the eastward road.

There was little to see. A farmer and his ox pulling an empty cart east, until they were a speck that turned north from the road. A pair of carriages riding into town from who knows where. Three Nirdac katarl, perhaps a family, carrying what looked to be their entire lives in sacks over their shoulders.

Tamed land to either side of the road was bathed in the golden light of evening. New buildings pushed the edge of Arnstead out to the east, over ancient farmland that had long since been abandoned from a hundred years of abuse. Quiet desolation coated in the bronze dust of progress.

Owen straightened himself as a gentle breeze pressed at his back and shoulders. He tucked his watch away and cast a defiant look at Oatmeal, who flicked her tail against the wind.

"Can't wait any longer, can I?" he asked of the horse. "Not if I want to catch them before they turn off from the road. I remember the witch and her lot came from the south, but that's all I've got to go on."

No response came from Oatmeal. Not so much as whinny.

That was not to say that Owen had expected anything. Once again, he spoke aloud to calm himself more than to interact with the horse. He engaged in the futile exercise of patting at some of the dust that clung to his trousers, then slotted his left foot into a stirrup.

"Be gentle with me, all right?" Owen pleaded, looking into Oatmeal's large brown eyes.

First one bounce, then a larger bounce. The third bounce gathered Owen's momentum and launched his right leg over the saddle. He came to rest on the seat with a plop. Oatmeal shook her head, rustling her brown, shaggy mane.

Terror gripped Owen. From his toes to the hairs on his head, nothing moved of his own volition. Any and all reaction to Oatmeal's movement was stifled. He was arrested in the saddle.

Owen had become a ten-year-old boy. The child who had been bucked from his saddle, who came crashing to the ground. Air had abandoned that child. His legs would not move.

A ten-year-old sack of meat that had to be dragged from under the raging horse. Dragged away by his cousin, his idol. At ten years of age, he had lain helpless while the horse kicked Cynthia to the ground and crushed her left leg under hoof. Infallible strength made brittle by a single step.

Light, vivid and full of promise, had been extinguished in the eyes of Cynthia Orland that day. The pained howl that accompanied the family doctor's call for amputation rang as clear in Owen's ears as it had fourteen years ago.

Oatmeal jostled to the left.

The gentle motion brought Owen crashing back to the present. So forceful was the return that he reeled forward in the saddle, clutching at the horn. Breath came to him in ragged gasps. He gulped at the air like a man nearly drowned. Sweat, cold and clammy, slicked his palms and neck. Owen felt his frame expand near to breaking with each greedy breath.

Potato and bile mixed in the back of his throat. Owen slapped the fist that held the reins over his mouth. The sore, still fresh from where he had bitten his lip earlier that day, came back to life like embers coaxed into a final burn. A new string of profanities spewed from pursed lips as he quarreled with his afternoon meal. Doubled over in the saddle, it felt to be a losing battle.

Chicken and potatoes were finally choked back to where they belong. A shaking hand wrapped Oatmeal's reins around the saddle horn and fumbled for a canteen. Stowed within easy reach of the rider, Owen clawed the cap off the metal container and cleansed his palette. Water streamed down the side of his mouth as Owen gasped in relief.

Owen sniffed at the smell of dust and horse. Through all his writhing and flailing, Oatmeal had remained calm. The animal was completely divorced from the anxiety of her rider.

"That's a good girl," Owen coughed. He gave Oatmeal a gracious pat on the neck.

All in the past, Owen thought. *Worry about now. Right now. Focus on now.*

Against all his instincts, Owen gave a gentle kick to Oatmeal's sides. Or at least he thought he did. It amounted more to digging his heels in than to sharp, direct action. The details did not seem to matter to Oatmeal. She began her eastward trot without pomp or fuss.

"Thank you, Marcus," Owen choked through another cough. "Leave it to you to find the most docile creature on the entire continent."

Restless legs ached to abandon the stirrups. Hands fraught with tremors pleaded to toss the reins aside. His sweat-soaked body agreed on all fronts, but Owen's mind had managed to wrest control. So distracted he was by the cry of every nerve in his body that Arnstead had become a speck over his shoulder before Owen considered picking up speed.

Stiff legs groaned as Owen stood in the stirrups. His desire to flee the saddle was outweighed by the need to stretch. He pulled his watch out and clicked the cover open as he sat back down.

"Can't imagine we're making *terrible* time. Let's see wha— how has an hour passed already?"

Excited words stretched out over fields that began to show signs of life. Owen snapped a quick look over his shoulder again. The sun did not seem like it had sunk so far, but he conceded to himself that he was not the best at deciphering the signs of celestial bodies. Looking back at his watch, spots in his eyes, confirmed it was past five-o-clock.

Slow and steady. That was what Owen's shot nerves desired. Time to adjust to this new reality of traveling on horseback for the first time in fourteen years. Time that Owen knew did not have to spare.

Owen leaned to his right. Far enough that he was able to get a good look at Oatmeal's face. He pursed his lips as he shifted his gaze to the eastern horizon.

"How do you feel about going a bit faster, yeah?"

Oatmeal released a conspicuous snort and shook her mane.

"I'm not happy about it either," Owen continued. "All the same…"

This kick was closer to its namesake. Feet splayed out on either side of the horse, then returned with a forceful prompt. Owen's heels dug enough for Oatmeal to take notice.

The resulting increase in speed did come in a sharp burst. Pace climbed at the steady grade that a name like Oatmeal would suggest. She carried herself like a horse who had known many riders. Seasoned equestrians and those who feared horses alike.

Grace and even temper were not enough to keep Owen's stomach from attempting another series of backflips.

Bile remained where it belonged. The mixture of half-digested chicken and potato stew did not rear its head. While there was a recurrence of cold sweat, this reaction was more tolerable than the first.

Clean air helped assuage Owen's animalistic response. The ever-present dust that lingered thick within Arnstead thinned as he rode away. The warm wind rushing through his hair lacked the sensation of fine sandpaper. Breaths were deep and taken with ease.

Green returned to the world as dust abated. First as patches of wild grass, then as farmland. Stalks of corn and wheat rustled by the unsullied wind stretched north and south to create their artificial horizon. Pockets of woodland separated farms and kept crops from intermingling with each other. Owen received a leisurely wave from the occasional farmhand while sunlight lasted.

Oatmeal afforded Owen the freedom to look about as he pleased. She found her own comfortable pace and stuck to the road. The maintenance required of Owen was to ensure that he didn't fall from the saddle. An act that, given Oatmeal's nature, would have required him to fall asleep in the saddle.

Though Oatmeal made the ride as carefree as she could, Owen could not find complete ease. One hand was always locked around the saddle horn. Both feet remained pressed against the stirrups, just in case a quick shift of weight was required.

The golden light of day melted into crimson twilight without incident.

Owen grew anxious as the rise of the moon replaced the fall of the sun. With dusk went light, and with light went sight. The waning moon afforded a measure of light in the cloudless sky. Stars offered what guidance they could, twinkling in far-flung galaxies. It was not so bright, however, that someone might lose sleep.

What Owen feared was a dark campsite. Tucked a half-mile or more off the road, shrouded in a veil of night. His eyes scanned the moonlit night for a campfire. A beacon to sound the end of his long ride.

Another fear prevented Owen from halting the ride. Though his legs and seat had grown woefully sore, and Oatmeal's pace had flagged back to a trot, he did not bring the creature to a stop. He knew deep down that it would be a battle to resume once he had dismounted to stretch. His body would fight the action, would beg for sleep before taking to the saddle again.

To stop without finding Devlin and Manda's camp would be to stop for the night. Owen was no better at tracking than he was telling time from the sun. If he did not find a camp near the main road before daybreak, he would either find himself lost amidst a desperate search or return to Arnstead empty-handed.

Sense had not entirely abandoned Owen. This effort was a fool's errand without assistance. He had hurried from Arnstead without a guide, knowing that Devlin had spoken of recruiting one. He did not even bother to check if Marcus had packed a map.

Owen grumbled to himself about the practicality of reading a map in the dark, or without knowing how to properly read a map in the first place.

Thoughts turned to how he would explain his absence to Aaron. This was a concern only if Owen returned on a shortened timeline with nothing to show. Knowing the lax nature of the Second Seeker, Owen would be surprised if the matter warranted a stern talk. A few notes about the value following order. Mention that their work, however dull and demeaning, was of great benefit to the people of Arnstead.

"If he manages to find his spine again." Owen took advantage of isolation to spit into the dark void. "Leaves me out to dry when I make a mistake, then refuses to let me help when he actually needs it."

Oatmeal flapped her lips at the sudden onset of noise.

"Exactly!" Owen replied. "Doesn't matter. Once we get this done, I'll be on my way out of that dead-end department. The Raulstone name will be known for more in Arnstead than paperwork. I won't have my father find me behind a desk."

Malevolence opened the door to further negative depths.

"Can already imagine his face, hearing I've been chained to an office chair. 'That's no place for a Raulstone. You should out in the field, climbing the ladder.' Ugh, your ladder can go fall down a well. This isn't the Federal Armies and I'm not on the officer track!"

Receptive night drank his howl.

"I don't need you to tell me what to do. Not you, not the First Seeker, and no one else like you! I am Owen first and Raulstone second. You hear? Owen!"

Owen's face had grown hot by the time he finished. The rant left him breathing hard, but overwhelmingly satisfied. He returned the wide smile of the moon as he basked in its glow.

A glow.

From the corner of his eye, Owen spied a glimmer to the north of the road.

"Whoa there, girl. I think I see a light."

Momentary confusion gave way to embarrassment as Owen remembered he was talking to a horse. Leather reins crinkled in response to Owen's pull. Metal clacked in the darkness to signal equine approval. Her steadfast steps came to a slow stop.

When he was sure that Oatmeal had come to a complete stop, Owen hiked a leg over the saddle and planted eager feet onto the ground. Relief was tempered by the immediate and forceful burn in his thighs and seat. The payment for his first solo ride in a decade came without mercy. From the feel of it, the ache intended to stay.

"Ah! Oh, oh my." Owen sucked air through gritted teeth. "Oh, that's awful."

Owen hobbled off the road and through the darkness, Oatmeal clopping along in tow, towards the glistening ember in a sea of black.

15.

TRAILBLAZING

Remnants of a dying fire crackled in an ink-black void. Enough life remained to foster the occasional pop and snap of a log. Sweet, pungent wood smoke mingled with bitter hints of coffee that was on the cusp of burning. Voices muttered indistinct nothings as the scrape of a tin handle against its pot cut through the calm environment.

Meat sizzled, freshly lain into a skillet. It had the distinct smell of pork, possibly bacon. Maybe sausage. The aroma was too faint to tell.

Something else bubbled and hissed. There was no smell to it. The fire roared as a new skillet was presumably laden with breakfast goods. Metal ground against metal. Whatever was in the skillet was being worked with fervor.

Numbness. Fingers pricked by needles and nails. There was too much pressure on one side, and a need to roll onto the other. Muscles lurched. Legs ridden raw protested movement.

"Up an' at 'em, Blue."

The warning preceded a boot into Owen's ankle. Without malice, but with enough force to ensure the recipient would awaken.

Owen shuffled with a start. Eyes, filled with sleep, snapped open to take in what his other senses had already observed. He propped himself up on an elbow. Fingers from his free hand rubbed at the blear that plagued his sight. A deep yawn on his back forced some smoke into his lungs. The sear helped to pull him into the land of the living. Another yawn arched his back. He leaned into the stretch and flung with arms out to either side.

Pale morning light gave new detail to the thin thicket of woods where he had found Devlin and Manda the night before. A bumper of trees between two farms, little more than a patch of green between fields of gold. Stalks of grain were clear to see fifty feet to the east or west. The brown of the road was not far south. Only north did the green stretch on as far as Owen could see.

There had been more in the patch to discover than just a Keeper of Many and a lieutenant of the Fourth Federation Army. Four others were present.

"Morning, sunshine," said the woman who had kicked Owen's ankles.

"Good morning, Mahika," Owen grumbled back as he cleared his throat.

Mahika was a Bangeli human who looked to be a few years older than Owen. She was short yet lithe. A compact container of early morning mirth. Long black hair was pinned into a tight bun. Painted freckles dotted her brown hands and face.

The familiarity between the two ended at their first names. Owen knew that much about the woman because she had been awake upon his arrival. Both her and Devlin chatted around the fire that Owen had spotted from the road. She had jumped to her feet, slender dagger in hand, at the sound of Owen's approach. Mahika had been a blade of bronze in the firelight, ready to tear at whoever might encroach upon a campsite in the dark of the night.

Murderous intent vanished when Devlin showed recognition. Cheer and a smile were on offer this morning, as though Mahika had no memory of baring her blade.

"Eggs, bacon, and a bit of bread. Coffee, too, if you have the taste for it," she said, walking to the fire. Logs and stones had been assembled, improvised chairs around a field kitchen. Mahika beckoned for Owen to join. "Come on, before these louts eat the lot of it."

"Look what rolled into camp."

Manda's unenthused voice signaled her presence before she was visible. She appeared from around a tree. Both hands were occupied with the effort of shoring up her trousers and fastening a belt into place. A loud crack erupted from her neck as she rolled her head from side to side.

The apathetic remark was all the attention she gave to Owen. No question as to why he had come or what his intentions were. Instead, she pulled a mess kit from her pack and took a seat next to the fire.

Of all the people who might have rejected his presence, Owen had expected Manda to put up the fiercest opposition. He had expected insults to be thrown without hesitation. At least a couple of punches now that Cynthia was not there to stop Manda's aggression. The complete indifference was somehow more uncomfortable. Complete dispassion from a woman who always exhibited extreme emotion.

Owen considered himself fortunate and grabbed his mess kit to join those around the fire. He lowered himself with tender care next to Devlin.

"How are the legs?" Devlin asked in his warm way. Steam wandered along the sides of his face as it rose from his coffee.

"Oh, so you couldn't hear my thighs scream as I sat down, then?"

Devlin snorted at the remark. Small bubbles churned in the black liquid at his lips.

"I'd thought we had everyone when we left town. This another one from the House, Sir?"

The question came from an unfamiliar face. A Zumbatran katarl with a braided mane of reddish-gold, he spoke in a rumbling bass. It was the sort of voice that a person felt rather than heard. Owen swore he could feel his bones vibrate at the katarl's every syllable.

Grand presence was somewhat diminished by the red apron that hung loosely around the katarl's neck. A bandana of the same shade was wrapped around his head. The cloth helped keep back the upper, unbraided portions of his mane as he leaned over the fire. In one hand was a cast-iron skillet. The other held a two-pronged fork that he used to manipulate sausage links. Grease popped as a deft motion skewered a pair of sausages, which he extended to Owen from across the fire.

"That's a joke, right? The man's wearing a Spellseeker uniform, Jabari!"

Last of the new faces, the incredulous jeers came from a Nirdac harn. It was difficult for Owen to tell if her face was scrunched with disbelief or if the look was natural. Her right eye darted from Owen to the katarl named Jabari. Where the left eye should have been was a scarred pit. Three jagged lines ran from the top of her head through to the bottom of her cheek. Pink flesh contrasted the marks against light brown fur.

"He was covered in a blanket until just now, Scarlet. Coffee?"

Jabari lifted the coffee pot from the fire and offered it to the harn.

"Get that outta my face," she spat. The scowl appeared to take permanent residence upon Scarlet's face. "You know I hate that swill."

"Suit yourself," Jabari shrugged. After topping off his cup, the katarl extended the pot towards Owen. "How about you, bluecoat?"

To hear the nickname bluecoat spoken without venom or malice was an unexpected turn. Owen had grown so accustomed over the past month to his uniform warranting insults that Jabari's flat use of the term came as a shock. Jabari had addressed an unfamiliar Spellseeker in the same manner that someone might have greeted an old acquaintance.

"If you don't mind," Owen replied and extended his cup.

"Not at all."

No point in questioning hospitality, Owen thought. If this stranger wanted to spend the next few days showering Owen with warmth and kindness, that was perfectly all right with Owen.

Heat pushed through Owen's metal cup as the coffee was poured. Fresh and scalding, he was forced to set the brew down for a few minutes before it could be enjoyed. Time enough to munch on the sausage link that had been so generously provided.

"And how about for you, Mr. Beech?"

Jabari raised the coffee pot to the last member of the group. A face that Owen recognized without assistance; one Mr. Joseph Beech, head of Beech Security Company. That was a face Owen had not expected to see again. Not for any thought of malice, but because he knew of no reason for crossing paths with the Nirdac katarl again.

"Oh, yes please," Beech responded. He did not attempt to hide just how eager he was to receive the piping hot beverage. Nostrils flared as he inhaled the bitter, slightly burnt aroma. "That is lovely. Thank you."

"No need to crawl up his ass, Beech," Manda grumbled, holding out her cup to be served. "Would be one thing if he knew how not to burn the stuff."

A sharp chuckle escaped Scarlet's twisted lips. Beech put on his best impression of a turtle, retracting his head between sullen shoulders. The others paid more attention to their meal than to the surrounding conversation.

Once the coffee had cooled somewhat, Owen took a timid sip. The temperature was perfect. Much to his displeasure, however, Manda had not been wrong. Burnt coffee coated his throat as Owen forced himself to swallow. Residue clung to his tongue as he passed it over his teeth. An unpleasant experience all around.

Expectant eyes looked at Owen from across the fire. Jabari awaited a reaction to his creation. Not wishing to waste the goodwill he had been shown, Owen met Jabari's gaze and smiled through another swig of the sad excuse for coffee. Jabari returned the smile was a satisfied nod.

A glance down at the remaining coffee in his cup told Owen that reaching the bottom would not be a pleasant endeavor.

Pockets of small talk emerged around the fire. Jabari discussed the finer points of meal preparation with an engrossed Beech. Some of the cringeworthy advice including that a pot of coffee's readiness was determined by smell alone, and that a healthy pinch of salt could save eggs that had started to turn. Talk that would make Marcus fall into an early grave.

Tales of past work were traded between Mahika and Scarlet. Narrow escapes from overwhelming odds. Feats of daring whit and subtlety unmatched by their peers. A bit of chest-pounding to pass the time.

Manda kept silent except to ask for more coffee or another spot of questionable eggs.

"I failed to mention it last night, but I'm glad you found your way to us." Devlin tapped his knuckles against Owen's knee. "Every pair of hands is a blessing. Regardless of who they're attached to."

The Keeper made a subtle, sweeping gesture towards the other side of the fire. Owen followed the motion and could not help but grin. Devlin returned a burdened smile.

"Good thing you kept a fire through the night. Was worried I might ride past you in the dark."

Owen choked down another gulp of coffee.

"You have our guide to thank for that," Devlin said. "Ms. Galloway was against the light, but he said it would help keep away creatures of the night. Proved enough to chew on to overrule our intrepid leader."

"Would that be our masterful chef?" Owen lifted his little finger from his cup to point at Jabari.

"Hmm? Oh, gods no," Devlin chuckled. "No, these are all Ms. Galloway's people. Our guide was my contribution to the group. I'll introduce you when he returns."

"Where's he gone to?"

"To scout ahead, he said. You wouldn't have seen it in the dark, but just up the road is where our carriage met its fiery end. Imagine he's doing his best to pick up Amalia's trail."

"That close? Hadn't realized I rode that far," Owen said, turning his head as he spoke. Oatmeal, as patient as could be, was hitched to a low-hanging branch. The grass surrounding her was notably shorter than the patches outside her reach. Bits of green protruded from her mouth while

248

she munched with contented abandon.

"I imagine he'll be just as excited to meet your horse as he will to meet you."

"Some sort of enthusiast?"

"Something of the sort," Devlin laughed.

It was clear that no more information was forthcoming. Rather than press the matter, Owen made another strike against the bitter foe in his cup. The battle grew more dire with each sip. Burnt coffee turned out to be no better cold than it was hot.

There was no sign of any guide or scout by the time the coffee pot was drained.

The camp stirred as breakfast came to a close. Metal brushes scraped grit and grime from pans and skillets. Water swilled about in pots before being tossed to the nearest tree. Bedding was rolled and stowed on horses, or ponies in the case of the harn. Horses and ponies were brushed and saddled. A single tent was broken down by Jabari and packed with care.

Mahika collected waterskins and canteens while others cleaned or packed their possessions. A vessel in hand, she would approach a tree and open the container. One finger was draped over the opening. Her spare hand was placed, fingers splayed, on the nearby tree. Light shone from her hands and was accompanied by the trickle of running water. A desiccated imprint remained when Mahika removed her hand from the tree. Mahika moved to a different tree with each new container.

"I try my best not to kill them," she had responded to Owen's questioning gaze.

Leaves rustled in the direction of the road as idleness began to stray into awkward silence. Owen paid the sound no attention. The wind had blown through underbrush all night and morning, and would likely continue to do so until the world ceased to turn.

It was when the wind produced a voice that Owen finally took notice.

"We have found the trail. We are ready when you are ready."

A voice like dry leaves rustled where Owen had thought there was only wind. He turned on his heel to see a man standing next to Oatmeal. One red hand tousled the horse's mane, while the other scratched above her shoulder. The half of his face that Owen could see bore no expression.

Pointed ears were a clear indication that the man was a kin. A Fieldkin, as evidenced by his red-orange skin. His face was long and sharp, framed by braids of long, black hair that reached over his shoulders and down to his breast. Thin lips were overshadowed by a prominent, hooked nose.

Of the few Fieldkin Owen had ever seen, this was the first to wear what Owen understood to be their traditional garb. Tanned deerskin leggings covered him from the waist down. A breechclout of the same material was draped over a rawhide belt. The leather was plain and devoid of decoration. He was bare from the waist up, save for a pair of beaded bracelets wrapped tight around his left wrist. Leather shoes that reminded Owen of slippers protected the Fieldkin's feet and were tied at the ankle.

Knowledge of the culture was not enough to prevent shock at seeing the man traipse around without a shirt. *It would have made some sense if the Fieldkin was fresh from a bath*, Owen thought, but to just walk around bare-chested? It did not look proper.

"There's the man of the hour," Devlin cried. His welcoming nature seemed to know no bounds. "This is our guide, Owen. He is called Igasho."

"Excuse me?" The fires of shame licked once more at Owen's when he realized this had been said aloud rather than thought.

"Your people call me Walks Far. It is acceptable."

If the Fieldkin had taken offense to Owen's sleight, he did an excellent job of concealing it. Weathered lines that cracked his face refused to stir. Chestnut eyes remained fixated on Oatmeal.

"You heard the red man," Manda shouted. "Trail is sniffed out. Time to saddle-up!"

Some weight was lifted from Owen after Manda spoke. Suddenly, he did not feel quite so bad about his transgression.

Owen and company had ridden from their campsite for half a day without major incident. Riders changed position as conversation pulled them forward or back. The only constant was Walks Far at the head of the pack. He set the pace, which Manda doggedly protested to be far too slow, and kept a steady gaze ahead.

What the man watched was a mystery. Owen tried his best to pick out any speck of consistent detail Walks Far might be looking for.

At first, Owen suspected the Fieldkin might be looking for burnt grass or farmland. The Cinder Witch had shown a limited ability for flight. Fire had propelled her through the air and somehow allowed her to alter course. It stood to reason in Owen's mind that she might have used this method of travel to keep pace with her mounted associates.

There had been some merit to the assumption. A clear trail cut southwest by south from where Beech's coach had met its eventual demise. The theory did not hold, however, as any indication of burnt grass had cleared away after about a mile's ride.

Walks Far showed no hesitation as the clear signs faded away.

The grass was tall where they rode. Their trail had taken back towards Arnstead and ran along the edge of tamed land. The farms furthest from town had been on their right. Wild fields stretched eastward on their left.

In these tall, undisturbed fields, Owen thought their path might have been dictated by bent patches of grass. A group of horses marching in single file must leave some clear sign of passage. Their own company left a thin trail of stomped grasses in their wake. It might have been possible that the Cinder Witch's band left similar markings.

Gentle encouragement pushed Oatmeal near the head of the company. As best as Owen could judge, there were no trail lines ahead.

Walks Far never so much as turned his head from side to side.

Half a dozen more theories popped up. None stood up to observation. They seemed to be riding based on clues that ran dry miles back. When Owen noticed a pair of figures working the nearest farm, he saw an opportunity.

"Manda," Owen called. Manda was three horses up and did not look at all pleased when she turned her head in response. Owen pressed Oatmeal to come alongside Manda. "Stop the group. I'm going to head over and ask those people if they saw the Witch come this way."

"Sure, whatev— Hey, what do you think we hired a guide for? Slow going as it is. Not about to stop for no reason."

"The guy has been staring dead ahead since we started riding," Owen said, his voice hushed. "What makes you think he knows where we're going?"

"And you're some kind of expert all of a sudden? Hey! I said no!"

Owen had already begun to steer his way toward the farm before the last question was out of his mouth. Two taps against Oatmeal's sides sent them speeding away from Manda's protests.

Too fast, too fast, too fast!

Haste to make distance had caused Owen to spur Oatmeal harder than he meant. Breakfast churned as Owen pulled back on the reigns. Oatmeal, capable of greater empathy than most people, slowed to accommodate her rider. Another tug at the reins brought her to a stop.

"How about we walk for a minute, huh?" Owen mumbled as he dismounted at the edge of the farm. Jelly legs approved of solid ground, though it took a few steps for Owen to find his normal stride. He kept the reins in hand so that Oatmeal would follow behind.

"Would be an awful lot faster if you rode your damn horse!"

Frustration rippled on the wind over stalks of barley. Manda made her impatience bare. Pretense, as was usually the case, was beyond her. The source of anguish was Owen.

All seemed right in the world once more.

"Hello there!" Owen called as he approached the figures, free hand raised in greeting.

A pair of humans, a man and a woman, both Nirdac with sun-kissed complexions. Sleeves that may have once been white were pushed up past the elbow. Wide hats of straw cast meager shade over their ears and shoulders.

Both looked but neither spoke, choosing lazy waves as their hello.

"Would you two happen to be the owners? Of the farm, I mean."

Heads were shaken in place of a no.

"Could you direct to me to whoever does? I have some questions I was hoping to ask, about an occurrence from a month or so back. Bureau business."

Two thumbs pointed west over shoulders.

"Fair enough," Owen said, tired of the tacit replies. "Thank you."

The quiet pair parted to make room for Owen. Their courtesy was rough. Manners learned from long days spent in large fields. An environment where every ounce of energy was put to use and nothing went to waste.

Rough courtesy, but courtesy nonetheless. Owen emphasized his thanks with a nod as he passed.

Down the dirt earthen path that bisected two fields was a farmhouse. A squat building, wood grayed by age and wear. White shutters were open to the fields and swayed with the gentle wind that made the fields whisper. Square posts supported a bowed awning that hung over the generous porch. Two rocking chairs lazed to the left of the open doorway, a small table between them.

In one of the chairs sat a withered Zumbatran human. Hands clasped over a round gut, his bare feet pushed back against his weight. Ancient floorboards groaned under the pressure. The gentle rocking motion suited his relaxed shoulders. Remnants of gray hair wrapped from temple to temple and down the back of his head, leaving the top of his dark head bare.

A small wave of guilt came over Owen as he approached. Whistled breath suggested the man was asleep. Or very near to it.

"Excuse me, sir?"

The man stirred slowly, like a confused child woken before dawn. His head lifted from the chair as eyes blinked at sharp daylight. Owen waited patiently for the man to realize he was there. Oatmeal scraped at the dirt in front of the porch. A short whinny brought the man over the edge from sleeping to wakefulness.

"Oh, morning there, Blue."

"Morning, sir," Owen replied. He didn't have the heart to tell the man it was half-past noon.

"Bit early to get my licenses done, isn't it? Violette send you?"

"Pardon?" Owen asked, head slightly cocked.

"The Woods girl, Violette. She comes out every fall to help me get the licenses for the tiller and thresher up to date. These old bones don't handle the trip to town so well these days. Real peach, going out of her way like that to help an old man like me."

"She is the helpful type, to be certain."

How much is that woman responsible for? Owen found himself wondering. *Monitoring Spellseekers, facilitating their correspondence, assistant to the First Seeker, and now licensing work?* The list of her tasks seemed to grow and grow.

"I guess you're not here to make sure the machines are up to code, then?" the man asked.

"No, sir. I'm here on Spellseeker business, trying to hunt down a fugitive."

"Really now?" The man's snowy eyebrows reached for the top of his head. "What's that got to do with me and my farm here?"

"Not much, I think," Owen said, raising a hand in reassurance. "Just wanted to ask a question or two, if you wouldn't mind."

"Mind? Violette's people are my people. You want to hitch your horse up and come take a seat?" The man leaned over to the vacant chair and patted the armrest. Before Owen could answer, the man had turned to shout through the open doorway to the house. "Hey Delilah, we've got company. Bring out the lemonade and glasses, would ya please?"

"That the Arlingtons?" The response wafted out from somewhere in the house on a thin, frail voice. "Jenny said they'd be out sometime this week."

"No, someone from the Arcane Bureau. What did you say your name was, son?"

"Owen Raulstone."

"Pleasure, Owen," the man said, stretching his hand out to Owen for a quick handshake. "Name's Salim."

Pleasantries went back and forth until a Zumbatran woman emerged from the farmhouse with a wooden tray. Lemonade glistened in a glass pitcher next to a trio of wooden cups. The woman carrying the tray, Delilah, beamed with a snaggled, gentle smile. Her skin was lighter than Salim's and her hair more gray than white. A slight tremor in her hands caused the contents of the tray to clink and clatter as she walked.

Self-conscious, Owen attempted to surrender his seat to his hostess.

"Thank you, sweetheart, but I'm not so old that I can't stand for a while. You go on ahead."

Dalilah poured a glass of lemonade for Owen as she spoke. Dauntless cheer in the face of age and a stranger in her chair.

Owen felt spoiled to receive so much kindness in one day while wearing his Spellseeker uniform. It was pleasant, but also a bit sad. The fact that simple hospitality felt like a royal welcome was not lost on him.

"Makes the best lemonade, she does," Salim said after a large gulp. He smacked his lips and exhaled blissfully. "About time we got your questions, huh?"

"If we could. I bet my companions are getting a bit antsy."

"Compan— well why didn't you say folks were waiting on you?" Salim took another deep gulp of lemonade. His protest was directed more at himself than at Owen. "Here I am going on about nothing. What do you need?"

"Quite all right," Owen said, taking another gulp himself. Salim was not wrong. The lemonade was the perfect mix of tart and sweet. Both light and refreshing. The sort of drink that did not make him feel ashamed to make Manda wait. "This fugitive I'm looking for, I think she might have come this way almost a month ago. I expect she would have been flying, low enough to the ground to catch field alight. She uses fire to push herself through the air."

"You're after that Cinder Witch woman?" Delilah cut in.

"Yes, as a matter of fact," Owen nodded. "Do you know her?"

"We know *of* her, yeah. Nobody we know hasn't heard of the messes she makes. You said a month ago?"

"Roughly, yes."

"Sal, I told you it wasn't a shooting star. Was too close to the ground!"

"You want me to believe that was a *person* zipping through the night?" Salim retorted.

"And why not? The time fits. And half the Arlingtons' field went off that night! They were lucky they managed to save a thing, how fast the fire came on. I bet it was that nuisance this boy is after."

"This streak," Owen asked from the edge of his seat, "do you remember which way it was moving?"

"Sure," Delilah said. She leaned into the word, hanging on it for a couple of seconds. "Was headed north to south. One-hundred percent."

"Exactly what I was hoping to hear," Owen said, ecstatic. He downed the remaining lemonade in his glass in a single gulp, the tartness contorting his face. "Thank you so much for your hospitality!"

"On your way already?" Delilah asked with a hint of disappointment.

Owen was already out of his chair and unraveling Oatmeal's reins.

"Afraid so," he sighed. "Places to be, people to catch!"

"Well, you make sure you to tell Violette we said hello, all right?" Salim belted as Owen mounted Oatmeal and turned to ride. "And tell her she doesn't need an excuse to come by once and a while."

"I most certainly will!"

The speed at which Oatmeal cut down the dirt path went unnoticed, quelled by Owen's excitement. This was real work. Speaking to people who valued his service, who had helpful information. Making headway on locating a dangerous criminal. His chance to smother an unruly flame was approaching.

Hope, fueled by progress, put a burgeoning wind to his sails.

Lunch was underway when Owen returned to his companions. The lot of them had dismounted and made themselves comfortable. Mahika was splayed out on folded grass, a yellow kerchief over her face to ward away the sun. Jabari and Beech sliced sausage and bits of cheese to distribute. Scarlet polished a caster rifle that stood a full foot taller than she did. Half of her attention was spent cleaning, the other half doing her best to keep the rifle from toppling over.

Engrossed in the pages of the Brahmzarrah, Devlin sat quiet away from the others. The occasional muttered word might have signaled to the faithful what passages the Keeper read. Owen was lost entirely. He felt it was best to leave the man to his book.

Manda, seated with legs and arms crossed, glared at Owen with raw malice. A face that said *this is your fault and I hate you for it.*

"Good news," Owen started as he dismounted. His bright disposition would not be quashed by a mean look. "The owners of the farm saw a phenomenon that matches what we know about the Cinder Witch. Confirmed she was traveling north to south, and leaving some carnage in her wake."

"So, we stopped for a half-hour just for you to figure out our guide was doing his job," Manda said as she continued to glower. "Sound about right?"

"Would be one way to put it, I suppose," Owen affirmed.

Manda stifled a scream behind pursed lips. Eyes rolled backward in frustration, her body imitating the motion until her back was on the ground.

A smile grew in Owen's chest that dared not show.

Theory-crafting brought nothing but frustration. By the time the day had grown long and the sun was ready to set, Owen had come no closer to understanding the Fieldkin's methods than when the day was young. There was a thread somewhere. Some piece of loose information to glean that would solve the riddle, Owen was sure. The trouble lay in finding that thread.

Walks Far kept to himself. While others changed position in line to discuss this or that, the Fieldkin remained at the front. He made a point of keeping a few horse-lengths away. If the pace of the company quickened, he would match. He slowed when the company slowed. Stopped when the company stopped.

It was a wonder that Manda had not noticed this tendency to match pace. Continued cries for haste fell on deaf ears. All she had to do was creep towards Walks Far to gain the desired speed.

Owen was content to keep the observation to himself.

A halt was called when the last golden rays of day bled into the crimson that signaled night's approach. The ride had lasted for as long as the sun would allow. What little light was left was spent making camp. Manda's people set to work without a word.

Mahika tended to the horses, securing their reins to stakes and providing feed and water. Manda herself unpacked bedrolls and folded grass. Preparations to make sleep accessible as soon as dinner was concluded. Rather than preparing a fire and sorting ingredients, as Owen had expected he would, Jabari made himself busy by pitching a tent. He was the only person in the company to do so.

Scarlet worked with a book of matches. There was not much to burn where the company had settled for the evening. Tall, green grass dominated the immediate area. The few trees nearby provided little in the way of kindling. She was able to gather some sizeable limbs and branches with help from Devlin and Beech, but not much that was small enough to help birth a flame. Brief sparks of flame turned to wisps of smoke as crimson skies slipped into purple twilight.

"Would you like some help with that?" Owen asked.

"What, you some kind of firebug?" Scarlet replied, her frustration evident in her ferocious emphasis on the word firebug.

"Something like that."

"By all means, then."

Scarlet pocketed the empty book of matches as she stepped away from the skeletal promise of fire and flung her hands to the sky.

Matches were fine tools. Simple, singular their purpose. Effective for those unable to focus the Flow into flames. Though Owen certainly fell into that category of individual, he had another plan in mind. Owen unholstered his caster pistol and opened the breech.

"We need a fire, Blue, not a crater."

Familiar scorn slipped into the term. It may have been Scarlet's nature as a whole, but her way of referring to Spellseekers fell neatly in line with the townspeople of Arnstead.

"Please," Owen said, maintaining a professional tone, "let me."

Crimson was the color of choice. Owen pulled the caster shell from his belt and slotted it into the breech. Glass tinkled against the pistol's inner workings as the cartridge settled into place. Metal scraped against metal.

Owen placed his thumb on the exposed piece of the cartridge with care. Flow channeled through his arm and into the receptacle. Light like a setting sun spilled from the chamber, illuminating the small pile of branches. The tool was ready for use.

"If you'll excuse me." Owen gestured for Scarlet to make room. Eyes rolled as she stood back in compliance.

When Owen willed the cartridge to work its purpose, a bright blue fire popped out from the muzzle of the caster pistol. The blaze did not shoot towards the pile of sticks and branches. It did not sputter and go out. Formed into a small cone the length and width of a human finger, the fire maintained its shape while Owen fed it energy. The fire hissed like a fierce wind through a penny-sized hole.

Dead twigs stood no chance. The fire caught within moments of Owen holding out his torch. The hiss of the pistol was steadily replaced by the crackle of a small campfire. Sparks flitted up towards the cloudless sky, joining the first stars of the night.

There was no approval on Scarlet's face as she eyed the caster pistol. No scowl, either. It seemed the closest to a compliment Owen might receive from the harn. He accepted with a nod. Scarlet muttered and scooped up her tools, plopping down by the fire to await the arrival of food.

Owen's mind no longer focused on its maintenance, the caster pistol sputtered and went out. He holstered the tool after a job well done.

Open flame drew the rest of the company. Warmth and the promise of food beckoned. Jabari, finished with his tent, had begun to extract pans and ingredients from his baggage. A grate was erected over the fire to house a kettle. Tea was on its way, courtesy of Mahika. The conversation broke out between Jabari and Devlin about what sort of tea to make. There were options aplenty, according to Devlin and his pack.

Everyone found some way to busy themselves around the fire. Everyone, except for Walks Far.

The Fieldkin kept a healthy distance between himself and the rest of the party. At the edge of the firelight, he looked more like a shadow than a person. A quiet observer of all that transpired. Not even the promise of food was enough to pull him away from the company of the horses.

Despite his isolation, Walks Far did not appear lonely. Quiet words were shared with his horse. What he said was lost to Owen. The language was one he did not recognize. *Must be his native tongue,* Owen thought. It was a language that flowed. Few harsh sounds fell from the Fieldkin's mouth as he whispered to his horse. To Oatmeal and the other horses, as well.

Watching the Fieldkin converse with the horses gave rise to more curious speculation.

Is it the horses? Owen wondered. *Are the horses telling him where to go? Maybe they see something we can't? Or smell something?*

A full day of questions had reached their boiling point. No longer atop a horse, Walks Far's imperceptible changes in speed could not maintain separation. Resolve to know more caused Owen to stir. He set his mess kit down by the fire and made his way over to Walks Far.

Four steps.

Horses veiled by night surrounded the Fieldkin. A mass of shadows that flickered at the edge of the light. One interconnected mass of horses, not a group of individual animals. It took four steps for this image to settle into Owen's mind. To become all that he could see.

The heel of the fifth step remained stuck in the earth.

Discomfort at the sight of an individual horse could be conquered. A group of horses, so long as there was a bit of distance, was tolerable. To ride Oatmeal had been a feat born of necessity. It was more than Owen had expected of himself. Life would have been swell if he had never climbed into another saddle for the rest of his days. Short on time and in need of speed, he had fought through that fear.

What he saw before him now was a nightmare put to the flesh.

Two days of reassurance with Oatmeal was a good step. Progress had been made. Tension eased enough to allow for new conceptions to be formed. There could come a time where thoughts of travel went first to horseback before resorting to a five-mile walk.

Two days was not, however, enough to crush half a lifetime's bias towards horses. Bones were brittle. Flesh was easy to tear. Visions of snapped, deformed limbs were still too vivid fourteen years later. Agonized cries of a loved one echoed just out of earshot.

Was it truly important to know how Walks Far knew the way? Doubt grew, a cold fist in Owen's stomach. Such knowledge seemed trivial in the face of roiling shadow.

"Do we frighten you?"

Half-whispered words slithered from the inky shape.

"W-what?" Owen stammered.

"You stopped. Do we frighten you?"

Rational thought hesitated to take root. The realization that it was Walks Far who had spoken, not the small group of horses, waited until the Fieldkin stepped forward. Firelight danced at his feet. Glistened in his eyes.

The congealed monstrosity was a group of horses once more.

"No, sorry," Owen said, finding his stride. "The uh, the horses. Horses disagree with me."

Thoughtful silence preempted Walks Far's reply.

"That is sad. This horse cares for you." The kin rested a barely visible hand on Oatmeal's neck. "Did you know her when she walked upright?"

Owen's silence was one of confusion.

"Walked... upright?"

"Yes."

The flat reply caught Owen off guard. He had expected some manner of explanation. Images of horses reared back on two legs came to mind. He did his best to block the thought from his mind.

"I'm not sure I understand," Owen said. He spoke clearly, with as much of a questioning inflection as he could muster. A child asking a stranger to read a sign or ask for directions. "What do you mean when you say horses walk upright?"

Another pause for thought. Walks Far might have been searching for the right words in the Federal tongue. Perhaps he was baffled by the lack of understanding. He grappled in silence long enough for Owen to single out Oatmeal. A childish piece of Owen was relieved to see that Oatmeal was, in fact, a single horse.

"A past life," Walks Far said. His voice was stern. A hunter speaking to one who had never held a bow. "When the soul of this horse belonged to a body that walked on two legs. Did you know her?"

This was not the explanation Owen had expected. He was not sure what he had expected, but this had not been it.

Owen cast a quick look back to the campfire in search of answers. None were offered. Beech and Devlin were busy scrubbing pans and rinsing pots. Jabari had disappeared, presumably into his tent. The women chatted about their plans after returning to Arnstead. What Owen discussed with Walks Far was of no concern to the others.

"So, when you say past life...?" Owen began tentatively.

"Our people do not share much beyond how we look. Your people say that a soul is crafted by your gods, that each body has a unique soul. We believe that souls return, in one form or another. A person that lives well is returned to us with four legs. We guard them, so they may live well once more and pass on to the plains above. A horse that dies a foul death becomes a person again."

"And if a person dies a foul death?"

"They return as a foul creature. Something that fears the light, that walks in darkness. Something that must be purged."

"And if you purge these creatures, do they come back as people?"

"Yes," was Walks Far's flat affirmation.

"So, when you ask if I know Oatmeal, you think that I knew them when they were a person?"

"Yes."

Owen learned more about Fieldkin in that exchange than he had known throughout his entire life.

The Orland influence extended beyond a distaste for Federation members with fur. With new land had come new peoples to look down upon. More fodder for exploitation and abuse. There had been no room in the house of Orland to learn more than was required. Extraneous detail ran the risk of facilitating empathy.

Raulstone legacy fared no better. A Raulstone had led the charge against the Seakin when the Federation first landed on the New World. There was a Raulstone when the Seakin were pushed from their homes and eventually wiped off the map. It was a Raulstone that led the Third Federation Army westward. That waylaid Fieldkin during their continent-spanning migrations.

Neither side of Owen's upbringing facilitated any love for the native inhabitants of the land. Even if that hadn't been the case, the idea of reincarnation through horses would have remained difficult to parse. A horse was an animal to Owen. Creatures that were broken down by the Federation races to serve. They were meant to carry burdens, to be ridden until usefulness abandoned them. Something to be replaced when an old one had expired.

The mere concept of showing reverence to a horse had never entered Owen's view of the world. It was an idea as foreign as the kin themselves.

"I suppose I've never considered it," was Owen's best response. True enough, and not a flat refusal of the man's beliefs. A solid middle-ground of an answer. Something that would not derail the conversation before Owen could ask his questions. "How would I know?"

"Time. A horse has its way of speaking to a rider. My son was quiet for two years before he spoke to me."

Walks Far gave a gentle pat to his horse.

"Your son?"

"He lived well, but not long. It is my place to guide him to the fields above. I cherish the burden."

The horse stamped twice. A pleased whinny shook the length of its body as it leaned into Walks Far's hand, he scratched at the horse's mane in turn. It brought a smile to the kin's stoic face.

Do you think this horse is your son?

Owen had better sense than to ask the question aloud. It would have sounded crass on his tongue. The sort of disbelief that rises from a drunkard proclaiming, for the third time in a week, that they had abandoned the bottle. A notion so bewildering that it had to be dismissed as false. Not the type of thought that Owen felt he could express with a civil remark.

Priests of the House spoke with similar conviction. Devout attendants would line pews of a House to hear talk of gods. Accounts of miracles performed on an unbelievable scale were a common point of discussion.

The comparison was not fair. Owen had seen miracles with his own eyes. Though the gods had never spoken to him personally, he had seen the fruits of prayer blossom into tangible manifestations. This talk of souls in horses was something else. How could a person prove the soul of a loved one occupied the body of a beast? To believe in such a thought so fiercely as one who routinely saw the works of a god was beyond baffling. It sounded of madness.

"You're quite forthright, you know that? Honest, I mean," Owen added.

"What reason do I have to lie?"

Dozens of examples flooded to mind. Owen made a point to keep that river dammed.

"Can I ask you a question?"

It felt safer to answer Walks Far's question with another question. Less room to say something regrettable.

Walks Far nodded, a slight gesture in the uneven glow of the campfire.

"You say that horses have a way of speaking. Is that how you've been finding the trail? Is your son... is he telling you where to take us?"

All of Owen's concentration had been funneled into saying 'son' where he had wanted to say 'horse'. The feel of the phrase in his mouth felt wrong. Owen was gripped by the sensation that he had told a father their son was due home from war any day now. Hollow words that brought brief respite, but would never amount to more than pain.

The laugh that roared from Walks Far was deep and sudden. Rooted in place, he clutched at his stomach. Grass crinkled as Walks Far plopped himself onto the ground. Steady hands wiped at his eyes until the laughter had subsided.

"I think you are much younger than you look," Walks Far said haltingly. He was still at war with laughter that had not yet died. Deep breaths fought against the urge to continue the raucous display. "You ask a child's questions with the sternness of a warrior."

"Excuse me?"

"We see with our eyes, human." Walks Far pulled down at his lower eyelids. A childish gesture to suit a childish question. He took another pair of deep, measured breaths before he continued. Freshly found light drained from his voice with each word. "Your people tear at the world when you harness its lifeblood. You grip at the veins and squeeze until the air is jagged and sore. We can see the mess you leave behind as easily as we see the water in a river. As easy as the dark when we close our eyes. I have seen how your witch tears; what she leaves in her wake. I could follow her if she flew to the end of the world."

"Fascinating," Owen muttered.

Drivel, he thought. *This was pointless.*

More talk of intangible nonsense. The patronizing tone Walks Far had adopted mixed with the dead-end nature of the conversation. Owen's inquisitive mood had soured into regret. Time spent spewing nonsense was time wasted, as far as he was concerned.

Owen turned without another word and sulked back to the campfire.

"Maybe lead with the pressing questions next time," Manda said. Her voice was gruff, trailed by an unexpected hint of consolation. She held a metal cup to Owen as he sat down. Vanilla and nutmeg wafted up from the black tea. "Save us all an hour."

"Time wasted, huh?" Owen whispered in sullen response.

263

16.

WOOD AND WATER

I need to ask about your reports from Monday and Tuesday. You advised that you were completing paperwork for ICFs and OCFs and that nothing noteworthy transpired. Aaron sought me out today (Wednesday) to ask if I had seen you, or if you had reported illness. He advised that he has not seen you since Monday.

Your report does not align with your senior officer's. I need accurate details regarding your accomplishments from Monday and Tuesday, as well as your current whereabouts. Please also advise why you reported false information in an official capacity.

If there is some kind of trouble, I cannot help you without full transparency. Report in person if possible.

Regards,

Violette Woods, Senior Administrator, Bureau of Arcane

Never before had a single piece of paper felt so heavy. It could not have weighed more in Owen's numb hand if it had been penned in iron.

False reports could only have bought so much time. Two days, it turned out. More than Owen expected. Less than he had hoped for. Violette was aware of his absence, and the lies made it clear that something was amiss.

Illness was an option unconsidered. The way Violette mentioned it so offhandedly in her message made Owen feel like he was an idiot. That road could have bought a week. Maybe more if a particularly nasty ailment had come to mind. Some kind of flu, or early onset of bone rust if he was feeling particularly grim. Haste had narrowed Owen's periphery so far that such ideas might as well have been dead and buried. They had certainly been forgotten.

The choice presented itself. Would Owen tell more lies to cover his tracks, or would he be honest with Violette?

Lies had proven successful thus far. Their lifespan was short but useful.

Perhaps he might say the illness he contracted was too embarrassing to share? Owen had spent time enough at the Creaky Board to sell that sort of falsehood. The fact that Violette had seen drinking down to his lowest low was yet more ammunition.

This was the sort of lie that would follow him for the rest of his time in Arnstead. If Violette bought what was sold, she would not look at Owen the same way. Owen would have to maintain the lie, as well. The thought would have to live at the forefront of his mind.

Truth bore its dissuasion. Owen could name a handful of conduct violations he had committed without much thought: abandoning his post; attesting falsehood in an official capacity; misappropriation of Bureau resources; disobeying a superior officer. More infractions would come to mind if Owen gave himself time, he was sure. It was already enough to see him stripped of rank and kicked out of the Bureau. That was if the First Seeker was in a good mood.

Prison, then, Owen thought. The idea of First Seeker Akheem showing lenience was laughable. There was no guarantee that Owen would see the sun's light again.

An unfortunately positioned branch ripped Owen from his brooding. The limb was as thick around as his arm, and its collision with Owen's skull made the Seeker see purple and yellow spots.

"Yeah, watch out for that one, Blue."

Scarlet snickered at her remark from the back of her pony. Small stature was in her favor at that moment. The branch was a couple of feet above her head. Whether or not she had noticed the branch before Owen found it with his forehead might have been questionable if not for the comment.

"Branch," Owen groaned to those behind him. A gesture of courtesy, as he was third in line behind Walks Far and Scarlet.

Woods had cropped up after a couple of hours' ride from sunrise. The last of the farmland brushed up against the thin tree line before vanishing entirely. Civilization had presented its border.

The message from Violette had arrived shortly after the incursion into the woods. Distracted, Owen had not seen the gradual shift in flora. Young trees that advanced northward gave way to century-old monoliths of bark and leaves. Trunks as wide around as wagon wheels, some wider still, surrounded the company. Light trickled down in sparse shafts through the green and yellow canopy. Saplings fought with all their might to reach the sky where gaps above were largest.

Leaf litter from years gone by crunched under hoof. A powerful wind whipped at the tree tops, showering fresh bits of green to the graveyard below. Chestnuts and acorns fell with a more noticeable impact. Sharp cracks signaled their descent as they were battered against tree limbs, ending with the eventual soft thud against the soil.

"First time in a forest?"

Owen looked down to his right to see that Devlin had come alongside.

"No," Owen replied, somewhat absent. "No, we had woods back home in Southport. Spent a lot of time there, actually."

"Wouldn't have guessed," Devlin continued. "What with how your mouth is hanging down to your saddle."

Sure enough, Owen's jaw hung slack as he took in the sights of the forest. An airy chuckle pushed out through his nose, the edges of his mouth curling upwards.

"Got me. I've just never seen trees this big before," Owen added.

"I wouldn't think so. Not in Southport, at least. The Federation was quite thorough when it landed on what became Southport and New Haven. You won't find a tree near those cities that's more than twenty or thirty years old. *At most*. Out here, though…" Devlin paused. If not for effect, then take a moment to look around with wonder. "Out here, you can hear the trees talk to one another."

"Too quiet, if you ask me!" hollered Mahika, a few horse-lengths back. "It's like there's nothing out here. I can hear the blood pumping in my ears!"

"Not for everybody, I suppose," Devlin whispered to Owen with a wink.

"The woods are loud if you know how to listen," Walks Far calls from ahead. He was five or six horse lengths ahead of the company. "Your cities are the problem. They are deafening. The woods will not speak to you if you stay in your cities for long."

"It's not home if I can't hear a barfight, a sermon, and blacksmith all at the same street corner," Mahika called, now twice as loud. "You can keep your quiet, kin. Makes my skin crawl."

"Does feel a bit ominous, that's for sure," added Owen. "Like the trees are staring down at us."

"You are right to be afraid. Make our fire today before the sun sets, not after."

266

Walks Far did not explain his order. Mahika and Manda both inquired after the cryptic remark but were met with firm silence.

It was possible that the Fieldkin did not care for dense woods. Little knowledge of the Fieldkin was required to know where their name came from. Infamous riders of the plains. Tribes were known to ride from the northern Kastkills down to Bottom Bay. Back before the Federation had staked claim over the land and begun to build.

Their territory was west of Arnstead now. The open fields of the Great Expanse were not their ancestral homes but seemed suited well-enough to the migratory Fieldkin. Sharp eyes saw rabbits dip into their burrows a mile off. Keen ears pricked at bison herds trampling hills and hills away. All common knowledge. The sort of stuff a child would learn when studying the history of the Federation's landing and the years surrounding it.

Densely packed trees must have been bothersome for the Fieldkin on two fronts. Clear sightlines were nowhere to be found. It was impossible to get a clear view more than a couple of hundred feet in any direction. That same obstruction would make it a challenge for horses to reach and maintain their maximum speed. Fair assumptions all in Owen's mind.

Pensive silence did not last long. Mahika saw to that by breaking into song.

I betcha a dollah, a dollah I do.
I betcha a dollah, so silver and true.
I betcha a dollah, I'll be home tomorrah,
To share a warm bed, with you.

"I betcha a dollar you can't shut up for five minutes," Manda called up from the back of the line. The smile in her voice was clear and bright.

A silver dollar flew through the air, from Mahika to Manda, just before Mahika began to sing the second verse. She did not sing alone for long.

"I mean, it's not *that* far."

Mahika did not sound convinced by her own words.

"Hah!" Manda could tell. "Well, after you, then!"

The company leaned over a perilous edge. Forest and earth alike gave way to a sheer drop. Orange rock stretched both left and right to either horizon without a clear path of descent. An odd root jutted through the cliff

267

face here and there, but not so consistent as to offer a natural ladder or stairway.

White foam churned in the river below. An ancient knife that carved away at the side of the cliff, its centuries-long work echoed upward. The forest returned to life beyond the far, rocky shore and remained level.

"Well," Mahika continued, "it's not like I said I'd jump or—"

"Hey, kin," Manda bellowed. "How far till we get to a way down?"

Walks Far had not joined the company at the edge of the cliff. He remained with the horses, at the point where soft soil turned to unyielding stone. Both hands rubbed methodically along his horse's neck. The circular motion was repeated as he muttered out of earshot.

"Hey! I'm talking to you, red man!"

"The cliff is long." Walks Far raised his head, opening mild eyes. "We would not find a place for the horses for a day. Maybe more."

"Oh, so we're supposed to climb down this thing? That it?"

"For someone who values haste, you do not seem to appreciate the straightest course."

Earthy green light shone from between Walks Far's fingers, like a leaf help up to the sun. The horse's hooves glowed the same color. With a kick, the horse began to trot towards the edge of the cliff. Then off the cliff.

Manda shouted.

Beech, whose whole body had trembled at the mere sight of the cliff, gasped in abject horror.

Mahika whistled.

Walks Far and his horse did not tumble over the edge of the cliff. Instead, the horse walked downward as if descending the side of a hill. Walks Far bent backward to compensate for the slope. He did not turn around, but Owen imagined a wide grin had broken the Fieldkin's stone-faced visage.

"We shall wait for you on the far shore," Walks Far called up as his horse rounded the bend of an invisible switchback. "Do not dawdle."

"Shut it!" Manda yelled after Walks Far. She plopped down onto the hard ground and muttered, "Great. Just perfect."

"Well, how much rope have we got between us?" Jabari thought aloud. "Enough to reach the bottom, you think? I know I've got a couple dozen feet or more."

"Another couple from me," Mahika chirped.

"I can check my pack?" Owen offered. "Might have some in there."

"There's a good lad!" Jabari said.

"That's all well and good if *we* get to the bottom," Manda interrupted, "but what about the horses? Just because I could lift one doesn't mean it wouldn't get hung on the way down. I'd rather not have my ride back into town kicking the bucket."

"Oh! I can stay!" Beech yelled. His large ears were pricked and pointed at the rest of the company. "Leave the horses with me and I'll watch them until you get back. I can watch anything you wouldn't want to be dropped, too!"

The slow, deliberate way that Manda turned her head gave Owen a shiver. He was glad to not be on the receiving end. Her seething glare was fixed on Mr. Beech.

"*Security,*" she spat. "Beech *Security* Company. You're supposed to be in this *with* us, not waiting for us!"

"I'll secure the horses. You said it yourself. Would be a shame if our rides up and vanished before we got back to them, right?"

"It's easier than getting the horses down, Manda," Jabari cut in. "Not like we were really expecting him to pull his weight, besides, eh? Now then, Scarlet, how about we get you cinched up and ready to rappel?"

"What?" Scarlet protested. "Why me?"

"You're the lightest," Mahika added with a devilish smile. She waggled her fingers as if threatening to scoop up a reluctant child. "Wouldn't struggle if I were you. Would be a shame if you took a tumble before we tied you up."

"All right, all right. Hands off."

That Scarlet was the smallest and lightest of Manda's people must have come up regularly. Once the point was made, the harn offered little in the way of protest. Reluctant sighs were in no short order.

"Does that mean I get to stay here, then?" Beech asked.

"Gods above," Manda grumbled. "Fine! Just make it work and tell me when it's time to go down. And toss me my hat!"

Eager to comply, Beech leaped towards Manda's horse to retrieve the wide-brimmed, brown hat. The implications of throwing a hat near a cliff were not lost on the katarl. He instead ran the hat over to Manda and placed it gently into her outstretched palm. It was clear that he did not wish to risk his newfound freedom.

269

Manda stretched out on her back to bask in the late morning sun. The hat rested on her face to shield her eyes. Open hands served as her pillow.

The rest of the company set about checking their belongings. Rope was the goal, but anything that could be tied into a knot was brought out. Leather belts and blankets were common amongst them all. A pocketful of handkerchiefs, Mahika's donation to the pile, was added in desperation.

"This is it?" Scarlet looked from the pile of odds and ends to each of her compatriots. "I'm supposed to get to the bottom with this? With bedsheets and snot rags? I don't think so."

"It won't be that bad, sister." Warm words from Jabari brought no ease to Scarlet. If anything, the relaxed tone seemed to further sour her mood. Jabari began to tie a section of rope to a bedsheet. "Look, nice and firm."

Scarlet's eyes grew wide with rage as the bedsheet slipped away from the rope like a greased pig fleeing a butcher.

"Owen, you don't happen to know any spells that might help out here, do you?" Devlin asked. "Maybe something that could fuse the ropes? Or make more rope altogether?"

The innocent questions, and the expectant look that accompanied them, were an unexpected blow. Owen had approached this problem the same way as the rest of the company. He searched through his belongings to find whatever might be long and sturdy enough to support a person. A length of rope had been tucked away at the bottom of his baggage. He was quick to donate his blanket.

More. It rang in Owen's mind like a funeral bell. *More. I should be able to offer more.*

An itch began to grow around his wrists. He could feel the slightest touch of his coat cuffs. Doubt gnawed at him like an army of ants picking at his skin, biting up his arms and onto his shoulders. Fingernails were powerless against this sensation. He could strip the flesh from his bones and still feel the crawl.

"No," Owen replied sheepishly. "Nothing like that."

"How about on your belt? Like that fire starter?" Scarlet asked.

"Uh, no. I don't think these shells would be helpful with a rope."

"What do they even teach you people at that magic school of yours?"

How to improvise.

Owen had to remind himself how he got his blue coat in the first place. Not through great feats of channeling the Flow, or through knowledge of spells. Such power was beyond him. There was no use in running away from that fact. What had gotten him through his tests, one after the next, was sheer willpower. The drive to apply what tools he could gather to the absolute limit of their usefulness.

Emboldened hands grabbed a length of rope. Quick fingers produced what might have been the ugliest knot to ever blight a braid. That did not matter. Owen drew his caster pistol before anyone could speculate as to the knot's integrity.

Sapphire light flashed under the sun as Owen slotted his chosen cartridge. The problem was one of binding, and Lionel's creation seemed like the right tool for the job. After all, what did it matter if the target was a person or a piece of rope? A knot that could not come undone would be a job well done.

Owen reached out to the Flow, grabbed what he needed, and let the caster pistol do its job.

Go!

Water spewed from the muzzle with enough force to push the rope away. It slid across the rocky surface towards the tree line. Surprised gasps popped out from Scarlet and Jabari. Mahika's reaction was closer to an excited giggle.

The second half of the cartridge's spell kicked in as reactions subsided. A sound like cracking glass popped when the water froze. Momentum carried the length of rope past the knot, which was now stuck to the ground. Another crack, the snap of the rope coming to a stop, caused another round of gasps. Owen sprang up and ran to collect his handiwork.

Both hands were required to rip the frozen knot from the rocky ground. Owen grabbed the rope from either end of the knot, planted his feet, and pulled with all his might. Credit was due to Lionel: the rope did not come loose without a struggle. Its eventual removal from the ground was as much a result of the blazing sun overhead as Owen's strength. A satisfying pop marked the release of the ice's chilly grip. The suddenness of the matter sent Owen sprawling backward.

"Nifty trick," Jabari said. Large hands caught Owen before he reached the ground.

"How long do you think it'll last?" Scarlet grabbed the rope from Owen's hands as she asked.

"Long enough for you to reach the ground," Mahika laughed. "One

271

way or the other."

"You're so funny, ha ha! Very reassuring."

"So long as we move quickly, it shouldn't be a problem." Owen did his best to sound confident. "The engineer designed it to retrain people. Weight won't be an issue. We just need to make sure the joints in the rope keep off the cliff face. Maybe we can wrap them in something?"

"Oh, that's easy. I've got handkerchiefs for days. What colors do we want?" Excited hands shot into Mahika's pockets. Strips of cloth in all manner of color and design burst outward in a rainbow shower of silk and linen. "Let's see we've got azure, cerulean, goldenrod, crimson, violet, teal... ah, here's a pink one! Some plain white ones. A bro—"

"The lighter the better," Scarlet interrupted. "Won't suck up as much heat that way."

It was difficult to tell if the agitation that dripped from Scarlet's every word came from the task at hand, or that Mahika seemed like she might have gone on listing colors until the sun set.

Efficiency was learned by doing. The first knot was the only one to be stuck to the ground. Mahika found the best distance to keep her hand from the knot. Not so far that the rope went slack, but not so close that her hand got frozen. White and yellow handkerchiefs were plucked from the ground where they could be found. Scarlet settled for pink or orange when her preferred choices dwindled.

Necessity gave birth to a monster that day. What the company had cobbled together would not have convinced a blind, handless man that the rope was sound. An amalgam of spare parts colored by desperation.

Despite the multitude of readily apparent flaws, however, the rope held weight.

"Let's get this done with, I guess," Scarlet grumbled. She sounded no more comfortable with the idea than she had before. Regardless, she had already assembled what gear she would be bringing to the bottom. "One of you bring the caster rifle down with you. Sucker is too big for me."

"I can do that, sure," Owen volunteered.

Scarlet narrowed her eyes. They darted from Owen's face to his boots and back again. She cut her silence with a pronounced sniff.

"Yeah, all right. You be gentle with my baby."

"Yes, ma'am."

A swift nod sealed Owen's affirmation.

"Let's get to it, then." Jabari pumped his arm as he spoke. A light gesture of enthusiasm to rally the company around the task at hand. "Mr. Beech, you'll want to watch this. You're going to be lowering the last person down. Since you're staying up top and all."

"I have to lower a whole person down? By myself?" Beech looked at each member of the company in turn. "And you're sending the lightest person down first?"

"Of course," Jabari replied. "We can hold the lightest for the longest. Give Scarlet here a chance to take it slow and make sure the way down is safe."

"Yeah, but…"

Rather than find words to fit his thoughts, Beech made a sweeping gesture that encompassed his whole body. A gesture meant to highlight his diminutive stature. The point was a fair one. Joseph Beech was a couple of heads taller than Devlin, quite short for even a Nirdac katarl. He was thin as a rail to match. Not the type of person that might be expected to support the weight of another person, even a small one, for more than a moment or two.

Jabari scratched at the back of his neck. His claws audibly raked across thick skin in contemplation.

"Why not just tie the rope off to something?" Owen asked "We can lower ourselves one at a time. Be responsible for our weight."

"A fine enough idea, but there's not much to tie to if you hadn't noticed."

Another fair point, this time from Jabari. To tie the rope off at the tree line would mean losing precious feet of rope. The rocks, while not uniform or flat, showed no jutting outcrops. The windswept surface was what the company had to work with.

"Hey Jabs, what about your tent stakes?" Scarlet asked. "Think Manda might be able to bulk-up and pound a couple into the rock?"

"Doubtful," he said. "They're wooden stakes. Would splinter the second she set her hammer to the head."

Stakes, huh?

Another idea came to Owen. He drew his caster pistol once more, this time slotting a jet-like cartridge into the chamber. It was the only shell he had not used since his departure from Southport. In his mind, this was the most dangerous shell. There had been no purpose for it in his mind other than as a last resort. A tool that could end a life.

New purpose came to life for the obsidian cylinder. Before today, Owen would hesitate to even touch this black vessel of death. Now he fed it energy with a smile on his face. He knelt and pressed the muzzle of his pistol against the rock.

Go!

Metal crashed against stone. It was not a sharp sound like Owen had expected. Not the clang of metal striking metal. This sound was heavier. Like men and women raising hammers in a quarry. Blows that sundered boulders as old as the earth. A thousand clay pots shattering all at once.

When Owen pulled his pistol up from the rock, it revealed a metal stake burrowed into the ground. Small, jagged cracks radiated from where the metal had pierced stone.

"Full of tricks today."

To Owen's surprise, Manda had risen and joined the onlookers. He did not notice while focused on his newest experiment.

"Trying to help, when I can," Owen replied

Manda snorted at the notion.

"Okay, let's see how steady this is."

Enough metal jutted up from the rock to allow a single handhold. Manda knelt and wrapped her right hand around the stake. It did not budge when she threw her weight it, nor did it budge when she pulled upwards. Manda spared no effort. Muscles bulged in her arm and shoulder as she grunted at the metal spike.

The stake remained in place when Manda stood, but she was not satisfied. Familiar light shone through the skin on her arms. Deep breaths rolled inward and were expelled with care.

Metal fought a valiant struggle to remain embedded in red-orange rock. A moment lingered where it seemed like Manda, empowered as she was, would not be able to dislodge Owen's handiwork. That moment passed. When Manda stood again, the spike was free from the rock.

Manda dropped the stake to the ground. Indents from where Manda had gripped the metal served as a chilling reminder of the power she commanded.

"Drop one of those closer to the edge of the cliff," Manda said, pointing. The hand wiped sweat from her brow when she continued. "Drive it in at an angle, so the rope doesn't get any ideas and jump off the stake."

"Glad you like it," Owen smirked. He could not help himself. It was the first time he could recall Manda having given him something that resembled praise.

"Cut the chatter," Manda snapped. "We've wasted enough time holding hands."

The curt reply did not embitter Owen. Two problems had arisen. He had resolved both of them and been thanked for it. Even the prickliest among the company had seen the value of his contribution. What better time was there to wear a satisfied smile? Owen chose to relish his continued usefulness rather than think on the matter.

Another spike was in the ground before long. This one was angled away from the cliff to act as a hook for the rope. If Beech was not going to monitor the last descent, it was best to stack as many boons in the company's favor as they could manage.

All that remained to do was done in haste. Belongings were gathered from saddles and stuffed into packs. Owen had scaled walls and repelled back down at Eastpointe, though rarely with a full pack of gear. The climbing walls had never been as tall as the cliff, either. Height was difficult to judge at a glance. There were no landmarks he knew the height of, and his best estimate at the height of trees across the river was just that: an estimate.

Owen made sure to pack light.

Unease was thick in the air. The enthusiasm Jabari had attempted to rally flagged and disappeared entirely. Owen made a show of freezing the rope to the newly planted metal stake. There was little reaction apart from a fragile smile from Devlin. Hesitation gripped them like classmates preparing to dive into a frigid lake. Rigid faces framed stiff looks.

Ice clattered against the rock when the rope was dropped over the ledge. A series of lifesaving marbles bouncing off an inverted table. Belt fasteners joined the cacophony as the shameful excuse for a rope reached its full length. The line wobbled, then settled into a rhythmic motion. Metal and ice scraped as the pendulum swung from left to right and back again.

Curious faces peered over the edge of the cliff. Most of the party had gotten down onto their hands and knees to look. Scarlet was on her stomach. Mahika, smiling like a woman gone mad, remained standing. She leaned over the fatal drop without an apparent care in the world.

"Doesn't look like it hit the bottom," Owen said, deflated.

"Nope," Manda grunted.

"Think it was close?"

"One way to find out," Scarlet said. Her hands were busy wrapping around the rope as she spoke. Loose dirt shuffled in response to her movements. Both legs were over the ledge before Owen could protest.

"You're still going?"

"I like getting paid," Scarlet grunted.

Those first few moments over the ledge would be the most precarious. Concentration meant the difference between a smooth descent and a fast one. Enough cadets had been sent to the infirmary on the account of a simple mistake. Owen fought against his urge to cry out.

Scarlet's head bobbed twice, then disappeared. There was no sudden rush of air. No cry of anguish or curses against a cruel fate. When Owen popped his head back over the ledge, Scarlet was already two arm lengths below.

"What if there isn't enough rope to get to the bottom?" Owen called, seeing Scarlet was well on her way. The descent was one matter. To climb back up such a tall cliff after having just come down? It did not seem reasonable. Owen's arms burned just at the thought of the strain.

"Then you lot get to pull me back up."

The response was muffled. Scarlet did not look up to those she addressed. Her words met the red-orange wall and bounced out over the river. The harn did not let her guard down. Though the hardest part had come and gone, a sudden gust of wind could dash Scarlet against the rocks. Hands could slip while her mouth flapped. Continued concentration was paramount.

It felt like a lifetime ago since Owen had last watched a person rappel from a dangerous height. Each breath had to be fought for. Tightness locked his chest in place. Subtle movements were lost to the eye as the person on the rope continued downward. Only the large, startling gestures were visible. Readjusting a leg when the climber hit a knot in the rope. Wrapping the line around one arm to give the other a break. What looked like a slip from the rope might be as benign a movement as easing down into a rocking chair.

Long stretches of doubt punctuated by brief moments of panic. Owen did not know these people. He got the distinct impression that Scarlet cared for him about as much as Manda. Still, they were living, breathing people.

276

No part of him wanted to watch Scarlet, or any of the others, meet their end. Much less in a state of utter terror.

Sweat-slicked palms greased smooth stone. Restless fingers played a silent symphony, backed by the rustling strings of wind in the trees. A heavy heart beat a reckless rhythm.

What broke the silence was not the screech of a harn losing her grip. It was not a random sniff, the scratch of stubble on rock, or the shrill cry of a red-tailed hawk. The sound that erupted from the cliff face was like one hand drawing nails down a chalkboard while the other scraped a knife across a plate at the same time. Owen slammed his hands against his ears to block the piercing barrage of noise. His eyes hammered closed, teeth straining against his clenched jaw.

"Ridgewing!"

A streak of orange darted from the cliff face as Devlin called its name. Thin wings, as wide as a human is tall, fanned out to catch the wind. The creature's body contrasted with the green of the trees below as it banked on an unseen current of air. It let out another ear-shattering cry and aimed its bat-like body at the cliff.

The sound was not as oppressive now that it was expected, but it still forced Owen to cover his ears. His eyes were free to watch the creature move with terrifying speed toward the harn dangling below. Scarlet had flattened her ears against the back of her head. One hand held her ears in place, while the other clung to the rope in desperation.

Wings like three-foot razorblades poised to slice through whatever they touched first. The rope would be cut, or Scarlet would be cut while protecting her lifeline.

What can I do?

Owen's hands moved even as he frantically dug for an option. The caster pistol was drawn. He did not see which shell was jammed into the chamber. It did not matter. Something had to be done and done quickly. He had no time to hesitate and ponder which shell might do the job best.

"Back off!"

Bloodlust dripped from Manda's guttural cry. Before Owen had time to channel into his cartridge, she had grabbed and launched one of her javelins. The force of her throw shook the stone at her feet. Air cracked and howled as it was forced away from the projectile. Manda glowed like a sun full of rage.

277

The javelin missed the ridgewing by a narrow margin. Though the attack went wide, the effort was not in vain. Pressure waves from the mighty assault rocked the ridgewing and forced it to change course. Nails shattered glass as the creature cried out in dismay.

Underneath the ridgewing's screech was another cry. Scarlet roared a battle cry of her own. The rope had found new life as a result of Manda's attack. Scarlet was swung from side to side along the cliff as the energy given to the rope slowly dwindled. Twice she bounced off the rock, sent into a dizzying spiral as she fought to regain control. Bits of the cliff crumbled away from the force of Scarlet's impacts. The pack on her back had popped a strap and dangled on one side.

"Quick, pull her up!" Devlin shouted. The call to action was spoken with fierce command. Owen was surprised to hear such a forceful voice arise from one who always seemed calm and collected. "Before the thing comes back!"

The Keeper had both hands clamped on the rope before he was on both feet. Owen rose to join him, and Manda piled on with her arms alight. The trio pulled in unison and heaved Scarlet upward with all their might.

"Stop!" Scarlet called. "I'm over halfway. Just keep the thing busy!"

Owen peered over the ledge to see the rope had settled. Scarlet had resituated the remaining pack strap so that it crossed her chest, allowing for the weight to be more evenly distributed. There was no pause. She did not wait for the company to agree to her demands. Scarlet was back on the descent as if nothing had happened.

Owen, Devlin, and Manda eased the rope back into place. They took care to make sure the frozen knot holding the rope to the metal stake was not disturbed. Satisfied, each readied themselves for the return of the ridgewing.

Metal ground against metal as Owen ripped open the breech of his caster pistol. Amethyst glinted in the sunlight. He counted himself lucky that he had the presence of mind to check, now that the time was afforded. The lightning net would have served no use here. There would be too much distance between where the spell was triggered and the intended target. The net would fizzle in the air. A pretty show of lights and nothing more.

Azure was out of the question. The wind cannon he had used to dismount the Cinder Witch would be too effective. Manda's javelin had caused enough of a disturbance just passing by. Pressure from the wind caused by the azure cartridge might rip Scarlet from the rope.

Crimson was too short on range. Water from the sapphire cartridge moved too slow, and there was no telling whether it would work on the ridgewing.

That just left jet. A metal rod through the spine would stop the ridgewing midflight. There was no doubt there. The true intention of the cartridge: to make sure the target never moved again.

Owen swapped the amethyst cartridge for the jet and jammed the breech closed. The Flow channeled through him as he lay back on the ground. He needed to steady himself as much as possible. The ridgewing was quick. Despite the creature's size, it would not present an easy target. He tried not to think about the alternatives if he missed his shot. Scarlet could be torn to pieces. Worse yet, the stake might bite into Scarlet if Owen's aim was not precise.

Another wail pierced the sky as the ridgewing banked in the air. Paper-like wings were invisible. Only the orange was clear to see. Black eyes, beads of night on the creature's pointed face, locked onto Scarlet like she was a fresh morsel waiting to be devoured.

Shouts filled the air. Something about the ridgewing. Approaching. Getting ready. Boots shuffled and scraped across the rock. Preparations were made as best they could.

All of it was noise to Owen. Collected bits of nothing that faded into the background. His attention was locked on the orange streak hurtling towards Scarlet. Eyes narrowed to focus on the target. Owen held his breath and waited for the beast to draw closer.

Closer.

Closer, still.

Go!

The ridgewing ceased to move the moment Owen launched his spell. Taught wings went slack. What had been a silent approach now sounded like a flag whipping on strong winds. The creature was dead, or very near to it.

Dead, and careening towards Scarlet.

Lack of life did not deter momentum from carrying the airborne corpse towards the cliff face. Exhilaration born from success was stamped out. Solving one problem had only created another. Manda let loose another javelin to intercept the dead ridgewing. It clipped one of the beast's limp wings. The missile of dead weight did not slow down.

The ridgewing colliding with rock sounded like slamming a raw steak into a stack of newspapers. Wet, crunchy, and soaked in blood. Red-orange rock streaked with crimson as the body hung in place, then began to scrape down the side of the cliff. It traveled for a few moments before detaching from the uneven rock. A wet sponge of blood and gore falling from a dust-covered wall.

It was impossible to see when the ridgewing hit Scarlet, but the muffled cry was undeniable. The body smashed into the harn and kept moving down. Weight and force from the impact combined into an obstacle Scarlet could not overcome. She was pulled away from the rope. Grasping hands were unable to find purchase. Rope uncoiled from Scarlet's leg, snapping her into a spiral as she began her fall to unforgiving ground.

Needles bored into Owen's cheeks. He felt the air rush from his lungs before he could call out for Scarlet. Horror locked his burning limbs in place.

Best efforts had failed. The rope had been secured. Packs were filled and strapped with care. Lightest among the company had gone first to check that the way was safe. None of it mattered.

Owen felt the muffled thud of bodies hitting the ground through every muscle and bone.

No one moved. Shock wrapped the company in a blanket of disbelief. Owen could not believe what he saw. Laid out before him, he could not process the mess. The fact that they had failed, that *he* had failed, would not process. Another error in the line of duty.

A fatal error.

Horror gave way to disgust. The all too familiar pit that took root in Owen's stomach. Another mistake. Another failure. Failure to protect someone just out of reach. Failure to plan for all contingencies. Utter, complete failure.

The dust settled at the base of the cliff.

"Is everything all right?"

Joseph Beech's timid question snapped the party from their collective trance. Its galvanized Owen to action.

"Put what first aid supplies we have into my bag," he said, voice quavering as he dumped the contents of his pack onto the ground. A rolled shirt tumbled off the ledge and was caught in the wind. "I know the basics.

I'll see what I can do."

He could not be sure that Scarlet was dead until he reached her side. A pulse might still course through her veins, however faint. She may yet draw breath. Seconds spent gawking were seconds wasted.

"Hurry!" Owen commanded when no one moved.

"Do it," Manda added hurriedly.

Bandagesand whatever else the group could cobble together were tossed into Owen's bag. There was no time to take inventory.

I'll figure it out once I'm down there, he told himself.

Weight was as much an enemy as time. Owen unfastened his sword belt and dropped the weapon on top of his other belongings. He did the same for his caster pistol belt. Any weight that he could shave would be a blessing. Adrenaline-fueled hands patted down trouser and coat pockets. The pocket watch could go. There was no immediate use for his message box.

Before he realized it, Owen was unbuttoning his Spellseeker coat. It crumpled over his things like a dense quilt. Idle hands rolled his shirtsleeves while Owen watched the company stuff his pack.

Gloves, Owen realized. Memories of recruits with raw, bleeding hands flashed before his eyes. Descending without protection was possible if speed was not a concern. Owen could have worked slowly, hand over hand until he had reached the bottom. There was no time now for such leisure. A few moments could mean the difference between Scarlet's life or death.

Hands rifled through belongings before a plan had coalesced. There had to be something Owen could use. If not among his belongings, then somewhere amongst the company's things.

Owen ripped his coat off of his pile. The coat itself was far too stiff and bulky to wrap around his hands. Even if it were more malleable, the woolen garment was not designed for the amount of friction it would subject to. Owen continued to dig. The rope could be looped through his belts to help control the descent, but would not protect his hands. The mess kit was useless. Matches, a small mirror, toiletries, all useless.

"The cloak!" Owen gasped.

Iron-heeled boots smacked against the rock as Owen bolted towards the tree line. Draped over Oatmeal's saddle was the cloak he had acquired from Collections. Its true purpose was to protect from the Cinder Witch's flames. After the first day of riding, however, Owen had begun to use it as a cushion for his saddle. He had completely forgotten why he brought it in the first place.

If it can stop a fire, it should help cancel the heat from friction!

The memory glass brooch, a ruby swallow laid into silver, was smooth. Rounded edges fit into the contours of Owen's closed hand. He wrapped the cloak around his right hand twice. Enough fabric to protect his hand, but not so much that Owen would be unable to hold the rope. Another wrap around his wrist and forearm. The rest would be for his left hand.

Preparation was complete by the time Owen returned. The party had packed and sealed his bag. Manda scooped the pack up as Owen approached. She held the bag in place as Owen slotted his arms through the straps and shouldered the pack's insignificant weight. It felt as if there had been little to pack.

Owen took the rope in his right hand and wrapped it once around his wrist. What remained of the cloak wrapped around his left hand. Then, with the rope in both hands, Owen backed himself towards the ledge. Subtle movements carried him backward until he felt nothing under his heels.

"As fast as you can without killing yourself," Manda half-whispered. "You're no good to her if you're dead."

Vulnerable. It was the one word that came to mind when Owen tore his gaze away from the ledge to look at Manda. For all her strength and tenacity, she had been rendered powerless. There was nothing for her to do but watch Owen descend. A feeble promise of aid dangling off a cliff.

"Right," Owen nodded.

Best circumstances would have allowed for the use of a harness. Clips of iron would have helped control the rope, allowed Owen to take weight off of his arms. He could have slipped down the cliff and struck the ground like a flash of lightning.

There was no assistance afforded to Owen that day. Hands alone would have to carry him to the bottom of the cliff. Buffered from the world's most unsettling rope by a cloak he *hoped* would protect his flesh, he had no other tool but the strength of his arms. Conviction would have to steel his fingers for the long descent.

That first step was always the hardest. A moment where weight shifted from vertical to horizontal. Gravity demanded that Owen's body plummet straight down to certain death. He could feel the call to fall in his chest. A sensation like he had already begun to fall.

Owen was out over the ledge now. The second step was a step down rather than backward or forward. His third brought both feet against the cliff face. Another pair of steps brought Owen's face below the ledge of the cliff. Steps after that were a blur. Concentration shifted from watching feet to channeling the Flow into the ruby swallow. Increased speed demanded protection against the accompanying heat.

Individual steps were abandoned for bounding motions. Owen would kick off the wall and allow the rope to slide through his hands. Pinching the rope brought him back to the cliff face. The process allowed for rapid descent while ensuring that Owen never built more speed than he could handle.

The first bead of ice came as a shock. Distracted by his channeling efforts and the demands of the descent, Owen had forgotten that the rope was not continuous. That it had to be bound together from multiple sections.

Owen encountered the first bead shortly after a kick away from the wall. Its sudden presence forced both hands open. Fear of the first step kicked Owen's heart up to his throat. Terrified hands fumbled to regain control of the rope. He clamped down hard on the hope, crushing the speed gained from freefall. The sudden change tore at every joint in Owen's arms. It felt like they were being ripped from his body.

With the sudden stop came a sudden slam. Owen was thrown against the cliff face. Breath funneled out in shock from the blow. The rock, rougher on the exposed face than at the top of the cliff, ripped at his skin. He felt abrasions open on his knees and right shoulder. Stone had bit into his flesh. The price for poor preparation had been exacted.

Teeth clenched. Fists locked into a desperate grip. Blood trickled down his shins, stained his socks. None of it mattered. He was still alive, and wiser for the wear.

Owen descended with greater control. He found the best balance he could between speed and preparedness. Connective ice would not throw him from the rope again.

A little more than halfway down the cliff face, Owen zipped past an open in the rock. It was after he had kicked off from the cliff. The speed of his descent rendered the opening visible for a couple of seconds. Enough time to see the shadowy suggestion of what looked like eggs tucked into a bed of sticks and leaves.

The nest was gone from sight before regret could manifest.

Speed was sacrificed for stability when Owen reached the transition from rope to belts. Ice beads had been enough of an obstacle when they came in intervals of twenty or more feet. Descending hand over hand seemed like the best course of action when the interval was reduced to just a few feet at a time. Leather groaned as the first belt took on Owen's weight.

When Owen reached the last handkerchief at the end of the line, the ground seemed to be about ten feet away. Maybe more. Close enough to see that Scarlet had begun to stir. Owen could make out disgruntled murmurs. Specific words were too difficult to make out, but it was assurance enough that the harn was still alive.

Owen took a thorough look directly below. The space was clear of any substantial rocks or other debris that might hinder his landing. Mangled remains of the ridgewing were splayed out away from the foot of the cliff.

Arms burned from the effort of the descent. Fists that felt like stone held fast, awaiting the command to release. Elbows extended like rusted chains until Owen's arms were at their full length. Anything to get closer to the ground. He took a deep breath through his nose, exhaled a heavy sigh, then let go of the last handkerchief.

Freefall enveloped every sense. That strange sensation where the body reached for the sky as it plummeted to the earth. Instinct replaced rational thought. Animal desire cursed the decision to fall. *We don't have wings*, the body says. *Why do we jump if we cannot fly? We must go back!* But there was no going back. The mind knows what the body cannot. That there is ground not far below, and that all will be well if the body cooperates. Feet must hit first. Legs tuck and the body rolls to dissipate its energy.

The ground drew close. Owen's mind forced his body to comply, to enact learned reflexes. He is prepared. His legs tuck as iron-heeled boots smash into the rocky ground. Stone swaps places with the sky as he rolls once, then twice.

His weight worked against him. After the second roll, Owen was unable to maintain his balance. Arms splayed out to protect his head as he unfurled. Rock bit and scraped and he slid across gravel. Owen coughed, both from the wind being knocked out of his lungs and against the dust stirred by his flailing. The dust coated his lungs and caused deeper, more painful coughs.

Owen rolled onto his back. The sun was bright. He blinked at the uncaring orb. Figures at the top of the cliff came into focus when Owen raised a hand against the sun. Little people shouting and waving their arms.

"Scarlet!" Owen coughed, remembering where he was.

Pained grunts slipped through gritted teeth as Owen rolled over, forced himself onto his hands and knees. The pack had slipped away sometime during Owen's fall. Maybe while he was rolling on the loose, rocky ground. A scraped and dusty hand reached out to grab the pack. It rose with Owen as he pushed off a knee to stand.

Bones creaked and muscles ached, but the sight of Scarlet's crumpled body sent a shot of adrenaline through Owen's whole body. He ambled over to her on unsteady feet.

Scarlet was in bad shape. Blood stained the base of her ears, which lay limp on the ground. An occasional twitch confirmed that they still had life. Such sensitive ears could not have handled the ridgewing's cry well, Owen guessed.

"Scarlet, can you hear me?"

Owen hovered over Scarlet, hesitant to lay a hand on her. What training Owen had in first aid was basic. Simple things like wrapping open wounds and tying splints to a busted limb. He had no way of knowing to what extent Scarlet's back or neck might be injured. Touching her could cause more problems than it might solve.

"Scarlet, please. Can you hear me?" Owen put his face in front of Scarlet's. Her eyes were closed, darting rapidly from side to side under their lids. Incomprehensible mutterings streamed from cracked lips. "Scarlet, if you can hear me, I need you to tell me what's wrong. Can you tell me what hurts?"

No response.

"I'm going to feel for any broken bones, Scarlet," Owen said. He raised his voice as if he were shouting across a room. "Tell me if you feel any pain."

Tender hands probed for injury. Owen felt for any telltale sign that something was not right. Neither of the harn's legs was bent at odd angles, so he focused on feeling things like swelling. Desire to avoid any unnecessary pain kept Owen's movements slow. A methodical search to find the smallest indication. Scarlet was clearly in pain. It was just a matter of determining the source.

Halfway up Scarlet's right shin was a damp spot. Her dark brown trousers had made seeing the spot almost impossible. Even knowing the patch was there, Owen had a hard time making it out. Owen applied gentle pressure to the spot and felt something raised. It was hard and sharp.

That's not good.

Something was in her leg. The fact that her pants were undamaged was puzzling, but Owen waved the thought aside. Her pantleg might have had ridden up as she fell. Whatever caused the injury might have become embedded then. There was no way to be sure without taking a look. As tenderly as he could manage, Owen started to roll the pantleg up until the injury was visible.

"Oh," Owen muttered, pulling back a bloodied hand to cover his mouth and nose. He had not been ready to see what presented itself.

The top of Scarlet's shin, broken and jagged, had punctured her skin. White bone gleamed under the noonday sun. Blood oozed from the gore-covered hole. Scarlet's fur was soaked through, matted with bits of dangling flesh.

"Oh," Owen muttered again. "Oh, gods."

Owen turned his head, collected himself with a breath, then looked back to the dire matter at hand.

"Scarlet, your leg is broken. I'm going to have to bandage the wound to stop the bleeding. This is probably going to hurt."

Still no response.

Dust flew from the pack as Owen ripped it open. Bandages were plentiful. The makings of a splint were visible, as well. Owen went to grab the supplies he needed but stopped short when he saw his hand.

Blood dripped from tremor-wracked fingertips. Red-brown splotches on the backs of Owen's hands showed where blood had met dirt. He eyed the clean bandages, then looked back at his sullied hands. There was no point in doing this if it was not going to be done well. He needed to do what he could to prevent infection. Each small decision would add up to whether or not Scarlet went home with one leg or two.

Owen refused to be responsible for the loss of another leg.

"I need to wash my hands first, Scarlet. I'm going to run to the river and come right back. Promise."

Gravel kicked up as Owen launched himself towards the running body of water. Little missiles flung into thorny bushes that dotted the riverbank. The rocks clicked and clacked against Owen's feet as he sped along. Rocks were soon muffled by the splash of water.

Owen fell to his knees and dunked both hands into the river. Water lapped at the blood and dust, pulling the grime downstream into thrashing torrents. He paid no attention to the massive boulders lodged into the river. Monolithic breakers that cut currents in half and sprayed water in all direction. He paid no attention to Walks Far, who sat atop his horse on the far bank with his bow in hand. Owen had eyes only for the last bits of blood that clung to his frantic digits.

Manda had reached the bottom of the cliff by the time Owen returned. The violet light from her arms, still aglow from a battle with the rope, cast an eerie radiance over Scarlet.

"What can I do?" Manda asked, out of breath. She did not remove her gaze from Scarlet's frail, twitching body.

"Make room," Owen said.

He did not know what to say. It had not occurred to Owen until after the ordeal that Manda was terrified. That her helplessness from atop the cliff had followed her to the ground below. What Owen saw at the moment was another obstacle. Someone that might get in the way of what he needed to do, that might obstruct his movement.

The words were forceful. Owen had no room in his mind for kindness. He was filled with an anxious rage at the thought of seeing Scarlet walk with a cane. There was no malice for Manda herself. She just happened to be in the way.

"I said *move*," Owen demanded, skidding to a halt.

Manda stepped away from Scarlet without protest.

River water dripped into the pack of supplies. Unsure hands hovered over the bounty while Owen fought through memory for what to do first. He shook the last remnants of water away, dug around for the most pristine bandage of the lot, and uttered the only prayer he could remember ever having made.

"Gods above, if you're listening, I could use a hand."

"What was that?" Manda spat. Loathing slipped back into her voice as it had never left.

"It's a figure of speech!" Owen howled. "Go… go figure out how to get her across the river. For when she wakes up."

Stammered phrases failed to form a cohesive whole. Bitterness and rage fought with a sheer lack of knowledge. Manda was torn in her response. After a string of half-curses, she stormed off to the riverbed.

Gravel was pulverized beneath her feet as she stomped. Violet light glimmered between the threads of her trousers. Manda had channeled more power through the Flow than she knew what to do with, it seemed.

She could throw a fit all she likes. As long as she did not stir up dust and kick rocks around Scarlet, Owen told himself, Manda could do whatever she pleased.

Distractions, Owen realized. He threw Manda's displeasure from his head with a vigorous shake. *Too many distractions. Have to focus. Focus on Scarlet.*

Sanguine streams continued to pour. Moments not spent bandaging Scarlet were moments tossed aside. Her life oozed from her leg. Around the glittering shaft of the bone. The gravel beneath the wound, a mix of gray and red-orange and white, shifted to an unsettling scarlet. It was the woman's very essence that had stained the ground on which she lay. Minutes of life drip, drip, dripped from the jagged protrusion. Seconds spilled away to feed what barren soil might rest underneath the rocky ground.

"What am I doing?"

Staring.

Owen realized, in horror, that he had been staring at Scarlet's wound. Not bandaging it. Not applying pressure to the injury. Not even raising the bloody gash above her heart.

He was just staring, mouth agape.

C'mon, you dumb idiot! Move those hands. Enough gawking!

"Right, the first order of business: secure the bone."

White linen crinkled and popped. A fresh bandage spoke with a new voice as it was unfurled for the first time. Owen folded the bandage down the middle and placed the free end along the exposed bone. He held the end in place with his thumb and began to wind the bandage around the bone.

As Owen completed his first turn, the bone was pulled a hair's breadth upwards. Scarlet sprang to life with a tempestuous scream.

"Stop!" she cried. "Oh gods, stop! Ah-h-h, bastard!"

Hands like hounds pounced at the wound. Scarlet grabbed at her leg on reflex. The madness of pain twisted her face into a snarl.

"No," Owen shouted. His hands dropped the bandage to intercept Scarlet. "No, stop. You're going to make it worse! I'm trying to patch you up."

288

"The hells you are!"

Thrashing ceased when Scarlet sat up far enough to see her bone. Her eye grew wide as saucers, then rolled back into her head with a whimper. What she said was indecipherable. A mixture of swears and curses muddled by disbelief perhaps. She splayed out on the ground again with as much warning as to when she had risen.

"That looks messy," Mahika grunted as she hit the ground. Lack of breath was enough to stifle her quips. She bounded over with a hollow smile. "Anything I can do to help?"

Owen nodded as he fiddled with the now crooked bandage. Mahika presented herself as a cool winter evening. Calm, collected, and ready to listen to what was said. The day to Manda's night.

"Yeah. Keep her shoulders pinned if you can," Owen mumbled. He went to wipe his forehead with a spare hand. Sweat was bleeding down his nose, into his eyes. The sight of the bandage in his hand reminded him to keep his hands as clean as he could manage. Sweaty forearms spread salty, stinging water more than it sopped anything up. "She regained consciousness when I tried to wrap the wound. The less flailing, the better."

"Easy enough," Mahika said with a relieved sigh.

Mahika turned Scarlet's limp head so that her nose pointed to the sky. She settled her knees onto Scarlet's shoulders. Next, Mahika restrained Scarlet's head with her thighs. She took Scarlet's wrists in her hands and squeezed.

"Perfect, thank you."

No more distractions. This time, Owen meant it.

Once again, the bandage crinkled and popped. Two full wraps around the exposed bone. Another for good measure. Pure white linen gobbled up blood on contact. Each wrap was soaked through as it was finished.

Scarlet did not move. There was no way for Owen to know if the pain had overloaded her and kept her asleep, or if it was the nightmarish sight her leg snapped in half that did the job. Not that the answer mattered. Could have been blood loss. Knowing the answer made no difference. All that mattered was that Scarlet was still and receptive to treatment. Thrashing and swearing would have done nothing to help, even as a short-term coping mechanism. Lights out were better than eyes on.

Owen moved to wrap the wound after securing the bone. Alternate wraps, first above and then below the wound, helped further fortify the injury while also staunching the flow of blood. This was where most of the bandage went. It took five laps above and below the bone before the bandage was not instantly soaked. Owen tied a knot just above the bone after the eighth wrap. He hoped that the constant pressure from the knot would help stymie the flow of blood.

"Are we good?" Mahika asked.

Her serene visage stood in stark contrast to the mess beneath her. Hands still as stone held Scarlet's sagging arms firm. Mahika's back was as straight as a board. The smile, hollow as it was, did not waver.

The dispassionate display unnerved Owen. His own hands dripped blood that was not his own. Despite his best efforts to wipe the morbid dye on his trousers, the stain remained. . It did not stop him from continuing to try. Though a vain effort, it helped distract from the tremors that wracked his hands. The burn that ran through his hunched spine.

Cleanliness was less of a concern now. The open wound had been thoroughly bandaged and protected from outside intrusion. He had done the best he could without soap to wash the wound. Next, it was time to secure the leg.

This effort was more straightforward. Owen grabbed a pair of wooden stakes from his pack and another bandage. The stakes, covered in dried mud and sprouts of grass, made Owen rethink his stance on cleanliness. Mahika offered a canteen when Owen explained he was off to rinse the bits of wood. He accepted without pause and began to douse the stakes. Pinching each one in the crook of an elbow, he twisted and pulled the camping gear across his sleeve.

Another piece of clothing ruined.

Satisfied that he dislodged the larger chunks of earth, Owen tied the stakes in place on either side of Scarlet's shin. He had propped the leg up onto his own to help expedite the process. The bandage was torn in half, one piece above the wound and one below. There was nothing pretty about the work. It was a job done in haste from memories that were years old.

That said, it was better than nothing. Owen took a moment to admire his slapdash improvisation before signaling to Mahika that she could let go.

"I'm going to go try and wash this off," Owen said, holding his bloodstained hands up for Mahika to see. "Keep an eye on her, yeah?"

"Oh, sure. I'll make sure she doesn't run off."

The wink Mahika added to her words deepened Owen's sense of

discomfort. Reactions must have been an alien concept to the woman. Whether it was being happened upon at night or seeing a friend bleed their life away, the smile always remained. An unchanging, infallible feature carved below glassy eyes that knew nothing but mirth.

Owen forced himself to stand, ready to get some distance from the whole scene. His knees fought against the sudden call to action. They had been folded closed for long that they had forgotten how to extend. The first steps towards the roaring torrent of water were stumbled. Not unlike the nightly trip from the Creaky Board to his room at the Orland house. These uneven steps came without the same price of admission. Fatigue was bought in this case by long stretches atop Oatmeal and lifesaving work on half strangers, not through wine and beer.

Home away from home, Owen snickered.

Thoughts of revelry lightened his steps. What glorious vices awaited his triumphant return to civilization? Fevered dances beckoned. Feet stomped on worn floorboards, more responsible for the beat of the music than the musicians who played. Drinks sloshed as people pitched from side to side. Those who were past the point of memory leaned on their neighbors for support. There were no strangers before that stage, only friends waiting to be made.

He resolved to himself that he would partake. The joy of complete release was one that Owen had always denied himself. At least, while he was in a state to remember himself. He had been too afraid to join in the mad rush of emotion with people he had never known.

Compared to nearly falling off a cliff in an attempt to save the life of a stranger, dancing in a room full of drunks did not sound so bad.

Cool water rushed over Owen's hands as he knelt in the fringe of the river. Silt-coated pebbles slid beneath his probing hands. He took handfuls of the stuff and scrubbed at his soiled hands. River slime rubbed off the rocks to reveal their rougher surface. Exfoliant stones that bit at the bloody surface of Owen's skin. That the repetitive motions began to hurt did not bother Owen. All that mattered was that the blood was coming off. It was okay if a little skin rode the current.

The water at the river's edge was clear as glass. Rapids stirred sediment and clouded water in the main channel, but that was expected. A different kind of dirty from the muddied intersection of the Rivers Ra and Ro at Arnstead. Muck made by humans, harn, and katarl. Refuse dumped where it did not belong.

Owen watched his hands, distorted by the shimmering surface, flex and unflex. His reflection caught his attention. Chin and cheeks past the point of stubble. Black and purple rings pulled at already burdened eyes. A streak of red cut a messy line across Owen's forehead. He had not noticed the crusted blood on his brow. From when he failed to wipe away the waterfall of nervous sweat, Owen guessed.

He sopped a few handfuls of water against his face. The clean water felt twice as cold on his face as it had on his hands. A refreshed shudder pulled at tense shoulders.

"To hells with it," Owen mumbled.

The river enveloped Owen as he eagerly plunged his entire head into the receptive basin. He stayed that way for a spell. All the world fell away amidst the muted rumble of the current. It was the best respite he could have asked for. Removed from responsibility and lineage. Nothing to fail. No one to disappoint.

Perhaps too comfortable.

When Owen attempted to take a deep, relaxing breath, he was reminded that he was still submerged. Water rushed up his nose. He jerked his head out from the water. The river dripped from his mouth down the sides of his face as he was wracked with coughs.

Owen squelched his way out of the river. That had been enough of a dip for his taste. Dry shoreline beckoned to him, asking to be stretched out upon.

17.

RESPITE

Plink!

Warm, afternoon sunlight pulled river water from drenched clothes. Sweat crusted on the edges of rolled-up sleeves. Owen felt the fabric crunch as he placed a hand over his eyes. Stubborn rays snuck between fingers as a mild, orange glow, but it was enough cover to allow clear sight of both the river and the base of the cliff.

Plink!

Jabari had been the last member of the company to rappel. The katarl carried more than his fair share down the cliff, something for which Owen felt a pang of guilt. What weight Owen had been spared on his emergency descent had to be picked up by those who followed. That no one had bothered to complain somehow made the guilt more poignant. A point of conversation left unsaid because all know its truth.

Conversation was shouted from the base of the cliff back up to Beech. Firm in his choice to remain with the horses, he asked whether anything else needed to be lowered. The rope could be hauled up and used to lower goods down without concern for another fall. A tempting thought. One that hindsight made more painful.

Something was shouted about not wanting to drop supplies.

"Trusted this thing more than enough already!" Jabari yelled. He pointed to handkerchiefs and belts that dangled overhead. "Just send it down!"

Ropes, belts, and handkerchiefs thundered to the ground. Dust flew up and around the coil as it formed. A metal spike encrusted in ice was the last bit of the line. It hit the rocks with a resounding thump. Jabari waved his approval skyward and set about undoing the various knots in the patchwork rope.

Plink!

Devlin and Mahika had busied themselves with the construction of a

293

basic litter. Trees were sparse on the northern bank of the river. That fact did not stop the pair from finding a pair of suitably sized branches to serve as handles. Jabari's tent canvas was volunteered to serve as the bed, a fact in which he was given no say. The katarl did not raise much of a fight. His protests came in the form of snide comments about how his poor tent would be useless by the time the company was through with its pieces.

The litter served its purpose well. Devlin and Mahika were able to transport Scarlet to the riverbank without causing any undue pain. Scarlet had not woken since she caught sight of her brutalized leg. Another stroke of luck so far as transporting her was concerned.

Plink!

"Easy now," Devlin cooed. "Down we go."

Rocks jostled beneath the Keeper as he eased Scarlet's feet to the ground. Mahika followed suit, gently laying her end of the litter to rest.

"Nicely done," Owen said. He offered the Keeper a drink from a replenished canteen. Devlin accepted and drank without a word. Thanks, came as grunts between mouthfuls. Owen chuckled at the display. "Don't mention it."

"Appreciate it," Devlin gasped, finally pulling the canteen away from his lips. Excess water dribbled down his chin to splat on the riverbed.

"Any chance Manus might hear a prayer?" Owen nodded towards Scarlet. "Now that we've got time to spare?"

"I could certainly ask," Devlin began, unsure. He rubbed his neck with both hands while turning his head from side to side. A series of snaps and cracks sounded his satisfaction. "I could not, however, make a promise."

Plink!

"Why not?"

"That's right. Not much one for prayer, if I remember?"

Owen scrunched the bridge of his nose, puckered his lips. The Keeper had remembered correctly. Owen felt no shame in the fact and so did not attempt to dodge the question. His look alone was enough confirmation for Devlin, who gave an understanding nod.

"Well, the first problem is the reagents." Devlin grew more uncertain as he continued. He wrung his hands together, shuffled the rocks beneath his feet. Slight nods accompanied every couple of words. "To ensure Manus heard my prayer, I would need the proper offering. These are not things the House affords to me as a Keeper. Second, I would need to know the prayers of healing. The words our priests recite to invoke blessings from Those Above. I know bits and pieces, but the healing rites are not ones that I have dedicated to memory."

Plink!

"Couldn't just take a crack at it?" Owen inquired. The specifics of prayers and rites were a mystery to him. He had seen some works done. Fortune, whether good or ill he had not yet decided, allowed him to experience one of these rites first hand. To have seen something so near and not understand it bothered Owen. "Is it a real problem if you don't know the words? You couldn't say what you know and hope Manus gets the rest?"

"It's a tricky thing, speaking to a god. We live in a wide world that's filled with a great many people. People asking the gods for fortune or health. Some ask with ill intent, while others would ask for nothing but blessings on their neighbors. I couldn't imagine trying to filter through all of that. Could you?"

"That does sound like a lot of noise," Owen conceded.

"Indeed. Now imagine some dolt who doesn't know the proper rites," Devlin pointed to himself with a sheepish grin, "using reagents to blast whatever drivel came to my mind into the ears of the gods. The gods may be patient, but one should always respect their time. Anger from any of Those Above is the *last* thing we need."

"Fair enough. You know better than I do on the matter, I'm sure."

Plink!

"Speaking of knowing better," Devlin grumbled, looking out over the river, "what is that woman doing? That noise is like a nail driving into my ears!"

"Taking my suggestion to heart, it seems."

Plink!

Manda was atop a large boulder near the southern bank. The unnamed river crashed around the perch. White flecks jumped from forceful contact and sprayed upwards. One misstep on her slick footing and Manda would fall into the current, pulled under the merciless rapids. Luck would have her resurface a mile down river and coughing the river up from her lungs. Poor luck, and she might never be seen again by the company.

The potential for a watery grave did not deter Manda. An established process had taken root. With Owen's caster pistol, which she did not ask to borrow, Manda planted a stake into whatever boulder she was on at the moment. If not the boulder on which she stood, then one near enough to reach. She would then holster the pistol and take hold of the stake with her left hand. A brace for what was to come.

With her right hand, Manda would strike at the metal stake with a formidable hammer. It was no common mallet used about a workshop or barn, nor was the tool of the variety that calls a smithy home. The hammer was a weapon. Owen had seen it dangle from her hip while the company traveled. Four square prongs rose from the face. Instead of a claw, the hammer had a curved spike.

Not the sort of thing you drive stakes with, Owen thought. Not that his musings slowed the visceral endeavor. Owen was not sure whether heat distortion around Manda was courtesy of the sun, or if it was a result of channeling the Flow. Her arm glowed bright either way. *Better the rock than me.*

Plink!

"Your things."

Sword, mess kit, and other things besides clattered onto the riverbed next to Owen. He started at the sudden crash. The Seeker coat, in which everything had been bundled, did little to stifle the noise.

Jabari eased himself to the ground adorned with a satisfied smirk.

"Thanks," Owen grumbled. His first and most natural reaction was to check his coat pockets to ensure everything was where had left it.

"Manda was the one that scooped your things up, brought em down," Jabari said. "You can thank her when she's done with... whatever she's doing. What *is* she doing?"

Plink!

Owen cast a quick look over to Devlin. Neither felt like explaining the situation. Both found the sentiment funny enough to warrant a chuckle.

"No idea," Owen said, failing to suppress his laughter. "You could go ask her. If you're feeling brave," he added. A feeble wave of his right hand accompanied the words. Now was a time for patience and empty-mindedness. Plans could wait for Manda's inevitable return.

There was any number of things that wanted to float to the top of Owen's mind, of course. Mainstays like returning empty-handed or not returning at all were easy to batter down. He had garnered considerable practice over the past few days. A lack of pathways left to explore on the subject was also helpful.

That day's events had given rise to plenty of new fodder for thought. Enough that keeping his mind quiet was difficult. Thoughts like what would happen to Scarlet if her leg got infected. Would someone take her back? Would the stubborn harn press on, despite her injury? Owen had grown invested in her situation through the treatment he applied. He felt responsible, in part, for whatever might happen to Scarlet going forward. At least, for anything that involved her leg.

Thoughts of care and infection led to thoughts of time. How long would it take for the company to find the Cinder Witch and recover the safety deposit box? Would they manage to find it at all? How long would they continue to search if Walks Far did not pull through? An extra day away from Arnstead could mean the difference between keeping or losing her leg.

Circular thoughts swirled with such dizzying intensity that Owen realized a still mind was not to be had. Not while he was hurrying up just to wait.

Manda did not force the company to wait long.

"All right," she called. At first near inaudible due to the river, her words became easier to hear as Manda approached the northern bank. She moved from boulder to boulder like a frog. Power gathered in her legs before taking to the air with mighty leaps. "Stakes are for you lot. I'm taking Scarlet over."

"What now?" Jabari asked. Confusion swelled in his cheeks and brow. Uncertain eyes peered at the metal stakes that had been driven into various boulders. "We can't all jump ten feet from a standstill, you know."

"I said to use the stakes."

"How exactly are we meant to do that, dear?" Mahika followed.

"I don't care!" Manda roared. Muscles bulged from her beet-red neck. Flushed cheeks sagged from the effort. "Hand-holds. Foot-holds. Throw a rope around them. I don't care. Figure it out."

The company exchanged perturbed glances.

"Okay, okay," Mahika said, her tone filled with reassurance, "we'll figure it out. Go ahead and do what you're going to do."

Manda did not look at any one member of the company. Her assenting grunt was directed to everyone at once. Wobbled steps carried her hunched frame over to Scarlet, where Manda knelt for a moment to gather breath.

Most of the company approached the riverbed to birth whatever plan they could. Owen was not among them.

"Manda," Owen whispered, "can I talk to you for a second?" He had waited for the rest of the company to get enough distance to allow for a private conversation. A look over his shoulder gave him the confidence he needed that he would not be heard. "I'm concerned."

"Shut your face," Manda grumbled between haggard breaths. "She'll be fine."

Owen paused before he spoke, unsure how to phrase his thoughts.

"I'm sure Scarlet will be fine," he began. "I'm not worried about her. I'm worried about you. That's not a normal red on your arms, is it? It's a friction burn."

"So, what… if it is?"

"Guessing your legs would have that same bright red if you rolled up a pant leg, wouldn't they?"

"Don't touch my pants, Blue."

"That's not…" Owen cupped his face in his hands, dragged them down the sides of his nose and cheeks. "I'm not going to touch you, Manda. I just think you need to be careful. You're not going to be any good to Scarlet if you fry your body."

"I'm fine."

Manda raised herself to her full height. She turned her head to Owen with slow indignation. Owen had not felt so threatened by a look since his meeting with First Seeker Akheem. Exhaustion gave way to pure malice.

"Sorry," Owen muttered. "I just—"

"Yeah, I bet you're sorry."

Without another word, Manda scooped Scarlet up from the riverbed. A brief moment of hesitation was the only weakness she allowed herself before leaping to the nearest boulder.

Owen let the breath he held escape in a low whistle.

"Well, okay then."

"Watch it! Every time one of you slips, it feels like I'm taking a hammer to my leg!"

This particular howl from Scarlet triggered as one of Jabari's feet slid from underneath. Terrain south of the river made a notable shift. Lightly trodden leaves and soft soil were gone. Gnarled roots and rocky earth had taken over. It was difficult enough to walk when every other step might slide out from under the company's feet. A task made more difficult for the pair that carried the makeshift litter.

Owen counted himself lucky that the present misstep had not been his own. Medical care and benevolent intent made no difference to Scarlet when either he or Jabari lost their footing. Both had been guilty of the act twice before. Scarlet, despite her condition, was more than willing to chew at their ears each time.

"All you have to do is walk," Scarlet continued. "Are your eyes closed or something? I'm tired of having to yell at you. Keep your head up and stop messing around."

The walk sounded simple when it came from Scarlet. As the only person amongst the company unable to walk, she had not been forced to endure the constant elevation change. What Owen had seen from the clifftop was a trick of the woods. An even canopy disguised the steep hills from which it grew. Flat ground was nowhere to be found. Combined with the awful quality of the terrain, it made for a slow march.

No time had been allotted for rest. Manda pushed behind Walks Far at a reckless pace and had done so since the company reached the southern bank. The others did not dare to stop her. Her cold ire was still too clear in Owen's mind. He had put enough of his luck to the test for one day.

Determination to press onward in silence did not quiet his screaming limbs. What rest had been afforded him on the north riverbank felt as if it had been weeks ago. A memory of a memory of relaxation. As if tranquil muscles and even breathing were a childhood fantasy. Owen had become acquainted with the feel of every tendon in his arms and hands, though their names remained a mystery.

There was no analog to the strain he endured. Owen had no landmark to which to compare this pain. Youth free of childhood labor had spared his early days. Drills at Eastpointe had been demanding but were always fair. Second Seekers at the academy pushed recruits to their limits. This march was beyond whatever limits Owen thought he possessed.

Green and yellow leaves faded from sight. Golden rays evaporated to leave a claustrophobic shadow. The ground was visible only so far as the next step as if walking through a dazed abyss.

Twigs no longer cracked or shuffled beneath stumbling feet. Birds stifled their songs. Owen felt his footsteps, heard them in his bones rather than through his ears. The only sound that could penetrate the shroud was the thrum of blood as it pounded through his head.

A death march.

Owen could think of no better name. This march would end in death. If not his own, due to misstep or a failed heart, then someone else. Perhaps the next false step would send Scarlet tumbling down a hill to snap her neck? Seemed plausible enough. With heads down, it was more than likely they could blow past the Cinder Witch and her people. It would be easy enough to torch an oblivious band of exhausted fools.

Possible reasons for failure were varied. They flowed through Owen's mind like water released from a dam.

The darkness that sapped at his periphery had encroached onto his mind. Black despair replaced words with enervation. Owen could no longer grip in his mind that he was tired. Too spent to ponder his situation, he simmered in his suffering. No words to coax his legs. No thoughts to ease his mind. Pain was all. All there ever was, all that had ever been.

Escape from this shell was not quick. Owen did not know his legs had stopped moving when the company came to a halt. More steps felt the same as no steps through numb feet. Cold sweat slaked his chest and back. Warm light from the evening sun could not pierce his stupor.

Open eyes perceived a void. Dark, senseless, and without direction. A placid lake of lukewarm water held up an unfeeling body, below a sky without stars. Black heavens met obsidian fields on an invisible horizon. Windswept fields of jet bowed to a breeze of shadow. Shadow? Yes, cast from the ember at the center of the world. Light thrown from so far away that it was not light when it reached Owen's eyes. Only the pale, gray suggestion of what had once been a gleaming jewel in the vast expanse of the universe. A sparking sapphire, painted blue-green by primordial seas, compressed from stardust into the home of millions.

Falling.

The glassy lake pulled away, dropping Owen into the world's womb. There was no wind to whip at his face. He could not tell how fast he was falling. No landmark proved his descent, but none of that mattered. Owen knew how it felt to fall. Elation and anxiety balled together before exploding throughout his body. There was no sensation like it in all the cosmos through which he tumbled.

Up, he thought. *I must be falling up.*

To start on a lake and fall towards the stars? For there were stars now. They passed by like a spark popped from fire and were gone just as fast.

300

Glimmering clouds of green and purple were leaves on a winter wind. Planets and systems vanished before they could be seen. All were transient save for the blue-green ember at the center.

The universe lost its appeal. Stars vied for attention but went ignored. Owen's eyes locked onto the ember and would see no other. Heavenly bodies came and went as the blue-green ember began to grow. Steady at first, then faster Owen could comprehend.

Hot air-filled Owen's lungs in desperate gasps. The tang of woodsmoke burned his throat, clinging to his tongue like a film of bad decisions. Tears rolled down salt-caked cheeks. His mouth watered with sour spit. One dry heave. Then another. More poisonous air funneled into his screaming lungs as fire licked at his face.

"Whoa there, partner."

Owen felt a hand plant against the center of his chest. It eased his wracked and heaving frame backward and upright. Aware of his hands again, Owen wiped away the murky tears that clouded his vision. His whole body rushed up to his face in a bid to leave the uncomfortable mix of sensations behind. The hand kept him from tipping forward. A gentle grip that stood as firm as a column of marble. His trembling hand wandered up to grasp at the stable presence.

A handful of coughs and a cup of spittle later, Owen felt strong enough to sit back. Feeble hands waved away generous support. The helpful hand withdrew from his chest after a moment of hesitation.

"Now keep your face outta the fire."

There was a voice connected to the words. No longer formless vehicles of thought, he recognized the speaker. Smoke-blurred vision cleared to show Manda Galloway. Her expression, lit by a crackling campfire, was a dubious one. Disbelief in Owen's ability to sit upright was neither hidden nor shied from.

"I'm fine," Owen rasped. Smoke hung heavy on his words. "Promise."

"Yeah, okay," Manda chuckled. "Here."

Something metal was forced into Owen's grip. It sloshed as it moved. Probing fingers found a cap and greedily spun it off. The disc clattered against the metal canteen. Owen slammed the vessel so hard against his face he thought he chipped a tooth. There was pain enough in his front teeth to convince himself of the fact.

Water!

Sore teeth were a small price to pay for clean water. Not some lukewarm swill from goodness knows where, but clean, crisp water taken from the river to the north. Owen had never known water to taste sweet. Each gulp made him yearn for more. He pulled and pulled at the canteen, throwing his head back, until he fought to catch the last drops on his tongue. Owen felt as if he had been reborn at that moment.

A small belch roiled up from Owen's gut to pierce the calm night air.

"Glad you liked it. Wish you'd saved a bit for me, though."

"Apologies," Owen replied, quite embarrassed. Sheepish hands offered the canteen back to Manda. Owen was not keen to lose his life so soon after restoration.

"It's fine. I've got a better one."

Manda pushed herself off the ground and carried the empty canteen to a nearby tree. Packs surrounded the tree trunk at the edge of the firelight. Canvas and cloth rustled as Manda fumbled in the half-light for whatever it was, she wanted.

Night encircled the camp like a thick curtain. The dense canopy of leaves and branches blotted out both moon and stars. What lay beyond the pulsing ring of firelight was a mystery of chirps and whistles. Wings fluttered somewhere out of sight. A bat or owl in search of a midnight meal. Crickets called to one another near and far. Though Owen could not see it, the forest was alive in the dark of the night.

Blankets rose and fell in time with easy breaths. Devlin, Mahika, and Scarlet each had found their nook between rock and root. Mahika in particular had contorted into a position Owen could not imagine would facilitate sleep. Back arched, legs splayed, and head lolled off to one side; comfort seemed the furthest thing from Mahika.

Walks Far seemed the most comfortable of the lot. He was leaned back against his sleeping horse. Even breaths from the horse raised and lowered the kin in a rhythmic pattern. The sight reminded Owen of a rocking cradle whisking a newborn off to slumber. A colorful blanket depicting fire birds and bears on two legs sealed the image. In his sleep, Walks Far was the pinnacle of peace.

The only person missing was Jabari. A realization that brought Owen discomfort. His mind returned to the death march as he looked about the camp a second time.

"Where's Jabari?" Owen asked, not seeing the katarl upon further

302

investigation. "I see everyone else. Is he all right?"

"Stubborn cat is fine," Manda replied. A hushed cry of exultation escaped her as she raised another canteen to the firelight. This one was smaller and suspiciously more flask-shaped. "He put up his tent somewhere out there in the dark. Said he couldn't find anywhere flat enough around the fire."

"Is that a bad thing?"

Owen thought it odd that erecting a tent to sleep in would classify the katarl as stubborn. Jabari had done so every night that Owen had been present.

"Guess we'll find out in the morning," Manda grunted as she lowered herself down by the fire once more. She held out to Owen a flask. "Want some?"

"Please," Owen said without hesitation. It did not enter his mind to ask what was in the flask. The cap was off the flask and the opening to his lips before the smell of whiskey had reached his nostrils. A familiar burn, pleasant and smokey. "What happens in the morning? Sounds awfully cryptic."

"Red said to stay by the fire tonight. Something about ghoulies or whatever. I dunno, Jabari's old enough to make up his mind. Might as well listen to the kin if we're paying for his advice, I figure."

"Huh, sounds spooky."

Manda raised her brow in a look of feigned terror, then held her hand out for the flask. Owen obliged. Three pulls from the flask in quick succession elicited a satisfying gasp from Manda.

"Yeah, real spooky," she scoffed.

Bugs sang their hymns while silence fell over Owen and Manda. A passing thought, whether all of those sounds were bugs or possibly something else, tugged at the back of Owen's mind. Ghouls seemed a bit of a stretch. The sort of story a vengeful mother told her miscreant children to ruin dreams. The stuff of myth and fantasy.

That was not to say that something else could not stalk their camp. Animals that mimicked the sound of another were not hard to believe. Ones that used such talents to sneak up on unsuspecting prey were even easier to accept.

Owen squirmed at the notion of some fanged beast hunched at the edge of the firelight, waiting for the last of the company to drift off to sleep.

303

"Can I ask a question?" Owen asked, as much to distract himself as to hear an answer.

"Shoot."

Manda did not look at Owen when she replied. Her attention was fixed on the crackling flame at the heart of the camp. Light danced in her dark brown eyes, windows to secret reflections at which Owen could not begin to guess.

"What's our plan?"

"Thought that was obvious," Manda said. Notes of condescension surfaced. A familiar tone that had been curiously absent until now. Her expression flattened into a blank slate. "We're going to grab the box and get the hells out of here. Nice and simple."

"Simple, yeah." Owen watched for any change on her face as he continued. "I guess I meant more like the specifics. *How* do we go about getting the safety deposit box back? We seem to be carrying some serious firepower, what with that caster rifle and all. A person could level a small house with one of those things."

"And?"

Manda's face remained flatter than Owen's employment prospects.

"Look, I understand that you're an officer of the Fourth. That grants you and your soldiers more leeway with magical weapons than your average citizen, but I'm not going to sit by while you torch a bunch of criminals. They need to be apprehended and allowed to receive judgment. Rogue mage or not. They're still people."

"People," Manda snorted. "You saw what that witch did to the carriage. What she meant to do to us. Cook us alive in a rolling tinderbox. She's an animal, at best."

"And what does that make you, if you plan to do the same to her and her people?"

Silence, weighted with expectation, filled the next few moments. The first crack in Manda's collected visage showed. A slight downturn at the corners of her mouth.

"It's like those folks at the House say," she muttered. "Do unto others, and all that crap."

"Well, that's comforting," Owen sighed. He could not muster the strength to sound convincing.

"What am I supposed to do? *Ask* for it? Walk up to the Cinder Bitch's door with my hands out like some street urchin begging for scraps?" That last notion carried a particular venom to it. It felt as if Manda spoke to herself more than Owen at that moment. "No, I don't think so. She already tried to roast two federal officers, and I don't plan to give the option again."

Manda flicked her thumb back and forth between herself and Owen. A Fourth Federation Army lieutenant and a Spellseeker of the Arnstead Arcanarium. The sort of pair that should mix about as well as oil and water. Both brought to an orange simmer in the light of the blaze.

"I guess not," Owen conceded. "All I ask is that you and your soldiers leave something left to arrest, all right? A modicum of restraint. That's all I'm asking."

Laughter was not the response Owen had expected. The bitter quality made sense, but that Manda would laugh in his face at the request? That felt uncalled for.

"Soldiers," Manda laughed. A limp hand waved fingers at Mahika and Scarlet. The other hand threw back another pull of whiskey before Manda continued. "These guys? They're not soldiers."

"What? You mean like they're fresh recruits?" Owen cast an unsure glance around the camp. "That sounds like a terrible decision."

"No, Blue. Use your ears. They're not soldiers."

Another laugh rolled up from Manda. She raised the flask, now capped again, before tossing it to Owen. The throw came as a surprise. Owen fumbled his catch, nearly dropping the flask into the fire before taking firm hold. Metal threads whined as he unscrewed the cap. The smell of liquid fire rose with a gentle caress.

Owen took a swig from the flask before handing it back. Leaning forward, arm at full extension, he used the effort to get a better look at Manda. Her face had been in profile for most of the discussion. There might be some hidden emotion on the far side of her face, he thought. Some key to helping understand what was going on. A fragment of betrayed thought on her features. Lines of consideration creasing her brow.

Whatever Manda's true thoughts were, she kept them well hidden. There was nothing to glean from examination of her face. Like the work of a sculptor who had forgotten how to convey emotion. She stared with her blank eyes into the core of the campfire, mesmerized by its glow. Amber droplets dribbled down her chin from another pull at the whiskey flask.

"I can keep guessing wrong answers all night," Owen ventured, "or you could save me the trouble."

The proposition hung like spoiled meat from a butcher's hook. Tainted, ready to poison the conversation that adopted it. The butcher was eager to see the item sold, but there was one buyer in the shop. Manda had no eyes for that line of questioning. Tacit concession showed that she was ready to field wrong answers until the sun broke through the murmuring leaves above.

Another uncomfortable silence filled by the doings of forest denizens. Owen wrung his hands to a chorus of cicadas. Their melody was harsh and grated the ears. It seemed that the further away Owen traveled from Arnstead, the louder the creatures became. They had certainly never been so loud back in Southport. Wails of warning served to turn away trespassers who ventured into unsullied woods. How the others had managed to fall asleep amid the cacophony of nature astounded Owen. There would be no drifting off when subjected to the call of the night.

Owen's head rolled like a clipper on stormy seas. He did not know where to rest his gaze. Darkness robbed the forest of visual interest. The company offered no new sights since daylight had faded. Crickets made their music away from the fire.

What remained was Manda. The occasional pull from her flask was the only motion, outside the occasional shuffle brought on by a dream. Subtle reactions to the whiskey had begun to fade. Manda no longer winced at each sip. She did not close her eyes against the burn of alcohol. A pass of her tongue over wetted lips caught lingering drops, now her only reaction. Eventually, the pulls stopped altogether. The empty flask knocked away sticks and pebbles where Manda dropped it.

Need drove Owen to stand. The need to end the suffocating stillness. If he remained in place, he would not be able to keep himself from staring at the intoxicated lieutenant. A stare that would be filled with wonder and disquiet in equal measure.

Firewood was a fair enough excuse. If Walks Far had said that the company should remain by the fire, it seemed fitting to ensure the fire did not go out. Not that the campfire was in imminent danger of sputtering out. The blaze crackled with a healthy glow. Still, there was no reason not to feed the flame. Owen considered it work done in advance should he somehow manage to fall asleep despite the sounds of night and his anxiety.

Handfuls of twigs littered the edge of the firelight. Better for starting a fire, they could still be pitched into the flame to burn for a minute or two. Owen made several of these trips before moving onto larger sticks and branches. The campfire flared with each handful. A voracious predator that devoured any scrap of wood that drew near. Logs popped and split as if the fire was asking for more.

Larger stuff was more difficult to come by. Logs within easy reach of the fire had either been fed to the flame hours ago or were used as seats. Owen had no qualms with sitting on the bare ground. Asking Manda for her chair, however, was a more discouraging thought. The grey border of light's edge seemed a safer prospect. Walks Far and his stories of monsters be damned.

Owen skirted the ring of light, prodding beyond with the toes of his boots. He found more fuel to feed the fire than expected. Whoever had gathered wood left plenty within reach. Enough to keep his attention from the brooding lieutenant.

The third trip brought a surprise. Something hard stuck into the ground. A kick did more to remind Owen how sore his feet were than to dislodge the object. He knelt to inspect the object, cursing his luck under his breath. Whatever it was had been bound in rope. Multiple lashings secured the rope in place. The quality of the binding was dubious, even to Owen's unknowledgeable hands. He did not need to follow the rope to know it led to canvas.

"That'll be Jabari, then," Owen whispered to the dark. "Guess I'll leave this spot be."

The light had spread far enough to see the corner of Jabari's tent after the fifth trip. The fire had fuel to last for hours, if not until sunrise itself. Owen dropped the last of what he had found near the fire and eased himself back down to the ground. Scarcely a minute had passed before Owen realized he needed another distraction.

Sleep was out of the question. His time spent wandering the stars had left Owen much more rested than he would have anticipated. Desire alone would not see him off to sleep, not after all the activity required to stoke the campfire.

Violette!

The thought cracked through Owen's idle mind like a bolt of lightning. He had forgotten to send a message back to the Arcanarium after the ravages of the day. Time spent in a state of delirium ensured the message was not sent by the time it was expected. Another mark against whatever excuse Owen might be able to conjure added to the fact that Violette was onto his lies. She had made that clear in her missive.

Owen fished the message box from his belongings. The simple box yawned open to reveal the silvered pen inside. Half-truths sprung from the depths of Owen's mind as he pulled removed the pen cap. No overt lies this time. Claims of paperwork in the Lost and Stolen office were not an option. Second Seeker Aaron saw to that with his inquiries.

Blank parchment glared up at Owen. He rolled the pen between the fingers of his right hand, waiting for some ingenious ploy to surface. Nervous teeth chewed at the pen cap. Thoughts of claiming illness were cast aside. Owen saw no use in mulling that one over again. It was not worth the potentially life-long backlash he would have to endure. Along that same vein, he discounted any claims of death in his family. His family names would render that excuse too easily verified. There had to be some manner of explanation. Something that suited that actual task at hand, but allowed enough secrecy to complete his objective.

Could tell her the truth.

Shame washed over Owen's face like a wave of boiling oil. The sort of tingling sensation that clung to his cheeks and refused to let go. It seeped down to his neck and chest. He curled his toes against the relentless discomfort brought on by the mere notion of transparency.

What would the truth look like? When written down in plain speech, free of trickery and deceit, how would the facts of the matter read?

No harm in writing it out, Owen thought. *Can always toss the draft into the fire if I don't like it.*

One thing was certain: the truth proved an awful lot easier to pen.

Metal scraped over parchment. The words were simple. Matter of fact and straight to the point.

Violet,

I have been pursuing Amalia Tennerim (alias: Cinder Witch) for the past three days. I intend to recover a safety deposit box the suspect stole from the Orland Bank. The box is a focus, therefore under the jurisdiction of Lost and Stolen. Will attempt to apprehend as well as recover the focus.

Traveling with a Keeper of Manus, a Fourth Federation Army lieutenant, and an independent security contractor. The lieutenant has three reports. Have not been able to verify their relationship to the lieutenant.

We traveled a day east from Arnstead, then followed the edge of cultivated land south until we reached woods. Continued south to a cliff that runs east to west. Descended cliff, crossed river, and have continued south on foot. Directions come to us from a Fieldkin hired by the Keeper. Currently have no reason to believe we are being led astray.

Will continue to provide daily updates at the regular time. Will contact you sooner if pertinent information becomes available.

Regards,

Third Seeker Owen Raulstone, Lost and Stolen

Owen turned the curled scrap of parchment toward the campfire for inspection. There were no factual errors, nor any mistakes in spelling. Detail had been provided without oversharing on the specifics of the expedition. Penmanship was not awful for having been written on his lap. A smudge or two that would be looked over given the contents of the message.

Shame had slipped away. Pins and needles fell from Owen's cheeks as he had written. Guilt transferred to facts once they reached parchment. Each word had bolstered the confidence of the next. By the time he had finished, Owen was quite pleased with what he had put together.

"Wish you'd said you were an Orland."

Soft-spoken words pulled Owen from his fit of self-congratulation. Lost in his predicament, he had forgotten he was in the presence of conscious company. Owen looked up from his message to find that Manda was watching him.

"Excuse me?" Owen asked.

"I said," Manda replied, more annoyed, "I wish you had introduced yourself as an Orland. When we first met, and all."

"Why's that?"

"Think we might've gotten on better, is all. Might not have started on the wrong foot or whatever."

Slurred words wafted on the fiery scent of whiskey. Alcohol was at least partially to blame for the sudden outreach, Owen was sure. That did not stop him from embracing the opportunity to learn more.

"Interesting that you'd say that, Manda. I'm used to folks not looking at me the same way when they find out I've got Orland blood. What I'm not used to is that being a change for the better."

"I guess that's fair," Manda said after a pause for deliberation. The gears were slow, but they still turned. "You hear stories. Things like burned houses and broken legs. That's the lucky ones."

"Yeah, I've... I've heard plenty of stories."

"You don't hear about much of the good stuff, though. I heard this one story about a pickpocket. Got her hand caught in the wrong pockets."

"Orland pockets?"

"Uh-huh," Manda nodded. She wrapped her arms around folded knees, then laid her head to rest atop the bony pillow. Brown eyes wandered around Owen. Indecisive marbles unable to find a place to rest. "This pickpocket, she expected consequences. When the lady explained her name was Cynthia Orland, the pickpocket expected even bigger consequences. That she might not have hands to pick with for much longer."

"Is that what happened?"

Manda shook her head with some effort.

"No. No, that Orland lady took the pickpocket home and washed her hands, gave her a place to sleep. The first time the pickpocket had a roof over her head since her bastard father went and died on her. The next day, the Orland lady offered the pickpocket a job. 'Join the army,' she said. 'Join the army and make friends. Get promoted. Help me make this town a place where young women like you don't have to steal from pockets to get by.'"

"That's some story," Owen said. He made his best attempt to pull Manda's gaze, show her that he was listening.

"It's the short version, anyhow. Makes you think the Orlands aren't all so bad. Not all of them." With those words, Manda finally allowed herself to make eye contact. "Scarlet and the rest, they're my people from before the army. Before I met Cynthia. I just... thanks. For doing what you could today, I mean. Appreciate that."

"Wish I could have done more," Owen said. A smile and a nod did a poor job of concealing the regret that plagued him. The mere mention of Scarlet and her injury reminded him of his ineffectual abilities. That the reminder came from genuine thanks only made the feeling more bitter. "I'm hoping she'll manage."

"She always does. Tough little runt."

"Does look like she knows how to take a beating. How did that happen?" Owen pointed to his left eye as he spoke. The image of a scarred pit where Scarlet's eye should have been came to mind. Grown-over and dull, it had not appeared a recent injury. "Do you know?"

"She was the last one to join the crew. Jabs caught her lifting food from our stash, let her have it a bit too hard. I wouldn't go telling Scarlet you know she's a pity case, though. A good way to wake up dead."

A quiet, shared chuckle led to silence. This was a different kind of silence. Before, the void of conversation had been pulled taught. A steal cable groaning under the weight of a heavy load, where one more utterance might snap the wire and cut everyone present. What was said was not important. The simple fact that the speaker had the audacity to make themselves heard was enough to warrant pain for those nearby.

Now the cable was at rest. Two people had marched in opposite directions, both holding an end of the cable in their hands. They sat back-to-back now. The cable was slack between them.

"Does this mean you're going to be nice to me now?" Owen jabbed.

"Don't push your luck, blue."

18.

IGNITION

Owen eyed the jagged, blue-green leaves in his palm. Though the serrated edges looked like they could pierce skin, they folded under the slightest pressure. A gentle press from Owen's thumb was enough to bend the points. The leaves, fresh-picked and full of life, regained their shape when Owen removed his finger. Fine hairs that rose from the leaves gave them a feel much like velvet.

"And I'm supposed to... chew on these?"

Disbelief was plain on Owen's tongue as he addressed Walks Far.

"Until they are like paste," the kin nodded.

"That's disgusting," Scarlet added under her breath. She was situated beneath Owen and Walks Far, who were both bent over the harn's injured leg. Bandages had been peeled away with care to reveal the wound beneath. Clots had formed to stifle the bleeding. Removing the bandages had revealed that the wound was still soft despite initial scabs. Flecks of dried blood coated white bone.

"He says it will help," Owen said, turning his head to Scarlet. He gave her a small shrug. "Has to be better than doing nothing, right?"

"Doesn't mean it's not disgusting," Scarlet grumbled. She gave her injury a hesitant glance before covering her mouth to stifle a heave. When the moment passed, she lay her head on the ground and covered her good eye. "Fine. Just make it quick."

"Perfect. That just leaves the doing," Owen said with as much cheer as he could muster.

The texture of the leaves remained unpalatable. He imagined it would not be far off from brushing a dog with his tongue. When rubbed between two fingers, the leaves made a sound, not unlike fine sandpaper roughing the edge from a plank of wood.

One look at Scarlet's mangled leg reminded Owen who had the worse end of the deal. He stuffed the handful of leaves into his mouth and began to chew.

At first, the process was just as unpleasant as Owen had expected. Velvety hairs made the leaves stick to his tongue. It was like licking an envelope that refused to let go. He had to shave the gnawed leaves off his tongue with his teeth. The process reminded Owen yet again of sandpaper. The top layer of his tongue felt as if it was being peeled away each time a leaf was removed.

A full minute of chewing made Owen realize that he had lost no flesh from his tongue. Instead, his tongue had gone completely numb. The slow onset of the sensation had tricked him into believing his tongue had been shredded.

Numbness spread as Owen continued to chew. First his tongue, then onto his cheeks and palette. Owen commanded his tongue to probe the inside of his mouth. He knew the action was executed only because he could feel his tongue rub against his gums. That connection led to numb teeth and gums, as well. The single sensation he felt in his mouth was a bitter chill with every breath.

"Niz iz kite afressing."

Owen was surprised by his garbled speech. A result of the numbing of his tongue, no doubt. While certainly comical, Owen could not help but feel embarrassed by the display.

"Very good," Walks Far laughed. "It is working. Chew a little longer, then place on the wound."

"Wha iz zis tuff?"

"We call it sage's mint." Walks Far rubbed some of the leaves together. The pungent, unmistakable scent of mint flooded the air. Notes of lemon gave the plant a refreshing aroma. "It is common in rocky woods like these. Good for pain."

"Less talking," Scarlet snapped, "more pain-relieving."

"Were, you hurd er." Mint leaves made a juicy smack as Owen gave the lump in his cheek an exaggerated chew. Lemon-infused spittle gushed from his mouth by mistake. Owen wiped the accident away on his wrist, then reached into his mouth to grab the herbal salve. "I jus shpread it on?"

"Around the wound, yes," Walks Far nodded. He pointed in a circular motion around the protruding knife of bone. Gentle authority hung from the words, like a grandparent teaching their grandchildren to sew. "Where bone meets flesh. Spread it evenly."

The blue-green wad pulled apart without resistance. Owen was able to take a small piece and dab it onto the tender wound. Scarlet recoiled from the touch but was able to contain her curses. Fibrous strands seemed to latch onto the exposed flesh. The plant, though rendered into a soft and pliable state, was resistant to spreading after it had been applied. Owen considered this for the next medicinal glob.

Owen had chewed enough mint to pack a complete circle around the wound, with some left over. The remainder was tucked into the spot where protruding bone overhung skin like a macabre awning. An extra buffer to protect against bone rubbing on flesh. The thought alone made Owen's skin crawl.

The effect was clear by the time the initial mint circle was finished. Scarlet was able to unclench her fists. Teeth withdrew from her lip, no longer needing to bite back howled protests. Ease flowed over her tense frame.

"Oh, that's actually pretty nice," Scarlet sighed.

"We'll shee if you pell 'at way when I wap you back up."

Owen grabbed a fresh set of bandages. Feigned madness rolled over his face in the form of a twisted grin. A playful gesture that Scarlet did not appreciate.

"No. Nuh-uh." Scarlet shook her head and raised a prohibitive finger. "Just… just let it breathe for a bit. Leg needs the air."

"Wush only joking. Jus make sure you keep it clean."

"Yeah, yeah," Scarlet grumbled. "You go take your funny somewhere else."

"I shink iss my turn up at da rocks, anywaysh."

Though the observation post was his end destination, Owen wanted first to grab a few things. The walk across camp also afforded him a chance to stretch his legs. Kneeling over Scarlet had put his legs to sleep. A bed of nails would have been more comfortable to walk on.

The walk was not long. Owen skirted the fire ring, built from stones found around the campsite, where Jabari sat with a ladle in hand. Steam rose from a pot as the katarl stirred in a methodical, circular motion. He hummed the tune of a field song. The occasional words he peppered into the song were once removed from being correct. Jabari was either unaware of the mistakes or simply did not care, as he hummed and murmured without much notice of the inconsistencies. Whatever it was that Jabari strewed smelled about as tolerable as usual.

"Your turn up at the rocks, isn't it?" Jabari inquired as Owen passed.

"Jus' grabbing my 'tuff. On my way in a minute."

The relative safety of an established camp had allowed Owen a measure of comfort. He did not keep his weapons strapped and ready for immediate use. The sword belt, caster belt, and dagger borrowed from Collections were buckled and slotted into their normal places. Their weight was a constant reminder that his mission might not have a peaceful resolution. It was a thought that plagued Owen each time he cinched the belts around his waist.

Water and bits of jerky carried no such sinister implications. Shifts at the post lasted hours at a time, and Owen was not about to be caught without snacks again. Late-night stomach growls were low on his list of desires and were easy enough to prevent. The fireproof cloak hung from one shoulder. Summer weather demanded that the bulky thing only be worn to stave off deadly flames. It also made for an agreeable cushion when splayed out in odd angles at the observation post.

Last he grabbed his message box. Today would mark the third honest transmission in a row sent back to the Arcanarium. Much to Owen's surprise, Violette had said little in response. Her responses had reverted to single phrases. Comments like, "So noted," or, "Update documented."

Owen had expected some level of protest. At the very least, he had thought Violette would demand his immediate return to the Arnstead Arcanarium. That some manner of reprimand would be promised. Violette made no such threats. No hint of discontent besides the short nature of her replies. It made Owen wonder what she was up to. He remembered the large map that Violette kept on her office wall, imagined a pin with his name being stuck into the wooded regions south of Arnstead.

Thoughts for later, Owen told himself. He snatched the wooden message box from his pack, spun it in the air, then slipped into a pants pocket. *I'll have all the time in the world to wonder when I get to the rocks.*

"Stay safe up there. Make sure you keep your head down."

Devlin waved as he spoke, wishing Owen well. Owen returned the wave with a confident smile and began the two-mile trek to the observation post.

Hills rose and fell along the rough trail. There was no even path to speak of. Notches cut into trees served as trail signs. The marks were large

315

enough for someone who knew what to look for, but not so obvious that they might stand out to a stranger. Their design was simple. Triplet scores that ran parallel to one another. Squirrels could leave similar tracks as they scrambled up to their nests. Larger, more obvious marks were cut deeper into trees with extra lines. Bark had been shaved away near these marks. Young bears might cleave into trees with their claws in such a manner. Inconsistency was key to ensure the trail would not seem unnatural or manmade.

Knowing where the trail turned did not make it a simple path to follow. It wound its way through dense brush and over fallen monolithic trees. Up steep inclines and down into a particularly steep ravine. Owen had lost his footing on his first trek and tumbled halfway down the hill. A rocky mistake he was keen to avoid today.

Light of evening helped ensure Owen kept solid purchase. His previous trip had been made with the meager assistance of a covered lantern. However precious light might be, it doubled as the surest way to be discovered. The final, treacherous climb up to the observation post had to be made in complete darkness at the midnight swap. Owen counted himself lucky that he had the sun to light his way today. The struggle that would be his nighttime return to camp was another matter. One that his nerves could stress about later.

When made during the day, and with ample attention paid to where he placed his feet, Owen found that he enjoyed the hike. It was a quiet time without obligation. Though his watch at the observation post would require silence, it also required full concentration. This walk allowed for peace of both ear and mind. Time away from the toils of camp and the stress of posting watch. He relished the time.

Memories of Pittwell Creek came to mind as Owen swung his weight around a tree to leap onto a boulder. The paths and trails had been clearer there, worn down from years of autumn hikes. Owen and Cynthia had marched those trails until the earth was pulverized to dust. Bits of dirty cloth, thrown out by Marcus and the rest of the Orland estate's staff, found new purpose as trail markers. The young cousins would tie the soiled flags to low-hanging branches to find their way back home.

Owen paused to run his hand over a set of scratches and sundered tree bark. Thoughts of home brought bittersweet feelings. A hollow half-smile completed his gloom.

"Still running trails for Cynthia," Owen whispered to himself. "So many years have gone by, but sometimes it feels like nothing has changed at all. She must hate that she can't be out here with us."

There were too many complications. If Cynthia had wanted to join the party on this expedition, Owen realized, there were too many responsibilities that rested on her shoulders. The Orland Bank branch was no small commitment of time. People of the town called for her time when she could spare it. Requests came from as high as the mayor of Arnstead, Owen recalled. Physical limitations were not even the top concern. Duty to town, business, and family were colossal in their own right.

Not that Owen had room to judge. This expedition was an escape from his responsibilities, he knew. A desperate attempt to change the lot that had been cast his way. He should be back in Arnstead with his nose buried in complaints. The next few days would determine whether or not this fool's errand was just that or a sound investment of time and resources.

Owen shook his head at the mounting guilt that rose in his chest. That he should be anywhere but here was a given fact. Dwelling on the notion did him no good. He pushed off from the tree where he rested and resumed his trek. The climb to the observation post was in sight.

Boulders mashed atop one another formed the climb. The observation post resembled gray and orange melons fit for a giant's feast. Individual boulders stood as tall as twelve feet. Those were the ones that stood on end. Gouges and imperfections on their wavy stone face allowed for a precarious ascent. Nooks large enough to fit a few toes. Narrow shelves might allow fingers a sure hold the second knuckle.

Though no spot on any of the boulders allowed for a good, clean hold, the climb was not a difficult one by the light of day. There was one spot in particular that Owen did not care for. He was forced to press his back against what felt like a loose chunk of stone to allow his feet to find better points of contact. The thought of a slip and fall twenty feet up was uncomfortable. Owen could imagine bouncing off each boulder he had climbed on the way up, shattering bones with every impact.

The ill sensation passed as Owen reached the top. He pulled himself over a rounded edge to a point where three boulders converged. Two formed a cradle of sorts, while the third formed a solid foundation. A natural window under the third boulder allowed a clear line of sight to the ravine below.

Manda lay splayed over boulders on a bedroll. Smaller rocks and fallen branches made it impossible to be comfortable while maintaining sight, but that did not stop the company from trying its best. She kept brown binoculars glued to her face as she acknowledged Owen's approach.

"Anything strange on your way here?"

Her words were barely audible. Owen might have mistaken her whisper for the rustle of leaves had he not been aware of Manda's presence.

"No," Owen replied similarly. "Nothing disturbed. Nothing tampered with. Your end?"

"No. Same faces performing the same tasks. Pair of humans brought back some racks of fish from somewhere east, so that's another source of food for them."

"They seem pretty comfy here, for living in a cave. Still can't believe they are hiding in a literal hole in the ground."

"The kin came through on his promise, for sure. Would have been a nightmare to find."

"Speaking of comfy, how're the burns? Friction healing well?"

Owen crawled on his stomach as he spoke. Buttons scraped on the stony ground as he moved, accompanied by the occasional clink of metal from his sword or dagger. All an effort to ensure he would not be seen by those below. Those who dwelled in the subterranean caverns. Members of the Radiant Circle. Amalia Tennerim's people. Lair to the Cinder Witch.

"Well enough," Manda whispered, taking a moment to look away from her quarry at her reddened arms. "It'll start peeling soon. Same as it always does."

The discomfort Manda felt at present must have been awful, Owen thought. Propped-up on elbows wrought with friction burn. Like prodding at a fresh sunburn. That she showed no sign of discontent was a testament to her concentration.

Owen slid into place next to Manda and situated himself atop his cloak.

"All right, I'm good." Owen held out his hand expectantly. "No need to wait around on my account. Whatever Jabari has cooking is probably done by now."

"What, is that supposed to be encouraging?" Manda grumbled. She placed the pair of binoculars into Owen's hand.

Manda did not wait around, despite the protest levied against Jabari's cooking. She crawled back from the natural window with her bedroll and disappeared over the rounded ledge. Not so much as a goodbye left her.

So went the only living interaction Owen expected to have until midnight.

Comfort came first. If he was going to be stuck here for hours at a time, Owen was going to make sure it was time spent comfortably. Both the sword and caster pistol belts came off and were laid by his side. Boots and socks were next. Any excuse to take off his shoes was a welcome one. The boots had been on so consistently and for so long that they began to feel like another layer of skin. Being able to rest his toes in the open air was pure bliss.

Fresh air became tainted with the smell of rancid feet. Owen had learned the hard way that his iron-heeled boots were not designed for the ups and downs of the wilds. They were a pair of city boots meant for brick and cobblestone. A day of moderate rest had helped the swelling in his raw heels, but the short hike to the observation had set his feet aflame once more. Owen added visiting a cobbler to the long mental list of errands to complete upon return to Arnstead.

Owen wiggled his freed toes as he pushed out folds and creases in his cloak. Folded over, it made an acceptable cushion. He kept one end bunched up to support his elbows while he watched. Owen settled into the nest he had constructed and began his shift.

Binoculars gave expressions to what would have otherwise been faceless mannequins. Two humans sat at the mouth of the cave. Orange and blue scarves, the recognizable headwear of the Radiant Circle, hung loose on their heads and shoulders. One was a Nirdac male, while the other was a Zumbatran female. Both were eased against the mouth of the cave. Idle chatter was passed between them with warm smiles.

All a familiar scene. Owen had never seen these two himself, but they matched descriptions provided by other members of the company. Though they were standing watch over the entrance, neither person bore any visible weapon. The pair seemed to pay more attention to each other than to their surroundings. As did the pair from the night before.

If they know we're watching, they're doing a fantastic job of hiding it, Owen thought.

Relaxation was a common thread that connected the Radiant Circle members. Whether they were coming or going, taking a moment to chat with whoever was on guard, or just spending some time outside the cave, they did not seem to have a single care amongst them.

The lack of tension made sense when considering their surroundings. Tucked down at the bottom of a steep ravine, the cave mouth was difficult to spot. Boulders and trees ensured camouflage when elevation could not. The high ground on all sides made the position awful to defend, but the Radiant Circle's demeanor told Owen that defense was not on their mind. The cave had been chosen as a place that would not need to be defended. A place that altogether should not be found.

To use nature as a shroud would have worked had the company not followed the direction of Walks Far. Tracks surrounding the cave were nonexistent. The members of the Radiant Circle did not see fit to carry weapons, but they were masters at covering their trail. Owen saw that they kept to boulders and smaller rocks where they could. Hard surfaces that would hide passage. Where no tough ground was available, they swept away evidence of their presence with pine branches.

Owen amended his previous assumption. The Radiant Circle did show one care: to not be found.

His mind was split on the assumption that followed. If they were so deep into the wilderness already, so far removed from civilized land, why go to all the trouble? Why work so hard to mask your tracks if you were so well hidden to start with? Such effort seemed like a waste of energy. There had to be some reason for the expenditure.

Are they sure they won't be found, or desperate not to be?

The thought simmered in Owen's head. No matter how he stirred, no matter the angle he looked from, Owen could not make sense of the question.

We wouldn't have found them without Walks Far, he thought. *I doubt they'd assume we hired a kin to help with our search. The Bureau typically doesn't accept help from outside parties. From what I gather about my reception as a Spellseeker, the House operates in much the same way. And anyone who knows a sliver about grandpa knows the Orland family doesn't care for katarl or harn, much less kin. No, a reasonable person would look at us on paper and laugh at the sheer impossibility.*

"I wonder," Owen mumbled.

He changed the focus of his attention. Hours had been spent on what he could see: the cave mouth; guards on duty; boulders and maples and pines. None of that helped put his mind to rest. Instead, Owen focused on what could not see. Something that had remained elusive, both from him and the rest of the company.

I wonder if she's even here.

Amalia Tennerim. The Cinder Witch. The one person he would recognize by voice or face remained unseen by the entire company. No walks in the woods. No trips to gather fish. Not even a quick trip to piss. As far as he could tell, Amalia was not here.

Could explain why they're so cautious, Owen thought. *Why they're making such an effort to hide their tracks. They know their resident force of nature isn't here to protect them if someone comes knocking.*

Doubt clouded his mind. Had Walks Far led them to the right place? It was true that the Radiant Circle was posted here, but what if the Cinder Witch had fled? What if the kin had missed another trail, one that led away from the cave to where Amalia Tennerim hid from the world while planning her next strike?

That would make retrieving the Orland lockbox a simpler task. As far as he was aware, Amalia was the only rogue mage in the Radiant Circle. Bows and arrows had been the tools of choice for the other members when they raided Beech's coach. Even Amalia had treated her command of the Flow as a last resort. Conventional weapons were a point where Owen excelled. If the band of thieving zealots did have swords and the like stashed away in the cave, Owen held supreme confidence the matter could be resolved without loss of life. His fencing skill would see to that.

Relief was tempered by the realization that no Cinder Witch would mean little to no clout upon his return to Arnstead. The meager offering of retrieving the safe deposit box could not measure up to the glory and recognition upon the capture of a dangerous and elusive criminal.

"Better we all live to see the sun rise than I get a promotion, I suppose," Owen sighed.

Conjecture had riddled his thoughts while he shimmied and rustled atop the observation post, but Owen knew he spoke the truth in that singular moment. He had not come here to kill anyone. Far from it. To bring the Cinder Witch to justice could very well prevent death at the woman's hands in the future. Her initial show of temperance had gone up in smoke along with Beech's coach. Whatever Amalia's end goals were, Owen had experienced the violence she unleashed to reach them.

The idea of returning with almost nothing to show remained a heavy weight. Moral high ground did nothing to lighten that load.

He could hear his father's voice, soft but stern, in the relative stillness of the woods. An imagined whisper that raved about ladders and how best to climb them. Owen had not yet learned to quiet that voice. It gnawed at better judgment. Poked and prodded decisions about which Owen would have otherwise been confident. The man was a whole continent away, but somehow still managed to influence the actions of his son.

Owen pulled his eyes from the binoculars and rested his forehead on his cloak. That his father held sway from so far away was a maddening prospect. Owen tapped the binoculars against the boulders in frustration. A subdued plink, plink, plink.

"That's enough of that," Owen resolved to himself. "Let's do something productive. That lot isn't going anywhere anytime soon."

He set the binoculars down and withdrew his message box. Better to get the day's report out of the way before it slipped his mind.

Not that there was much to say.

Violette,

Situation remains unchanged.

We continue to observe the supposed hideout of Amalia Tennerim (alias: Cinder Witch). No sign of her, despite heavy Radiant Circle presence.

Under suspicion that Tennerim is at another location. Will share the theory with my associates and discuss immediate retrieval of stolen focus (Orland safe deposit box).

Will send an additional report if situation changes.

Regards,

Third Seeker Owen Raulstone

Owen rolled the missive and slipped it into the message box. An overloud clap bounced between trees. He had snapped the box closed out of habit, his mind absent. Silence had slipped from his thoughts.

Binoculars snapped up to alerted eyes. The action was so swift and forceful that Owen smashed the device against bone. Lightning shot through his forehead in a violent arc. He sucked his teeth at the pain but did not dare lower the lenses. He had to be sure that none below had noticed his lapse in judgment.

Smiles and laughter. Abandon that walked hand in hand with ignorance. Owen's mistake had gone unnoticed.

He cursed himself under his breath, heart pounding as he massaged his forehead. That had been a dumb mistake. One that could have, and should have, been avoided. Owen considered the pain to be his reprimand and did his best to move past the episode.

Owen grabbed the message box and jammed his thumb over the facetted memory glass. The Flow warmed his arm as it passed through him to the gem. It was a warm gesture steeped in the comfort of familiarity. Transference of power through his body to a chosen utility. Comfort that his talent at channeling the Flow could be put to some kind of use, even if he lacked the concentration to craft a spell of his own.

Aptitude at channeling the Flow proved to be a blessing. The amount of energy required to send a message to Arnstead had grown considerably with distance. Each day added tens of additional minutes to be allocated to the task. Points on Violette's office map sprang to mind. Some colored dots had been a week or more away from Arnstead if Violette's measurements were correct. Owen assumed that they were.

"Must take an hour or more when they're out that far. Long time to focus on doing nothing. I'd probably lose my mind trying to dial in for that long."

By the time the channeling had finished, Owen's fingers had begun to tingle. This warmth was a more unpleasant one. It was as if he had dipped his hand into boiling water for a split second. Patience would have yielded a more pleasant result. Owen could complete the task without injury. Each minute that passed while he channeled, however, weighed heavier on his mind. Time that should have been spent watching the Radiant Circle's hideout. Their lax nature did not mean there would never be something worth seeing.

A muffled swish sounded at the end of the process. The message had been sent, and Owen was free to resume his watch over the cave. This time he made a point of not jamming the binoculars into the bridge of his nose.

"What in the hells... am I looking at?"

Owen may not have jammed the binoculars into his face, but now found they were boring into his eye sockets all the same.

"Breathe first, son. *Then* talk."

Devlin clapped a hand on Owen's shoulder. Owen felt the gesture, but the words did not register. Stammered approximations of words spilled out of his mouth like vomit. What came out was just as unclear to Owen as the expressions on everyone's faces.

"The hells are you yammering about," Manda said, "and why are you back here? You're not done at the rocks until midnight."

Manda's hand took a more forceful grip. Both she and Devlin watched Owen with looks that were worlds apart. Confused aggression was as plain on Manda's face as it had been in her words. Devlin offered a softer expression. One that favored curiosity with a mild hint of concern, like how he might view a child lost in a crowd. With wild eyes darting from person to person and a face wet with sweat, Owen looked the part.

The manic flow of blood to his head thrummed in his ears as Owen fought to form a proper sentence. After another string of failed attempts, he dropped the attempts altogether and pulled the one word he had come to share more than any other.

"Beech," he gasped.

"As in Joseph Beech?" Mahika asked, pushing a canteen into Owen's trembling hands. "That do-nothing katarl?"

"What about Beech?" Manda followed.

"Cave," Owen replied. He took a deep drink before offering a whole two words. "The cave."

"That sounds like a problem," Jabari offered.

The gathered members of the company looked from one another back to Owen, whose head had slumped down between his knees.

"You think he came all this way by himself and then just ran into the cave? Are you really *that* dense, Blue?"

Harsh criticism from Manda was lost on Owen. He knew what he had seen atop the rocks. Through the binoculars, conversing with the guards like they were old friends, Joseph Beech was impossible to mistake. More importantly, whatever Beech had said to the guards darkened their mood. The members of the Radiant Circle made their first display of outward concern.

Half a canteen later, and after a series of questions that missed the mark by miles, Owen was able to speak his mind.

"He knows them. Beech knows the Radiant Circle. He walked up to the guards on duty and started chatting them up like old friends. What's worse is that, by the time he was done talking, the guards had a real serious look. Like something was wrong. I think he told them about us. As much as he knows, anyway."

"I'm not in the mood for jokes, Owen," Manda said. She put her frame directly in front of Owen. White-knuckled hands clasped each other with rage on the verge. It looked like Manda was using every muscle in her body to hold herself back. "If you're trying to get off watch duty, now's the time to come clean."

"No jokes," Owen replied, shaking his head. "Can't say why he did it, or how he knew where they were, but I know what I saw. He betrayed us to the Radiant Circle."

"Might be one of them, d'you think?" Mahika asked

The question was innocent, as were Owen's earnest statements, but Manda did not take them well. What control she had held was lost when she stood. Flow channeled through shaking arms. Manda approached the nearest tree and threw her fist through the trunk. Chunks of bark and splintered wood rained over the campsite. The tree did not fall, but a crater the size of a cast-iron skillet remained as a testament to frustration.

Bits of wood raining down without due warning prodded the one member of the company unable to run to Owen's side.

"Hey!" Scarlet howled. "What's the matter with you? You *trying* to tear me open again?"

"I'm gonna kill him." Manda spoke to herself without regard for Scarlet's demands. "I'm gonna grab his neck, wring it, break it, and tear off his gods damn head!"

Another cry served as a brief warning before the second shower of wood flew about the campsite.

Protests ceased after the second punch. Scarlet, Jabari, and Mahika made a point to not look at their leader. A slight twinge from Scarlet was the only reaction to a third punch, which Manda followed with a pained series of swears.

"Somebody grabs me a bandage," Manda muttered, her rage spent. She dropped herself next to the campfire with an exhausted grunt. Blood oozed from abused knuckles. "Get some rest. We're dealing with this at sunrise."

Sleep came in waves. Owen was not ready to surrender himself to the night. Unanswered questions gnashed and bit, a colony of ants that had invaded his mind. Accumulated fatigue held no power over the throes of an anxious man who could do naught but think.

Why had Beech shown up at the cave?

To warn the Radiant Circle we're here. That one's easy.

Why would Beech want to warn the Radiant Circle?

Tougher. He's one of them, I'd guess. A sympathizer at the very least, though what there is to champion in a religious zealot that waylays innocent travelers I have no idea.

What does the warning mean?

Preparedness. What surprise we had been gone. There will likely be search parties come the morning to try and weed us out.

What can be done?

Manda has the right idea. We need to act before the Circle does. It's a short window, though. We don't have the familiarity of the terrain that I assume the Radiant Circle does, so acting at night is out of the question. Early twilight is our window. I hope these people aren't early risers.

Questions rose and fell with consciousness. Short gaps in thought allowed for the slightest rest. It was the tossing, turning sort of sleep that never fell into true sleep. That sweet state of total oblivion where not even the mind could trouble Owen. Where he was safe from himself and the prickly thoughts he could bring to bear. The briar patch of self-reflection, where the occasional flower was far outweighed by dense thickets filled with stabbing thorns.

Perception of his surroundings, hampered by his half-sleep, trickled in around questions and silence. The fire crackled in a pit that no one watched. Feet shuffled rock and twig in preparation to move. Devlin competed with a screech owl as he snored. Belts were buckled and boots were strapped. The night was quiet, yet somehow filled with noise.

Filled with the sounds of people?

People moving, Owen's muddled mind managed to notice.

Discordance grew in the disorganized, but otherwise calm, landscape of shadow. Owen blinked against bright firelight that encroached on his tenebrous respite. Knives of orange and gold slashed at eyes that winced. Clamping his lids shut caused tears to well faster rather than ward them away.

Stillness met Owen when he managed to clear his beleaguered eyes. Whatever shuffling had penetrated his sleep must have subsided well before he woke. Save for Devlin rolling-over near a root cluster, the camp was empty.

"Must have imagined it," Owen grumbled as he rolled over, not yet ready to relinquish his weak grasp on slumber.

Owen snapped upright.

"Where is everyone?" Frantic looks around the camp confirmed what a near unconscious mind had perceived. "Why is nobody here?"

Feet failed to find to purchase on the treacherous soil when Owen sprang from where he laid. His attempt to launch up from his bedroll backfired, with his chin finding solid ground first. Blood formed into small droplets on the fresh abrasion. Fresh air stung as he pulled away from the earth. Pebbles and stone bit into his palms as Owen once again tried to force himself up, this time finding success. He was careful not to eat the dirt a second time.

Owen wiped his chin with the back of a hand. The crimson stain was a brief distraction from panicked thoughts. His eyes danced back and forth between his blood and the emptied camp.

The absence of Manda and company had an explanation within arm's reach. Cratered tree trunks served as a stark reminder of the rage that had been put on display. Blood was on Manda's mind as much as it was on the back of Owen's hand. Real and plain to see. There was no doubt in Owen's mind where Manda had run off to and pulled her backup in tow.

Rushed musing could not make sense of the absence of Walks Far. The kin had shown no outward desire to participate in bloodshed. Owen expected to see him asleep with his horse.

"No time," Owen realized. He dropped his sword, swore as he fumbled to don the belt in uneven light. "No time for this. Have to move. Devlin!"

Owen hopped on one booted foot towards the sleeping Keeper, struggling to pull the second boot into place without courting the ground with his face. He shouted the Keeper's name twice more before kneeling next to the peaceful harn. Consideration for slumber was not at the forefront of thought. Perceived lack of time suffocated Owen, hurried his breaths and movements. Vigorous, bloodstained hands shook Devlin with the sort of force brought on by a house set aflame.

"Come on, wake up!" Owen shouted. "They're gone! We need to get to the cave. Before they do something stupid. Wake up, gods damnit!"

Wakefulness came to Devlin no faster than it had come to Owen. The Keeper's eyes creaked open like shutters after a dust storm. His head craned upward to peer about the abandoned camp as if to confirm the words filtered through ears clogged by sleep.

"What's all this noise about, son?" Devlin croaked through a yawn. "You're going to wake the camp."

"*We* are the camp, Devlin. Everyone else is gone!"

"Gone? What do you mean gone?"

"I mean *gone*. Look around!"

Owen stumbled back to his pack, satisfied that the Keeper had begun to stir, to grab the rest of his gear. Dagger, cloak, pistol, anything that might be useful in case Manda made a terrible decision.

"Where has everyone gone?"

"I don't know," Owen snapped. "The cave, I'm guessing."

"What? Without us?" The question trailed off as Devlin asked it. Stumbled realization reached the Keeper. The speed at which Devlin leaped up from his blanket caught Owen by surprise. "No time to lose."

Spare clothes flew from Devlin's pack, his head and shoulders lost inside. Owen was lost in his pack up to his shoulder. Both came to a sudden stop when the night shuddered.

Black night cried out in pain. Owen felt the agonized wail reverberate in his chest. Warm gusts of wind rolled through the camp. It felt as if a roaring fire had been fanned into Owen's face. Too warm, even for a summer night near an open fire. The kind of heat that brought sweat without physical exertion. Then, as quickly as it had come, the heat wave passed.

What did not fade was the orange glimmer to the south. Faint at first, but growing in intensity with each moment that Owen stared. A midnight sunrise climbed until the bright fire was visible over the nearest hill.

"We need to go, Devlin," Owen called out, deflated by what he saw. "We're already too late. Whatever we have will have to do."

"Not without a light."

The Keeper had not been afforded enough time to slide into his chainmail and assortment of plates. He had instead grabbed half a dozen pouches that he lashed to his belt. Some were cloth, others leather. Ingredients for whatever miracles a Keeper might call upon. His mace was slotted through a small leather loop on the same belt. The heater shield, sized for a harn, had been strapped to his left arm and was ready for battle.

Devlin opened one of his belt pouches and grabbed two half-burnt branches from the campfire. His right hand dug into the open pouch and produced some kind of sand or grain. The substance drained between the fingers of a closed fist. Before his hand emptied, Devlin cast the reagent over the smoldering ends of the branches.

"Guide us, Sisir, through this blackest night. That we might find those who cry for help in the darkness and banish the evils that beset us. Sisir, hear my prayer!"

Without hesitation, Devlin clamped his free hand over the flickering embers at the end of each branch. He did not recoil in pain or cry out. Instead, blinding light exploded outward from the branches, as if small stars had been born before their eyes. Devlin tossed one of the beacons to Owen, who had to shield his eyes against the light. So aggressive was the light that Owen nearly fumbled the branch.

"Now we run," Owen commanded. He took off towards the flaming horizon, Devlin close behind.

Torches proved to be a miracle in the truest sense. Two days spent walking about had not been prepared for a mad dash through the dark. Lack of light would have meant a slow crawl across terrain that posed a challenge in broad daylight. Timid steps would not have carried Owen and Devlin to the cave before sunrise. From the vicious boom to the crackling over hill and rise, all signs indicated that dawn would be far too late an arrival.

Light from the torches gave Owen, who maintained his position in front, a moment to plan his movements. A warning of roots that would trip his feet and send him tumbling down. Whether that meant forward, back, or to either side depended on where he was on the trail.

Signs and markers posed a new challenge. Difficult enough to spot during the day, Owen had distant landmarks to note his passage. Guesses and estimates were all he had to go on. A feeling of how far he and Devlin had come, and which trail marker he should expect to see next. The problem was compounded by the fact that he could not spare glances upwards for long. His attention was forced to bounce between ground and tree.

The task was difficult. Twice Owen was forced to stop and second-guess his intuition. The first was a good call that saved the trail. He did not know where he was headed, but doubling back spared him from finding out.

Doubt wormed inky tendrils into his mind after the first error. Second guesses and challenges arose where conviction had previously allowed for none. The second stall proved to be nothing more than a waste of precious time spent looking for the correct path, when he had been leading in the right direction to start with. Devlin offered breathless condolence.

"The dark plays tricks. No shame in that."

Owen heard the words but did not listen. Haste pushed away thoughts that came from without, stopped his ears so that instinct might resume its control.

Stones crunched underfoot as the race resumed. Fear was the wind that caught Owen's sail, that demanded speed where caution was preferred. A primal reaction not driven by the darkness or where a slip might send him. His fear was born of helplessness. The knowledge that Manda was tearing through whatever remained of the Radiant Circle with no one brave enough to stay her hand. He feared a slaughter that he was powerless to stop.

Hands that tore living trees as a nail dropped through wet paper. A rage that was kept in check by a lack of hostile nearby throats. Great imagination was not required to picture the scene at the cave. The images assembled themselves in Owen's mind without effort.

There would be no forgiveness. Owen knew this was his fault. He had chosen to sleep rather than return to his watch, half-convinced that Manda would not have moved before dawn. Trust in that dangerous woman was undeserved. A measure of confidence had been bought by honest words and a shared flask. Such meager offerings had caused Owen to lower his guard. His failure to keep watch had allowed Manda and her people to move unopposed.

Owen cursed himself as he ran. Firsthand he had seen the carnage that Manda was capable of when she set her mind to violence. That unrestrained onslaught was her first, and seemingly last, choice of action was a known factor. A common factor from one encounter to the next.

Lack of concentration claimed its price. While Owen was preoccupied with self-degradation, an errant root grabbed his right foot. The attack was sudden and caught him by surprise. Time froze for an instant. Space long enough to realize his left foot would not be fast enough to break the impending fall. Owen tensed his muscles in preparation for a fall into the shrouded rise.

The blow that followed was not the result of a hapless body crashing to the earth. Pebbles did not bite. Stones did not scratch. Instead, it felt to Owen as if Manda had swung a railroad tie like a club. His shoulder caught the brunt of the assault. The force carried Owen up and away from the ground in a tall arc before he crashed downward.

Darkness obscured the height of the fall, but to slip from the roof of a home could not have felt worse. The wind rushed from Owen's lungs upon impact. He had no air to swear away the pain of the ordeal.

What breath might have remained was sucked away by the gut-wrenching cry that pierced the chaotic night. The sound froze Owen's crumpled body in place. His mind wanted to check for broken bones, to stand through any injury, and press on towards his goal. Cold terror kept his body in check. An orphanage set ablaze could not have mimicked the panic-inducing wail that rose from the edge of the light. The urge to act was stymied by an overwhelming thought that could not be evaded.

What could I do?

It moved unlike anything Owen had ever. Halting, shaking like a beast frozen to its core. Six shuddering legs supported a chitinous mass that bulged and contracted without rhythm or cause. From the nearest end rose the torso of a human, or something very near to one. Trembling arms, swollen to the point of bursting, dangled from lopsided shoulders. In the center of what might have been a face flickered three amber eyes, terrible and unblinking.

No mouth was visible on the creature's ghastly grey head, but that did not prevent its howl. An unreal sound to match an unreal visage. There was nothing about the monstrosity that suggested it could be a living creature.

What could I do?

The thought wracked Owen's body in place of pain. He could see the creature, whatever it was, skirt the edge of torchlight. Life-saving light had been knocked from his hands. The creature had left him curled-up in darkness, severed from protection. Owen assumed that light would mean safety. Something so unreal could exist when exposed to pure illumination. The thing that skittered towards him on fleshless legs must be a trick of the light. No other explanation made sense to a racing, terrified mind.

"Stand, Seeker!" A clarion call that cut through shadow and fear like the dawn. Devlin shouted the words with uncharacteristic vigor. His torch had been dropped in favor of his mace. Powerful legs catapulted the harn across fields of torchlight straight at the ashling, allowing Devlin to strike the unsightly creature with a sickening crack. "Leave this one to me. Go and save them from themselves!"

Placing himself between Owen and the unnatural beast, Devlin unleashed a guttural cry against an oncoming blow. One of the bulging arms lifted Devlin from the ground. The pulsating mass clanged against Devlin's heater shield. A sound that joined the chain of impossible that formed the ashling. The flesh should not sound like one sword striking another. It *could not* make that sound.

The Keeper had been ready for the strike. Rather than fall to the ground like a sack of bricks, as Owen had, he tumbled in the air and landed on his feet. A few steps backward allowed the momentum of the blow to dissipate.

Against all logic, Devlin rose onto the balls of his feet and spread his arms wide. The Keeper made himself look as large as possible before shouting another primal challenge at the flickering abomination. A challenge that pulled the gaze of all three amber eyes toward himself. Imagined bones cracked and buckled as the ashling wrenched its head towards the harn.

Weight lifted from Owen. The moment the ashling shifted its gaze, Owen felt a rush of warmth over his entire body. Freedom of movement returned to his paralyzed frame. He was able to stand. His legs shook and remained bent, and his hands refused to leave the comfort of solid ground, but Owen was up and on his feet. As he stood, his eyes remained fixed on the thing that stalked around torchlight. It probed at the edges for a place where its shifting arms could reach Devlin.

"Go!" Devlin commanded. His mace smacked the chitinous body of the ashling, forcing it to recoil. Distinct emotions were unclear in the thing's hollow retort. The ashling was just as likely joyous as it was pained. Arms twitched as they lurched about in search of new sensation. "Before it changes its mind, take a torch and go!"

Nerves screamed in protest before Owen had even leaned towards the stalking, impossible mass. Away. Away was the only direction that made sense. Left or right was irrelevant. North, south, east, and west were just words. Meaningless concepts in the face of so primal a fear.

Another decipherable blow of arms to shield rung through the night like funeral bells.

The noise, scissors of sound, cut the cord that bound Owen in place. Though the fear did not leave him completely, he was able to dash towards the nearest of the torches. It sat on an island of safety. Pale, white light bathed the ground in a peaceful aura. Owen snatched the torch from where it lay and held it between himself and the ashling. A hollow gesture. The abomination remained fixated on the Keeper, who continued to brandish his weapon with brave tenacity.

Owen loathed taking sanctuary from Devlin. Between the light and the mace, Owen felt sure that the shining beacons were what kept the ashling at bay. Removing one of the torches from Devlin's manufactured sanctuary felt like cleaving a lifeboat in two.

"I owe you tea!" Owen called with his shaken voice. "Don't die on me!"

A vicious battle cry was the best response Devlin could provide.

Owen tore himself away from the scene. Truth rang in his ears, that Manda and company had to be saved from themselves. The selfless Keeper knew what must be done and was willing to sacrifice himself to see that it happened. At least one of them needed to arrive at the cave whole enough to make a stand. Devlin's place was with the unholy amalgam of limb and shell. Serving justice to those who abused the Flow to harm others was Owen's.

Sounds of struggle faded beneath the clomp of iron-heeled boots. Demands of the trail prevented backward glances. Reassurance came only in the occasional clang of metal against goodness knows what. Those, too, were drowned by footfalls in time.

19.

INFERNO

Before long, the crackle and pop of woods aflame stifled all. Ragged breaths were first to be silenced. The rustle and whip of his cloak followed, and his heavy footsteps soon after. Roiling inferno consumed sound and tree alike in a cacophonous roar. A wild symphony of unbridled destruction.

Heat set in as Owen approached the observation post. It felt as if he was walking straight into a massive oven. The stony climb was a ghastly chimney silhouetted by fire. Foul deeds glimmered just past the monolith. Fire coiled up and around tree trunks, flared as its engulfed leaf and limb. Cinders rained down from the crackling canopy like caustic rain from malevolent clouds. The angry scraps of life nipped at Owen's head and shoulders as they fell.

Owen raised the hood of his cloak as he shook cinders from his hair. Taking the clasp, he fed energy into the cloak to ward off the fiery debris. The effect was immediate. Heat vanished. It was as if the fire he saw burned with a cool radiance. The air he breathed was still hot and dense with smoke, but the majority of his body was spared the pyre's onslaught.

Opening the cloak allowed a rush of hot air to envelop his torso. It could not be helped. Owen needed the freedom of movement to climb up to the observation post. There, he assumed, lay his first order of business.

Light from the torch mixed the with blaze's glow to signal a clear path upwards. Long, unsure strides were traded for obvious handholds. The backside of the observation, not yet wreathed in flame, remained cool to the touch. Adrenaline pushed Owen to reach higher, push faster than on his previous climbs. Maintaining three points of contact with the rockface was a luxury for calm days.

Hand over hand, Owen pulled himself towards the top. Legs pushed with ferocious might to skip safe handholds. Speed had become favored over personal wellbeing.

The torch fell victim to haste near the edge of the observation post. It snagged on a small overhang and was wrenched from between Owen's teeth. The strobe-like pinwheel turned end over end over end until it bounced on the stone below. Wood thrashing ground was barely audible above the inferno.

Devlin's gift of light sputtered and went out. The last few feet of the ascent were made by the sinister light of burning trees.

Luck had cursed him yet again. Owen had made the climb a handful of times. Enough trips to become comfortable with routes to the top, but not enough to memorize the paths. Three to five feet separated him from his goal and he might as well have had his eyes closed.

"Gods damn it," Owen grumbled. He mustered air to yell and let forth a frustrated cry.

Some part of him hoped that beseeching the night might bring a stroke of fortune. A small part that spurned logic and demanded a fair fight. Demands that nature, upset by the wicked machinations of Manda and her people, extend a moment of clarity. Fire might chew through enough foliage to light his way if Owen waited. Another few feet back the way he came and the trees could illuminate pathways to the top.

Time. The thought rumbled between his ears. *No, I can't just wait here. Even if I trusted my strength to hold out.*

The last variable seeped between tired knuckles. The adrenaline from the ashling encounter had run its course. Tremors worked into his arms. They were mild at first but promised the wait would not grow easier as time passed. A body abused showing the initial signs of revolt.

Panic, refreshed by the dire assessment of the situation, started to rise. Owen felt a hypothetical fall like a knot in his chest. The idea clutched his lungs and forced air to come in small, desperate gasps. Smoke mingled with the meager air in his lungs. Coughs wracked his body as fingers clung with waning might to the rockface. Owen focused on keeping himself to the rocks while the coughing fit subsided.

Owen cast a deflated look upwards. His left hand fumbled over dim stone. Stretched high over his head, the search was made by feel alone. Smooth stone to his left and directly above. There was a crevice that ran up from his right, but it was too small to be of use. His fingers could not worm deep enough to find purchase.

The lip of the observation post was almost close enough to reach if Owen pushed up with his left foot and allowed his right to hang. Close, but not quite there. A foot or less taunted Owen and his best effort.

I can jump that, he thought, easing himself back down to three solid points of contact

Spite fueled the notion as much as reason. A gap so small would not prevent him from securing the observation post. Even if there had been no response to cry, Owen knew there must be someone at the top. The level of destruction set upon the woods told him that Scarlet's caster rifle was in play. It was the only conclusion Owen could reach without extensive knowledge of Manda's crew.

Owen had to be sure that there would not be a second shot. Each second spent in deliberation was another that might see the rifle unleashed a second time. The whole forest might be lost if shots were fired without obstruction, to say nothing of the people that were likely trapped inside the cave.

Time spent in deliberation would not make the task easier. The decision had to be made, there and then.

Hands slotted into the best holds unobscured by night. Fingers drummed with nervous expectation. Feeling secure, Owen extended his arms and allowed his weight to slump down. The motion reversed when he reached full extension. Arms became bent as his left leg feigned a jump.

One.

The cycle of motions was repeated. Tests that ensured the necessary range of movement was available.

Two.

Crackling wood quieted, overcome by the harsh beat of an unsure heart.

Three!

Left leg pushed while both arms pulled. The concerted effort launched Owen up through thick, simmering air. Both hands reached upwards to clutch whatever they might find. A narrow crevice. Maybe the lip of the observation post itself. Anything that could hold a human desperate to make a difference. Owen hoped against hope that the weight of his indecision would not bear him to the shadowed ground below.

The left hand found nothing but smooth stone. No rung or long-dead root to snag. No slot into which fingers could be jammed.

Nothing.

The right hand found something.

Fingertips slid over the lip of the observation post. A tenuous hold had been established.

Elation was knocked quickly aside by the crushing realization that all of his weight, weapons and all, was supported by the mere tips of four fingers. Owen's body caught on quick, cementing those lifelines in place. Those fingers clung to the uneven stone-like ticks burrowed into a gargantuan deer.

A labored cry erupted from Owen when his mind had a moment to catch his body. Not a cry of pain, but one of strain. He could feel the muscles in his arms stretch against his weight. His hand felt as if it had been turned to stone.

Scrambling feet looked for purchase somewhere on the stone wall. The instinctive need to alleviate the strain on his right hand was powerful. Owen's left hand swung up to the ledge through no conscious command of his own. His body was working frantically to save itself from the brutal fall that would result from failure. Unfortunately, the grip of his left hand was no surer than his right. Eight fingertips fought in unison against the savage wills of gravity. Another labored cry rumbled from Owen's chest as he failed to pull himself upwards.

Another cry pierced the crack of fire of darkness. From above, Owen saw the glimmer of a slip of metal raised over the ledge. A dagger was pointed at his tenebrous connection to the observation post. Poised to sever the ties that bound Owen to fleeting safety.

A face followed the dagger over the ledge. One that was filled an alarm melting into surprise. As if sour expectations had been met by a pleasant outcome.

"Blue?" Scarlet said, her voice elevated above the roar of the woods. "The hells are you doing here? You're supposed to be watching camp with the Keeper and the kin!"

"Less talking," Owen grunted. "More helping."

"Oh, yeah, sure!"

Scarlet tossed her dagger over her shoulder. The weapon clattered atop the observation post before coming to a metallic stop. Her hands, small yet confident, gripped at Owen's wrist. Her one good, powerful leg planted itself in place.

"All right, up you go," Scarlet groaned.

Hidden strength pulled Owen's left arm up and over the ledge. His constant state of panic made way for a sliver of surprise. Not that Scarlet was helping him in his moment of need, but that she was able to in the first place. She pulled and pulled until his shoulder was up to the ledge. All the while she spouted scraps of encouragement, her arms now wrapped tight around Owen's.

That brief respite gave Owen a chance to root his legs. Scarlet's efforts had raised Owen high enough to find new footholds. First his left foot and then his right. The weight of the world shifted from weary arms to stalwart legs.

"You good?" Scarlet asked. Owen assumed she noticed the weight change. The harn now supported one arm rather than the whole body.

"Yeah," Owen gasped. "Yeah, I think so."

Owen tugged lightly against the harn's death grip. She released him with an embarrassed titter and pushed herself back from the ledge. Owen was able to scurry up and over. That he was not the exact picture of grace was the last thing on his mind.

Once over the ledge, Owen gave himself some time to breathe. He rolled over onto his back and let dirty, smoke-tainted air flow freely in and out of his lungs. Any air Owen could find was good enough. It stung his throat and coated his lungs. Problems for later. He watched fire dance through the canopy above as he sucked down the poisoned concoction.

Bright lines painted the back of Owen's eyelids, remnants of the fiery waltz that consumed the trees above and the ground below. Closing his eyes offered no escape from the severity that surrounded him.

"Whatever brought you here, your timing is good. The rest haven't come out of the cave yet and I doubt I could get down by myself. Even if I slid down the front."

Owen snapped upright at Scarlet's words.

"The caster rifle," he demanded. "Where is it?"

"Mounted-up on the post. Overlooking the cave."

"Good." Notes of disgust tainted the retort. Owen did not care if his displeasure showed. "I'll get you down the front. The rifle stays here."

"The hells it does!" Scarlet yelled. "I was halfway through charging another shot. What happens if Manda isn't the person that walks out of the cave? Or Mahika, or Jabari?"

"Doesn't matter."

"Doesn't matter? Of course, it matters!" Scarlet continued at a steady yell, though the strain on her voice was imperceptible over the crackle and pop of the woods. "I can barely walk. I'm not dropping down from here if I can't defend myself."

"Defe—" Owen started. The word caught itself in his throat. It was a concept he could not fathom. "*Defend* yourself? With a *caster rifle*? That is not self-defense! Do you even know how many people you killed with that thing tonight? Gods damnit! I should have confiscated that thing the moment I saw it. Thrown it off a cliff. Something!"

"Hey, come on, man. We've got a job to—"

"No!" Owen howled. "No excuses. You've lit the whole gods damn forest on fire. Whoever didn't know we were here full well knows now. And that says *nothing* for how many people are going to end up dead. There could be innocent people in that cave, Scarlet. Gods forbid, there might even be children! We have no idea."

"Stop it! We didn't see any—"

"It doesn't matter, Scarlet! The problem is that we don't know. We don't…" Owen trailed off. He had not noticed himself stand. Aggressive steps toward Scarlet had also gone unnoticed. He towered over the injured harn now, teeth and fists clenched in equal measure. Poorly disguised fear flickered in her eyes. She winced away when Owen held out his hand. A new wave of heat rose from his chest, driven up by shame rather than the surrounding flame. "It's not all right, but it's a conversation for later. I'll get you down. Rifle stays here."

Owen knelt low to offer his hand again. He tried to fight his nerves to make the gesture welcoming and smooth.

"I'm going to help you down, Scarlet," he said. "After that, I'm going into the cave to see what I can find."

"You're not going to stab me or anything?"

"Wha— no!" The remark caught Owen off-guard. Anger and aggression had not vacated him completely, but murder felt like an unwarranted jump in logic. "Worst I'd do is arrest you, but we don't have time for that right now."

Doubt remained over Scarlet like a raincloud. Dark uncertainty, unsure if there was lightning on the horizon or just a trickle of rain. An understandable reaction from a person who had been raised by thugs on the streets of Arnstead. Understandable, but still problematic.

I don't have time to win you over.

The thought served as a call to action. Owen realized he did not have the time to break down the barriers built by a life lived on the edge. A few warm words would not keep Scarlet from looking over her shoulder, much less help lower her guard amid panic and danger. Warm words offered at the tip of a sword, turned white-hot by rage, were even less helpful. What the moment required was action over words.

With his outstretched hand, Owen reached for Scarlet with slow determination. The motion was plain for Scarlet to see. No hidden intention or secret purpose. An offer of safety, as much as could be offered in the present circumstances, with no strings attached. No payment required.

Tacit and gentle proved to be the better approach. Though Scarlet did not reach out for assistance, she did not withdraw from Owen's touch. He was able to pick her up with one arm. It felt like scooping a frightened, human toddler. Scarlet weighed more, but not by a large margin. Owen found himself thankful that Nirdac harn were smaller than their Zumbatran relatives. Lack of physical stature was a blessing that day.

"Don't drop me," Scarlet muttered, wrapping her hands around Owen's neck.

"Haven't dropped you yet," Owen replied, confident. "Not about to start."

Long ears flattened backward as Owen tucked Scarlet into the cloak. Another burst of Flow from his free hand renewed the cloak's spell. Hot air was expelled in a rush to leave behind a cool haven.

"Oh! You've got all sorts of goodies, don't you?"

Owen snorted at the notion, followed by a chuckle.

"Suppose I do."

Sliding down the front of the observation post towards the Radiant Circle cave did not pose the same challenge as ascending the rear, even burdened as Owen was. The gentle slope stuck out in Owen's memory from shifts on watch. Where the back of the post imposed a sheer climb, the front was not so steep. Owen was able to lay down on his back and ease his way down to level ground.

Two sound legs were the key to a smooth descent. The slope was approachable but was by no means flat. Shale mixed with twigs and dead grass to reach impressive speed. Larger rocks served as footholds to break up the slide. Traveling from the observation post all the way to flat ground in a single slide might have matched the gallop of a horse in speed.

Light as she was, Scarlet would not have been able to make the descent without help. The effort would have demanded too much of a person with one good leg.

The momentum died without assistance as Owen reached flat ground. Dust from the descent mixed with smoke and heat to further sour the suffocating cocktail. The pleasant air within the cloak did not protect his exposed face. Beads of sweat swelled and stung his eyes as they dribbled down his forehead. Breathing felt like raking fingernails along the insides of his lungs. The ensuing coughing fit felt like it made the problem worse.

Owen felt Scarlet pound a fist against his chest before her words were clear. Thin suggestions of ideas fought to reach his ears through the chaos that surrounded them. 'Safe' was key among shouts.

"Not safe," Owen hacked, tucking his face into a covered elbow. "Not safe, but stopped. Find somewhere safe. Don't leave the light."

Unsure how much got to Scarlet through his coughing, Owen rolled to one side. A slow and gentle motion with Scarlet cradled in one arm. Owen rested her weight on the ground before poking his head into the cloak. Any trace of composure had left the harn's face. Fear and confusion dominated her typically indignant features. Eyes like moons reflected scraps of firelight that clawed through the cloak.

Looks were somewhat deceptive. Despite the terror that gripped her, Scarlet had enough presence to nod in response. She let go of Owen's neck and supported her weight.

Good enough, Owen thought.

Responsibility for Scarlet's wellbeing slipped away with her weight. Though the harn herself was no heavier than a child, Owen had felt the weight of her deeds around his neck. He had carried to safety an individual willing and able to burn an entire forest to the ground. Owen could not say whether the cost of those actions pained Scarlet or not, but the fact remained that she had committed the atrocious crime against nature. That was nothing to say for how many people might have died, or would still die, as a result.

It felt wrong to let Scarlet go. She should not be tied to a burning tree but letting her hobble away unattended left a foul taste. Owen did not like the thought of Scarlet surviving him to go unpunished. He watched her crawl out from his cloak and away from the cave wishing he had time enough to see to all things that needed doing: bind Scarlet; staunch fires and make the area safe; deal with Manda and the rest of her people; grab the safety deposit box; apprehend the Cinder Witch. Days' worth of effort that all needed doing in the same instant.

Owen was forced to pick his battles with care that night. Scarlet would have to be dealt with later. Those running amok in the cave had to come first.

Flame constricted the mouth of the cave. The fire was unlike that natural blaze that consumed trees and brush. Fires that chewed on fuel and spread from tree to tree. Expected behaviors of a ravenous flame. What choked the cave clung to bare stone and did not move. It was as if the rock bled oil. The flames did not waver when wind whipped through the hellish valley, nor did they dimmish with time.

Owen kept the cloak wrapped tight around his person as he approached the unsettling scene. The Flow moved through him to the cloak's clasp in regular intervals. Pulses of cool air kept Owen comfortable. The exterior of the cloak kept the flames at bay.

Through the mouth of the cave lay a broiling corridor. Much like the mouth of the cave, these flames raged where no fire should. Owen made a mental note to retrieve the caster rifle and its cylindrical core. No layperson should have access to that kind of destructive power. He could think of no purpose beyond violence for an explosion of flame that did not dissipate.

The path forward concerned Owen. Flames above and to his sides had proven to be no threat. The cloak saw to that. What about the fire from below? The heat was expelled well, but would that hold true to constant flame? He would be exposed from his shins to the soles of his boots, as well. Drawbacks of a cloak not cut to fit him.

Seconds wasted gnawed at the back of his mind. A quick test sprang to mind. Something to put his nerves at ease.

Owen stamped at the ground around the mouth of the cave. A simple yet practical attempt to smother the unnatural flame. Simple and ineffective. Stomp as he might, the fire would not be doused. Dirt kicked at the flames was no more effective. The blaze seemed to seep through whatever was thrown its way.

Well, I'm sure they're in there, Owen thought. *Either they have some secret they stashed away to protect them from the fire, or there's space enough inside to be safe from the flames.*

"Here's to hoping it's the latter," Owen cried as he ducked through the mouth of the cave and into the heart of the Flow-infused flames.

The first few steps were timid. Probing strides that assessed the grade of the cave passage, which was not so steep. It was not like the terrain that led from the observation to the cave mouth. This rock was solid and unmoving. Long strides could be taken in quick succession without fear of sliding or gathering too much momentum.

The grace of easy passage was countered by the heat. Owen found this was neither the place nor the time for unsure steps. Those first few steps, slow as they were, allowed a swell of broiling air to climb up to his midsection. A focused pulse of Flow pushed the air out before it could roast Owen where he stood. However, the pulse was not strong enough to cool his feet and lower legs. He realized that a slow pace would result in his feet being cooked inside his boots. He broke out into a run as the image of being melted in place burst into his thoughts.

Despite the light of the fire that surrounded him, Owen had no clear sense of when the passage would end. A wall or sharp turn could have been just outside arm's reach and he would not have known until the moment of collision. The light was too much. Too bright to see by, and too hot to keep his eyes open for a good look.

Isolation of this kind was a new sensation. To be lost in a place that was so well-lit was a bemusing notion. Owen had always imagined that blindness would be dark. A world of shadow that encroached upon open eyes. That his own eyes could be open and see nothing but white was beyond belief. It was as if yellow and orange had been drained from the fire. All that remained was a white, hot intensity that pierced closed eyelids. Terror squeezed at Owen's heart as he feared that sight had melted from his skull to dribble over the stony floor.

Tongues of flame scratched at his cheeks. With the hand holding the cloak closed and the other wrapped around the neck clasp, Owen had no way to keep the hood held tight around his face. Skin screamed for shelter that was just out of reach.

His mind reeled at the lack of visible safety. Determination had given way to panic in the face of fire and pain. Owen whipped his head from side to side. Fear prevented him from gathering his senses. Fear that his hands would touch charred skin, blistered and useless. Fear that he might feel nothing at all.

Without warning, the claustrophobic coil of fire and madness opened into an antechamber. Space was well lit by fire that had been pushed to the walls. Ten feet separated the floor from the ceiling. At the highest point was a naturally formed chimney through which smoke was able to ventilate. Breathing remained an unpleasant endeavor but was not so impossible as it had been in the passage that led there.

Signs of habitation, blasted into pieces by Scarlet's spell, littered the room. Remnants of wooden chairs. What might have been a fire ring, though scorch marks seemed to be the rule rather than the exception. Some cookware that had been bent or melted. Fragmented ash whirled about the room and up towards the chimney. Owen imagined clothes, books, and the like to be among them. He feared that remnants of bone and sinew would be muddled within those ashes.

As welcoming and free of immediate danger as the cavern room was, Owen found his attention split between two things.

First was a gut-wrenching commotion that rose somewhere from his immediate left. Sounds of struggle, like tools striking against stone, intermingled with sporadic cries for help. The exact source was difficult to determine at a glance. Scarlet's unnatural fire coated the walls, as well as some of the floor and ceiling near the sounds. Whatever passageway might lead to the source was obscured.

The second was the trio that stood on the right side of the room. Horrible flames showed Manda and Jabari, arms crossed, near a preoccupied Mahika. Water rushed from Mahika's left hand in a powerful jet. She used the stream to move Scarlet's flames around as she pleased, explaining how the trio had managed to push through into the cave. What made Owen fling back his cloak and draw his caster pistol rested in Mahika's right hand.

"Stop!" Owen commanded. His voice echoed around the chamber in a desperate bid to be heard over fire and terror. "Stop, Mahika! Let him go!"

"Oh, hello there!" Mahika called in response. The flow of water from her hand sputtered, then dribbled down her wrist. She waved as if she had passed by an acquaintance in the street on a sunny afternoon. "Almost done!"

Owen heard the words without truly hearing them. Another source of noise to add to the sick and twisted confusion. His attention was fixed on Mahika's right hand and the desiccated ankle she clutched.

Shriveled on the floor next to Mahika was the body of a man. Orange and blue scarves obscured much of his face, but what skin could be seen was repulsive. Raisin-like eyes dangled from dry sockets. His forehead resembled farmland that had been plowed into dust after years of misuse. The man's calf, just visible under Mahika's hand, was in no better shape. Pork salted for winter had more moisture than the crinkled husk of a leg.

Mahika stepped closer to a flame-drenched archway. When she pulled at the shriveled man's leg, it ripped loose at the hip. Out it popped through the man's trousers with a sound like deer jerky being ripped apart.

A dry, dusty, but unmistakable groan slipped out from between parched lips. The man from the Radiant Circle was still alive.

"Ah, this one's broken, too." The torn limb was dropped as Mahika addressed everyone present. She continued to speak without compassion. Concern showed only for the job to be done. The man at her feet seemed to be nothing more than dust to her. "Help me find another one, will you?"

Go!

Wind whipped from the caster pistol with violent crack. Fire and screams were drowned by the noise of the spell that reverberated within the enclosed space. Silence reigned for a breath before the inferno resumed its roar.

The powerful rush of air lifted Mahika off her feet and threw her through the archway she had attempted to clear. Her passage cleaved the wall of fire in half for an instant. Mahika was lost from sight when the blazing wall reformed. The cave had swallowed Mahika, closing red-hot teeth to trap her inside.

Manda was on Owen before he could level the caster pistol. A terrifying blur, Manda allowed no time to react. She pointed the caster pistol to the ceiling with one hand. The other hand wrapped its menacing digits around Owen's neck. Owen knew that fighting her flow-infused strength was a futile effort, but that did not quell the reflex to grab at the hand around his neck. Wild eyes glowered at Owen through enraged confusion.

"I don't care what your last name is," Manda spat. She drew her face closer to Owen's as she spoke. Crackling fire lit her face in a hellish manner. "If you attack one of my people again, I will *break* you in half. You can take that to your cousin's bank."

"Manda, I can't see her," Jabari called. "I can't see Mahika through the fire!"

Manda whipped her head around long enough to shoot Jabari a look. The katarl recoiled.

"Then get in there and look for her. And find the damn box while you're in there!"

"The fire—"

"I don't care!"

Owen felt the grip around his neck tighten as Manda's fury intensified. Blood welled in his face. Owen felt that his head might pop. It wasn't until Owen tried to step away that he realized his feet were no longer on the ground. He kicked at the air in a panicked attempt to reach the solid stone.

Words gargled in Owen's throat. Ideas that failed to reach his lips and died without reaching Manda. Spots began to blot out portions of Owen's vision. They flashed between bright white and deep violet. He abandoned efforts to reach the floor and flailed his feet at Manda. Weak kicks flopped against an iron torso. Manda was a pillar of strength from which Owen hung limp.

The hard-stone floor rose to catch Owen all at once. Feet, hands, head, and the rest crumpled to the ground. Sharp pain from the collision went unnoticed. All his attention was focused on sucking down as much air as his lungs would allow.

Gathering what sense, he could, Owen looked up to see Manda stepping away towards Jabari and the flaming archway. She showed no hesitation to turn her back to Owen. Her point had been made.

"I'm not—" Owen began, coughing as he spoke. The faltered speech was punctuated by gasps for air. "I'm not going to let you people murder anyone else."

"Do what you want," Manda called without looking back. "Just don't get in our way."

The fire snapped and danced as Manda approached the archway. A barrier to stop the faint of heart and the indecisive. Manda was neither of these. She rocked on her heels once, twice, then launched herself through the opening towards uncertain ends. The wall of fire sputtered at her forceful passage before reforming yet again.

Jabari looked about the cave and swore. A dozen thoughts seemed to swirl about him all at once before he resigned himself to follow his leader. Though less confident than Manda, his resolve was unbroken by the trial.

With both Manda and Jabari leaping through fire to locate Mahika and their prize, Owen was left to contend with the muffled screaming alone.

"No one else dies here today," Owen said as he drew himself up. Pride welled in his chest. He spoke to the yawning fire through which Manda had disappeared. "Not while I'm standing."

This rush of pride came as much from his show of defiance as it did from an idea that had sprouted. Watching Mahika's deplorable acts, ghastly as they were, had inspired Owen.

The fire that enveloped the cave was resistant. It proved difficult to smother or extinguish in a meaningful way. Rather than quench the flame, Owen thought he might be able to move it as Mahika had done. He pulled the sapphire cartridge from his belt and swapped it with the azure cartridge already in the pistol. The work of Lionel Eilhart would save lives once again, or so Owen hoped.

Energy passed through Owen's arm and into the sapphire cartridge. The Flow moved at a constant, accelerated rate. He intended to blast the spell continuously, to fully charge the cartridge even as its power was expelled.

"You helped power a whole train," Owen whispered to himself, a half-hearted reassurance. "You can keep a tiny, little piece of glass charged. You have lives to save."

Go!

Water gushed from the caster pistol in a short burst. However hard Owen focused, he could not override the nature of the spell to shoot a continuous stream of water. Such was the limited nature of a focus. What he could do, Owen found, was charge the cartridge so quickly that the spell might as well have produced a continuous jet of water.

Short streams, punctuated by shorter gaps, pelted the fire-coated stone floor. Owen let his spells loose far from the screams at first. There was no sense in making a terrible situation even worse with a decision made in haste. He would not allow duress to render the situation unsalvageable. Whoever was trapped behind the flames needed calm, measured assistance, not a rushed solution that caused more problems.

Scorching stone hissed. Steam erupted wherever water met fire and rock. Yet more obfuscation to cloud the already murky cave. Smoke and steam rose together, mingled in the natural chimney as they sought to escape.

Through veils of smoke and steam, Owen was relieved to see the fire recede in response to his spell. That the water evaporated before it could form into ice was irrelevant. The inferno could be controlled to an extent. Moved in a way that suited Owen's needs, though not snuffed in its entirety.

Good enough, Owen thought.

Owen peeled fire away from the sounds of struggle. Cries for help became clearer, spilling out from a small opening in the cave wall. It was just above the height of his knees and was a few feet across. Large enough for a person or two to scamper through at a time. Faces, distorted by fire and desperation, peered through the crawlspace. They had taken note of Owen and waved for his attention. Frantic, pleading gestures that dropped Owen's stomach to the floor.

"Hang on!" he reflexively cried upon seeing the display. "Just hang on. I'm getting you all out of there!"

Flow coursed through Owen's veins as he resumed use of the caster pistol. Water punched at the flames guarding the crawlspace.

"Stop!"

The word rang out from the trapped survivors. It tumbled out of one after the other amidst coughs and screams. Owen's surprise at the request was short-lived. Their reason was plain to see after the last blast of water.

As with Mahika, his spell did not extinguish the flames. His best efforts could do no more than move the fire. Shift the flames from one area to another. This posed no problem when clearing fire away from walls or clearing a patch of exposed floor. Angles were plentiful and Owen could manipulate the magical fire as he saw fit. With the crawlspace, his options were limited. Water shot at the floor pushed flames deeper into the space behind the opening.

Owen could not see how large or small the space was. At best, those within would simply need to move further back to allow for rescue. The worst case, however, far outweighed the good in Owen's mind. Space might have been small. People might be packed from wall to wall. Pushing flames further into such a confined area would cook the poor souls alive.

The words of those trapped were of no help after their discordant cry for Owen to stop his spell. Fevered calls for help resumed, drowning out any useful information that might have been shouted from the group.

"Hang on, hang on," Owen found himself mumbling. Empty words meant to carry him from his last good idea to the next. He looked around the barren, broken room for something useful. Anything useful. His head snapped from one direction to another with the frenetic speed of a squirrel that heard the screech of a meteoric falcon. "Hang on. Just hang on."

Lost. Owen was alone in the middle of an empty room set alight. The only people nearby that could offer help or suggestion were either panicked out of their senses or sniffing around for job security. Help had to come from within.

Oppressive heat weighed on his thoughts. The combination of fueling the caster pistol and the cloak at the same time had proven too much. It felt like his blood had turned to pulverized glass as it ran through his arms, forcing him to focus on the pistol. Owen sought the comfort of the cloak again now that the pistol served no apparent purpose. He holstered pistol and clutched the memory glass clasp with a sweat-drenched hand. The rush of cool air might spare his mind, Owen thought. A source of relief that might lead to revelation.

The cloak!

The obvious struck Owen like a brick to the head. Around his neck was draped a fire-proof cloth. He pushed aside the shame of not realizing this sooner and whipped the cloak from his shoulders.

His mind moved at full speed now that Owen had the makings of a plan. With the clasp tucked firmly into his hand, he wrapped the cloak around the length of his right arm. Cloth-covered every inch from his shoulder down the tip of his middle finger. No portion of his arm was left exposed to air or fire.

"Take my hand!" Owen called through the crawlspace. He knelt and channeled the Flow into the cloak. "I'll pull you through. One at a time!"

Looking past how the fire burned without any obvious fuel, Scarlet's spell seemed to function as a normal blaze. The fire produced heat and smoke. It spread to natural fuel sources like wood and dried leaves or grass.

Most important of all was that it took a moment to catch. Manda had jumped through the spell without hesitation. While Owen was certain there was a kind of violent madness about the woman, she had yet to show that she did not value her safety. That must mean that Scarlet's fire was normal in that sense. Something could pass through briefly without suffering irreparable, life-altering damage. The members of the Radiant Circle should come through with nothing worse than sunburn if Owen could pull fast enough. Assuming the person being pulled would help, with a push or by kicking off, Owen knew he could pull these people to safety.

Owen eased his arm through the gaping mouth of flame. Heat crept into Owen's shoulder the closer he drew. Sweat beaded on his brow and the back of his neck, but, try as it might, the fire could not penetrate the cloak.

"Take hold," Owen called. Scalding rock sizzled next to his head. He could feel the heat tear at his exposed face even as someone took hold of his arm. "When I pull, you push-off!"

There was no verbal response. Instead, Owen felt a pair of hands squeeze tighter around his wrapped-up arm. Calls for help had subsided. Screams fell away amidst the roar of the fire. Those stuck in the crawl space must have focused all their attention on the gamble that played out before them. Tacit hope permitted deep within the belly of a crackling oven. Owen took hold of his sleeve in his open hand, covering his palm with the thin fabric. Preparation to against the searing wall in an attempt to muster as much force as possible.

Every muscle moved in concert. The right arm pulled as the left arm pushed. His fluttering chest tightened to produce torque. Both legs pushed away from the crawlspace, working against the weight affixed to the right arm. What felt like the weight of the world reduced to nothing as Owen pulled and pulled and pulled.

Out from the crawlspace popped a trembling, gasping pile of shot nerves. A Bangeli katarl. Broad shoulders heaved as his core fought to expand for each breath. He lay on his back next to Owen, stunned eyes peering up at the smoke-obscured ceiling.

"Are you okay?"

Owen's question snapped the katarl out of his stupor. The katarl shook the confusion from his pace and patted at singed patches of fur.

"Fine, I'm fine," the katarl rumbled. After clearing residual embers from his striped fur, his attention moved to Owen for a moment before turning to the crawlspace. "There's seven more of us in there. I'll help you pull!"

Questions like, "Who are you?" or, "What are you doing here?" were absent from the katarl. Curiosity was overridden by the will to survive, the need to save those who remained. The katarl's immediate command of the situation impressed Owen. An introduction would come later. There were seven more lives to save. For now, Owen simply nodded and pushed the Flow back through the cloak.

Powerful arms wrapped around his waist as Owen reached back through the opening. When he felt a new set of hands squeeze around his improvised mitt, he issued a guttural command.

"Pull!"

Both Owen and the katarl pulled in unison. Owen pulled at the stranger

350

clinging to his hand, and the katarl pulled at Owen's waist. Being caught between the two was a whole different experience from pulling alone. It felt like he was being torn in half. After the initial kick-off with his legs, Owen was no longer in control of his motion.

The positive effect of the uncomfortable situation was that the human popped out from the crawlspace in half the time. The fire had not time to bit at her as it had the katarl. The three crumpled atop one another, sprawled out over the cavern floor. A writhing pile of ragged breaths and emboldened determination. All three were on their feet after a brief pause. No words were dispensed. The newcomer followed the lead of Owen and the katarl. Their added strength went unnoticed by Owen, as did the additions of the next four Radiant Circle members, but he could not have dissuaded them even if he had wanted to. One after another they emerged through fire. One after another they took up the cause of pulling their comrades away from certain and gruesome doom.

Elation was brought to an unforeseen end with the second-to-last survivor. Hands did not tighten around Owen's arm. He reached further into the crawlspace, as far as he could. The skin on his cheek burned when it contacted the wall. Owen forced himself to resist the urge to recoil.

"Take my hand!" Owen called. His words were distorted by a cheek pressed against the scalding stone. "Hurry!"

"He's— he's not breathing," was the uncertain reply. "James isn't breathing!"

"Just grab him, Elena!" roared the impressive katarl. "We'll pull you and Jim out together."

"Before we *all* stop breathing!" Owen added.

The fire continued to burn, unwavering and merciless. The chimney tucked into the ceiling helped clear some of the smoke away at first. As the efforts of Owen and the Radiant Circle drew out, the efficacy of the chimney diminished. Hungry flames must have found more natural fuel. Boxes, books, foodstuffs. Anything that a militant group of religious extremists might have about their encampment. The specifics were irrelevant. What mattered was the smoke working its way down from the stony rafters.

The urgency of the situation seemed to sink in for this Elena. The woman on the other side of the crawlspace had taken hold of Owen's wrapped arm. He only felt a hand this time. Quivering fingers latched onto the folds in the cloak, a tentative grip unsure of its anchor points.

"Pull!" Owen shouted.

Owen pulled. The katarl pulled. Some number of the other Radiant Circle members pulled, though Owen hadn't stopped to count how many helped. It was hard to tell whether the combined strength of the group ripped Owen from Elena's grasp or if she had let go to pat at the flames. Whatever the answer, the result was indisputable; a woman writhed and screamed in the fiery crawlspace. Owen and the Radiant Circle, now without the resistance of two bodies to match their pull, crashed to the floor.

With Elena was the body of an unconscious harn. Primal desire to survive fought against the will to save her helpless comrade. One hand clung to the harn, while the other flicked about the crawlspace to find a handhold.

Horror, thinly masked by a heart-stopping roar, thundered out from the katarl. He had released Owen's waist and scrambled towards the flame-engulfed pair.

The roar snapped Owen from despair and guilt. He pushed off the ground and towards the crawlspace with the same effort. It was a clumsy motion that brought Owen to his knees just as he reached the katarl. Thought of harm was pushed aside as Owen reached into the crawlspace with both hands. His left found immediate purchase, though the mitten-like right hand struggled to grab either Elena or the harn.

A synchronized effort was no longer on the table. Owen and the katarl pulled and pulled, desperate to wrench the still-screaming Elena from the blaze. The human woman clung to the harn with all her might. Frenzied legs kicked at the crawlspace, an attempt to help her saviors in their efforts.

By the time Elena had been extracted, black patches of charred skin were visible through burned clothing. Cooked flesh mingled with burnt hair, both hers and the harn's, to concoct an offensive aroma. The woman trembled with pain as she struggled to find quaking breaths. The harn in her grasp remained unconscious and oblivious to all that had just transpired. Blistered skin raised from where his fur had burned away.

"Hold on," Owen half-whispered to the woman. "I'm getting you out of here. Getting all of you out of here."

Adrenaline wracked his hands as Owen unbound the cloak from his arm. *Better on her than on me,* Owen thought as he held his cloak. Soothing chill from the Flow-infused garment might help stabilize the burned woman. A chance to prevent her wounds from worsening. The thought was kind, but it did not will Owen's shaking hands to move faster. He felt as if he was working underwater.

"I said, 'What's the plan, Seeker?'"

Owen pricked up at the words. A quick, searching glance showed the katarl to be looking at Owen. The expectation was clear in the katarl's grey, steadfast gaze.

"What?" Owen replied. He had heard the katarl full-well, asking the question more as a reaction than to hear the katarl repeat himself.

"Seeker," the katarl repeated. Likely for the third time, Owen realized. The katarl followed the title by pointing at the badge on Owen's belt. "You said you're getting us out, but we might have more people alive down here. And we need a way out once we find them. The tunnel is full of fire."

The katarl waved a clawed hand over his shoulder. His gesture encompassed the entryway to the cavern, the archway through which Manda and Jabari had disappeared, and another archway Owen just now noticed through smoke and fire. It had not entered into Owen's mind that could be more people yet to find. Given the state of the harn, they might not be able to call for help either.

First thing first, Owen told himself through shaken nerves. He finished removing the cloak from his arm and wrapped it around Elena and the harn. A blast of energy into the clasp ensured that some level of heat regulation could be applied to the burn victims. It was not enough, Owen knew, but it was the best he could do at that moment.

"Keep them wrapped in that cloak," Owen said, meeting the katarl's gaze with a commanding response. "If anyone among you can channel the Flow, have them push energy into the clasp. It should help keep these two keep cool."

The katarl nodded before turning to the scattered members of the Radiant Circle. They had dispersed in search of a way out besides the tunnel. Some called the names of others who might yet be trapped somewhere deeper in the cavern.

"Jwala!" the katarl snapped. "Get over here. Channel into this brooch, Seeker says it'll help Jim and Elena."

A Bangeli human gave up on her calls and approached. Long, black hair fell over her shoulders as she knelt and began to administer energy to the memory glass clasp. She whispered soothing words to Elena, who sobbed within the cloak.

"Now we get you out," Owen said. He unholstered his caster pistol and began to channel into the Sapphire cartridge. If he could clear fire away from the crawlspace, he saw no reason why the same wouldn't be true for the tunnel. "Gather your people. I'll clear the way."

"Wait," pleaded Jwala. "There are more of us, somewhere inside. We can't abandon them!"

"We won't, but I need to get you out of here. There are more people here besides me," Owen said with a glance towards the archway. "Dangerous people. I'll look for the rest of your people once you're outside the cave. Okay?"

Jwala did not look convinced, but the katarl spoke before she could protest.

"I'll hold you to that," the katarl said as he rose to his full, imposing height. His next words rang with an authority that chilled Owen to his core. "We're leaving! The Seeker will find our people while we tend to the wounded outside. Move!"

Motion followed the command. None among the Radiant Circle questioned the katarl once he had spoken. The katarl himself scooped Elena and Jim into his arms and fell into step behind Owen, who approached the entry passage to the cavern. Jwala remained attached to the katarl's hip as she channeled the Flow into Owen's cloak.

One last glance over his shoulder confirmed for Owen that the Radiant Circle had corralled themselves at his back. He turned his attention to the fire that coated their exit. The passage did not hold the same power over his senses as it had before. Knowing there was a solution, the caster pistol in his right hand, bred confidence. This would not be a desperate run through a passage of unknown length, hungry flames biting his ankles the whole way. . Anxiety left steady hands in its wake as it abandoned the Spellseeker, melted by the scorching expectation of those relying on his skill to survive.

Owen ignored the pain brought on by channeling the Flow in haste. He pushed aside the sensation of pure energy grating against raw flesh, refused to acknowledge it. All that remained was the need to evacuate the people at his back as soon as possible.

Go!

Water shot from the caster pistol with redoubled vigor. Each powerful blast of the spell pushed fire further up the tunnel. Owen edged forward in the short space between blasts. Little by little, he worked his way through the passage unimpeded. The members of the Radiant Circle followed close at his heels. One heavy, reassuring hand, belonging to the katarl, rested on Owen's shoulder. Gentle confirmation that those behind kept pace as the huddled collection of souls pressed through remnants of flame and steam.

The passageway felt an awful lot shorter to Owen when he was not running headlong through open flames.

Strain from continual charging of the caster pistol kept efforts focused on the immediate path. Though the way was shorter than he remembered, for he could see the mouth of the cave shortly after their crawl began, he did not feel comfortable wasting energy. Flames that coated the walls and ceiling continued to burn. Avaricious fields of orange and yellow that threatened to reach out and ignite loose scarves or shirt sleeves. Bodies huddled together into a vulnerable mass, seeking to keep as much distance from the near-omnipresent fire as possible.

Reaching the mouth of the cave, Owen could see the fire had spread further into the woods. The patch of flame he pushed away from the cave felt like a joke. A thimble extracted from a lake of fire.

Those behind Owen paid no mind to the scale of the blaze as they poured out from the deathtrap that was the cave. Jwala, the katarl, and all the others found a patch of stony ground not consumed by flaming debris and set their wounded down. The katarl looked up at Owen long enough to offer a short nod of thanks before busying himself with his people.

Owen allowed himself space for a few breaths to gather his nerves. He holstered the pistol to examine his right hand. On the surface, there was nothing to see but the scuffs and scrapes from scampering over stones and fallen trees. Those marks did not explain the pain as he clenched and unclenched his hand. Fingertips that tingled could not feel the palm of his hand. As proficient a channeler as Owen was, the consequences of his actions were beginning to make themselves plain. Valuing haste over precision came with a cost.

"Can't stop now," Owen told himself. He continued to prod himself as he flexed his right hand and attempted to shake the pain away. "Not yet."

The way into the cavern remained clear. Owen tucked into the flaming tunnel and sped down the passageway to make good on his word.

Sweat poured down Owen's soot-smudged face. Drenched sleeves did little more than smear the grime together. It felt like the cave was trying to extract every last drop of moisture from his body. Mild dizziness crept up to his forehead. His tongue, parched and swollen with thirst, sat heavily on the floor of his mouth.

Owen took a quick survey upon reentering the main chamber of the cave. Two options presented themselves; push through the archway the Radiant Circle had gathered around, or go after Manda and the rest. That Owen was the only person in the main chamber told him Manda was still tucked away where Mahika had been blasted. A guilt-fueled fear clapped cold hands onto Owen's shoulders. Not a fear that he had harmed Manda and her crew, but that he may have exposed more of the Radiant Circle to Manda. Clear visions of Manda tearing through trapped, seemingly defenseless people played across Owen's mind. Those thoughts made his choice a simple one.

Once again, Owen drew his caster pistol. Sensations like sandpaper against exposed flesh renewed as he charged the sapphire cartridge's spell. How many times had he cast Lionel's spell this night? The number was lost amidst confusion and pain. Useless information served only to distract from the tasks at hand.

Fire gave way to the watery deluge that exploded from the caster pistol. The archway was wide enough that Owen could approach from various angles, clearing a path without pushing flames further into space. A lack of cries for help gave Owen time to rest his nerves. This effort could be completed with some measure of precision. Owen had the archway open for passage with a few well-placed casts of Flow-infused water.

Through the archway was a storage area. Crates and chests lined the natural stone walls as best they could. Though some had been spared Scarlet's wrath, many of the wooden containers that made up the majority of storage had been set ablaze. Several had been ripped open by the force of the initial blast to reveal the supplies within. Food, bedding, clothes were turning to ash. Craftsman's tools and sundries, nails and screws and the like, had been thrown about the room.

At the center of the room was a waist-high ring of stones. Manda stood at the far edge, hoisting something up with a rope. A few seconds revealed her prize to be a bucket. Manda pulled the bucket from the well and dashed its watery contents over a prone Mahika, whose limp arms rested above her head as if she had been dragged into place. Manda tossed the bucket away in frustration when the water did not rouse Mahika from her daze. The wooden vessel splintered against the cave wall.

Furious as Manda still appeared to be, Owen was relieved to see her without some stranger's necks crushed beneath her bootheel. Owen holstered the caster pistol when Manda noticed his presence. The knife-like stare she threw was enough to make Owen raise his empty, open hands in a gesture of peace.

Jabari was too preoccupied to notice that Owen had returned. The katarl lumbered between boxes and chests. Never staying in one place overlong, he peered inside containers that had not yet been claimed by the blaze. Owen assumed he had been tasked with finding the Orland lockbox now that Mahika had been accounted for. An unenviable task in the current climate.

The safety deposit box was not an immediate concern to Owen. That task could be left to Manda and her people. Something simple that did not require a delicate touch. Preservation of life, however, was a task that Owen knew fell squarely on his shoulders.

Leaving Manda and Jabari to their mission, and seeing no one that required his aid in the storage area, Owen stepped back into the main chamber. Another wall of flame barred entry further into the cave. Exhaustion, refreshed by the thought of channeling more spells, hung on Owen's right arm like a solid weight. Owen drew the device with his right hand and transferred it to his left. The process would be slowed. Used to channeling with his dominant hand as he was, Owen suspected it might take twice as long to channel. Possibly longer.

No good to whoever I find if I can't lift my arms, Owen resigned. *Long overdue to balance out the strain.*

Owen closed his eyes to the swirling inferno that reached up to the ceiling. The harsh light of the fire was reduced to a faint, shimmering glow through his eyelids. Smoke and soot vanished. Probing hands and menacing glares became memories smothered by the persistent crackle of fire. All that remained in the warm, monotonous void was the Flow.

Gentle at first, the Flow swelled within Owen. Orange and yellow gave way to vibrant purple. The Flow was deep here, in this sequestered cave. Owen felt the river of energy envelop his legs. It rose to his waist as the current gained strength. Through his mind's eye, Owen could dip his hands into the raw energy and watch it splash over him. He was an ancient boulder weathered by the river of infinity.

Energy seeped through Owen's flesh. It oozed into every pore and welled in his chest. The raw power was hot, a purple sun that carved out a place in his breast. The raw power that he could command. Owen pushed the energy from his chest through his left arm, focused it into sapphire caster shell. He opened his eyes. The spell was ready.

Owen's heart stopped.

Through the wall of fire stepped a human figure. Wreathed in flame, they paused in their stride. Their head snapped to the right; the crawlspace. Then their head snapped to the left; the storage area, where Manda and Jabari scoured for the Orland prize. Last, the flame-shrouded head turned to Owen. A slow, deliberate gesture intensified by obscurity.

"I let you live."

The trembling words that came from the fiery figure were a stark contrast to the figure itself. Before Owen stood the personification of rage. A roiling, human cauldron of hate and power.

Tears hung in that voice.

Her voice.

"I am Third Seeker Owen Raulstone, of the Arnstead Arcanarium." Owen plucked his badge from his belt. He raised both the badge and the caster pistol so they were level with the Cinder Witch's chest. "I am placing you under arrest. Your crimes are assault with deadly magics, assault of Bureau of Arcane officials, and theft of focuses. Resistance will be met with force!"

"Got it!"

Reflex took over. For the slightest moment, Owen looked to his right. His head remained in place. Just a quick flick of his eyes to see Jabari holding a small, wooden box over his head with both hands. A triumphant pose.

Owen realized his mistake too late. He looked back to the Cinder Witch to see she had taken flight. Explosive force erupted from her hands with a thunderous noise that shook the cavern. The spell propelled her through the air. Sleek and low to the ground, the Cinder Witch looked more like she was skating across a frozen lake than flying through the air. Her trajectory would carry her past Manda and straight to Jabari.

The caster pistol spewed forth the spell that Owen had been fueling. A vain attempt to knock the Cinder Witch from her flight. Water splashed against the archway a foot or more behind and above Owen's target. He cursed his aim as he channeled another spell's worth of energy into the cartridge.

Manda was in no better a position to stop the Cinder Witch's assault. She was in the middle of shouldering Mahika when Jabari found the Orland box. Presumably, to carry her to safety while Jabari continued the search. Regardless of her intention, Manda was weighed down by the unwieldy load of an unconscious body when the Cinder Witch launched through the air. An exclamation of surprise and a hasty attempt to set Mahika down without causing injury was all Manda could manage.

A horrific crack sounded the collision between the Cinder Witch and Jabari. She had raised her knees and met the side of the katarl's head. The force of the blow lifted Jabari off his feet and sent him sprawling into a huddle of storage crates. Half-broken boards caved under the weight of impact. A bloom of splinters and soiled linen rose to fall on top of Jabari.

The Orland safety deposit box flew from Jabari's hands to strike the cave wall. The katarl's tongue hung from his slack jaw as he lay unconscious.

Channeled energy shone from Manda's arms as she rested Mahika on the stone floor. Manda dashed towards the Cinder Witch the second her hands were free. Momentum and Flow-infused strength combined when Manda cocked her right fist for a wild hook. Manda moved like a manarail engine that had hopped its tracks. A terrifying force of nature that stood against the graceful power of the Cinder Witch.

For all her strength, Manda's swing was obvious to read. The Cinder Witch ducked the attack. Manda stumbled to catch herself without a solid object to meet her fist.

The Cinder Witch capitalized on the whiffed strike. With the momentum of her downward dodge, along with an extra push from hands that exploded Flow-infused fire, she rocketed a heel up to catch Manda square in the temple. This blow made a solid thud rather than a crack. It did not quite lift Manda from her feet, either. Rather it sent Manda stumbling until she toppled over a knee-high chest. The resulting slap of her body meeting the floor was a sickening one.

Whether Manda had been put down for good or was merely stunned, Owen could not tell. All he could be certain of was that the distraction offered by Manda and Jabari had allowed enough time to channel the sapphire cartridge's spell. He let the water fly just as the Cinder Witch was recovering from her kick. The spell caught her in the back and went to work without fail. A ring of ice bound the Cinder Witch's arms to her torso.

"You are under arrest!" Owen took a few tentative steps towards the Cinder Witch as he spoke. He continued to channel energy into the sapphire cartridge, hoping to bind the Cinder Witch's legs in addition to her arms. "Do not resist and you will not be harmed. You have my word."

Another snap of water jumped from the caster pistol and make contact with the Cinder Witch's ankle. Just as with the target dummy at Research and Development, the spell brought both ankles together and encased them in a ring of ice. The Cinder Witch did not mimic the dummy, however, and fall to the ground. She maintained a rigid balance.

Amalia Tennerim stood proud, a confident pillar amidst a swirling torrent of chaos.

"You will not bind me, Spellseeker."

Her words crackled like fire as the Cinder Witch turned her gaze to Owen. Flames that coated the walls flickered and whipped, as if a hurricane had forced its way inland to the cave. They did not sputter and go out. Instead, the flames were lifted from where they burned. Around the room, they spun in clockwise rotations. Slow at first, but faster and faster as the flames progressed, they formed a hellish vortex around the Cinder Witch.

The Flow-infused ice that bound her arms melted away at the barrage of encroaching fire. Freed from her bonds, the Cinder Witch stretched her arms in a grand gesture. She turned to face Owen. Ribbons of fire danced around her body. The words that spilled from her, despite the inferno of which she had become the epicenter, were detached and cold.

"You will not stop me."

The gesture was slight. A mere flick of the Cinder Witch's wrist. It was command enough to send one of the ribbons of flame lashing out at Owen. Fire given solid form wrapped around Owen's wrist. His exposed flesh sizzled under the searing heat. Owen reflexively pulled away, but the Cinder Witch had taken hold of the ribbon of fire. The resistance she offered was firm.

Another flick of the Cinder Witch's wrist sent a second ribbon forward. This one coiled around the caster pistol just Owen let loose a blast of water. The shot went wide, vaporizing a third dancing ribbon. The Cinder Witch wrenched the drained pistol from Owen's hands with a mighty pull. It skittered away into some shadowed corner of the storage room.

Panic flickered. Owen had been disarmed of his most powerful tool. With a whip of fire wrapped securely around his wrist, he knew he could not evade the Cinder Witch. A contest of strength was pointless. Even if Owen was stronger than the Cinder Witch and was able to twist the fiery binding to his advantage, he would not have much of a right arm left by the time the tactic paid its due. White-hot pain taxed his ability to formulate options. Owen needed something simple and fast.

The dagger!

Owen twisted his left arm, free of binding for the moment, behind his back. The hilt of his dagger was within easy reach. So little use had he found for the tool since his arrival at Arnstead, Owen had almost forgotten its purpose. There was more to the dagger than just a sharp edge.

The small piece of memory glass faceted into the hilt-ring of the dagger was cool to the touch. It accepted the energy Owen channeled with voracious hunger.

When the Cinder Witch flung another fiery ribbon to bind Owen's left hand, he was ready. A quick flick of his wrist caused the dagger's edge to meet the ribbon mid-flight. The Cinder Witch's spell over the flame was broken on contact. Puffs of ash and smoke were the only remnants of the spell. Owen utilized the visible surprise of the Cinder Witch to force more energy through the dagger and slash the ribbon that bound his right arm.

The first ribbon left a more lasting impression; blisters and burns swelled where the ribbon had bound Owen. A painful reminder of Owen's disadvantage. Pain that doubled when Owen rolled his wrist in response to newfound freedom.

With her moment of shock passed, the Cinder Witch pressed towards Owen. She seemed to abandon fire and spells, proved to be uncertain options by Owen's newly remembered variable, in favor of a traditional frontal assault. There were no visible weapons in either of the Cinder Witch's hands. Owen assumed she meant to pummel him as she had done Manda and Jabari.

Whether the Cinder Witch chose to bear a weapon or not was her decision. Disadvantaged as he was, Owen felt had no option but to fight through pain and draw his sword. The sharp motion sent tendrils of agony from the tips of his fingers to the top of his shoulder. Friction burns from his overuse of the Flow combined with the exterior burns of the Cinder Witch's spell. Owen knew he would not be able to utilize the sword to his best ability. He felt it more likely that the sword would be little more than a sharp shield in his current state.

That doesn't mean she needs to know that, Owen demanded of himself as he adopted a defensive posture with both sword and dagger.

The Cinder Witch did not falter. She charged at the raised blades at full speed. With her left hand, she reached out to grab the sword and push it aside. All a fluid, singular motion to close distance and expose and armed foe. There was no doubt in Owen's mind that the Cinder Witch was an experienced warrior.

No amount of experience could save exposed flesh from a honed blade. So Owen thought as he dragged his sword-hand down to slice the Cinder Witch's hand.

I'm not so weak that I can't drag my sword across a naked hand.

Sparks showered from the Cinder Witch's hands. They were as much a surprise as the feedback of the blade. The sensation of dragging the blade down the Cinder Witch's hand felt more like a clash of blades than a sword cutting through flesh. A pig's carcass was the closest thing to a human Owen had cut ever cut through, but it was close enough a proximation to know that something was wrong. Owen looked from the cold fury of the Cinder Witch's eyes to the gleam of her hand.

Gleam?

Owen knew the Cinder Witch to have a strong Zumbatran complexion, but her hands darkened to the likeness of obsidian. They shared the gloss of the volcanic stone. Much to Owen's dismay, her hands shared the iconic edge of the black stone, as well. Rounded fingertips had been replaced by gleaming talons. One set kept Owen's sword preoccupied while the other swung for his face.

The first thought was, *What?*

A close second: *When?*

Both initial reactions were pushed aside by protective instinct. Owen raised the dagger to intercept obsidian talons. Energy flowed through his left arm and into the dagger, ready to shatter this new spell that weaponized the Cinder Witch's flesh.

A new shower of sparks erupted next to Owen's face dagger collided with talons. He winced at the orange rain that assaulted his eyes. That brief moment of blindness ended with a foot planted deep into Owen's gut. Breath left Owen in a ragged gasp as he was pushed back from the Cinder

Witch. *Better than missing an eye*, Owen consoled himself through the dull pain in his gut. He drew himself up with a fresh breath to face the disarmed Cinder Witch.

Except she had not been disarmed. Gleaming talons remained where dark flesh should have been. Another shot of panic pierced Owen. His spell had been loosed from the dagger. Cutting into the arm should have—

It didn't cut. Panic escalated. *The dagger couldn't cut. It couldn't cut her arm, so it couldn't break the spell!*

Whether by luck or calculated guess, the Cinder Witch had nullified the last advantage in Owen's pocket. She seemed more a mountain to Owen than a person now. Insurmountable. A stone-plated assailant who grew as Owen shrank. An obstacle that would require days to scale rather than the moments Owen felt he had.

Owen readied himself for another barrage of blows. With sword and dagger raised, he watched the Cinder Witch prowl just out of reach. Her demeanor could not have been more foreign to Owen's. Where Owen was lowered into a defensive stance, the Cinder Witch stood tall with arms lowered to her sides. Every small noise, from the crackle of fire to the Cinder Witch's shuffled steps, caused Owen to twitch or recoil. The Cinder Witch herself flowed through one step to the next. Her focus was locked on the Spellseeker before her.

It was much to Owen's surprise, then, when the Cinder Witch flinched. Owen had made no sign of aggression. He did not have the strength to waste on feigned strikes that would just return to his defensive stance.

A violent roar that rose above the din of the inferno made clear what the Cinder Witch had perceived. She half-turned, facing both Owen and the newly- returned threat. Owen looked past the Cinder Witch to see Manda dashing across the main cavern chamber. Blood coated the side of Manda's face where she had been kicked, and her eye on the same side was swollen closed. The vicious, clawed hammer was in her right hand and poised to deliver a devastating blow.

The hammer fell just as the Cinder Witch raised an arm. Claws on the hammer's face had gripped the Cinder Witch's stony arm to impart as much force as possible. The ring of metal striking stone pierced through all other sounds to hang in Owen's ears. A shrill, painful sound that caused him to wince.

Unlike with Manda's first attack, the Cinder Witch was unable to mount a counterattack in response to the hammer blow. Her left knee buckled from the sheer force of impact. A grunt of pain mixed with the subtle crack of stone. Brute force had won over clever tricks.

Owen pressed the opening Manda had forged. He kept his sword raised to shield his advance. With his dagger, channeled full of energy, he cut at the Cinder Witch's thigh. A shallow, clean cut resisted by thin cloth. The Cinder Witch had not thought to encase her legs in the same black stone as her arms. Owen felt the energy leave his dagger and flow into the Cinder Witch's exposed flesh.

A short gasp, sounding more of surprise than pain, escaped the Cinder Witch. She whipped her right arm at Owen. Her forearm met the blade of his sword, while her clawed hand dug into Owen's cheek. The strike would have been devastating if not for the dagger. By the time the Cinder Witch had struck Owen, her spell had already shattered. Bony fingertips replaced obsidian knives. The attack amounted to little more than fingernails raking across Owen's face. Owen dragged his blade down the Cinder Witch's now bare arm in response.

The Cinder Witch recoiled from Owen's draw-cut, attention now evenly split between two assailants. Her demeanor changed as if a switch had been flipped. Cold eyes flitted back and forth between enemies on either side. She took steps backward towards a wall to reduce possible angles of attack. Rather than down by her sides, one arm was raised against Manda and the other against Owen.

No sign of surrender. Though she was outnumbered and backed into a corner, the Cinder Witch did not concede defeat.

Manda had bought time with her sudden intrusion and devastating blow. Time for Owen to formulate a plea. Some kind of offer to stop the violence before someone was fatally injured. What could Owen say that might quell the rage of this cornered criminal? He put himself into the Cinder Witch's boots as best he could.

She had walked through fire to see her base of operations in ruins. Unless there were others beyond the final archway Owen had not explored, there was no sign of survivors. Her entire retinue could be dead and gone for all she knew. Strangers and government officials were picking through her supplies. Strangers that were armed to the teeth presumably destroyed the place she calls home.

It was no wonder to Owen why she would have attacked. Criminal or not, Manda and her people were violent aggressors. Owen imaged he looked no different to the Cinder Witch than Manda or her people.

"Your people are still al—"

Owen's attempt to calm the Cinder Witch was cut short. The moment the Cinder Witch flicked her eyes to Owen in response to his words, Manda reared back to strike. Time for goodwill and negotiation would not be allowed. Not while Manda continued to draw frenzied breath.

Thunder rolled through the cave. A deafening ring that heralded a missed strike. The Cinder Witch had ducked Manda's swing, causing the hammer to clang against the stone. Claws wedged themselves into the cracked wall. Manda tugged at the hammer but it would not come loose. The weapon was embedded into the cave wall. Nature had claimed its prize and would not release the destructive tool.

"Stop!" Owen cried.

Both women were deaf to the plea. Manda abandoned her hammer to the wall, but not before the Cinder Witch had launched a retaliatory strike. The Cinder Witch kept her center of gravity low. She forced a leg between Manda's and planted a hand on Manda's face. When the Cinder Witch kicked her leg backward, her hand drove Manda's head into the ground. The momentum of the kick followed into a second. This one came up to kick Owen's sword from his hand. Another weapon was stripped away.

"Run her through!" Manda commanded.

The second blow to her head had not put Manda down. She was tenacious if nothing else. Manda wrapped her arms around the Cinder Witch. Her arms glowed as she locked their mutual adversary in place. The Cinder Witch kicked and howled, but was unable to move her arms. Overwhelming, Flow-infused strength kept the Cinder Witch at bay.

"Stab her," Manda repeated. "Finish this!"

Matter-of-fact words were spoken by one used to killing. Accustomed to murder. Owen did not hear the desperation in Manda's voice. What he heard was impatience. Desire to be done with an inconvenience and move on to the next task.

Owen looked at the dagger in his hand. Streaks of blood dribbled down one edge. Fresh evidence of the wound he left on the Cinder Witch. On Amalia Tennerim. A human who continued her fierce struggle to the last breath. Bound as she was, the Cinder Witch did not reserve an ounce of her strength. She was a wounded wolf. The last of her pack and aware of the fact. Caught in the iron jaws of a jagged trap.

Still, she fought.

Still, she struggled.

Light glowed anew from Manda. Her grip around the Cinder Witch tightened like a vise. Bones crunched in response to the added pressure. Manda, seeing no action from Owen, was attempting to crush the Cinder Witch with her arms alone.

Pain, pure and intense, poured out from the Cinder Witch. There was no surprise this time. She understood her position. Likely knew she was powerless to change the situation. That did not stop her. She continued to kick and howl and flex her restrained arms. Wild efforts to find something, anything to turn the tide.

"Enough."

As the single chilling word reached Owen's ears, distracting him from his indecision, all the fire that remained in the cave flickered in the same direction. Pulled by some unseen force, the blaze flowed to a single point at the back of the cave and coalesced into a sphere. The fiery orb was about as large as a football. It hung motionless in the archway through which the Cinder Witch had initially come.

Now the sole source of light in the cave, the sphere of fire revealed something awesome. Someone. Both awesome and terrifying.

In the archway stood a slender figure. Over her shoulders was draped a single, black robe of no special description. It clung loosely over skin that was green and yellow. Scales gleamed up to the figure's neck before melding into fair skin. Vestiges of lips signaled where her mouth began, but the corners of her mouth reached near to her ears. Luxuriant auburn hair tumbled down over her shoulders until strands wound together into crimson vipers. The snakes followed the green gaze of their master, swaying gently of their own accord.

A gorgon.

The ball of fire hovered just above the gorgon's open palm. She took a few silent steps towards the trio of humans. When she spoke, her wide, unsettling mouth revealed a large pair of fangs folded into the roof of her mouth.

"I'll have no more violence in my home."

Measured and calm, the gorgon spoke as if her home had not just been soaked in flames. She continued to walk toward Owen and the still-grappled pair that was Manda and the Cinder Witch as if speaking to rowdy house guests. The unexpected tone was enough to force Owen to cock his head.

One final crack, accompanied by an anguished cry, sounded the end of the Cinder Witch's struggle. Her arms had finally snapped under pressure and could offer no resistance. Manda tossed the woman aside like a wet dishrag and staggered to her feet.

"Keep out of my way," Manda demanded as she fought to catch her breath.

No master of subtlety, Manda had pulled her hand back for punch before she finished speaking. A fresh glow of channeled energy shone through her right arm as she launched her fist at the newly revealed gorgon. Manda seemed to have adopted a strategy of subduing her foes first and asking any questions after the fact. The sheer abandon with which she attacked the gorgon almost impressive.

The gorgon did not share Owen's sentiment.

Green eyes flashed as the punch neared the gorgon's face. Manda's hand might have screeched with how suddenly it was brought to a halt by thin air. The gorgon placed her hand lightly onto Manda's.

Owen never forgot the horrified scream that followed.

A sound like sandpaper scraping over rough wood was the first indicator of what had transpired. At first glance, Owen could not guess the source of Manda's anguish. It was not until the gorgon ran her hand over exposed flesh that the situation was made clear.

Skin peeled away from Manda's hand. Like ashes caught on a breeze, those bits of flesh floated away and dissolved into nothing. The spot where the skin had been was now gray and porous. Another gentle swipe of the gorgon's hand revealed yet more patches of grey. That same hand tenderly folded Manda's shirt sleeve up to the elbow. Skin continued to wash away from the arm all the while.

The discoloration stopped at Manda's elbow. A clean line formed where natural flesh met what the gorgon had turned to stone.

Manda made feverish attempts to remove herself from the nightmarish situation. Too afraid to strike at the gorgon, she grabbed her stony arm and tried to pull it away. She poured energy into her free arm and wrenched with all her Flow-infused might. The portion of her right arm that remained flesh pulled and pulled. Her arms rivaled the sun in brilliance as Manda fought to wrest herself from the delicate clutches of the gorgon.

Though the gorgon had no visible hold of Manda or her stone-encrusted arm, Manda could not pull the arm away.

At the height of the struggle came a wet popping noise. Relative stillness gripped the room for a moment before Manda collapsed to the floor. Half of Manda's arm, still cased in stone, hung freely in the air. Droplets of blood pooled at its center as the last bit of flesh that remained turned to stone. Manda toppled backward and laid motionless on the floor. The end of her fresh stump had been sealed in stone that clung to red, agitated flesh.

The gorgon looked at the free-floating arm and gave a dismissive wave. As had Manda's skin, the stone fell apart into ashes and dust.

"I assume we have no quarrel, Seeker?" The gorgon gestured to Owen's badge as she spoke. Her tone was that of a person answering the door to find a stranger calling in the dead of night. Apprehension with a subtle undercurrent of curiosity.

"None," Owen sighed. The dagger slipped loudly into its sheath on his back.

"Excellent." The gorgon smiled. She extended her hand in search of Owen's. "I am Melowyn. Welcome to my home."

20.

HOUSE OF STONE

"Manus, hear my prayer. I offer you these worldly goods that you might hear me. I offer you this lifeblood that you may empower me. Wield through me your power to knit flesh. Wield through me your power to mend bone. I am your servant and vessel. Manus, hear my prayer."

Divine healing surged through Owen. Both his hands were placed neatly in Jwala's, who recited the prayer to Manus with a practiced inflection. There was no doubt that this was a prayer she had spoken many times. The speech did not bother her, nor did the beheading of a small rat she found scurrying about the cave. Lifeblood left alone for this purpose.

Once the incantation was completed and the healing began, Jwala could not contain the wide smile. Thin lips parted to reveal immaculate, white teeth. The feature was quite disarming.

"You sure this is all right?" Owen asked, uncomfortable with the silence.

"We're both adults, Mr. Seeker," Jwala chuckled. "Or are you unaccustomed to holding another's hands?"

"That's— that's not what I meant."

"Oh, come now, don't deprive me of my fun. But no, everything is all right," she added. A serious touch marred the last.

"Are you sure?" Owen asked. He looked around the main chamber of Melowyn's cave. Others, in much more dire straits, lay on fresh litters of grass and leaves. A single mattress was made available to the most devastatingly injured among them. "Plenty of folks here need your attention more than I do. And I'm at least partially respons—"

"It doesn't matter why you came here," Jwala interrupted. Owen felt her give his hands a tender squeeze. "What matters is that you saved lives. Mine, and several others besides.

"And burns are no minor thing," Jwala added after a heavy pause. "Especially not the sort that makes blisters. Like the ones on your right arm here. Leads to infection. Nasty business, that. I've stabilized the worst of the others, so no worries there. We don't have the materials to ensure everyone is in tip-top shape, but I can guarantee no further loss of life or limb. A trade anyone should be happy to make."

Never before had Owen felt so withering a guilt. The sort of feeling that made his body want to melt into the floor, through some hidden crack in the cave to never be graced by the sun again. He knew that he was responsible in part for the events that had transpired. The destruction that was brought down on the heads of these decent people. Pleasant consolation, however tender it might be, could not wipe that thought from his mind.

"Well, thank you, then," Owen murmured with a nod.

"I should be thanking you," Jwala replied. "You are most welcome."

It was no trite offer of thanks. Between moving the Radiant Circle back into the cave and restraining Manda's crew, Owen had not paid much heed to his injuries. Finding and corralling Scarlet was a whole other adventure. Now that he had time to sit and rest the pain was excruciating. A sharp throb in his right wrist radiated through the rest of his arm. Just as he felt he had the pain under control, a new wave of agony would ignite his suffering anew.

Aid from Jwala was like a cooling balm being smoothed over his entire arm. Knicks and cuts sealed well enough to not be a source of discomfort. Blisters receded as red skin shifted back to its natural hue. A welcome but slow process.

What time is it?

Relative quiet, and the regression of pain, allowed for idle thoughts to bubble. The wave of tiredness that washed over Owen drove the inquiry. He had not had the presence of mind to check the time when he woke to find the camp deserted. *Must have been sometime around midnight*, he guessed. Time enough for Manda and her people to be sure that Owen and Devlin were fast asleep.

Another survey of the cave disproved his initial theory. Shafts of golden light trickled through the entry passage to warm the stone floor. It would have to be mid-morning for the sun to have climbed over the ridge that surrounded the cave. Knowing the time somehow made Owen more tired. He fought the reflex to rub the sleep out of his heavy eyelids. The yawn, however, he was unable to stifle. One of those yawns that nearly unhinge the jaw and beckons to every fly in a two-mile radius. Owen gave his head a quick shake to rid himself of the vulgar display.

"Keeping you awake?"

"Not at all," replied Owen in the middle of another yawn. "Completely awake. One-hundred percent."

"Of course, you are." Jwala snickered.

An open recipient to sarcasm was a nice change of pace for Owen. It felt like he hadn't had a carefree conversation since leaving Arnstead. Perhaps even longer, if he was honest with himself.

"Suppose I should play host, then," Jwala continued. The third yawn seemed to be her tipping point. "Can't have you falling over and cracking your head open. Enough work to go around as is."

"I am sorry, truly," Owen attempted to reply through the end of that third yawn. "Didn't have much sleep last night."

"I'm sure, Mr. Seeker," Jwala said, adding a bright laugh for emphasis. "Can't say I slept much either."

"Ah— yes, you're right. That was stupid of me," Owen mumbled as his head sank between his knees. He had meant that his sleep schedule had been disrupted by odd hours on lookout and long days of travel. The words had failed to link together how he wished as they dribbled out of his mouth.

"How about the basics, then? I don't think I've caught your name yet. Would be an awful shame to call you nothing but 'Mr. Seeker', don't you think?"

"I suppose that's fair," Owen conceded, lifting his head from his knees. "My name's Owen."

"Any family, or is it just Owen?"

"Ah, Owen Raulstone. Owen Jay Orland Raulstone, if you feel like being fancy."

Though the light was poor, Owen did not fail to see the hint of shadow overtake Jwala's face. He had overshared. Exhaustion had clouded his mind, perhaps. A lapse in better judgment. Owen knew what his full name meant to people. Given the trouble the Radiant Circle had caused for Cynthia and her business in Arnstead, Owen cursed his stupidity twice over. He felt the goodwill he had earned the night before slip away like leaves on a breeze.

"No need to be too formal, I don't think," Jwala replied. A seriousness had slipped into her once bright tone. Seriousness, but no accusation or malice. "Just Owen, then? Right?"

"If you wouldn't mind," Owen said with a pleading smile.

Perhaps not *all* of the goodwill had been lost.

The remainder of the interaction was conducted in silence. Cautious inquiries as to how Owen was feeling, and his timid replies might as well have been nonexistent. They lacked true substance and served only to punch the occasional hole in an uncomfortable void.

Once Jwala had completed the task, she advised that Amalia was through the archway at the back of the room. The passageway directly opposite the cave entrance.

It was a mental struggle to identify the Cinder Witch as anything but her title. Owen was tired enough without having to concentrate on relabeling a wanted criminal in his head. Her alias had been burnt into his skin. Healed as they were, Owen could still see a discoloration where the Cinder Witch's— where Amalia's, he reminded himself— spells had blistered his flesh. The last stages of healing would be natural. Those reminders of the Cinder Witch would be around for several days to come.

His curious nature pushed some discomfort out of his mind. Why the Cinder Witch —*Amalia*— wanted to speak with him was an easy guess. Owen was part of the company that had kicked down the proverbial door of Melowyn's home. Reclamation of the Orland safety deposit box, and the arrest of those involved in its theft, were the obvious intents of Owen and company. None had concealed why they came.

Knowing all this made Owen wonder what Amalia might want from him. The rational part of Owen knew that he was one of the more amenable among the company, and so might be easier to extract information from with a gentle touch. Another part of Owen thought the Cinder Witch may just want an outlet on which to vent her frustrations.

All capable hands that could be spared were set to work. As Owen strode through the main room of the cavern home, he saw faces both familiar and new. People he recognized from the crawlspace. Others that must have been tucked elsewhere in the cave. They tended to the wounded, fashioned new beds from unspoiled remnants of the storage room, prepared morning meals. Some had bandages wrapped around burns and cuts. Small injuries left to heal naturally due to a shortage of supplies.

Members of the Radiant Circle nodded politely as Owen passed. A handful spared the time to wave and wish him a good morning. He returned the gestures with a guilty conscience. As responsible as he knew he was, there was no sense in being rude. Even if wishing the Radiant Circle well felt somewhat hollow.

Sequestered near the entrance to the crawlspace were those deemed dangerous by the Radiant Circle. Scarlet, who gave a fierce struggle throughout the night, had been bound back-to-back with Jabari. The more sedate katarl served as an anchor to keep Scarlet rooted in place with minimal effort. Mahika remained lost in her twisted world. Bound at both her wrists and ankles, she idly knocked her booted feet together while humming an unfamiliar tune. She seemed quite content despite the circumstances.

Manda was the only one among her crew that acknowledged Owen as he passed. A disgusted snarl twisted her features. Unlike the rope bindings fastened about her crew, the Radiant Circle had bound Manda in heavy chains. The one good arm left to Manda was cinched to her torso. Chains wrapped from her ankles to the middle of her thighs. Loose around the stub of her right arm was a white bandage littered with small splotches of red and brown. Around her ankles were fastened the one pair of manacles that Owen had brought on the journey. They served as a safety measure to ensure Manda could not channel enough strength to break her bonds.

Owen turned his eyes away from the seething glower that Manda wore. He bore enough guilt without having to look at his sorry travel companions.

The heated conversation was overheard before Owen had stepped through the archway. A one-sided conversation, as far as he could tell. The only voice he heard as he approached was that of the Cinder Witch.

"—to deal with him alone. Me. *Me.* A young Keeper, unproven in every aspect. The priests had none of it. They wouldn't have given me the time of day if I had told them the drapes in the dorms were hung upside-down, much less if I came to them with accusations against the Pontiff! I needed someone who would listen to me. Someone I could trust to speak on my behalf. But what did you do when you finally hauled your sorry ass to Arnstead? Nothing!"

Those in the main chamber had stopped their tasks. The whole room was still for a moment after Amalia had finished.

Owen stopped short of the entryway and rested a shoulder against the cool cave wall. He was still out of sight from those in the next room. *If there was a right time to enter*, he thought, *this certainly is not it.*

"It's all right, Mr. Seeker. You're free to join us."

The smooth voice of Melowyn carried the words to Owen, almost like a whisper in his ear. Owen felt his throat constrict. Shoulders tensed as a boy caught eavesdropping on his parents. He took a deep breath and fanned his fingers, then rounded the edge of the archway into the backroom of the cave.

A reluctant turn around the low archway revealed that this space had not been spared by the inferno. Black scorch marks marred what might have once been a beautifully polished dining table. The long table could have comfortably seated ten or more before one of the corners had been eaten away. There were not enough chairs to seat the handful of people that were now gathered around. Melowyn stood with her back to an unnaturally smoothed wall. Devlin sat in a blackened chair, and across from him were seated Amalia Tennerim and Joseph Beech.

The whole room seemed unnaturally smooth compared to the chamber that preceded it. Both in that the walls were smooth to the touch and they were flat. A practiced mason could not have made a more perfect surface. There were no markings to suggest that a mason had present at all. Nails, from which hung remnants of singed and wrinkled parchment, were the only imperfections on the otherwise clean surface.

"Go on, have a seat," Melowyn said, her voice sounding more distant and concrete. She twirled a finger indicating a spot to the right of Devlin, then turned her hand over and raised finger as if commanding someone to rise. A faint, yellowish glow surrounded her green fingers. Up from the flat floor rose an armchair of stone. The process was unsettlingly quiet. It sounded more like sheets of paper being stacked and aligned than stone grinding against stone. Melowyn gestured towards the chair with the smallest smile her enormous mouth could manage.

Owen nodded his assent and eased himself into the Flow-constructed chair. Much to his surprise, the stone reacted to his body to produce a more form-fitted seat.

"Glad to see you're still kicking, Owen." Beech was the first to break the silence brought on by Owen's intrusion. The katarl was more himself now than when he had been traveling with Manda's retinue. He held his shoulders higher and made eye contact as he spoke. Beech was no longer a quivering mass of fur doing his best to go unnoticed, though that behavior made a great deal more sense now. "I'm sorry you got mixed up in this mess

374

again. Wasn't our intention. You never should have been involved, to begin with."

"Kind of you to say," Owen replied with a forced smile. "So, when you say 'our', you mean—"

"Yup," Beech nodded emphatically. "I'm with the Circle. Have been since you met me. I'm typically our eyes and ears in Arnstead. Gathering news of Orland transports and the like. Help us find our targ—"

"That's plenty, Joseph. Mind yourself."

Though she spoke to Beech, Amalia stared at Owen as she spoke. She placed a firm hand on the katarl's arm to emphasize the command.

"Right, sorry," Beech replied with a more downcast tone. "Anyways, glad you pulled through the night, Owen."

"I want to know two things from you, Seeker," Amalia continued. Flat, expressionless intonation masked the contempt Owen knew must be there. "Where are the rest of you, and what does the Bureau want from us?"

"The rest of us?" Owen raised a brow in honest inquiry. His mind went first to Walks Far. The kin was the only member of the company who Owen had not been able to locate. His whereabouts were as much a mystery to Owen as they must have been to Amalia or Beech. What could the Radiant Circle want with a lone kin? "I'm... not sure I follow?"

"No lies, Seeker." The thin veil of dispassion pulled back to reveal a venomous fang. Amalia sneered as she continued. "I can guess why the rest are here, but you're out of place. Worse, your kind hunt in packs. I don't know why you came in here without the rest of your wolves, but I know they're out there. Tell me where they are and what the lot of you want with me and my people. I won't ask again."

Owen watched Amalia while she spoke. Her shoulders tensed as she went on, an action that caused her arms to wince. Both arms had tight bandage-work wrapped around the upper arm. Bandages that needed changing. Splotches of brown formed messy rings that circumvented Amalia's arms. There must have been some kind of ruptures that accompanied shattered bones. Manda had left devastating marks on her opponent; injuries that would leave ugly marks if they were ever to heal.

The Cinder Witch had shunned all but the barest of healing. Snippets about there not being enough supplies to go round had been caught amidst the din of people at work. Jwala had fought to seal the wounds, at least. The bones remained unset at present.

Intimidating as she was, Owen could not help but respect the composure required to function through that amount of pain.

"Speak."

Percussive, Amalia's command snapped Owen from his thoughts.

Simple and honest.

"I am Owen Raulstone, Third Seeker with the Arnstead Ar—"

"You mentioned," Amalia interrupted. "Get to the point."

"I wa—" This time Owen cut himself off. Protest welled in his chest. Unproductive speech would worsen an already fractured relationship. He took a calming breath through his nose before he continued. "I represent Lost and Stolen. I'm here for the Orland lockbox you stole at the written request of Cynthia Orland. I'm he—"

"I said don't lie to me."

"Let the man speak, Amalia," Devlin interjected, his words soft and reassuring.

"I've heard enough from you, coward. Your time to speak passed the day you left," Amalia replied. It was Devlin who finally pried Amalia's eyes away from Owen. The moment was brief. Her words to the Keeper were slow and seemed to cut down to the bone. Devlin slumped in his chair as if he had received news of a death in the family. Amalia slid her attention back to Owen upon seeing Devlin's retreat. "I've been hammering that witch since the day that false Pontiff signed his soul to her. She didn't break down after all these years because of one box."

"I have a signed request in my coat. It came with the rest of our supplies from our camp to the north. More than happy to show you."

Amalia snorted at the notion but did not press for proof.

"As I was saying," Owen continued, unable to stifle a triumphant huff, "I'm here for the box. Lost and Stolen is a small department so I was forced to come alone." This caused another snort of disbelief from Amalia. Owen allowed a moment to pass in allowance for any protest, then proceeded when none arose. "Cynthia Orland advised me that she had people en route for the same purpose and requested that I join the company in an official capacity. Your capture would make a nice feather in my cap, but my primary concern is the safety deposit box."

"It's just him, Am," Beech offered. The conversation drew out some of the katarl's more passive nature. He drummed his clawed fingers on the defaced table to a nervous beat. "If there were more bluecoats, I never saw them."

Cautious words were spoken by a cautious man. Tension remained palpable in the room, but Beech had managed to lessen the strain. It was clear that Amalia placed at least some trust in the katarl. That he was a spy for the Radiant Circle proved as much. His confirmation seemed enough for the Cinder Witch to entertain a belief in Owen's words.

Wood screeched over stone. The sudden, jarring noise that accompanied Amalia's swift backward motion caused the Seeker to start. He realized the concern to be unwarranted. Amalia had simply given herself enough room from the table to place her right ankle atop her left knee. The sudden nature of the action must have resulted from her inability to use her arms. It felt almost pathetic to Owen when he realized the reason.

Looking around the room, Owen noted he was not the only person to feel relieved. Beech had let out a deep breath from between pursed lips. Devlin, as well, seemed to perk up as Amalia showed signs of calm. The gorgon, Melowyn, was too far out of sight to survey casually. Owen assumed that her steadfast warmth and welcoming demeanor had not flagged in the slightest.

Owen was the last to relax. He had not realized how tightly his fists had curled, hidden by crossed arms until he allowed them to unclench. It was as if the entire room had taken a long, tranquil breath all at once.

"I still don't know what we're going to do with you."

The breathy statement left Amalia as she tilted her back to gaze at the rough ceiling. Bumps and crags on the surface added texture to what otherwise would have been a room of alien uniformity. A pair of brass lanterns dangled from high points in the ceiling, casting conical shafts of light down at the table. The gentle movement of air through the cavern caused the lanterns to sway. Shadows bowed back and forth across the faces of everyone gathered in the room.

"*You* won't be doing anything with him," Melowyn noted after a brief pause. She stepped forward to place a hand on Owen's shoulder, an action that sent a chill down his spine. "Just as he won't be apprehending anyone. You're all guests in my home. While you remain, I expect your courtesy to each other to mirror your courtesy to me. Is that not fair?"

Melowyn looked down to Owen, who nodded acceptance without delay. She moved her gaze up to Amalia. The expectation of affirmation was evident. The host would not accept refusal.

377

"What about them?"

Amalia deflected the question rather than provide her acceptance. With a tilt of her head, she indicated the rough location of Manda and her people. Melowyn's eyes flashed in the light as she craned her neck to watch the Orland crew.

"They are my guests, of course," Melowyn murmured. "Though I shall have to have another chat with them. They can remain bound until they have accepted my hospitality, as you all have."

"Fine," Amalia relented. The single word came after a pensive click of her tongue against the back of her teeth.

"Imagine they'll be tied up for a while then, huh?" Beech cracked, raising his eyebrows to Owen.

"That's their choice," Melowyn admonished. "Well, now we that have our terms settled, I imagine the Keepers have plenty left to discuss. Let's give them some space, shall we?"

Owen felt a light squeeze on his shoulder. He looked up and was met with the gorgon's massive grin. Welcoming as she might be, her presence remained a somewhat unnerving one. Owen did his best to hide his discomfort with a casual nod of agreement.

"Yes, ma'am," Owen added.

"Right, come along then. Just this way."

Silent footsteps carried Melowyn across the room to a small, round doorway sealed by a thick door of oak. The gorgon seemed more to glide than walk as she moved. Black cloth billowed behind and snapped as she came to an abrupt stop at the door. One hand grabbed an iron ring at the door's center and pulled the slab of wood inward, while the other beckoned for Owen to join.

"Go on, lad," Devlin whispered. The Keeper must have sensed Owen's hesitation to leave the table. "Lady Melowyn is right. Amalia and I have plenty left to discuss. Not the sort of business you want to get involved in. Or... more involved in, I guess. House business and all that."

A light pat on the shoulder was Devlin's final input on the subject.

Amalia glared as Owen stood.

Beech waved as Owen left.

Stepping through the circular doorway revealed an area untouched by the ravages of flame and smoke. Unlike the previous room, furniture had been cut or molded to match the natural growth of the cave. Wooden bedposts ended as if their tops had been swallowed by the low ceiling. A nightstand and vanity curved in line with each minute jut and crevice of the walls they were set against.

Bookshelves carved into the walls and the flat stone floor were the only signs that space had been substantially tampered with. A casual snap of her fingers from Melowyn ignited a series of memory glass spheres faceted into the ceiling. The light revealed that room made up for its shallow height with considerable depth. Owen had seen substantial houses with smaller floorplans than this single room. What at first appeared to be walls across the room were rectangular pillars.

The simple bed and associated furniture near it felt out of place once the room had been lit. This wide, low space looked more like a personal library than a bedroom.

Along the shelved walls, which Owen was sure were walls thanks to the light, were gaps. Thick parchment spanned these places and was nailed to the wall at each corner. Markings and names became clear as Owen approached the parchment nearest the door. Small clusters of trees illustrated over vast swaths of green. Perilous mountain peaks accented by tiny, unfamiliar birds. Names that Owen recognized, written in sure and luxurious script, hovered above small depictions of cities and towns. New Haven and Southport stood out from the lot.

"A map of the eastern coast?" Owen asked, unable to hide his puzzlement. He looked over to Melowyn as she closed the oak door. "This *is* the eastern coast of the New World, yes?"

"It is," Melowyn replied. "Do you like it?"

"Do I... Do I *like* it?" Owen looked back to the map. Straining his eyes, he drew close to the map. Rapt attention scoured every pen scratch and pencil shade. "I've never seen a map this detailed before. I'm no expert, to be sure, but these are... can maps be captivating? Is that an odd thing to say?"

A mellow chuckle permeated the room.

"No, I suppose not, though I should hope they are detailed."

"Why? Were they expensive? I could see that."

"Because I've had a few hundred years to make them."

"You... made all of these?" Owen made a sweeping gesture to encompass every map pinned to the stone walls.

"Was that an odd thing to say?"

Owen raked self-conscious fingers along the back of his scruffy head. Each word that Melowyn spoke was uttered with the same evenness. Coy indifference hung about her like a thin but ever-present mask; enough substance to hide intent, but not so much to obscure her subtle warmth. Whether she spoke in offense or jest was impossible to tell.

"Fair turnabout," Owen muttered through a nervous laugh. "I guess I just never imagined someone so important doing something so mundane."

Laughter sliced through the air. True laughter this time, not a cheap imitation meant to sell ease and comfort. Melowyn threw her head back, mouth open wide, as she devolved into an amused cackle. One hand gripped her shaking stomach while the other wiped the beginnings of tears from her narrow eyes.

The gorgon made her way to Owen's side as the laughter subsided. A small titter escaped between every few footsteps, but Melowyn had regained her composure by the time she reached the map.

Silence echoed through the chamber as the pair gazed at the map in silence.

"I suppose I was important, once. A long time ago." There was a hollowness to Melowyn's words. Not a lack of sincerity or meaning. Perhaps it was that she had dropped the warmth from her words, Owen noticed. More honest than hollow. Her split cheeks sagged into a slight frown. "A Keeper for the wrong god at the wrong time."

"I'm sorry if I've upset you."

"No, you've said nothing wrong," Melowyn replied, shaking her head. "You're quite restrained compared to most. The questions that some people ask… absolutely baffling, the nerve."

"And what is it I might have asked, were I less restrained?"

Melowyn lulled a leery eye at Owen.

"Simple things," she sighed. "Did you see the Upheaval with your own eyes? Were you there to witness millions perish at the hands of cataclysmic, continental destruction? Did the gods truly vanish? Are they dead? Can you still hear the gods while we cannot? Does Damarae whisper to you in your nightmares."

"Do people really ask that?" Owen probed after a beat had passed.

"Sometimes it feels like it."

Owen gave a somber nod.

The pair moved to a new map at Owen's request. Names of places he recognized on this new map were dwarfed by those he did not. A landmass that was unfamiliar, both at a glance and upon a thorough examination. Zumbatra was among them. Far to the east on the map was Bangel. Lands lost to the Federation. Lost to the world.

"Why blue?"

"Pardon?" Owen asked, turning his to Melowyn.

"I was still a prominent figure when the Federation landed on the shores of the new world. Helped found new cities and lead exploration to the west. Back when the armies still wore red. Raulstone Red, they called it. Thought for a moment my eyes had gone bad when you said your name."

"Ah, why a Spellseeker, you mean."

"Why blue?" Melowyn repeated softly.

It was not the first time Owen had received the question. The legacy of the Raulstone name stood, without question, in the shadow of the Federation armies. His father was a ranking officer in the modern Third Federation Army. Achievements burst from the man's resume like the ink could not stand the page; led two campaigns into the reptile-infested swamplands of the southern peninsula; quelled a workers' strike in New Haven that had stifled manarail construction for months; repelled dozens of raids conducted by the grey savages from beyond Misty Lake. All of that came after a stellar career as an enlisted man, during which he was awarded four silver stars for bravery and a Thomas Havernash Medal of Peace.

The only failure of his father's that came to mind was that he had not reared a child willing to carry the Raulstone legacy on through a new generation.

Most asked the question of Owen in a sidelong manner. They might question how long he intended to stay with the Bureau of Arcane and their Spellseekers. The more verbose in his circles would ask what about the Bureau of Arcane garnered his interest. Cunning and on the prowl for whatever advantage could be had, those who went by the Orland name merely wished Owen well and offered favors should they ever be needed.

Why blue?

A question so direct it hurt. Melowyn knew the history of the Raulstone family. If not in whole, then certainly in large part. The question might as well have been, "Why not red?" It was the sort of question that made Owen fidget. Questions about him and his father.

"When I think of a soldier," Owen began hesitantly, "I think of someone decisive. A sword that cuts through the wilderness to find a way for the Federation. Brave people, who face the unknown without trepidation. That can stand tall before the most terrifying creatures. Solemn men and women that can take a life when they have to. To spare a weaker person the strain on their soul. I think of people like my father. Like his father. I don't think of people like me."

"An aggressive definition of a soldier. Broad, but not without some truth. Still doesn't tell me why you chose blue. What truths do you know of Spellseekers that do not also hold for soldiers?"

"I suppose I see a Spellseeker more as a shield than as a sword. Seekers protect people from those who would abuse the Flow. We regulate the violence and corruption that spreads when power grows unchecked. It's a different kind of bravery. We don't stand against the enemies of the Federation. It's more like we stand against the rot that hides within."

"Is that so?" Melowyn asked, arching a hairless eyebrow. "And you came all the way out to the frontier for that?"

"Didn't really *choose* to be assigned to Arnstead, if I'm being honest. And if I'm being *really* honest," Owen sighed, "I don't even know if blue was the right choice. The people out here, the Seekers I mean, they're violent. All I've seen from them is aggression, shutting people down with threats and hate. A bit of cowardice is sprinkled in there, but not in any place that shows on the outside. Those that don't fit the mold either die or get swept under the rug."

"Sounds rotten, don't you think?"

"It does," Owen mumbled with a sullen nod. "Worst of all? I wanted in. When I got here, to Arnstead I mean, I wanted nothing more than to be a part of the club. I saw myself on the Violent Offenses team. Dreams of taking down criminals and cleaning the streets. Making the place as safe as I could and earning recognition while I did so."

"And now?"

The pull of Melowyn's words was irresistible. She was engaged in the conversation without chiding Owen for his flaws. Thoughts and desires seemed to roll through the gorgon and then back to Owen with added clarity. It was difficult. Enlightening.

Owen did not want to stop.

"I just want to help people. If that requires violence, if a conflict is unavoidable... I understand. What I can't understand are people that just

382

seem itching to kill other people." Owen waved a limp hand to the wall in the direction where Manda and her people would have been. "They don't care who it is. If someone gets in their way? Dead! Like there were no other options. It baffles me."

"I know that feeling," Melowyn whispered. She ushered Owen to the next map down the line, speaking as they walked. "The Upheaval was a violent, bloody mess, but there was purpose. We were being wiped off the map. All signs of our existence were turned to ash and dust. Settling the east coast, though. That was different. We made our homes despite the SeaKin. When we pushed west, we did so against the FieldKin. By the time we had reached what became the Arnstead you know, I had grown numb to the violence."

"And so, you left?"

"I ran," Melowyn corrected. "I didn't try to fix the problem. I just abandoned the Federation. Left the people to their will, to blaze their trail in search of the horizon. Many have died by my hand or as the result of my actions. Many more, I assume, will die from my inaction."

"Why not go back, then?" Owen softened his voice. He did not know what value he could provide to this ancient being, but he wanted to try. That much he felt he owed Melowyn. Both for her hospitality and her intervention the previous night. "The fact that you're talking about it, even after considerable time… you obviously care. Don't you?"

"It would be so much easier if I didn't. Care, that is. No, it's simply that I don't belong anymore. I felt my last shred of humanity crumble when loss of life no longer brought me pain. The kin may not be human, but they are closer than a harn or katarl would ever be. Yet we treated them like the demons that robbed us of our homes across the ocean. *I* treated them like demons."

The two remained quiet as they stopped before another map. Wrapped in pensive tumult, processing everything that had been shared by both Melowyn and himself, Owen failed to notice that this new map differed from the others on display.

Grand did not begin to describe the scale of this map. Other maps in the chamber were no wider or taller than an adult human. Their details were lush and filled with painstaking attention to detail. Each map occupied a space of its own as if they were exhibitions of a high-class art gallery.

This new map was, to begin with, not a single map. A moment of scrutiny was enough to determine that the patchwork assemblage of canvases and parchment all radiated from a single point in the middle of the space. Trees and mountains were nowhere to be seen, nor were there any roads or buildings to suggest the map depicted a sprawling city. The passageways on display wound about each other. Some crossed over or under others. Intersections led to winding ways that thinned and widened without obvious patterns.

The most apparent difference, plain at first sight, was the sheer size of the map. Any single map from around the room could be swallowed by the patchwork map without notice. The space the large map occupied must have been more than thirty feet in length. Paper and parchment touched the floor, and other scraps curled up onto the ceiling.

"What is *this?*" Owen could not help but ask.

Somber notions were pushed gently to one side in favor of raw, unfettered curiosity. A hint of relief was the only emotion Owen could perceive when he turned his gaze to his host. The phantom frown vanished without a trace.

"This?" Melowyn said playfully. She lifted a single finger from her crossed arms to point at the hive of passages caught on paper. "Would you rather I told you or *showed* you?"

"Oh, and you may need your things."

The sudden realization flashed over Melowyn's face. Her hands moved as she spoke. Fingers rolled and flicked as she traced an unknown pattern in the air. Part of a spell, it seemed, as her fingers glowed a soft pink. Fresh rose petals could not have flashed a more luxuriant hue. Particles of light dripped from each twirling finger to the stone floor. Drop by drop, the outline of a sword, pistol, and dagger materialized.

Recognizing his weapons, confiscated by Melowyn for an assurance of harmony amongst guests, Owen unshouldered a leather pack. Melowyn had provided the pack, stuffed with rations and other goods to last a few days at most. Pickings were slim. The fire had consumed much of what Melowyn had stored in her larder. Slivers of cured meat and dried pieces of fruit were a minor portion of the foodstuffs. Those prized goods were cradled on all sides by bundles of hardtack.

Owen was more than happy to set the pack down and fasten his tools on either side of his waist. It was a small pack but managed to be remarkably heavy. Waterskins, full to the point of bursting, contributed most of the weight. Each was fixed loosely to the outside of the pack and swung wildly with Owen's natural stride. He was thankful for the recovery of his Seeker coat. It offered considerably more padding for his shoulders than the thin, cracking pack straps.

"Is that everything?" Owen asked, slinging the pack back onto his shoulders. A question that he felt needed to be asked, but one he was afraid to hear the answer to.

"I imagine so," Melowyn replied with renewed warmth. "If it takes this long to remember, it's probably not worth having."

Owen failed to suppress a sigh of relief.

"Fair enough," Owen nodded. "So, we've got supplies for a few days. What exactly is it that we're doing?"

The pair walked while they talked. Provisions were assembled and packed in the larder. Their path took them through the main chamber, past the scorched dining room where Devlin and the Cinder Witch conversed in hushed tones, and back to the room that more like a library than the bed-chamber it was.

"Earning your keep. I have no objection to guests, but those who would stay more than a day or so," Melowyn gestured to Amalia and Beech as they cut through the dining room, "are encouraged to help me with my work."

"And your work is?"

"You saw the maps, yes? Our work lies below."

"I did see the maps, yes," Owen grumbled. The shifting weight on his back limited his patience for the gorgon's roundabout answers. "And what exactly is it that we are meant to be doing *below?*"

"Well, some have lent me their blood, sweat, and prowess. Like Amalia. Others have allowed me to borrow their sharp eyes or keen smell. Some have offered a depth of knowledge that rivals my own. Others still," Melowyn added with a playful glance back at Owen, "have lent me their shoulders."

An honest answer was not in the immediate future. Owen resigned himself to the role of pack mule as they ducked through the round door and into the library.

Books now drew attention. Between the maps and conversation with Melowyn, their nature had gone unnoticed. Hard, leatherbound covers were universal. The exquisite craftsmanship was apparent without having to handle a single volume. Books with paper backs and covers would not do for such a room.

The contents of most books remained a mystery. A large number that Owen passed had no title engraved into their spines. Others merely had dates stamped where a title should have been. Dates that stretched nearly a hundred years back in time.

Despite the room serving as Melowyn's bed-chamber, she did not mind sharing the space. Owen saw a small, round table of carved stone. It was off to the left once past the bed and tucked into a little corner. The memory glass bulb that illuminated the space was particularly bright. At the table was seated a member of the Radiant Circle. Three volumes were stacked atop one another on the table. A fourth was in the intense grip of the Zumbatran harn. The occasional flip of a page resonated throughout the silent room, an impactful offbeat to the matched strides of Owen and Melowyn.

So, it really is *a library,* Owen mused. His eyes flitted from one shelf to the next. The promise of shared literature set his mental maw to watering. *Does that privilege extend to all of her guests, I wonder?*

"I don't know how interesting they'll be to you, but you're welcome to peruse my collection when we've returned. If you have the energy."

Melowyn had caught Owen in his hunger for potential knowledge. A feeling that left him bare, though not at all offended. He gave an embarrassed chuckle at the gorgon's offer, acceptance that hid just how appreciative he was of the gesture.

"Mostly ramblings of a half-mad immortal. The peace and quiet that are typical of self-isolation are fine, but even hermits value an occasional conversation. Even it's just with the other side of a mirror."

"I can't imagine the life and times of a gorgon to be boring," Owen replied, unable to control his piqued interest. "The wealth of knowledge that comes with such... impressive age must be monumental."

"Impressive age," Melowyn cackled. It was bitter, toxic noise that soon subsided. "*Old* suits me just fine."

"The House, especially, would go mad for that kind of documentation." Owen nodded towards the individual seated in the corner of the room. "I don't know how many can say they have met a gorgon before. I couldn't have said that before stumbling into your home. To hear about the gods from someone who was there at the end—"

"Could lead to savage disappointment."

Those words carried a foreboding sense of finality. Owen dropped the subject and remained silent, noting the occasional date or rare title that he would explore upon his return until he and his host came to an abrupt stop at the edge of a massive hole in the floor.

Dread rose from the gaping hole like a noxious fume. Ten feet across and without any guard rails to speak of, the black abyss instilled a sense of falling before even stepping over the edge. The light cast from nearby memory glass bulbs thinned before evaporating in the wide portal. Even the bulb directly above the hole did little more than highlight the unfamiliar, runic symbols that crowned the hole like an ancient halo.

Owen peered at the runes with intense curiosity. He knew there had been languages unique to the regions. A few hundred years ago, a Zumbatran might not have understood the words spoken by a Nirdac. The races within regions had further variations still upon their base dialect. An old system was brought to an end by the same cataclysm that forced the surviving peoples of the Old World to congregate on the isles of Nirwa.

"Careful now," Melowyn whispered. The sound was uncomfortably similar to that of a coiled snake . A warning that trespassers should come no closer if they value life and limb. She placed a firm hand against Owen's chest. "Not too close, now."

"Are those symbols one of the original languages? From before the Upheaval? I've never seen anything like them."

"A good guess, and not entirely wrong," Melowyn replied. "God runes. Similar to the demonic alphabet you might see on a relic. They bound miracles to places just as demons bound the flow to objects. . One of the many secrets that Damarae granted her brood before she sacrificed her body."

"And what does it say?"

"Ashlings beware. None may cross these runes without permission. Death awaits those who trespass against us. Damarae lives through me. I am your bane."

Pale green light flickered around the edge of the hole as Melowyn spoke. A sickly light like some fetid dough poured into an intricate mold. This light was no devoured by the darkness of the hole. It reflected off the glassy ceiling to reveal a new source of terror. The rim of the hole was neither clean nor uniform. Deep gouges had been struck into the surface.

"Claws?"

The words left Owen without consent. A thought so ghastly that Owen could not contain it within his head: Melowyn's bed was a matter of feet from an open passageway to the World Below.

"This won't be your first time below, will it? I can see it in your face."

"No," Owen replied. "No, we have a passageway to the World Below at the Arcanarium in Arnstead. We keep rogue mages and confiscated focuses down there.

"Not a terrible idea," Melowyn noted, rocking head gently from side to side. "Not the sort of place your average person is dumb enough to brave alone. Today's venture is a necessary one, sadly. The Keeper in your company advised that an ashling had reached the surface near here."

"The ashling..." Owen said breathlessly. "Just the thought of it—"

"Makes you sick, doesn't it?" A quick nod from Owen was answer enough for Melowyn before she continued. "Nasty things. Roamed in packs of thousands after the Upheaval. I've been mapping the passages below to learn as I can and sealing exits where I find them. You and I will be looking for any holes that might need some patchwork."

"Oh, lovely..."

"Raise your chin. You've done better than most could hope to. Devlin told me of the one that was prowling above, and that you stood your ground. An impressive feat for a blasphemer." A wry smile crept over the gorgon's wide mouth. "Most folks don't live to see a second ashling."

"And what happens to that small percentage? The ones that stand their ground and have a second encounter."

"If they survive the second?" The thought teetered behind eyes that rolled pensively. "Well, I suppose most of them become Keepers, now that you mention it. That, or they go stark, raving mad. Can you slow your fall, Seeker?"

"Excuse me?"

The disconnect between Keepers and a steadied fall was jarring. Owen blinked at the thought for a moment while processing the question.

Melowyn, wasting no time, took the silence as a 'no'.

"Not everyone can picture themselves falling like a feather, and for an indeterminate amount of time at that. Take my hand. There's no ladder or stairs, so we'll be going straight down."

God runes. Ashlings. Unexplored labyrinths of the World Below. The sort of things Owen never expected to see in person, much less all in the same place. Curious nature lost ground to an anxious thought. Owen remembered just how terrible it had been to look upon the ashling in the dead of night. Without Devlin at hand, Owen knew his life would have ended at that moment.

You're not alone, Owen reminded himself.

Next to him stood the closest thing to a god that any member of the Federation had seen or spoken to in the past three hundred years. She held her hand out to Owen. A warm, open invitation to explore a world of unfathomable horror and wonder. Melowyn held a booted foot over the lip of the hole. Sickly green light from the god runes peeled away from their master's incursion.

"I guess the exits won't be sealing themselves, will they?"

"That's the spirit," Melowyn replied with a smile.

Hand in hand, the pair stepped over the runes that crackled with warning and began a controlled descent down into the ink-black void of the World Below.

21.

RESONANCE

Only in regards to silence could Owen compare Melowyn and Lionel. The comparison stopped at the silence itself, however, as the quality could not be more different. Confident and fearless, Melowyn was a predator stalking her territorial grounds. Any creature, ashling or otherwise, that stumbled across her path would have begged for mercy.

The cave system offered more to see than the one in Arnstead's Retentions department. That space had been an open, vaulted area with a ceiling unreachable by the brightest light. Scroll racks and tagged relics lined shelves that stretched on to what seemed like infinity, though Owen knew better.

Twists and turns were intimate below Melowyn's home. Passages wound above and below each other. Sometimes one corridor might fall into another; treacherous pitfalls that nearly snagged Owen more than once. Moments like those reminded Owen that he brought along for little more than the company. That, and his sinewy shoulders that carried enough goods for two or more. It was his place to walk behind Melowyn as she navigated the sprawling complex by memory alone.

It truly was a *complex* more than any natural formation. Some paths hid their nature better than others, with walls and ceilings that looked as if they had been formed by the subtle passage of water for millennia. Other sections were not so cleverly disguised. The intersections of passages were the most egregious offenders. The walls, floor, and ceiling were all smooth as glass and rigidly even. Owen thought he might even be able to see his reflection in the torchlight when looking at the floor.

At first, Owen thought that Melowyn might have smoothed over the passages she walked the most. It made sense that someone would want to ease passage in a high-traffic area. Melowyn had displayed a plethora of stone-shaping skills that might have been able to produce similar results.

Similar.

The one word caught in Owen's mind. What Melowyn had crafted above was similar, but not the same as the most obvious sites of reformation in the World Below. The walls down below were too perfect. Too smooth. They had an eerie quality, the source of which Owen could not quite put his finger on.

Visions of chitinous beasts swarming the clean and ancient stone, skittering across its smooth surface as their human-like torsos wailed in suffering at their malign existence, gave Owen chills. He did his best to push the notion away whenever it arose.

It was on the third day that Owen and Melowyn found what they sought; a passageway once blocked by a collapse of stone had been. The barrier, made of rocks and rubble that Melowyn must have dropped from the ceiling, had been picked apart. Clean was not the right word. What had resulted from the effort of removing rubble from one spot and depositing it in another was more of organized chaos.

However, Owen chose to look at it, the way was now open for passage.

Time was not wasted on niceties. Owen set down their pack and began to heave stones he could manage by hand. Melowyn channeled her stone-shaping prowess to move larger boulders into place. A process that left both participants drenched with sweat and heaving for air. Dust and grime caked Owen's face and arms.

Another layer was added to the refreshed barricade after the pair had finished replacing the original stones. Rather, Melowyn melded the outer stones into a single sheet of rock. The strain must have been monumental. Owen could see it in the contortions of the gorgon's face. Rocks small and large glowed with a sickly purple hue as they melted and reformed. When Melowyn had finished, the passageway was blocked by a wall.

"Might be best to do that for any other entrances? Harder for things to get out that way."

Melowyn leveled a feeble glare at Owen, who had spoken innocently enough.

"Of course, my prince," she muttered through strained breaths. "Right away."

"Oh, come now," Owen replied, also struggling to find where his breath had gone, "I didn't mean right now. A project for another time."

"As you command."

Melowyn proffered an exaggerated bow.

Once the pair had caught their breath and shared a small meal, they began their trek back to the entrance from which they started. This journey was shorter than the slow, probing expedition that had come before. Melowyn knew where the entrance was relative to their current position. All that remained was to walk.

Half a day's walk saw them returned to the entrance to the World Below. Owen stood in the cylindrical shaft, with his head craned backward until he could see the ceiling. It felt almost looking up through a dirty chimney; dark, covered in some kind of ill-defined soot, with memory glass bulbs that twinkled like stars in a cloudy night sky. The rim of the shaft framed the image well enough to bring a light smile to Owen. That he was about to be rid of the wretched world behind him played a role in summoning that smile, to be sure.

The journey up played out just as the journey down. Melowyn took Owen by the hand, interlocking his fingers with hers. She closed her eyes and mumbled something to herself. Owen strained to catch a shred of what the gorgon whispered. Despite his best efforts, the words were too quiet to gather any complete phrases. He questioned whether or not Melowyn had spoken in the standard language at all.

With her channeling complete, Melowyn ascended the shaft. Owen, connected by a firm grip, was carried along for the ride.

It was an odd sensation. Owen knew that Melowyn was not holding him tight by her strength alone. There was no pull-on Owen's shoulder. The firm grip on his hand was not squeezed for additional anchorage. Whatever spell Melowyn had woven onto herself also trickled over to Owen. Floating up from the bottom of a lake was the nearest comparison Owen was able to draw, but even that did not feel quite accurate.

At the top of the shaft came the most curious part of the spell. When they both stopped, level with the lip of the hole, they were able to tread on air as if it were solid ground. This allowed them to step lightly away from the hole and back into the library. The only other time could recall having seen such a spell was quite recent; when Walks Far had ridden off the cliff and across a river without ever touching the ground.

Diversity in spell craft was always impressive, Owen knew. The greater the gap between the spells, the greater the spell caster's power. To switch from molding stone to becoming lighter than air was no small gap to bridge. A new light of appreciation flickered in Owen's eyes as Melowyn led the way back through the round door to the main chambers of her home.

The savory aroma of roasted meat wafted through the doorway. Exhaustion was soon smothered by excitement as Owen quickened his pace through the scorched meeting room and into the central chamber. A four-legged beast, Owen assumed it to be a deer from the length and shape, was spinning on a spit over a crackling fire. Amalia moved her hands around the base of the fire. Splints had replaced the cloth bandages that hung from her neck, and she seemed to be using the newfound freedom to sculpt the open flame. She moved like a potter at her wheel.

Most surprising was that who turned the spit: Walks Far.

A thousand questions flooded Owen. Where had the kin gone during the fire? Why was he not present to help? What had he been doing in the days following? How long had been here with the Radiant Circle, talking and laughing like he knew the lot?

Two spies in one group? Owen wondered. *Was all that talk about seeing disturbances in the Flow a lie? Did he just...* know *where the Cinder Witch and her party were from the beginning?*

There would be no answers had by standing at the edge of the room. Owen pushed off from the dining room and over to where the Radiant Circle had gathered – around the food.

"Ah, the Blue one!" Walks Far proclaimed, noticing Owen's approach. He flung a hand out in invitation, while the other continued to rotate the sizzling carcass. "Come. The meat is almost ready. We will celebrate your return."

A few of the Radiant Circle members emulated Walks Far's tempered elation. Waves and quiet 'hello's drifted up from around the fire. Most seemed too intent on the cooking meat to pay the rest of the world any heed.

Amalia turned her head far enough that the corner of one eye could catch Owen and Melowyn. The look did not linger.

"Glad you're back, and in one piece."

The ambiguity of the statement left it to Owen to decide whether he was included. It was a safe assumption, he believed, that he was not. A vague display of courtesy was better than outright hostility, however. Owen chose not to prod the matter as he found a seat at the fire next to Devlin.

"Didn't doubt you for a moment," the harn smiled. A light clap on the back met Owen as he found his seat. There was no mistaking the genuine nature of greetings from Devlin. The man could keep a secret, but he had

393

never seemed the type to lie. "See anything interesting down there?"

"Thankfully, no," Owen returned with a warm smile of his own. "Just a busted barricade. Guessing that thing we met by the camp made the hole, and we just happened to find it at the wrong time."

"Demons are not stumbled upon." The somber words came from Walks Far. "Demons stalk. Demons wait. They are known when they want to be known."

"Knows his stuff, he does," Devlin added. An indicative thumb pointed lopsidedly to Walks Far. "Showed-up out of the darkness to help slay that one. Was a big help. Then he vanished like he was never there."

"Went to find more," Walks Far said with pride. "Where there is one demon, there are often more. Should not leave to chance."

"Well," Devlin sighed, "thankfully it just turned out to be the one. I'm getting too old for this kind of ashling work. That's what we have the young ones for."

Devlin pointed a foot towards Amalia. She did not need to look to know that she was being singled out by the Keeper. An amused snort was her only reply to the suggestion from Devlin. Thin tendrils of fire reached up to caress the cooking deer as Amalia refocused her efforts.

The circle of people around the fire was a touch wider than Owen had expected it to be. Looking around the gathering revealed two surprising faces had joined the group; Jabari and Scarlet. They sat quietly next to each other. An occasional utterance was passed between the two, but they otherwise remained still and silent. Their greeting to Owen was tacit. A brief moment of eye contact before withdrawing back into themselves.

As moody and brooding as they were, Owen was pleased to see they calmed themselves sufficiently to be untied.

Mahika and Manda remained bound as they had been when Owen had last seen them. Three days of being confined by taut ropes and heavy chains. A whole three days to stew in whatever thoughts wracked their minds. For Mahika, you could not tell. That distant, dissociative smile must never have left her visage the entire time Owen had been gone. It would explain why she had not been untied.

Manda seethed.

There was no better way to describe it. Owen felt he might get burned just by looking at Manda, so hot was the contempt that boiled on her face. Furrows deeper than oceans rippled across her sweat-crusted brow. Some part of Owen, a part he never let see the light of day, wished she would remain tied there forever.

Chatter flitted around the room as the food was eventually passed around. Meat peeled away from the deer without resistance. Cooked to perfection, each bite melted like butter on a hot sidewalk. Steamed carrots and smashed potatoes rounded out the meal. Wholesome and filling. The world stepped away for a moment or two to allow a measure of comfort in the lives of those gathered around the fire. A measure of time to forgot how many had died just days before in the very same room.

"We need to talk."

Owen had been dreading those words. They came after the evening meal had been picked down to the bone when bellies were full and eyes became heavy. The only other noise, beyond the mild din of pre-sleep chatter, was a pair of Radiant Circle members washing cookware over by the well.

The words came from the Cinder Witch.

That the words were spoken was no surprise. When Amalia had finished her task of roasting the deer, which she had done expertly, she planted herself next to Owen. Her presence was unnerving. She sat quite still and in near-perfect silence. The small, direct movements she did make were to eat. The rip and tear of meat was the only noise she produced. It was like she was barely alive, all her efforts focused on remaining conscious for as long as possible. Fragile was not a word Owen had expected to assign to Amalia, but there it was. The one descriptor that came to mind.

The silence built towards those four little words. Innocuous in a small group, the phrase carried significant weight in light of the situation. Amalia could have openly declared that she would beat Owen until his face turned purple, that she would rip his arms from their sockets. None of that would have been more troubling than those four simple words: we need to talk.

Words did not come readily for a reply. Simple affirmations caught in Owen's throat and refused to sully the important invitation. "Yes, ma'am," and, "Right away," held no weight.

A meager nod was the only response Owen could muster at the time.

Rather than speak her mind, Amalia rose to her feet. It was a belabored effort without the use of her arms. She was forced to rotate her crossed legs behind herself to rise to her knees. A small push with her left foot took her up to a standing position. About as graceful as could be managed given the situation.

Amalia patted the dust and soot from her pants, gingerly executed, and started towards the entrance passageway.

"I thought you wanted to talk?" Owen croaked.

"Not here."

Most members of the Radiant Circle made a concerted effort not to look up from whatever conversation they were in the middle of. Jwala failed that consideration. A troubled glance bounced twice between Owen and the Cinder Witch. She opened her mouth to speak but seemed to think better of it before any words had slipped out.

Before Owen had realized, his mess kit had been pulled from his hands. He looked in surprise to where the plate, utensils, and cup had been before turning to look at Devlin. The Keeper held a collection of cookery and seemed to be on his way over to the well.

'Go on' was what the Keeper said with a gentle tilt of his head.

The Cinder Witch had reached the passage that led outside by time Owen looked her way again. Red-gold rays signaled the end of the day and wreathed Amalia in a fire of light. She did not wait for Owen but pressed on through the passage and out of sight.

More out of reflex than desire, Owen took hold of his sword and pistol belts. He had taken them off for the sake of comfort while eating. A nagging voice in the back of his mind prodded and poked. It whispered warnings of ambush by a wounded wolf. Retribution at the hands of one who had been faulted.

"You won't need those," Devlin reassured. A gentle hand came to rest on Owen's back. It carried the comforting weight of safety, but also a morsel of judgment. "Time for fighting is over. She knows just as I do."

A queasy sensation gripped Owen's full stomach. Something akin to guilt, but a bit sourer. He could not place his finger on what it was.

"Mind them for me, then?" Owen asked.

"Of course."

Owen pushed himself up from the warmed, stone floor, taking full advantage of both working arms. His left hand wandered to the hilt of the dagger fixed at his lower back. When looked down to Devlin, he was met with the same stare of mild accusation.

It was with heavy hands and a reluctant heart that Owen pulled the dagger, sheath and all, from his belt and left it in the care of the Keeper.

The absence of his tools somehow made Owen's stride feel heavier rather than lighter for the load. He was thankful for the words of reassurance from Devlin, but they were not a promise. Security of his person was in the hands of the demonstrably skilled and dangerous rogue mage that desired a secluded chat. A prospect that did not thrill Owen in the slightest.

Pushing his reservations aside, Owen strode off towards the entry passage.

This marked the first time Owen had left the cave since the hard-fought battle. Assisting the Radiant Circle with their clean-up efforts and joining Melowyn in her work had taken all free time Owen might have been afforded. A rush of fresh air barreled down the passageway as Owen took his first steps.

Owen reached out without thinking and ran his fingers along the passage wall as he walked. The surface was smooth and cool, but somehow unpleasant to the touch. It was covered in some sort of film. Owen withdrew his fingers to see that the tips were covered in soot and ash. Remnants from the battle that had not yet been cleaned away. The grime might have been in a heavily trafficked area, but it was of no inconvenience to those who passed. It must have been deemed not worth the effort to clean. Owen could hardly blame the Circle for such a decision. He still felt mentally drained from the ordeal and it was half a week past.

Morbid thoughts welled up from the dark recesses of Owen's mind. He gazed with disgusted intent at the mess on his hand. Was the soot on his fingers the simple remnants of an unnatural fire, he wondered? Was there more to what remained? Perhaps the last evidence of a Radiant Circle member, incinerated while walking the passage, had just been smudged by wandering digits?

The thought was sickening and caused Owen's stomach to turn. He resumed his faltered pace to suppress the unwelcoming idea.

Hushed voices rolled down through the passageway. At the mouth of the cave, Amalia was speaking with the two sentries. Owen recognized one as the harn named James. The other was a new, unfamiliar face.

James had been astoundingly full of energy considering the state from which he had been extracted from the crawlspace. Owen assumed he had received the most treatment from Jwala and her prayers of anyone else gathered below. Large patches of his body were missing fur, signs of where the blaze had ravaged his small frame. These spots, once dry and black, were now a tender pink. A minor source of agitation that would soon be covered by the return of a furry coat.

Though Owen had not heard what the trio discussed, the nature of the conversation became clear after a moment of silence. Both James and the other sentry gathered their belongings and meandered down the passageway. Both offered a polite 'hello' as they passed Owen on their way down.

So, it's guard duty, then, Owen realized. *One way to get a quiet conversation.*

Owen tilted his head from side to side as he measured the sense of the plan. Standing guard outside the cave was not how he had wanted to spend his first night back from the World Below, but allowed that there were certainly worse alternatives. Anything that got him away from Manda's carving glower had to be considered a positive.

Outside the cave waited yet another stark reminder of the vicious siege. Trees stood tall over the small ravine in which the cave mouth was tucked. Once proud and majestic, they were now broken and hollow. Not a trace of greenery remained on their blackened bodies. Limbs had been stripped away. Obsidian spikes reached for the dimming heavens, coated in the creamy red-orange glow of the setting sun.

Some trees had not managed to weather the storm. Colossal pillars of charred wood hung over the lip of the ravine. A handful had tumbled their way down towards the cave mouth. Gentle breezes bore ill tidings. Those trees that remained crackled and popped at the slightest provocation. To stand out in the open, Owen felt, was a disquieting endeavor.

Amalia seemed at home among the obsidian monoliths. Broken and ready to collapse. Utterly spent by the demands of the world that surrounded them. She eased herself down onto a smooth rock to stare out at the desolation.

"So..." Owen began as he approached. Unsure of what to say next, he let the word hang in the open air. It whipped on the unobstructed wind that tore through the plucked ravine. He continued when it was clear that no reply was forthcoming. "You wanted to talk?"

"If I gave you the box, would you leave me and my people in peace?"

"I, uh..." Owen stuttered. The forthrightness of the Cinder Witch was disarming. Sincere and powerful, she did not veil her desire behind pretty

398

words. "You don't mince words, do you?"

Amalia turned a neutral look to Owen in place of a verbal reply. "Well?" she seemed to say.

"I suppose I did come for the box, didn't I?" Owen continued. A nervous chuckle cut through the cool tone he attempted to maintain. "You'd just hand it over then and let us walk away? After all the effort in getting the thing in the first place?"

"I've done what was necessary. The next person to open that box will be wreathed in a consuming fire."

The Cinder Witch did not waver as she spoke. Her eyes remained locked on Owen's. Backed by honest and straightforward speech, the woman proved unnerving to speak to. Her presence alone was enough to inspire a small measure of awe.

"Excuse me?" Owen could not help but ask. "You said the next person that opens the box will... be burned alive?"

"That's correct."

"And you want me to—"

"Return the box," Amalia interrupted in confirmation. "I want you to return it to its owner, so they might check the contents of the box."

"And be burned alive?"

"Correct."

"So, you're admitting to me— a Spellseeker— that you intend to commit another criminal offense. Utilizing the Flow. With *my* assistance." Owen was unable to contain his disbelief as he spoke. "I have that summed-up about right?"

"All correct, yes."

Air rushed through Owen's pursed lips, which flapped like a horse. He could not bear the weight of the admission. Tired shoulders found purchase along the mouth of the cave. A lot of information had been dropped onto an already full lap. More surprising than the information itself was how willingly it was supplied. This was the type of information that necessitated a dark room and an assortment of rusty pliers, not given for anything less than the threat of death.

The beginning of words formed a handful of times. One attempt to question the validity of the information that Owen could *feel* was true. Another couple of attempts to contextualize the information. A few other strings of thought that he could not quite qualify. None of them made their way up his throat to cross his lips.

Owen was stunned. Plain and simple.

"I appreciate your honesty," was what Owen settled on. "I do, but I can't help you with your revenge plot. Blowing up the people that named you a heretic won't change that fact. It *is* for someone at the House, yes?"

"It is," Amalia replied. The refusal of her request brought no perceptible change to her tone. "For the Pontiff, Isaac Avendale. But not for revenge."

"For what, then?"

"To save the people of Arnstead. To wipe his heresy from the House so that the gods might return to us. I would hear the gods speak if I could."

"I'm not exactly what you would call religious, but aren't the gods dead?" It was Owen's turn to speak with unbridled sincerity. "I don't think murdering a man would bring them back to life. And even if it did, I doubt that would put you in their good graces. Your plan sounds flawed. I mean no offense."

Amalia allowed her gaze to drop, at last, from Owen. She scanned the charred stones at her feet before turning her head up to the sky. The first signs of night had begun to reach over the ravine. Dim stars ignited on a violet tapestry. The moon just barely crested the lip of the ravine. All these grabbed at the Cinder Witch as she pondered what to say next.

The brief respite was not lost on Owen, either. A discourse of this nature, even when spoken plainly and without subterfuge, was a daunting task. Each word carried the weight of a life. Respect for all considerations had to be given.

What caught Owen's attention was not the moon or stars. Amalia dominated his periphery as she stretched her back amid a wide yawn, but did not control Owen's attention fully. It was the observation post that drew his sight. The spot from which he had helped plan the attack on the Radiant Circle. The sacking of Melowyn's home. Consideration of his actions, whether or not he intended the results that had ensued, made present conversation feel all the more weighted. Another look at his soot-covered hands reminded him just how dirty his own hands were.

"Have you visited the House in Arnstead, Owen?"

The question hung in the cool evening air. Amalia kept her gaze fixed on the growing moon that crept up over the ravine and into full view. There were no clouds to mar the beauty of the oncoming night.

"I have," Owen replied flatly.

"Tell me what you saw. Tell me what strikes you about the House of Arnstead. Unusual or otherwise."

"What stands out, you mean?"

"Yes," Amalia nodded. "Tell me what stood out when you visited."

"Well, again, I'm not a religious man… but I suppose there were a couple of things that seemed odd to me. I've only ever seen one other House from the inside, back in Southport. I don't remember it being as big as the one Arnstead. It certainly was not as beautiful. The House here in Arnstead is a real marvel to behold."

"So, you perceive the opulence," Amalia noted. "What else have you perceived?"

"Expensive?" Owen added with rising intonation. "I'm not sure if that's the right word. I got medical attention from the Arnstead House after our first encounter. Was something like twenty silver dollars to treat mild burns and lacerations. The sort of thing that would heal on its own in a couple of weeks, if no infection sets in. Probably could have seen a doctor for less. But they had already treated me, and I wasn't about to *not* pay them. You know what I mean?"

"I do." An amused snort from Amalia cut away some of the tension Owen felt in his chest. "Two fine points," Amalia continued, "both perfect examples. The House of Arnstead was small before Isaac Avendale was installed as Pontiff. His coming was a wind of change. Grandeur replaced simple efficiency. Services that had always been free to good, honest people became locked behind a desire for wealth. No person should have to pay for a miracle. The whole purpose is to give second chances to those who need them. All that goodwill ended with Avendale."

"Wait…" Owen wondered, "you're trying to tell me that *massive* building was bought and paid for by the congregation? And anyone that needs some kind of healing? I don't buy that. You don't get that level of decadence from taxing the desperate of one town."

"An excellent observation." This marked the first change in Amalia's tone. A sense of bitter mockery broke into her otherwise neutral speech. "Normal cannot afford what Avendale desired to become. The House itself was largely bankrolled by the Orland Bank. I did not joke when I said that he was *installed*. Cynthia Orland had the previous Pontiff, a good man, removed so that she might tighten her grip further over Arnstead."

"And you have proof of this?"

"I do, Owen Jay Orland Raulstone." The slow, deliberate tilt of

Amalia's head was unsettling. It felt to Owen as if her eyes drew a knife down the length of his face. Mockery was gone from her voice. All that remained was bitter and rough. "I saw it. With my own two eyes. The murder of the former Pontiff. I spoke out as Avendale ascended to the vacated post, but none would hear me. I was too young, untested. It was a trifle for the new Pontiff to have me labeled a heretic, and so I was cast out for the crime that is witnessing a murder and having the integrity to speak."

Owen thought back to the few words he had caught when Amalia spoke to Devlin. A discussion that seemed to hang on these very notes. Bitterness over having been abandoned, both by Devlin and by the House at large. Owen could not help but take the words of the Cinder Witch on faith. Her spite felt too genuine to be ignored.

"That's…" Owen mumbled, "that's awful. I'm sorry to hear that."

"Of course, you are," Amalia replied under her breath. She turned her wroth back to the moon. "Of course, you are."

"Did you consider reporting the Pontiff to the Fourth Federation Army? I'm sure they could have someone from a Civil unit investi—"

"Please don't insult me, Seeker. The moment I was branded a heretic it became my word versus that of the entire House. I don't have the clout for that kind of fight."

"Maybe I do?" Owen said with a note of hope. "Well, not me personally, but my name carries weight. It would be nice to put my name to good use for once."

"What are you getting at?"

"Come back with me." The words left Owen in halting, unsure fashion. "Surrender. Let me protect you with my name and position until you have a chance to speak. You've stolen a focus and channeled the Flow to do it. You fall squarely into my jurisdiction. No one could reasonably claim otherwise."

"Are you that naïve? You think I could walk into Arnstead and live more than a night? You might be family, but I doubt something as fragile as blood ties would stop the wolf from pouncing."

"I can speak with Cynthia," Owen added, now less sure of his offer. "We have history together. I might be able to get her to listen."

"I'm sure," Amalia huffed. "And what of my accomplices? Can you guarantee their safety? Can you promise them a return to normal life after having aided me in my damned crusade? No, it would be better if you just took the box. End Avendale's reign over the Arnstead House and send a message to your precious family with one swift motion. Remind the Orlands that the House is not a toy to be played with."

"I can't knowingly endanger someone like that, Amalia. And not just because I'm a Spellseeker."

The words grew soft as they spilled out from Owen. He felt backed into a corner, unsure of where next to drive the conversation. What the Cinder Witch said could not have been truer. Owen knew his cousin. He knew how goal-driven she was and had seen her success within Arnstead. There was no way she would not protest if her means were threatened. Owen refused to believe she would go so far as to order the death of another, but there would be a reckoning of some sort. Of that much Owen was certain.

"You say you cannot knowingly endanger someone," Amalia began after a heavy pause, "but you would march me through the streets of Arnstead like some prize. The person who conquered the Cinder Witch, brought her to heel. I'm sure that would look good on your resume, regardless of how long I survived."

Owen opened his mouth to speak, but found yet again that he was unable to voice his thoughts. He wanted desperately to refute the accusation that Amalia had leveled. He wanted to but knew that he could not. The Cinder Witch had seen right through Owen's intentions and labeled him for what he was. Owen could not bring himself to refute the claims, to lie to Amalia's face.

The conversation had begun to make Owen itch. That odd sort of discomfort that arises when a person had been caught in an argument and has nowhere to run. A sort of burning shame that rises from the gut to leave crimson marks on the face. Owen shuffled uneasily against the smoothed mouth of the cave.

Silence appeared to be enough of an admission of guilt. Amalia gave Owen an understanding nod and left the conversation at that. There was no sense in pursuing the points any further. Both sides had said what needed to be said, and neither had gotten what they desired.

Bare traces of sunlight remained by the time the conversation ended. Stars littered the sky through the barren boughs of cremated trees. It was the first clean sky he had seen for almost a week. There was no light of nearby towns or cities to mar the milky tapestry above.

Between raw night sky and the accusations from Amalia, Owen had never felt so small.

22.

RECKONING

"Ready to switch, Owen? You've carried your fair share by now."

"No, quite all right, Ishir," Owen grunted. "We're not so far from the cave now, might as well see it through to the end."

"I like the confidence," the Bangeli katarl laughed. "Let's see if your shoulders can hold up your words, Mr. Seeker."

Owen shrugged against the staff leveled across his shoulders. With arms draped up and over the staff, he struggled to maintain the balance of his load; a bucket of fish hanging from either end of the staff. The result of a day spent with Ishir, the Bangeli katarl he met during the initial incursion of the cave, fishing at a nearby stream.

The stream was tucked into another ravine a handful of miles from the cave. According to Ishir, the stream ended in a small, stony opening that led below ground. It provided fish above ground and fed the well in Melowyn's home.

Ishir proved to be a font of knowledge. Not only for the surrounding area, but for the members of the Radiant Circle, as well. He helped Owen become acquainted with some of the more distant members of the group. A bright and sure introduction from the katarl gave Owen a leg to stand on rather than approaching as a stranger. There were quite a few new faces to meet. About half of the surviving members of the Circle had been sequestered in Melowyn's library when Scarlet's spell blasted the main area. Those tucked into the crawl space, which turned out to be a sleeping area for a large number of guests, had been lucky to have a half-wall separating them from the explosion.

"So, Mr. Confidant," Ishir began, "how long do you plan on staying with us? We're coming up on a week now, aren't we?"

"Has it—" A pair of stumbled steps brought Owen's attention back to his own two feet. Panicked breaths subsided as he regained control. "Has it been that long already?"

Ishir brought himself back up to full height. He had adopted a stance that would allow him to support Owen if necessary. It was an instinctual change made without fanfare and was abandoned when Owen showed signs of secure footing. The katarl smiled as he recounted the past week with clawed fingers.

"Well, there was the first night, the night of the fire. Then you spent three days down below with our host. Guard duty the night after that. A day of rest, followed by a day of fishing with your friendly neighborhood katarl. Makes for almost a full week."

"I suppose—" Another shift in balance. Owen grunted from the effort of course correction. "Suppose it does, doesn't it? Well, as soon as your boss undoes whatever it is she did to the Orland lockbox, I can take the thing and be on my way. Any chance you might put in a good word for me? Help get me out of your hair?"

"Not likely," Ishir chuckled. "Even if I agreed to try, changing Amalia's mind is like trying to move a mountain with your bare hands. The woman is about as stubborn as she is strong. And I mean that in the best way possible."

"So that's a no on the good word, then?"

The katarl did not speak, instead acknowledging the notion with another baritone laugh from his gut.

Chatter slowed to a crawl. There was plenty left to be said. Owen had no doubts there but was appreciative of Ishir for allowing full concentration on the task at hand. Walking with the suspended buckets was difficult enough without having to think about what to say. The fact that the live fish were not content to leave the lid of either bucket alone added another facet of challenge to the task.

Moments between violent outbursts from the fish allowed Owen to focus on more than just the next few steps. The terrain from the stream to the cave was not unlike the path to the abandoned campsite. Uneven, rocky terrain mixed with loose soil to create an uncertain ground. Attention had to be paid to each step even when not carrying buckets-worth of meals.

Green and brown dominated the area around the stream. Healthy trees provided an abundance of natural shade. Melowyn had caught the blaze before it could stretch too far beyond the ravine. Her mastery over the Flow spared the fate of the greater woods. Walking from the cave to the stream felt something like walking backward through time. Black and charred monoliths slowly gave way to living bark and leaf-covered branches. Bushes and flowering plants were abundant near the banks of the stream.

The walk back to the cave, on the other hand, carried with it a sense of foreboding. It felt to Owen like he was stepping into a graveyard. Towering gravestones denoted where life had once flourished. Blackened, soot-covered stones blasted by the terrible decisions of Manda and her people. An uncomfortable openness lingered in the air where boughs should have swung in the wind.

It was clear that Ishir felt the same way. Owen could see that the katarl's shoulders had stiffened since returning to the desolate space surrounding the ravine. Carefree steps became heavy and laden with purpose. The ravaged land must have weighed on Ishir, Owen thought, to make the katarl seem so grave where before he had been a wellspring of mirth.

"Hold," Ishir muttered, as much to himself as to Owen. A large, clawed hand rose to the height of Owen's chest and held him in place. "Set the fish down."

"No, I already told you, I'm quite all right. We're almost ther—"

"Quiet!"

Ishir now spoke in a violent, commanding whisper. The realization that Ishir's mood had not been affected by the surrounding desolation came slowly to Owen, like warm water gnawing at winter-chilled hands. Owen did as Ishir requested and set his burden down on the ground. The reason for Ishir's tension was revealed the moment Owen was able to look more than three steps ahead.

Standing at the lip of the ravine was a fragile silhouette. The frame of a human swayed in the gentle, unobstructed breeze. Their dead eyes looked through both Owen and Ishir to rest on nothing in particular. A red-brown gash crossed the length of the woman's neck. The same red-brown color stained her brown neck. Blue and orange scarves, cut in the same place as the gash on the woman's neck, were stained with blood. Trails of blood ran down her shirt to her waist.

Despite the mortal wound, Jwala stood over the precipice to safety. She titled her head backward, a move that caused the gash in her neck to widen, and let forth a gut-wrenching howl.

A black and orange blur launched over the lip of the ravine. It hurtled up and over with a startling speed. There was not time enough between its reveal and when it landed at Ishir's feet and drove a sword through the katarl's chest. The sound was wet with a subtle crunch. Bones gave way to the powerful thrust that ended Ishir's life on the spot. Owen had only managed to half-draw his sword by the time Ishir had crumpled, a blood-sputtering mess, to the stony ground.

"Relax," came the voice of the assailant. "We're here to clean up your latest mess."

The voice was familiar, but only just. It took seeing the owner's face to recognize the speaker. Owen would have been hard-pressed not to remember the tendrils of scar tissue he had left on this Bangeli katarl's face.

"Chitra!" Owen gasped. It was a raspy sound. The mixture of effort from carrying the fish buckets melded with the surprise and alarm of the sudden attack.

"Come on, the rest are at the cave," Chitra commanded. She paused for a moment to kneel and wipe Ishir's blood from her blade. Life had already faded from Ishir's eyes. He could not protest that Chitra used his clothes to wipe away his blood. "And put your sword away. Your work is done, and I'd like to avoid any fresh scars, thank you."

Third Seeker Chitra, dressed in her Seeker's blues, turned to leave a stunned Owen where he stood.

Shock pulled Owen's mind in too many directions to function. He tried desperately to rationalize everything that had transpired in the past few moments. Jwala was dead, yet she moved and screamed as if alive. Ishir was dead at the hands of a Seeker who should be in Arnstead. There was a clear suggestion that *more* Spellseekers were waiting for him down by the cave entrance.

The first scrap of information that Owen's befuddled mind could act on was Ishir. Owen knelt next to the katarl in panic. Shaking hands checked for a pulse, one hand at the katarl's neck and the other under an armpit. Nothing. A glance at the wound in Ishir's chest showed that his heart had been pierced. Wide, unfocused eyes and an open mouth framed a look of surprise that Ishir was unable to form into words. There had been no time to do so. Chitra's strike was too precise to allow for any last thoughts.

Owen had only just met Ishir. They had been acquainted for less than a week. Even so, Owen felt the loss. The katarl had borne a commanding presence laced with unabashed kindness. It was an unfitting end for a man so trusting and warm. Owen unbuttoned his Seeker coat and draped it over Ishir like a sheet. It was the most respectful thing Owen's reeling brain could come up with.

"I'm sorry," Owen muttered. "I am so sorry."

A new figure had appeared on the lip of the ravine by the time Owen stood and made his way over. A Nirdac human; this man was wholly unfamiliar. He, too, wore the coat of a Spellseeker. Two six-pointed stars on his shoulder indicated that the man was Second Seeker. A mess of oily blond hair trickled down into what must have been several days' worth of stubble. Delicate hands draped themselves over Jwala's shoulders. The touch was tender as if he was placing his hands on his child.

"Quite the little sentry, isn't she?" the man asked as Owen passed. His voice possessed the same oily quality as his hair. "Nabbed the sentries from the cave. Now they're *my* sentries. Couldn't let them go to waste."

"I see that," Owen mumbled, unsure what else to say.

"Second Seeker Donovan Reign, by the by. Violent Offenses," the man followed. He extended one of his hands to Owen. Donovan's chin took up the perch made vacant by his hand. Furthering the look of a man embracing his child, the Seeker tilted his head so that it made gentle contact with Jwala's. "Pleasure to make your acquaintance."

The easy smile slid off the man's face as Owen failed to contain a rising sense of disgust. Owen stepped past him without taking the outstretched hand.

"All right," Donovan added, "suit yourself. Keep an eye out, would you, love?"

Disgust fermented into utter revulsion. This was not the first time Owen had encountered a person raised from the dead. He understood the purpose behind the action, and that a lifeless marionette could be used to help better the Federation. Corpses had been used to build the manarail. They could raise towns and cities in half the time required of a living workforce.

What bothered Owen here was the lack of decorum. There was no way, Owen imagined, that Jwala would have agreed to allow her corpse to be used in such a manner. Even if Jwala was one of the few followers of the House that did not mind, Owen was sure she would not have agreed to be used against her friends in life. Topping the whole mess off was just how close this Donovan was to Jwala's corpse. He might as well have been cradling Jwala with how invasive his actions were.

Owen kept his complaints to himself. Apart from his reports to Violette, these were his first interactions with the Bureau of Arcane in almost two weeks. He had learned by now that his opinions held less water than a leaky bucket with the Arnstead branch. There was no sense in starting a fight that he was sure he would lose.

The view from atop the ravine was no more pleasant. Chitra worked her way down to the mouth of the cave, which was surrounded by an additional five Seekers. Only one of the Seekers was recognizable from the bunch. He was the one Spellseeker that Owen had wished not to see.

First Seeker Akheem Albarn turned his head towards the sound of Chitra's descent, then up to Owen. The black coils that made up the bulk of the First Seeker's hair bounced from the snap. Wide shoulders were raised to strict attention. Everything about the man was as imposing as ever. Rather than speak, he waved for Owen to descend and join the gathering of Seekers. Owen did not have the strength of will to disobey.

Owen worked his way down the ravine with practiced steps. The way was familiar, though the destination was no longer an inviting one. Dust, ash, and soot kicked up behind with step.

First instincts told Owen to stop an arm's length from the party of Spellseekers. He readily assumed that he did not belong among the congregation of veteran personnel. They all carried the same electrified presence as the First Seeker. A Nirdac katarl, two Bangeli humans, and a Zumbatran harn, all unfamiliar faces despite the working relationship that was shared between them and Owen.

A short wave from the First Seeker beckoned Owen to draw closer. One arm's length was too much, it seemed. Owen stepped forward until he was within reach of First Seeker Akheem. The imposing man took a deep breath, then exhaled slowly through his nostrils.

"You abandoned your post, Raulstone," Akheem began. Each word felt to Owen like a frigid chain wrapping itself around his spine. "You lied to your handler regarding your whereabouts. You disobeyed my direct orders. Negligence like that is lucky to be met with court-martial. I *should* let Chitra take a piece out of you and report the Cinder Witch killed you. No one here would dispute that."

That sense of cold that Owen felt doubled. The chain froze itself around his spine and tried to drag his core down into his boots. He could not bring himself to look the First Seeker in the eyes but rather locked his gaze on an unassuming boulder. Owen braced himself for another barrage when First

Seeker Akheem took another labored breath.

"That said, fine reconnaissance work, Seeker. If you plan to pull a stunt like this again in the future, which I *expect* you won't, run it by me first. This is the sort of work for Violent Offenses, First Division." The First Seeker made a sweeping gesture when he said First Division. "Not a lone wolf."

Ice chipped away from his mind as the gears in Owen's head began to turn. He realized that his notes had not stopped at Violette Woods for mere documentation. Though she had never said as much, Violette must have passed those daily reports directly to First Seeker Akheem. There was no other explanation for how a whole division of Spellseekers had been dispatched to the hitherto unknown location of the Cinder Witch. At least, no other explanation came to Owen. It must have been his letters that led the Seekers here to the cave.

Sudden pride instilled by rare praise from the First Seeker was short-lived. New guilt, more poignant than any Owen had felt to this junction, bled into focus. He could not keep himself from casting a withering glance over his shoulder. At the top of the ravine stood the unwavering corpse of Jwala, a woman who had shown Owen nothing but kindness. He felt the weight of her death on his shoulders. The body of Ishir carried the guilt deeper into his core.

There was no rationalizing. No words came to mind. Nothing to soothe Owen's nerves or deflect the self-loathing. It was different from his feelings about the initial siege of the cave. His contribution to the success of Manda and her people was questionable. The presence of half of the Arnstead Violent Offenses division, however, was unquestionable. They would not be here without the information that Owen had provided to Violette in his evening reports. Jwala and Ishir would still be alive. Their deaths rested on his shoulders, made his legs quiver until they gave out and Owen fell to his knees.

Owen felt the cold collection of eyes that surrounded him bore into the skin like icicles. He sat where he was, too limp to care about the judgment cast his way. His ears were deaf to the general chatter that consumed the group.

"That's two of yours now, Cinder Witch." The voice of First Seeker Akheem, dominant and impatient, cut through the dull drone like a razor. "Wait all you like, but even gorgons have to eat. She won't be able to protect

410

your people when they come out searching for food. Get out here and answer for your crimes with dignity."

Those words cracked the ice that bound Owen in place. A sudden warmth rushed from his heart up to his face. A warmth that quickly rose to a wave of anger that burned his cheeks.

No more, Owen told himself. *No more death.*

The thought shattered his bonds. With great effort, Owen forced himself up onto his feet amongst the pack of ravenous dogs that surrounded him. All their attention was focused on Melowyn's cave. A lone Seeker out of his depth was not worth their time or focus. Owen must have seemed littel more than a child in their eyes.

What the other Seekers thought of him was not important. Their condescending judgments were irrelevant. They might snicker and joke as he walked, but it would not stop him. Steeled as he was, Owen would not be stopped.

"No more death," Owen said aloud as he took his first step through the crowd of Seekers. None stopped him as he strode through the cave entrance. His echoing footsteps were the only sound to reach his ears and he walked with furious confidence down the passageway and into the main chamber of the cave.

Those of the Radiant Circle that yet lived had gathered together at the back of the main chamber. Shortbows were knocked with arrows. Nervous hands quivered as they held daggers and logging axes. It was a sorry sight. The band of zealots who commanded so much respect back in Arnstead feared for their lives. They were not fighters. They never had been. Here were collected a group of people who thought that Amalia Tennerim was in the right, and they were willing to do their best to bolster her cause.

At the head of the group stood Amalia herself. The light of the Flow, orange and yellow, pulsed through her arms. Sparks sputtered from her fingertips as Owen reached the main chamber. Gouts of flame ripped and roared until they stabilized in helical formation around splinted arms. She stood like a bastion between the Radiant Circle and those who would do them harm.

Owen raised his hands above his head, open palms facing Amalia and her people.

"I'm not leaving," Amalia said in a flat, collected way. "Not until Ishir and Jwala are given back. I'll walk out with the Orland people once mine

411

have been returned."

"They're dead, Amalia."

The words struck Amalia like a hammer blow. Owen had not pulled his punch, nor had he offered to warn of the news to come.

"What do you mean?" Amalia asked, stunned.

"I mean they're dead. Jwala was dead when we got back, and they killed Ishir before I had time to speak. They're not coming back, Amalia."

"That's... no," Amalia stuttered. Hairline cracks rippled throughout her composure. Owen swore he could hear her nerves break at that moment. "They're Seekers. Why would they do that? Kill innocent people on sight?"

"They're Radiant Circle, Amalia," Owen murmured. "You're all good people. I know that, but you're not innocent. They're treating you like the threats you presented yourselves to be."

"But without warning—"

"I didn't say I agree!" Owen shouted. His composure was shot. The time for decorum had passed, giving way to simplicity of thought and speech. "I don't want to see any more of you die. I really don't. And the only way I see that happening is if you surrender, Amalia. If you come quietly, I'll try my damnedest to protect you. Please."

Owen drew his sword with his right hand. A slow, deliberate gesture so as not to alarm anyone present. He pointed the tip of the blade up towards the Spellseekers gathered outside. At the same time, he offered his empty left hand to Amalia.

"Please," Owen said again. This time it sounded more like an apology than a request, a subtle change that was not lost on Amalia.

"Do as he says, Cinder Witch," came the cold voice of First Seeker Akheem.

"Shut it!" Owen snapped. He whipped his head around to ensure that the Seekers had not followed into the cave. Satisfied that he had not been followed, he turned his attention back to Amalia. "Well?"

Never before had Owen seen someone so visibly torn. Amalia shifted her weight on her heels as she looked back and forth from Owen to the cave mouth and the collection of Radiant Circle members at her back. Her brow crinkled and smoothed as she struggled with the implications that either available choice carried.

At the back of the cave rested Melowyn. Her haunting gaze was locked on the entryway to the cave. The light of the Flow pulsed in her arms, ready to be called upon if it was needed. She seemed intent on ensuring that the cave itself remained a neutral zone.

The sound of rustling fabric and clattering metal drew the attention of all who were assembled in the main chamber.

Tucked away in the storage area were Jabari and Scarlet. Each was digging through a separate pile of goods. Jabari was elbow deep in a pile of goodness knows what. The entirety of Scarlet's torso had vanished inside a chest, leaving only her sporadically kicking legs visible to the group of onlookers. Jabari had stopped moving once he noticed ponderous stares. Scarlet was too invested in her search to stop.

Now!? Owen thought to himself in pure disbelief. *You're rummaging for the lockbox now, while a division of bloodthirsty, federally endorsed headhunters are knocking at the door?*

"Fine." The single word sounded like a shattered windowpane. Owen turned his attention to Amalia in time to watch her hang her head then snap her attention back to the plunderers. A heavy sigh seeped out before the Cinder Witch resumed her usual, neutral tone. "The box is in the rightmost crate, tucked under the sacks of flour."

Scarlet's lively legs stopped, finally realizing she had been caught in the act. Jabari pointed a sullen finger at the rightmost container. He raised an inquisitive eyebrow.

"Yes," Amalia sighed again. "Yes, that's the one."

"Then you'll surrender yourself?" Owen asked hesitantly.

"Do I have any other option, Seeker?"

The world seemed to turn faster after the agreement had been struck. Motion filled the cave as idle hands found ways to busy themselves.

Jabari and Scarlet, no longer under constant scrutiny, set about releasing Manda and Mahika from their bonds. It was not a sly endeavor. The pair of miscreants likely could not have made more noise while freeing their counterparts if they had tried. At least that was how Owen felt about the matter. He injected himself into the process to assert that Manda should behave. The Fourth Federation Army officer promptly spat in Owen's face.

Members of the Radiant Circle set about gathering supplies for travel. They set aside what they knew they could spare for those leaving the cave, and a little more that they could not afford to spare.

Amalia spoke with members of her troupe about plans for their future. Something about returning to the West. Traveling to the Gods' Fingers.

413

Owen was not able to catch much detail. The Cinder Witch spoke in hushed tones meant only for those to whom she spoke. Occasional nods and notes jotted onto scraps of paper signified complete attention on the part of the subordinates.

Melowyn had stepped out of the cave to meet the Spellseekers at her door. What was discussed was a mystery, but the subject matter had left the gorgon pale and distant. All were packed and ready to leave by the time she returned.

"Feel free to drop by, if you ever have the time," Melowyn said to Owen in passing. "It's not often I meet a fellow lover of literature who can stomach time in the World Below. I'd love to have you again."

"If I'm ever in the neighborhood, I'll be sure to give you a knock," Owen replied, realizing how stupid he sounded only after he had spoken.

"A simple 'no' would suffice," Melowyn offered with a warm smile. "I don't plan on moving anytime soon, should you change your mind."

"Ma'am," Owen said, followed by a slightly ashamed nod. Melowyn nodded in return and went about speaking to her other departing guests.

Though Owen and Amalia dragged their feet on departure, Manda and her people were not so coy. They remained busy picking over Melowyn's larder until the gorgon had returned. Bits of extra food and simple traveler's clothes were their prizes. Items to replace what had been lost during the initial raid on the cave. In some cases, they were simply retrieving things that had been taken from them.

Manda and company took to the cave entrance as soon as they had finished raiding supplies. Scarlet was happy to relinquish her pack to Jabari after the katarl made the kind offer. Manda shirked the same offer, insisting on packing and shouldering the bag alone with her one good arm.

"C'mon Blue," Manda grunted as she passed Owen. "Time to get the hells out of here and not look back."

"All right, all right. You ready?" Owen asked as he turned back to Amalia.

"As I'll ever be."

"Just say what I told you and you'll be fine," Owen said in his best at reassurance. "I'll be standing between you and them, so don't let them provoke you. Keep your head on your shoulders."

"You're one to talk," Amalia scoffed.

A fair point. Owen could feel the sweat on his palms. The First Seeker had just gotten through telling Owen not to pull any more stupid stunts, which Owen was fairly certain this qualified as. Owen did not understand the inner workings of the Arnstead Arcanarium. Not fully. Their standard practice might have been to blow away rogue mages on sight and file the paperwork in a way that made it sound like an accident. They might paint Amalia as the aggressor, even if she did not throw so much as a single punch.

To make matters worse, Amalia was still injured. Scrapes and bruises had come and gone. Fractures in her upper arms, however, were still in the process of healing. More than a week was needed to get the Cinder Witch back into fighting shape. The sleeves on her shirt barely hid the outline of the splints meant to keep her arms in place.

If the Violent Offenses division decided to blow past Owen and have their way with Amalia, her chance at a solid defense was minimal.

All this negativity and more manifested itself in Owen's face. The sheer audacity of the plan was more than he could contain. Clenched teeth. A smile crooked with doubt. This was possibly the biggest lie Owen had ever attempted to sell, and his body knew it.

"Last thing," Owen said as he produced his lone pair of manacles, freshly removed from Manda's ankles. The reaction from Amalia was immediate, a subtle shake of her head. "We've got to sell this as hard as we can. If they see you wearing these, they'll know you couldn't possibly channel the Flow into any kind of spell."

"And then they'll rip me apart because I can't defend myself."

"They'll have to kill me first."

"And I'll be right there, as well," Devlin chimed in as he stepped towards Owen and Amalia. "I won't leave you to face the world alone. Not again."

Amalia rolled her eyes at the implication. Still, after a series of grumbled half-words, she held her arms out. Owen bound Amalia's arms with the lead-lined restraints to hamper any attempts at a spell. The trio bid their last farewells and set out through the entry passageway. They neared the cave mouth just in time to hear a brief exchange.

"Lieutenant Galloway."

"Seeker Akheem."

The familiar tone of the exchange caused Owen's heart to sink. Not only was almost half of the Arnstead Arcanarium present, but they were also on speaking terms with Manda. Any prospect of a clean return to Arnstead slipped that much more through clenched, desperate fingers.

It doesn't matter, Owen told himself.

It certainly did matter. This was a fact, no matter how much Owen would have liked to dispute it. Owen knew this despite what he told himself. His attempt to convince himself that everything would be all right was what allowed him to put one foot before the other. The driving force behind his ability to face whatever the next few minutes would bring to bear.

Nervous, shallow breaths shortened and shortened until Owen forgot to breathe entirely. The light of day burned as Owen stepped across the threshold of Melowyn's home and out into the scarred ravine. Expectant eyes fell heavily upon him and his prisoner.

The whole world grew taught as a wire, ready to snap at the first uttered word.

A semicircle of Spellseekers formed around the cave mouth. They were clad in pristine uniforms. Each bore a sword on their hip that, apart from Seeker Chitra, they did not bother to draw. Silvered buttons glinted in the sunlight. Five Third Seekers, Second Seeker Donovan, and First Seeker Akheem Albarn.

Flow glowed in each member of the Violent Offenses division. Some carried the energy in their hands and arms. Chitra's power shone through the threads of her pants, indicating some kind of strength or speed. An explanation for how she ascended the ravine so quickly to fall upon poor Ishir.

Ishir!

The recently deceased katarl stood just behind Second Seeker Donovan. The Seeker seemed to have called Jwala's corpse down from her post on the ravine. Both former members of the Radiant Circle flanked Seeker Donovan. Their movements were uncanny; a twitchy series of jerks and jolts. There was no way to make their animation look natural. The dead were dead, no matter how much Flow had been pumped through their veins. Constant reminders of the fate that awaited Amalia should the plan fail.

Past the line of Seekers were Manda and her people. The bulk of the group had set down their packs to reorganize and shuffle gear around. Scarlet in particular had pawned her caster rifle off to Jabari yet again.

Manda herself stood just behind First Seeker Akheem, with her hungry eyes locked onto Amalia.

Come on, Owen thought at Amalia. He did not dare take his eyes off the half-ring of Seekers spread out before him. Speech was beyond him, as well. Owen feared any action might come across as provocation. The only option left to him was hope. A hope that Amalia would feel his thoughts and remember the lines she had been given. *Come on, out with it.*

"I am Amalia Tennerim," were the first words to shatter the silence. Neutral as it was, the utterance caused half of the Seekers to start. None went so far as to draw out a spell or attack. Their movements were kept to nervous jitters. "I am better known as the Cinder Witch. I surrender myself to arrest under the protection of Third Seeker Owen Raulstone. I am charged with the crimes robbery and assault, though I do not admit guilt for these crimes."

It was not perfect.

The short speech lacked some of the finer points that Owen had provided. There had been no mention of a trial before a court of law, nor had there been any words on the manacles that bound Amalia's access to the Flow. The crimes Amalia had listed were too pedestrian. She had not mentioned that her use of the Flow is what placed under the jurisdiction of the Seekers gathered there today.

All of that aside, Amalia had more or less done as she was asked. Her temper was even. There was no hint of rage or discontent. The cold composure that Owen had come to associate with the Cinder Witch remained sound.

"I accept her surrender," Owen followed. Amalia had done her part. Now it was his turn. "As a Third Seeker of the Arnstead Arcanarium, I offer her my protection until she is tried in a court of law. I will ensure that she lives to receive a fair trial so long as she remains peaceful. Any who object must speak now. Silence will be treated as acceptance."

"Are you serious?" The exasperated words came from Chitra. Comic disbelief and pure disgust fought for dominance over her features. "Is he *serious?*"

The second question dropped any pretense at humor. Disgust was in full control of Third Seeker Chitra. Her inquiry was directed not at Owen, but First Seeker Akheem. Owen realized he was not worth the time or effort it would take to question him. At least, that was what Chitra's actions seemed to indicate.

No answer came to the question. Not immediately. The First Seeker's complexion was contemplative. He examined Owen, Amalia, and Chitra all in turn.

"You serious?" Chitra asked of First Seeker Akheem. "You're actually thinking about this?"

"You object, then?" Akheem asked in return.

The First Seeker was calm in his retort. There was no spite in his speech. It was a genuine question that he raised to Third Seeker Chitra.

This might work! Owen thought. *The First Seeker is* actually *considering the proposal!*

Owen was nothing less than astounded. He had expected immediate refusal, and that there would be violence to follow. Parts of the Cinder Witch would be scattered across the rocks as she put up the best defense possible. Restraints would have made her success impossible. A new wave of guilt would have washed over Owen in that failure. He would have told himself that this was not his business, that he should have left Amalia to her own devices rather than intercede with a failure of a plan.

With the First Seeker entertaining the notion of an arrest, Owen figured that his odds of success had improved to that of a coin flip. Certainly not the best odds he could ask for. Still, it was better odds than asking a pack of wolves to not devour an injured sheep.

"Of course, I object!" scoffed Chitra. "This runt doesn't deserve the credit."

The First Seeker looked back to Chitra. Whatever the man might be thinking, his face was still as stone. He raised an open, level hand towards Amalia. It reminded Owen of the gesture that Marcus, the Orland butler, would make to announce that a meal was served.

A bright flash of light was the only warning that preceded Chitra launching herself towards Amalia. The speed of the attack was incredible. It was impossible to tell when she had raised her sword into a thrusting position, so quick the motion was. Chitra had turned herself into a living spear that was thrown by the Flow itself. Speed was her strength, just as Owen had guessed.

It was that guess that allowed Owen to move. Having seen her speed twice now, once on the bridge in Arnstead and again when she assaulted Ishir, Owen was prepared. The speed was a known and expected quantity.

Steady was the hand that slipped down to grab the caster pistol. Steady, but by no means slow. Flow rushed through his arm even before Owen had set a finger on the pistol. The energy jammed into the cartridge that was loaded. It moved with such a speed that it burned Owen as it passed from his hand and into the weapon. Never before had Owen channeled with such speed that he immediately felt associated friction. He didn't care.

Go!

The thought howled inside his mind. The tip of the barrel had only just cleared the pistol's holster when the thought rang out. Owen did not realize it at that moment but called the one word aloud as the thought fought for freedom.

"Go!"

Wind rushed from the pistol. The ferocious jet caught Chitra, who was a single step away from piercing Amalia with the leveled blade. It was not a clean hit. The rush of air caught the Spellseeker in the shoulder instead of her chest. Owen had hoped to flatten Chitra where she stood. The katarl only seemed to have lost her balance.

Owen heard several sounds after the shot of his pistol. They happened in such proximity to one another that it was difficult to tell which happened first.

A shout. It came from behind Owen. The voice was recognizable. Amalia had let go a pained cry, which was accompanied by a subsequent shuffling of feet. *The reaction to a blow?* Owen wondered. Had he been too late?

Metal clattered against stone. It must have been Chitra's sword, Owen reasoned. Unless one of the others had drawn their sword and joined in the fray, there could be no other explanation. But why had her sword struck stone if it had been driven through the Cinder Witch? That morbid thought led to the processing of the final sound.

Crunch.

It was a sickening sound. Bone snapping from the application of astounding force. The sort of sound that lived deep in memory. Owen had heard that sound when Cynthia's leg was crushed by a horse so many years ago.

When Owen turned to see the situation behind himself, he almost wretched.

Amalia was more or less fine. The sword had cut through her sleeve and left a new injury just above the site of her fracture. Painful no doubt, but the blood dripped with a slow trickle. It was a wound that could be

419

mended.

The sword that bit into Amalia had fallen to the ground. Chitra's hand had gone limp and allowed the blade to fall. Here was the source of the crunching noise. Chitra. The Seeker's face was planted into the stones that made up the cave mouth. Apart from an occasional twitch, the katarl was motionless. Blood poured from a fissure in her forehead to pool on the rocks below.

Chitra had split her skull and lay dead against the mouth of the cave.

"Are there any *further* objections?"

Dispassionate words from the First Seeker brought Owen's waning energy back to focus on the Seekers before him, rather than the one that lay behind. None among the Violent Offenses division moved. Only First Seeker Akheem dared to move in that moment, and only to take account of his subordinates.

Deliberate steps carried First Seeker Akheem to Owen. Unable to tear his eyes away from the mangled body of Chitra, Owen felt the First Seeker's presence before he saw him. The sort of invasive presence that demanded acknowledgment. It subjugated Owen's presence of mind. When he finally turned to see the First Seeker, it was not of his own accord. Owen's body demanded what his mind refused to command.

"You staked your claim," First Seeker Akheem declared as he placed a powerful hand on Owen's shoulder. "Chitra made her choice, and she bore the responsibility. You did only as you said you would. Nothing more to the matter than that."

"Sir..." was the only dejected form of acknowledgment that Owen could muster. He looked up with hollow eyes to meet the surprisingly understanding gaze of First Seeker Akheem. "I didn't... I don't—"

"We've all taken a life, Seeker." The assurance came with a light pat on Owen's shoulder. "Even Second Seeker Aaron, though you wouldn't guess it by looking at the man."

"What happens now, sir?"

"After we get back to Arnstead? A regrettable amount of paperwork, unfortunately. But after that, it's back to business as usual. We get a new Seeker to fill the vacancy in Lost and Stolen, hit the streets, keep folks out of trouble. That whole bag."

"Vacancy in Lost and Stolen?"

Owen thought he misheard the First Seeker. His hands still quaked from the rush of adrenaline, still burned from the quick channeling of Flow. His mind still reeled from the settling reality that Owen had added yet more blood to his already stained hands.

"When it comes to Violent Offenses, I prefer to hire from within," First Seeker Akheem said. It was the first time Owen had ever heard a hint of light in the man's deep voice. "Unless, of course, you'd rather stick with Aaron and the Lost and Stolen division."

"What, me?" Owen asked, pointing a shaking finger at himself. "I thought you said I wasn't fit to be a Seeker."

"I'm allowed to change my mind."

"I just... I just *killed* a fellow officer, sir."

"You were in the wrong the first time you stared down Chitra. This time, you were in the right. She had no business objecting to the arrest. Not with the Cinder Witch there being as passive as she was. She attacked out of spite and vengeance. Not the sort of qualities that keep a Seeker on the force for long." The First Seeker paused for a moment as if caught in revelation. "Not turning down a promotion, are you, Seeker?"

23.

SOLACE

Light peered through ratty, moth-eaten curtains. The green fabric gave the small room a sickly hue. A hue with which Owen had become familiar, courtesy of the east-facing window. Some days he could push past the early light of dawn to rise alongside the blare of his small alarm clock.

Today was not one of those days.

Owen rolled over in his small twin bed and yanked the lone sheet over his eyes in a single motion. The hand that did not clutch the sheet fumbled around on the nightstand for the signature bells atop the alarm clock. Groggy fingers wrestled with the mechanism until it had been switched to the off position. Just because he rose with the sun that day did not mean Owen had to wake his neighbors with him. The heavy hand that operated the clock slumped off the bed and down to the warm, wooden floor with a thump.

It was not until the sun rose to the perfect height that Owen finally yanked himself from bed. A hole in the curtain allowed the full strength of morning sunbeams to splash over Owen's face. There would be no combatting the sun itself.

Reluctant feet slid out from atop the lumpy mattress and planted themselves on the floor. Owen lifted the clock, as he had set it face-down on the nightstand, and immediately jumped out of bed. Both feet struggled to gain traction on the slick floor as Owen realized he had managed to sleep past his designated alarm. He flew with frantic energy about the one-room apartment. Noise was no longer a concern as he jumped out of his nightclothes and into his Spellseeker uniform.

Coat. Pants. Boots. Sword. Pistol. Pocket watch.

All of the necessities were gathered and flung onto Owen's person, even as he stepped out his door and down the stairs.

"Morning, Blue," said the baker, noticing Owen rush down the steps next to the counter. The Zumbatran's warm face was cracked with age as he

422

smiled. "Sunday usual?"

"Please!" Owen replied as he cinched his sword belt into place. He fumbled around his pockets for three copper pennies and two silver dollars. "The month's rent in there, as well."

"That's what I like to hear. I've got your cheese danishes right here. Two wrapped, one not; just the way you like it."

"Thank you!"

Owen jammed the unwrapped danish into his gob as he wove through a line of people who seemed unhappy that a Spellseeker was receiving special treatment. A muffled 'excuse me' spoken through a mouthful of pastry did not help the matter, but Owen was in a hurry. Manners could wait.

The bakery where Owen had taken up residence was located in the Eaststead district of Arnstead. It sat on Main Street, just a few streets east of the Bridge on Main. Across from the bakery was a messy general goods store called Robin's Field Goods. On either side of the bakery were a butcher's shop and a tailor of adequate skill. Both the tailor and butcher had residences for lease above their stores as the baker did. The space above the general store was kept by the amiable Nirdac harn that ran the place.

It was a busy time to be on Main Street. Those who sought congregation at the Arnstead House were out and about in the streets. Fishermen were staking their favorite places on the banks of the Rivers Ra and Ro. Those who missed prime real estate on the twin rivers found places on the convergence of Sisir's run.

Farmers trickled in from the eastern edge of town. Carts loaded with all manner of food and unprocessed goods tottered on the uneven road, ready for the Sunday market. Those who worked for a wage would flood the streets in search of the best deals to be had. Noon would see the market at its peak. People released from worship at the House would mingle with those who favored a secular way of life. The farmers did not care either way. Money was money, be it blessed or blasphemous.

It was onto the thickening Main Street that Owen turned. His destination, the Arnstead Arcanarium, lay across the Bridge on Main. Right at the heart of the Weststead district.

Time spent in the wild had taught Owen a certain appreciation for crowds. Densely packed streets were his home. Buildings jammed close enough together that they nearly joined was his norm. It felt good to be back in a town. A place where he knew which turns led to what ends. Shadows were reserved for darkened alleys and belonged to humans or katarl or harn. The worst nightmare to be realized in those back alleys was nothing compared to the darkness of the southern woods.

Not even the haughty stares or spit at his boots tore at Owen's spirits. The disrespect had simply become a part of the job. There was nothing personal about it. Those who spat did not do so to spite Owen, they did so out of loathing for the station. Owen recognized that much and did not allow it to bother him.

The rushed walk to the Arcanarium was uneventful. Locked doors yielded to Owen's brass badge despite it being a day of rest. As Owen knew, the Arcanarium would not turn away a Spellseeker who wished to put forth the extra effort. There was always some manner of work to be done around the town.

Owen relied on the fact that others might be present. Specifically, he hoped that Violette Woods would be tucked into her office. Whether she was working on something or simply enjoying the solitude was irrelevant. She just needed to be there.

Footsteps echoed in the empty reception area. Ropes tied to brass posts marked the passage of citizens who were not present to queue. The only sound to be heard was the tick of four clocks, one for each wall in the roughly rectangular room. Sundays were Owen's favorite days to walk through the front of the Arcanarium. No vile whispers. Not a single cursed remark. Steadfast clocks were the only sound to hear. Vacant space was the only thing there to be seen.

Foreboding red gave way to ethereal blue as Owen applied his badge to the door in the back-right corner. The passage was free. The door closed with a muffled click after Owen had walked through. He continued past the first door to stop at the second. Bare knuckles rapped on the door to the office of Violet Woods.

Owen did not bother to speak. The tell-tale sounds of notes being sent to, and received from, message boxes clicked through the door. Footsteps followed the knocking after a moment's pause. Trot, trot, trot, right to the office door. Measured steps that made their way with utter precision. Metal clacked and ground upon itself as the knob turned and the door swung inward.

"I thought as much," were the first words to leave Violette's thin lips.

"Every Sunday, like clockwork."

"So, you'll let me in?" Owen smiled sweetly.

"I'll not be bought with a smile, Raulstone," Violette grumbled. She held out an expectant hand. A hand into which Owen placed his second cheese danish. "Not a word to anyone."

Violette took a decisive bite out of the pastry as she stepped past Owen into the hallway. Her destination was the same as Owen's; the door to Violent Offenses. Specifically, the doorway to the first division. A room for which access had not been programmed into Owen's badge. The sort of place he would need outside assistance to reach.

Once she had unlocked the door, Violette slipped her fingers around the chain that bound Owen's pocket watch. Nimble digits popped the clasp to open the clock. She took a glance at the time before holding the clockface up to Owen's nose.

"Fifteen minutes and not a second more."

"Yes, ma'am," Owen nodded. "Thank you—"

"Starting now."

"Right!"

Owen reclaimed his watch and loped off to the back of the impressive workspace that belonged to the first division of Violent Offenses. The door at the back of the room was not locked. This lack of redundancy allowed Owen to descend to the floors below. Layer upon layer of holding cells spiraled down from that door at the back of the room. Sconces filled with purple flames lit the way.

Four whole floors were descended before Owen stopped. On this fourth floor rested his goal. He stepped out into the long hallway, four minutes already having passed before Owen reached the desired cell.

All the surrounding cells had been kept empty. The entire fourth floor was barren save for a single soul tucked at the back.

"Rise and— oh, looks like you're well awake already."

Amalia Tennerim, the Cinder Witch, was busy doing push-ups on the stone floor when Owen arrived at her cell. The baggy stomach of her beige, standard-issue shirt touched the ground each time she lowered herself to the floor. An indecipherable grunt accompanied each upward push. Owen thought he heard a three-digit number under Amalia's breath, but was not quite certain.

"Brought some breakfast. For when you're done that is," Owen added, setting the danish down on Amalia's side of the bars. He squinted his eyes at his pocket watch. The dim, purple light made reading difficult. "I've got something like ten minutes before I have to leave. How's the cell? Are they keeping you fed down here? Haven't forgotten about you?"

"You don't— have to do this— you know," Amalia said between pushups. "Coming to see me— every Sunday."

"How else are you supposed to keep track of time down here?"

Amalia snorted at the notion. Not a dismissive sound, but one of shared humor. Another snort put a stop to the rhythm of push-ups. Amalia pulled her knees forward and sat on her feet. Beads of sweat trickled down from her neck and forehead. One baggy sleeve, the left, was given clean-up duty. It whisked away from the droplets before they could fall into Amalia's eyes.

She did not say much during the visit. That kept in kind with all of the previous visits. Amalia took hold of the danish and munched in near silence as Owen excitedly prattled on about the goings-on of Arnstead. The subject was not as important as the act of talking itself.

"They said I'll be seeing a judge soon," Amalia interjected during a brief pause in Owen's ranting.

"About time!" Owen groaned. "We're going on two months now. It's absolutely absurd how long they've kept you down here."

"Sounds like the judge is coming to see me, not the other way around."

"Still won't let you see the sun, huh?"

Amalia shook her head. It was a weak gesture. The shake of the world-weary person denied the warmth of the sun for two whole months.

"Well," Owen started, "it's better than nothing, I suppose. In the event that there's a next time, do you want something different?"

Owen pointed at the wrapper for the cheese danish, then held his hand out to receive the evidence of his visit. Amalia deposited the scrap without fuss.

"Bacon," Amalia chuckled. She leaned heavily into the 'B' in bacon. "The crunchy kind, none of that half-raw stuff."

"I'll see what I can do," Owen returned with a smile.

"So, how's your friend? The one downstairs."

Second Seeker Aaron Connolly looked up from the mess of forms and folders that cluttered his desk. Though there was mirth in his voice, the Nirdac harn bore a face of utter exhaustion. Ears hung limply behind his

426

head. Cheeks sagged. His mouth hung open slightly when not engaged in speech. Below the neck, the man's shoulders slumped so far that it seemed his arms were trying to escape their sockets.

The only part of Seeker Aaron that showed real signs of life was his right hand. Silvered pen held tight, he scrawled endlessly. Whether it was copying notes from an Initial Complaint Form to an Official Complaint Form, providing signatures where they were needed, or jotting down notes on separate pads of papers, the pen flowed with furious vigor.

"Haven't the slightest idea what you're referring to," Owen replied with a sly grin as he stepped in the Lost and Stolen division's excuse for an office.

"Of course not." Aaron turned his head back to his paperwork. "Here to help thin the backlog, by chance?"

"I'll file forms until my hands bleed… while I'm on duty."

"Tomorrow, then?"

"Tomorrow," Owen confirmed.

"Haven't come with lunch, by chance, have you?" One of Aaron's ears perked at the thought. He allowed his eyes to trail up to Owen. The harn even set his pen down in anticipation.

"It's not even eleven, sir."

Aaron nodded, crushed thoroughly by his expectations.

"So, to what do I owe the pleasure, then, Owen?"

"Came to grab a certain OCF," Owen said as he began to dig through boxes. "I made a promise to someone that I would like to keep. Where would I be, sir, if I was the OCF that had been followed-up on in my first month here."

"That you completed?"

"Yes."

"Before your little escapade."

"Yes," Owen replied with a slow nod.

It was not the first time that the subject of absence had arisen. The matter had cleared both Violette and First Seeker Akheem, so there was nothing in the way of reprimand. Aaron did not seem to care much for the nature of the absence, either. He would occasionally refer to it. A remark slipped into a discussion, or to use the absence as a reference for time. Owen was unsure as to whether his superior had nothing to say or simply chose to say nothing.

Either way was fine by Owen. The less he had to talk about that sequence of nightmares, the better. An ordeal of blood and sorrow that he was happy to leave in the past.

"I'd start there." Aaron indicated a stack of boxes with his pen. "Best guess would be the box in the middle, but I'd suggest checking above and below if you don't find the OCF in that middle box."

"Yes, sir. Thank you, sir."

How the boxes came to be organized remained a mystery. The only spells Owen had ever seen Second Seeker Aaron utilize were a small lick of flame and a gentle push to flip the latch on the windows in the hall. It left Owen to imagine that the harn was manually stacking boxes. An image to parse, as the boxes were not light. What's more, was that the tallest stacks towered twice as tall as the harn. Not an issue for Owen to navigate, but the struggle for Aaron must have been very real if there was no Flow involved.

Owen pushed the comical thought aside and organized the three boxes he had been directed to. Sure enough, the first box to be indicated contained the Official Complaint Form that Owen had been looking for. More impressive than the stacks themselves was Seeker Aaron's ability to navigate the absolute chaos of boxes. There had been no date or numbering system on the box in question, nor on the boxes that surrounded it. Seeker Aaron had simply picked the correct box out of all the possible choices available. The harn was either exceedingly lucky or had a memory to put any scholar to shame.

Scribbles and scratches permeated the air as Owen put the boxes of documents back as he had found them. Aaron had resumed cuttings swaths through the piles of pages on his decrepit desk of boxes.

"Be seeing you tomorrow, then?"

"Bright and early, sir. I'll chew through forms until my fingers bleed as promised," Owen added with a certain lightness.

"Go on," Aaron said with a smirk, though he did not bother to look up. "Go help whoever it was that caught your eye."

The streets of Oldstead were crowded with a mass of people ready to hit the riverside markets. It was just past noon. The congregation had come to a close for the day, and the House released its followers to do as they would. Some of the devout might have remained for divulsion. The rest had places to be and deals to find.

People poured around Owen as he cut through the crowd. His destination lay against the flow of traffic. The odd, cheeky individual took advantage of the anonymity offered by the stream of bodies to nudge Owen a little more forcefully than could be construed as an accident. Another joy added to the daily life of a Spellseeker in Arnstead. That was how Owen rationalized the minor affronts, at least.

It felt good to be among people. Even the ones who wanted to elbow Owen in the ribs while he was not looking. A thick current of people meant all was right in the world. No imminent threats to the people of Arnstead. No buildings aflame or killers running rampant in the area. Relative peace was at hand.

The deluge of people thinned as Owen approached the House. By the time Owen had reached the building, he was able to breathe deeply without inhaling the sweat of those around him.

Gleaming in the noonday sun, the white bell tower of the Arnstead House climbed high. A pristine pillar that served as a landmark for any who might have lost their way. It was visible from almost anywhere in Oldstead. The twelfth chime of the great bell still rang in Owen's ears as he passed the building by. His destination lay further still from the center of town.

Alleys that wound and coiled like snakes were the path of the day. The rigid planning of the Weststead district was nowhere to be found on the streets of Oldstead. Corners appeared where they were convenient. Dead ends were commonplace. Plazas were erratic, knowing no standard size or shape. Oldstead was everything that an architect saw in their nightmares. It was the dream of thieves and scoundrels; everywhere seemed a great place to hide, while also allowing for multiple avenues of escape.

Oldstead did not make sense.

Luckily for Owen, this was not the first time he had visited his destination. This was a repeat visit to uphold a promise made months ago. That did not make finding the place Owen sought easy by any means, but it did help make it possible to find in the first place.

The bell tower called out the first hour of the afternoon by the time Owen had managed to locate the residence he sought. Knowing who called the place home made the decrepit state of the dwelling all the more heartbreaking. There were even more boards falling from place than the last time Owen had visited the hut. He was careful not to knock too hard for fear of toppling the tottering building to the ground.

"Just a minute!" came a frail voice from within the hut.

Wood clacked on wood. The sound of an oaken cane colliding with creaky floorboards. Doddering, shuffled steps accompanied each smack of the cane.

"No rush, Julia," Owen called in response.

When shuffling steps finally reached the doorway, the doorway was pulled back to reveal a grey-black, Zumbatran harn. Her face lit up when she got a good look at Owen. The light of recognition mixed with the fulfillment of a promise.

"I recognize you," the elderly harn creaked. "You're the one who said he was gonna find my magical thingy. The focus! That's it. Have good news for me, son?"

"Well, I couldn't find what happened to *your* focus," Owen began, offering a poorly crafted faux frown, "but I *did* find a replacement."

Owen pulled a small cube from one of his coat pockets. No larger than two inches on any of its size, the object had proved a difficult find down in the depths of the Arcanarium's Retentions department. The base of the cube was carved from purpleheart. Silver filigree surrounded the emerald piece of memory glass faceted into one side. Owen held the small device out to Julia for inspection.

"Oh dear," Julia gasped. A hand reflexively thumped against her chest. "Well, that one looks an awful lot fancier than the one I had. I couldn't—"

"It's a gift," Owen interrupted. "Rather, think of it as an apology from the Bureau of Arcane. For taking so long to get you squared away."

"You sure nobody's gonna miss something so fancy?"

"Absolutely."

Wide-eyed, Julia examined the object in Owen's hand. The way the light glimmered in the multi-faceted gem of glass. How the thin bits of intricate silver wove around the socket. Even the deep shade of purple from the wood seemed something worth marveling at.

"Well," Julia started, pulling joyous attention up from the focus, "don't just stand there. Get your skinny butt in here and help me set the thing up. There's lemon cake in it for you if you do a fine job."

"Yes, ma'am," Owen said with a smile as he crossed over the threshold.